White Lies and Dark Chocolate

VALLEY COMMUNITY LIBRARY
739 RIVER STREET
PECKVILLE, PA 18452
 (570) 489-1765
 www.lclshome.org

DANA LYNNE PITELY

Copyright © 2012 Dana Lynne Pitely

All rights reserved.

Grateful acknowledgments is made for Aesop and his wonderful Fables. Specifically www.aesopfables.com

Publisher's Note

This is a work of fiction. Names, characters, places and incidents are either the product of the author's imagination or are used factiously, and any resemblance to actual persons, living or dead, business establishments, events, or locales is entirely coincidental or completely and totally on purpose.

Cover was sketched by the author and implemented by Amy Fedele.

ISBN-13: 978-0615736471

The scanning, uploading, and distribution of this book via the Internet or via any other means without the permission of the publisher is illegal and punishable by law. Please purchase only authorized electronic editions and do not participate in or encourage electronic piracy of copyrighted materials. Your support of the author's rights is appreciated.

For my mother, who gave me a dream and told me to dance. I am so proud of you.

With boundless thanks to:
God; My parents and family for their support and encouragement throughout my life; Aesop, Abdul and Yacou for their courage and strength; Shabana Kayum, my patient and kind editor, who let me keep a few ellipses as well as my love interest; Ryan Joseph for his singular epistemology; Elizabeth Griffis for her daily supportive emails; Christopher Augustine and Sarah Sleboda for their very cute Chips; Michael Stephen Fuchs for his advice in formatting and submitting works without zombies; David McKenzie and Brent Swalis for an inspirational article on CNN.com; and Quetzalcoatl and his swift morning star.

PREFACE
ANDROCLES

A SLAVE named Androcles once escaped from his master and fled to the forest. As he was wandering about there he came upon a Lion lying down moaning and groaning. At first he turned to flee, but finding that the Lion did not pursue him, he turned back and went up to him. As he came near, the Lion put out his paw, which was all swollen and bleeding, and Androcles found that a huge thorn had got into it, and was causing all the pain. He pulled out the thorn and bound up the paw of the Lion, who was soon able to rise and lick the hand of Androcles like a dog. Then the Lion took Androcles to his cave, and every day used to bring him meat from which to live. But shortly afterwards both Androcles and the Lion were captured, and the slave was sentenced to be thrown to the Lion, after the latter had been kept without food for several days. The Emperor and all his Court came to see the spectacle, and Androcles was led out into the middle of the arena. Soon the Lion was let loose from his den, and rushed bounding and roaring towards his victim. But as soon as he came near to Androcles he recognized his friend, and fawned upon him, and licked his hands like a friendly dog. The Emperor, surprised at this, summoned Androcles to him, who told him the whole story. Whereupon the slave was pardoned and freed, and the Lion let loose to his native forest.-Aesop

Abdul slowly pushes the heavy branch down to get a closer look at the sleeping lion. He is not sure about its size or its age. He can only hear his breath, the snores that both start and finish with a deep bass purr. While holding the branch down, Abdul fights his instinctually frightened body to take one step closer. He picks up his right foot and moves it a few centimeters forward. He starts to duck underneath the branch as he moves his left foot. *Snap.* The lion wakes, and so does Abdul.

The boys laugh as Abdul's body jars itself awake.

"Scared?" Arnaud says over the other boys. "Relax, it was

just a dream."

"Nah, I wasn't scared," Abdul answers as he sits up. He leans back on his arms and looks down at his bright orange shorts as he retrieves the purple T-shirt that he uses as a pillow. "What time is it?"

"Breakfast," Yacou answers. "You'd better hurry. It's almost gone."

"Abdul always misses breakfast. He likes to sleep too much," Daouda teases.

Abdul, in a panic, leans over to his right and then swings his legs to a crouching position. He knows his friends are telling the truth about him. He does like sleeping; he *really* likes dreaming. Abdul exhales deeply as he rushes to stand from his sleeping mat. He picks up his machete, "Did I miss the fried bananas?"

"You're not late," Yacou announces. "I'm joking. It's actually early. We might be the first there."

Abdul turns to look at his sleeping mat and sighs deeply. *Can I return to the dream?*

The seven boys leave their hut and make their way to the tent for breakfast. It is early enough to hope that they might get fried bananas this time. Unfortunately, only fish gallets are offered today – fish gallets and a bag of water, half frozen. They sit outside of the tent, near the left netted wall, close to each other as they eat their first meal of the day. They share a high spirited banter as they yell out to the boys from the other huts as they make their way to the tent. Within ten minutes, the number of boys grows to nearly fifty.

Abdul eats his allotted fish gallets and drinks a quarter of his bag of water. He knows he must conserve his water; it is already hot and he knows that it is only going to get hotter. As Abdul watches his friends talk and joke, he notices a white stranger talking to the man who pays for his food. "Who is that?" Abdul asks Ishmael.

Ishmael shrugs, "A liar."

Abdul unconsciously tries to rub the dirt off his legs as he spies the white man talking to his task master. "Yeah, but what is he doing here?" Abdul asks, looking back at Ismael, "Lying?"

He looks around the troop gathered around him, wondering if any can offer another explanation. Those closest to him, those who heard his question, just shrug their shoulders. Abdul returns his attention to the white man and then to the tree tops above them. His mind naturally begins to see both animals in the leaves as well as animals made out of leaves.

The boys finish their meals quickly and begin to stand. The simple lesson they have learned in their young lives is that it is better to be ready when called than to be seen as lazy. The boys pick up their day's water and their machetes and start to walk down the densely wooded path to the cacao trees. One of every four stop to pick up a large wooden box as they make their way to the section next to where they worked the day before. Two by two and four by four they choose their tree and immediately, without prompting, begin their shift.

Abdul is still small compared to many of his friends; he is also younger. He is rarely responsible for carrying the filled boxes. His job is clearing paths as well as cracking open the cacao pods. He is good at his job because he thinks ahead. Abdul is on a return trip from clearing a path when he, again, spies the white man talking to his boss. He puts his bean bowl at his feet and leans to the left to get a better view. He tries to cover his stealthy observations by taking a few pods down from a tree on the edge of the newly cleared path. He pretends that he is doing what he is supposed to be doing. Abdul squints his eyes to try to find something he cannot see. To Abdul, the white man doesn't appear to have eyes. He cannot see them – at least not from this distance.

Abdul notices the reporter noticing him. The reporter is pointing at him as he speaks to his field guide, Abdul's boss. Both start walking on the path, in his direction. Stunned, Abdul stands still, unable to move as they approach him. *I am not scared,* Abdul says to himself. Abdul's boss introduces the white man as a reporter. He tells Abdul with his voice and a penetrating stare to tell the reporter the truth about himself and his job.

The reporter shakes the hand of his field guide, then nods as he leaves. He immediately changes his countenance to address Abdul. "Hello. My name is David. How are you? For starters, let's see, what is your name, how old are you, and how long have you been working here?"

"My name is Abdul and I am ten," Abdul says. He looks at his bare feet covered in mud. He doesn't mind the color; he thinks of it as body paint. He wiggles his toes, smiles and then looks up at the tree branches, blocking the sunlight. "I've been here for three years." To distract the reporter, a cunning Abdul holds the yellow cocoa pod in his left and hits it twice with his blade. He snaps it open and dumps the milky white beans into his hollowed wooden bean bowl at his feet. This is all done without looking at anything other than the strange eyes of the reporter. "I'm good."

Abdul looks past the reporter to his friends, his tribe, the only family he has known for the past three years. They are all staring at him as he talks to the reporter. He is amused by them as they watch while squatting just a few feet past the white man, on the other side. He listens to the reporter's questions. Abdul tilts his chin toward the reporter and tells him that when his mother died, a man he did not know, a stranger, brought him to this farm. Abdul notices the reporter looking at his torn, yet colorful clothes and his hungry eyes. Abdul can try to guess what the reporter is thinking; however he does not need to know; he is content with his own thoughts. Yet he guardedly decides that Ishmael, who is two years older, is probably right in saying that he is not to be trusted.

Abdul tells the reporter that he really doesn't mind the work. "It helps me fall asleep at night." Abdul does not tell the reporter about his big, colorful dreams and how he looks forward to them every night. The presence of the reporter remains as he takes another pod, cracks it, snaps it and cleans it. This time he takes a scoop of the succulent milky white beans and offers a taste to the reporter. The reporter is gracious and takes a few from Abdul's hand.

"This is very different from chocolate," the reporter responds. "Have you ever had chocolate?"

Abdul looks confused as he shakes his head. "What is chocolate?"

One of Abdul's closest friends, Yacou, steps from the gang toward Abdul and the reporter, seeking attention. Yacou loves attention. The taut and sinewy child proudly tells the reporter that he is sixteen and that he was brought here from Burkina Faso by his mother after his father died.

"Sixteen?" The reporter knows that he cannot be much older than Abdul.

Yacou nods and lifts his leg to scratch the machete scars.

"Where did you get those scars?" the reporter asks.

"I can't clear grass without cutting myself," Yacou responds candidly.

Abdul laughs. "I'm much better than he is. I'm good." Abdul demonstrates that he has far fewer scars. He playfully pushes Yacou and the two run around the closest cacao tree.

The reporter stops their play and asks, "Is there anything you want to do?"

Yacou answers, "I wish to go to school. I want to read and write."

"Sure you do," the reporter comments with an almost sincere tone. "Have you ever been to school?"

"No." Yacou abruptly looks to his right as if he spotted a dangerous predator. "No, I have never been to school. I'd like to go. I want to learn how to read. My brother can. He tried to teach me. He's dead now."

Abdul watches and listens to the conversation and the reporter's condolences. He notices the reporter's shoes and their thick, rugged soles. He notices the metal jewelry on the reporter's wrist showing what Abdul already knows – it's noon. Above all, Abdul notices and is mesmerized by the blues and whites of the reporter's eyes.

The reporter feels the child's stare and turns to him. "Abdul, do you want to go to school?"

Abdul is silent. He already decided to not share his dreams with the white man. He emotionlessly returns his attention back to his job and with minor movements suggests to Yacou that he should do the same. Abdul and Yacou rejoin the line and work for another six hours – clearing, carrying, cutting, snapping, cracking and sweating.

At the end of the day, this troop has put in very long, hot hours harvesting cocoa. They are tired and hungry. Abdul sits with his friends and enjoys his simple evening meal of fish, bread and water before finding his favorite spot under the stars to sleep. Abdul knows it is far too hot to sleep in the hut on this night and this puts a tender smile on his face.

Tonight, he will dream of valiantly protecting his friends against a ferocious lion in front of tons of spectators. After defeating the lion, he will be rewarded with robes of heavy green silk and an endless feast, including fried bananas. But no chocolate.

Abdul has never had chocolate.

***

The reporter does what he can to obtain enough printable information for his story. He is writing a follow-up exposé about the world's chocolate industry. He knows that eleven years ago the world's largest chocolate industries signed a formal promise to stop the worst forms of child labor "as a matter of urgency." As a vetted international correspondent, he understands the players on the board and the insurmountable obstacles in West Africa. He has covered them. He has covered the wars, the poverty, the political unrest and those industries who seemingly take advantage of these weaknesses. He knows the promises of these players are empty; he knows the promises are absolutely senseless to children like Abdul and Yacou. He surrenders his story to CNN, hoping that it will make a difference – somewhere.

CHAPTER 1
THE ROSE AND THE AMARANTH

AN AMARANTH PLANT, whose flower never fades, had sprung up next to a rosebush. The amaranth said, 'What a delightful flower you are! You are desired by the gods and mortals alike. I congratulate you on your beauty and your fragrance.' The rose said, 'O amaranth, everlasting flower, I live for only a brief time and even if no one plucks me, I die, while you are able to blossom and bloom with eternal youth!" –Aesop

"Do you know what she is going to do?"

Rose Isope knows what the conversation is about. The ladies in line behind her are gossiping about Lindo Mei, the owner of the dry cleaning establishment across the street. Lindo just won twenty million dollars from a lottery ticket, given to her as a token of gratitude from a customer who required a rush job on an intricate Halloween costume. *Joy Luck.* Rose is happy for Lin and her family. She is also confident that Lin will do the right thing, whatever that is.

Clutching her watered down espresso, Rose grabs the chair of the small table nestled between the humidor and the dairy counter with a speed that suggests she is not drinking coffee for the caffeine. The table is not her favorite in the small café, yet it does afford an excellent view of the entrance. She is waiting.

Rose sets her coffee down before taking her seat. She scans the café for regulars and sees none. She hears Lindo's name again, echoing from the opposite corner. She reflects on Lin's windfall. The body conscious Halloween costume was an elaborate Chimera: the lion's head had fur and suede, the goats head attached to the back was made of suede and velvet, and the snake tail was covered in sequence and crystals. She heard from Lin that it took almost twelve hours to clean.

In Lin's telling, she was fascinated by the costume; she

immediately fell in love with it. The costume was designed in the 20's for an obviously wealthy New York socialite. Its construction was master level and reminded Lin of home. She accepted the challenge. She wished she hadn't. Rose knows the story because Lin was upset that they chose to tip her with a lottery ticket. She would have preferred cash.

Rose smiles as she lifts her Americano to her mouth. *She would have preferred cash.* Lin wants to contact the costume owner to thank them and also ask whether they would like anything in return. Rose thinks this is a mistake. Her pessimistic advice to Lin - "I think you already learned from them … Give an inch and they'll take a mile." Rose watches the corner table for a few more seconds and then quietly reconsiders her position. *Good Luck Lindo.*

She picks up the newspaper she brought from home, her daily gift to the café. Rose reads the paper because she heard from a reliable source that reading current events makes social interaction easier. Social interaction is easy for her – understanding the day's current events – impossible. She wants legends and footnotes. She wants a running tally at the top of the World section that states exactly how many people have died in America's current "skirmish" since its inception. She really does want to know just how many civilians, soldiers, freedom fighters, terrorists, journalists, women, and children have died. The numbers are always senseless the next day, not meaningless. She also wants a citation denoting how many sources were checked prior to printing. She is not sure if this will help her understand any better; however, she would be able to at least obtain a few facts.

After situating her belongings to signal that the table is occupied, Rose stands up, walks to the corner shelf and places the paper in its proper recycling space next to the magazines. She is aware that every step of this daily routine is antiquated – no one gets the actual paper anymore.

She steps in line to get her second cup – cappuccino with

one packet of raw sugar. When she has the stir stick in her mouth, the last phase before pure cappuccino enjoyment, Aristotle Irwin arrives. She slides into her chair and motions with a grandiose gesture where he is to sit.

Aris is always about four or five minutes late for their Tuesday night conversations. He does this to signify that he recognizes her admiration of punctuality and that he will always let her down a little. Without a word, he sets his coat down across the seat of his chair and steps to order a Turkish tea. He turns to her with a "Let's sit outside."

Rose immediately responds. She moves their gear to an outside table. There is a heating lamp under the awning that produces just enough heat to comfortably sit outside, even in November. Aris meets her in their new location with his tea. Rose can tell he is a bit happier with the new seating arrangement. He sits with his back to the stucco wall and looks out over the natural landscaping of the isolated café. She, of course, looks at him.

The initial few moments of these "dates" are always a bit awkward. Rose has been in love with Aris since the day after he broke up with her, nine years ago. So, for Rose, she must go through feelings of interest, attraction, puppy love, friendship, rejection, understanding, history and acceptance before she can utter her opening sentence, "Cat got your tongue?"

"Not so abrasive... How are you, Thorn?" he says with a sharp glance and a relaxed jaw served precisely while stretching his legs. Their relationship, suggestive of an Aesop Fable, can best be canvased as a relationship between two animals – a horse and a camel. Each animal is capable of great social contribution, speed, and intelligence. Both the horse and the camel can respond and adjust their contributions based upon terrain and necessity. The two can fairly compete in the same field as well as excel in their individual ways. Yet, wisdom dictates they are two entirely different animals. This distinction is easy for Aris. Rose, on the other hand, has no other choice but to confuse this deep understanding with love. Rose wishes Aesop did write this fable. She may have been better prepared.

Rose coyly lowers her head and smiles in response to her nickname. "The world stinks!" is her reply.

Aris mocks her by taking a deep breath. "I smell coffee and the Fall. I think the world smells good."

Rose takes a breath of her own. She looks to Aris and tries to mimic his posture. She is too short.

"Okay, Rose. Why does the world stink?" Aris says with a baited tone.

Rose has never been much of a tease. Yet, she tries. "Abdul has never had chocolate." She returns to her original posture. "Sweet, huh."

"I'll bite. Who's Abdul? And why has Abdul never had chocolate?"

The rant begins. "I decided to eat lunch at my desk today. I went to CNN and read the day's headlines."

"Thorn, I thought you were being serious. You're never going to get your legends."

"CNN is accurate and credible, right?" she flutters her eyelashes. It is dark enough that he may not have seen it. "Anyway, the news wasn't the story – the story is the lack of understanding of the reporting of the news of the story."

"Am I going to need a spelunking helmet to follow this?" Aris shifts and accompanies his response with slow, silly miming gestures. Using American Sign Language he signs, "What?"

"Was it the words you did not understand, or the delivery?"

"The story is what?"

"The story is ...the story is that Abdul has never had chocolate."

Aris just shakes his head as he pours the remaining liquid of his pressed pot into his cup and then thoughtfully takes it back to the barista counter. He returns with a couple of individually wrapped dinner mints.

Rose begins, "Abdul, a 10-year old who has been working in the cocoa fields for 3 years, has never even tasted chocolate. He has never had chocolate and he's never gone to school."

"Okay, now I am with you. Abdul has never had chocolate."

"Like I said." Rose laughs a little and continues in a much slower pace. "The CNN article was about Abdul and other children who live in the Ivory Coast. Apparently, the Ivory Coast and Ghana produce 70% of the world's cocoa." She looks at Aris. "Sometimes I hate how ignorant I am. How did I get to be this age without knowing where cocoa comes from?"

"I think I remember learning that cocoa requires a very specific climate to grow."

"How did I not know?" Rose aggressively kicks a few small pea stones with the toe of her shoe. "Maybe I just didn't... Anyway, it makes me mad. As of 2011, there are almost 2 million children working in cocoa agriculture."

"I am not exactly sure how you missed that information either. It's common knowledge," Aris says coolly.

"What makes me mad is the information they didn't report." After a brief pause and processing exactly what Aris said, she begins to raise her volume louder with each sentence. "It's common knowledge? It's common knowledge? I think it's closer to...to," she quiets down and grinds out the word, "...*commonplace*. After all, it's not the chocolate companies' fault. They would get their cocoa from another place if it grew there. They really have no choice, right? Kids. Kids with machetes. These candy companies are putting machetes in the hands of children. They do this stuff and come out smelling like... like a..."

"True," he interrupts in a voice that only she could decipher. He utters the word with a twist, an echoing of a wood screw. Unlike Rose, who often talks to hear herself talk, Aris does not waste words expressing himself. His natural demeanor and mode of expression create a visual component that utterly fascinates her. She has spent many hours wondering how it is that he has this majestic speech. Never quite sure how to ask how he does what he does, she contents herself with the explanation that he must simply think before he speaks. He smiles. "I love the smell of chocolate."

"Apparently men like the smell of chocolate chip cookies too." Rose adds conversationally, "Hey, this is something interesting... I recently read a definition of truth, well sorta...Actually it was a definition of falsehood. Falsehood neither creates anything new, nor restores anything. Interesting, right? It sounds true?"

"You are thornier than usual."

She wants to reply with something clever – pointed, beautiful and poetic. Instead, she excuses herself to get a glass of water. She brings back two, sits down and brushes her lap as if she were covered in bread crumbs. She repositions again, takes a sip of water, exhales and looks toward her evening's companion.

"What do you want to do?" he asks.

Not even pausing to think he might actually want to do something like play a game of pool or get a bite to eat, Rose continues, "What do I want to do? I want to... No, I need to give a piece of chocolate to Abdul." She runs a heavy hand through her strawberry blonde hair. "I think what I am experiencing right now is a moment of clarity."

"A moment of clarity? I find that phrase untrustworthy." He laughs at himself and takes a sip of his tea. "Do you think you are confused most of the time, part of time, rarely, always?"

Rose rolls her eyes. "What I mean is... it's clear to me... I think... I think I found this article because I was supposed to. Like everything I have been doing up to now has led to me finding this one particular article – this one particular issue." Rose looks out over the darkened landscape. "It is calling the Aesop in me... Anyway, I have to get a piece of chocolate to Abdul."

"Calling the Aesop in you," Aris mutters in understanding.

Both Aristotle and Rose took it upon themselves in their early childhood to understand the meaning of their namesake. Rose has read and studied each Aesop fable; Aris has read and studied everything Aristotle has ever written. Although only verbally discussed once in their entire relationship, it is their deepest bond; it is the root of their connection. Aris surmises, "A Eureka moment, perhaps."

"Archimedes!" Rose says flirtatiously. "Stop trying to distract me. I am trying to have a life altering conversation here."

"Sorry." Aris laughs. "Abdul has never had a piece of chocolate. You want to give Abdul a piece of chocolate."

"Nice summary." Rose smiles wryly. "And in order to do that - I must first familiarize myself with the Harkin-Engel Protocol."

Aris smiles at her tone and further engages himself in her conversation by cupping his ears with his hands and serves what he thinks is a funny pun. "Speak up Sonny! What'd ya say?"

Rose lobs a return by forming a megaphone with her two hands. "Friends, Romans, countrymen, lend me your ears – the Harkin-Engel Protocol. It is a promise made by the major chocolate companies stating that they would stop using children. It had six objectives. It was signed in 2001. Eleven years ago."

"Eleven years ago Amnesiac was released. That may explain things."

"Oh, I see, they forgot." Rose laughs. "How about - Hail to the Thief?"

Aris is pleased with her Radio Head lob. He returns with a few idioms for her pleasure, "Why buy the cow... no honor among thieves...it is like stealing candy from a baby..."

"Six objectives and eleven years. For some reason I am picturing Moses descending from the mountain and asking Aaron, 'Yo Bro- what happened? I asked you to do this one thing...'"

Aris grimaces at her bad allusion yet cannot resist, "I bring you these fifteen... oops... I mean these ten commandments."

She pauses to notice the curves of Aris's face and the color of his eyes. "Chocolate."

"This is like blood diamonds."

"It's worse. Chocolate is so much more valuable." Rose huffs and then takes another breath. "So yeah, anyway – back to the Cocoa Protocol – the six objectives. There are three active objectives and three passive ones. The active ones are the first, fourth and sixth."

Rose laughs. "And do you know the one they are concentrating their efforts on?"

Aris smirks. "Let me guess – six?"

"According to the industry – the real challenge is finding quantifiable and verifiable ways to ensure that the chocolate we, law-abiding westerners, are eating is not harvested by a child. That is the challenge? THAT?"

"So what you are saying is... the problem is child slavery, not certification?"

"The difference is so ridiculously subtle. You see, starting with 6, they can continue to use children until they figure out a way to not use children. Yep, subtle... the difference is subtle...Excuse me waiter, there is a fly in my chardonnay."

"Who put their chocolate in my peanut butter?"

"I don't understand...?"

She shifts her eyes inquisitively to Aris thinking that he may actually know the answer to her next question. "I was wondering...Do children working on Amish farms in Pennsylvania Dutch country violate child labor laws? I am pretty sure that they do work on their family's farm. Aren't they learning the skills they need to provide for themselves in their adult life?"

Aris shakes his head and then says, "I can say that I am pretty sure that the Amish are not guilty of child trafficking."

Rose accepts his answer. "Anyway, this certification thing... well, I think this is an example of – putting the cart before the horse. You can more easily certify that the children are not in the fields, if they are in the classroom. Right? Build the schools first. This is not rocket science; it's elementary…elementary school."

Aris huffs, picks up a mint and works on the wrapper with his fingers before using his teeth.

"I am glad you are here," Rose says abruptly.

Rose knows that most people find her both exhausting and arrogant. Aris, on the other hand, understands her. In addition to the burden of her name, he understands her mind and its musings. When someone asks him how it is they met, he refers to a game of pool where he used his favorite pick-up line of that year and asked her to describe her personality to him in two sentences. Rose only paused briefly before answering, "I am a genius. It's just no one believes me."

He did believe her that night and almost every night since. He knows she is a daydreamer; she dreams of a better world and he loves this about her. Most people are content with a relationship, a social circle and a professional ladder. Rose is not most people. Aris knows that at age 32 she has not even started to give up. Aristotle fully understands this and can only safely describe her as *scary*.

For now, Aris realizes Rose only needs a small bit of encouragement. "It's not Rocket Science?"

"It's simple. You see, not only can a school provide a future other than farming; it can also instruct safer practices to the children who must work on their family's farm. A school can teach them that protective gear should be worn when working with pesticides."

"I see your Rocket Science and raise you a space suit?"

"Nah, I just need a giant rocket launcher." Her eyes take on a sinister glare as she mimes the weapon at her shoulder. "My target – Hershey's." Rose aims the imaginary air canon at a not too distant tree. "It is either funny or ironic that Milton Hershey built a school for orphaned boys 100 years ago and they find themselves in this jam today. The Hershey Industrial School is still very active and successful today. Is it funny or ironic?"

"Both, I suspect."

"I guess I am going to ask them, urge them, to continue their founder's legacy and build new campuses in West Africa. I will suggest that they pay for it by packaging special Hershey's Kisses to sell specifically as a world-wide fundraiser to raise awareness of the…" she holds up two fingers and produces an air quote "…commonplace problem."

"Personally, I think these eight companies, companies like M&M /Mars, Nestle, and Callebaut could and should pull their resources and make the best schools in the world. Because there are eight - they could partner in pairs. One pair will pay for technology, computers and the like. Another pair will pay for the construction…"

"Hi, Handsome. I've been looking everywhere for you," Nora says, sneaking up on the pair and planting a surprise kiss on Aris's cheek.

"Nora. Hi," Rose says.

"I didn't see you out here. It's dark," Nora replies.

"It is really crowded in there," Aris says as he grabs her hand from his shoulder and pulls her around to his lap. "Ready to go eat?"

"Where are you guys going?" asks Rose.

"The sushi place at the square," Aris responds.

Rose tries to hide a look of disappointment in her eyes by playing with her drink napkin.

"Rose was just telling me about cocoa fields in West Africa and how they are using child labor."

"Huh," Nora says. Her eyes inadvertently try to size the threat of her boyfriend's best friend by scanning her clothes and hair.

Rose stands and grabs Nora a chair and sets it down close to Aris. "I am not trying to be rude – but these chairs… well, 250 is their max."

Nora glares for a moment before recognizing the truth of her statement and shifts her weight onto the chair. "Thanks."

"So schools... One pair would pay for construction..."

"One pair could pay for staff and the last pair could pay for adult programs and agricultural research. So yeah, building the schools...." Rose ploughs the pebbles with both of her feet, clearing a rectangle space approximately two feet long. "This fulfills objectives one and four... and paves the way to accomplish six."

Aris lifts Nora's hand to his mouth to kiss it.

"I think I would call the schools, 'The Fields,', or perhaps even more romantic, 'The Tuskegee Fields.' However, I suppose I should ask the kids what they want to call it." She recovers the trough. "Anyway, Aris, that is what I want to do," she says with the tiniest hint of vulnerability.

Aris lifts his right cheek, stands and snaps his watch. "Booker Washington – and it only took you a half of an hour, give or take. Excuse me, Ladies." He kisses the top of Nora's head.

Rose's eyes follow Aris until he turns the corner leading to the loo. She breathes a few more times and even takes one or two deep breaths. "Sushi," she whispers to herself. She wonders whether she should compliment Nora on her footwear or tritely comment on the weather.

"Are you talking about that article on CNN?" Nora asks.

"Yes." Rose's mood lightens considerably. "I am pretty fired up about it."

"Aris told me you get that way."

"Yeah. I pretty much go whichever way the wind blows."

Aris returns and grabs Rose's right shoulder with his left hand and gives a gentle squeeze. "We should probably get going. I am pretty hungry." Aris looks at Nora. "Are you ready?"

Nora nods.

"Specially packaged Kisses. I'd buy a couple of bags," says

Aris.

"Thanks. Thanks for your support." She resumes her normal posture.

"What are friends... fore!" He swings a pretend golf club.

Rose watches the pretend golf ball fly. "Isn't it obvious? Copious amounts of cheese and chocolate, of course." Rose looks down and then up at the couple standing very close to each other. "Hey, thanks for listening. I know I talk too much"

"Talk too much? No, Rose, the truth is, I don't talk enough." Aris is quoting Rose from a previous conversation.

"True."

"By the way, did Lindo call that costume guy?" Aris embraces Nora from behind while looking at Rose.

Rose shrugs. "To be continued..."

"Not tonight. Same time, next week? Want us to walk you to your car?"

Rose declines and points to the empty table inside. She grabs her purse from under her chair, collects her keys and stands with both hands behind her back.

After taking a few steps toward the parking lot, Aris turns again. "Rose, be humble in your arrogance, please." He takes a few more steps backwards. "And just so you are prepared...What happens when Hershey's says 'No'?"

"You mean paradise is actually lost? What did he say, that Milton guy, he said something like, 'Can make a heav'n of hell, a hell of heav'n?' No way. This Aesop says that ain't no moral."

"I'll look forward to an update next week," Aris says while placing his hand on the small of Nora's back.

"Next week."

"So what's the fable?" Aris asks with a tone of genuine interest and is immediately met with an impatient look from Nora.

"I was thinking 'The Rose and the Amaranth.' I will find the flaw in the beauty and the beauty in the flaw." She says while rocking from her heels to the balls of her feet. She strikes a balance and yells to her distancing friend, "The moral, the moral is that there is a penalty to greatness."

"Good night, Rose."

"Have a good dinner, and a good night, and…" Rose whispers, "… and do you think it's true?"

CHAPTER 2
THE SERPENT AND THE FILE

A SERPENT in the course of its wanderings came into an armorer's shop. As he glided over the floor he felt his skin pricked by a file lying there. In a rage he turned round upon it and tried to dart his fangs into it; but he could do no harm to heavy iron and had soon to give over his wrath. –Aesop

"You are sitting outside of Hershey's right now?" Aris asks.

"I am," Rose answers into her cell phone, all the while glaring at the entrance through her windshield. "I am going to submit this idea to their marketing department."

"You are at Hershey's headquarters in Hershey, PA. In the parking lot?"

"Yep. There are still leaves on the trees here."

Aris laughs. "You're stalking them."

"I'm not. Maybe I am sizing up the enemy. It is a pretty big building."

"Well, you are certainly not wasting any time," Aris comments.

"As I see it, they have had eleven years to do something… obviously they need help."

"How did you get out of work?"

"I am flying out tonight so I have the day off."

"Where are you going?" Aris asks.

"Milwaukee," Rose replies. "I love Milwaukee."

"America's best kept secret," Aris quotes Rose. "What are you going to say?"

"I dunno. I think I'll wing it."

"You can't do that."

"Aris, geez, I pretty much have it all written out in a formal proposal. So technically, I do not have to say anything. I could just hand them the file and walk out. I hope I get a chance to talk to someone though. I think I could sell this idea if given the chance."

"So you have actually thought about this."

"Duh. How long have you known me?"

"Long enough. I know that you sometimes don't look before you leap."

Rose smiles. "Good idiom."

"Tell me, for your sake, what is your plan again?" Aris asks.

Rose looks at the folder in the passenger seat and grabs the corner to open it flat on the seat. "It's the specially marketed Kisses," she resounds. "I twisted the vintage advertisement campaign Hershey used in the past. If you are really interested, you could type 'vintage Hershey ads' in Google to find the ones I am talking about. Although I am pretty sure that you have seen them before."

"Vintage Hershey ads? Phew, so you have a plan." Aris sighs. "I was a bit worried."

"I don't get it. How could you think that I could… you seriously thought that I just woke up this morning and decided to drive to Hershey's?" Rose huffs. "I'm not that crazy."

"Gotcha. You are so easy."

"Easy as a nuclear war," Rose lobs. "A Duran ran ran, a Duran ran."

"Classic," Aris says. "So you are using their own words against them, eh? Classy and Classic."

"Yep. Remember? Falsehood neither creates anything new, nor restores anything. Anyway, the first vintage ad I feature is 'Hershey is first in favor and flavor! Hershey Leads Them All!' I am sure it's obvious to you what I say about it. I mean how perfect is that? They launched an ad campaign calling themselves leaders. Granted, it was like decades ago – World War II."

"Are these the fighter pilot ads?" Aris asks.

"No. Same vein though, probably the same artist."

"Hershey leads them all. Got it. I am looking at the ad right now. But it only looks like they are talking about their other chocolate bars," Aris sums.

"I twisted the ad – a little. Anyway, they are the first signature of the protocol and they really should be leading. The second vintage ad is an ad for Hershey Kisses. It's a picture of two children, and the little girl is feeding the little boy a kiss. The ad reads, 'A kiss for you.' I was thinking that marketing could rework the ad to have the little girl delivering a kiss to Abdul. That ad is easier to find."

"I got it. So the plan is that you will just walk in there, hand them your plan, and they will say something like, 'why didn't we think of it?'" Aris prods.

"It's possible," Rose answers. "The genius is in its simplicity."

"I looked up the fable 'The Rose and the Amaranth' after our conversation last week," Aris says. "The penalty of greatness... My guess is that Hershey doesn't want to draw attention to itself. People may blame them and they will be the only one who suffers the consequence."

"I have moved on from there. I am now thinking about the Serpent and the File. The moral of that fable is that it is useless attacking the insensible."

"I don't know that one."

Rose retells the fable from memory.

"Who is the insensible in this scenario?" Aris asks.

"Isn't it obvious – it's Abdul!" Rose barks.

"Ouch." He laughs. "Ask a stupid question..."

Rose huffs. "Sorry, I am really angry about this. And if I don't do something I will have to stop eating chocolate in protest. And I don't want to have to stop eating chocolate."

"Noted. So your true feelings and real motivations come out."

"Eleven years! How does it take eleven years in today's

society to make something publically known?"

"It is not that simple, Rose. I am sure they have loads of stuff to consider."

"Or cover," Rose mutters quietly. "BTW, where are you?"

"ATL," Aris responds. "I'm flying to DC."

"I missed you this week," Rose says and milliseconds later wishes she hadn't.

"Yeah, well, business happens," Aris responds.

Rose quickly changes the subject. "I drove by Hershey's school today. It really is a beautiful school. And the fact that it is there makes me even angrier." Rose looks at her fingers gripping the steering wheel tightly. "It just really makes me want to nail their expletive."

"I don't think I will ever quite understand how you can get so worked up over things. Nora thinks you need to get…"

"Over things? Children and chocolate… these are beyond… things," Rose interrupts. *Wait.* "Nora thinks what?" Rose thinks she already knows what Nora has to say about her. She decides she would rather not hear it.

"I was reading about chocolate – it has a very interesting history," she powers forward before Aris can respond. "Cocoa has its roots in both the Mayan and Aztec civilizations. The Mayans thought the fruit of the cocoa tree represented life and fertility. The Aztecs attributed the creation of the cocoa plant to Quetzalcoatl, a god who descended from heaven on a beam of a morning star carrying it."

"Quezalcoatl. Great name."

"Keysol, for short? Pretty." Rose continues with a serious laugh, "Hey, I am not kidding around. Stop trying to distract me."

"I really think Quezalcoatl is a good name."

"And he carried the cocoa plant. What I am trying to say is… I really do think cocoa is divine, like water, and apparently many civilizations agree with me, many great civilizations. As a theologian, I would argue that chocolate is a symbol of the divine, carried by civilization, much like music and language. A symbol carried in God's time."

"The fruit of the cocoa tree carried by civilization in God's time. Come on, Rose. Seriously?"

"Did you know that cocoa beans were also used as currency to purchase prostitutes, slaves, horses and rabbits? It was literally and factually a cash crop. That's crazy, right?" Rose pictures a white suited man paying for Abdul with a few cocoa beans.

"No, I guess I didn't know that." Aris sighs. "But Rose..."

"Anyway, for some reason cocoa, Theobroma Cacao, the food of the gods, is now principally, almost entirely, being grown in Africa. Why? I think it is a sign. A sign of where we are supposed to be looking."

"Looking for what? Slow down. I understand that this is a dynamic issue, particularly for you. And obviously you put a lot of heart and soul into this already. All I am saying is, what I am trying to say is...Look Rose - it's foolish to think that you can do anything about it. It's out of your control. You cannot solve the child slavery issue from your car in some parking lot."

"Out of my control?" Rose begins to yell, "Notifying the public that major chocolate companies are using slaves. I beg to differ, Darling. It is not out of my control. What if my control is to point out that it is well within *their* control. And Pumpkin, I am planning on getting out of my car as soon as we finish this conversation." She tries to rein in her emotion and volume. "It is not out of my control."

"Listen Rose, there is obviously a reason that it is not done." Aris continues in his role as devil's advocate and as her best friend. If she were really listening, she could hear the smile in his voice.

"Really?" Rose says disdainfully. "I think there is a dissertation here: "Slavery: How it happens in the age of text messaging. The same as it ever was. Byrne baby burn."

"The old new wave," Aris chuckles as he realizes he cannot

cut her passion. "So what you are saying is, this time we forgot our vow-els?"

Rose melts. "Can you hear me now?"

"Almost."

Rose sighs. "Just checking?"

"To see if my ears are working?" Aris sighs. "Why can't you care about normal things? It would be a lot easier."

"What's on TV tonight?" Rose says with an ironic tone.

"Reality," Aris says dryly. "You really are exhausting."

"So now I am easy and exhausting."

Aris laughs. "And just a tad bit crazy."

"It just might be a lunatic you're looking for," Rose sings.

Aris laughs.

"So I was thinking about my exponentially great grandfather. He was a slave who was given the opportunity to learn because of his display of intelligence and wit."

"So the story goes," Aris says in his way.

"Well, I guess my thought of the matter is this… he must have been pretty darn precocious to let his masters know his mind and wit. I imagine he also took a good many beatings because of it."

"I don't think you mean precocious, maybe audacious. What you mean is that slaves aren't, or weren't, supposed to be sensible?" Aris digs. "Am I right?"

Rose paradoxically laughs as she looks at her own chewed-off nails. "He probably bit that file until it broke."

"So you're going to march audaciously into Hershey's and hand them this suggestion," Aris says trying to jokingly temper his friend for battle.

"I am. Yet, how does one march audaciously? Any suggestions?"

"Are you wearing a skirt?"

"Yes. A pencil skirt."

"Then I don't think you should march audaciously. It

would be unseemly."

"Okay then, I will boldly march. I am pretty sure I can boldly march in a skirt. Although just walking in a pencil skirt can pose a few problems. You almost have to walk heel-toe in a pencil skirt, heel-toe with a twist."

"I didn't know."

"The things I could teach you," Rose says. "Important things – like how to walk in a pencil skirt."

"Need to know stuff." Aris laughs. "You do realize they will more than likely take your proposal and throw it away in the closest receptacle."

"I do. Do you think I should attach a post-it reminding them to recycle?" she jokes.

"Rose, if you know that they are going to throw it away, then why are you there? I cannot believe you drove all the way there."

"Abdul and Aesop. I am doing this for them. They are worth the extra mile, or 200."

"In that case, call me and let me know how it goes?" Aris says sensitively.

"Of course. I have a layover in St. Louis around 8ish. I'll text. How's Nora?"

"She's fine. Good. Well, actually, the holidays are a bit rough on her. Her father passed a couple of years ago around this time."

"I am sorry to hear that. I didn't know. How is it that you never told me?"

"I just did," Aris snaps. "I don't tell you everything. I'm allowed a private life, and she certainly is." Aris says defensively.

"Sorry. You're right. Wait. Hold on a second." Rose notices a parking lot security guard taking notice of her presence. She awkwardly waves at the uniformed man and then flashes her phone in an attempt to explain her loitering. The officer gives a gentle salute as he drives by. She decides she will say something to him the next time he drives by. "Sorry. I am back."

"Anyway, she's good. She is also a bit sad."

"Understandably."

"She is with her mom now. However, she is spending Thanksgiving with my family. Her mom is going to visit her brother."

"You have a plan for her return, a special dinner maybe? My guess is that she is having an emotional time and might need a bit of comfort when she gets back."

"I am making spaghetti and meatballs. I'll buy good Italian bread and wine. She really likes my spaghetti."

"Sounds good. I would suggest flowers, too. So you are going home to your folks? You must be looking forward to it. Oh, by the way, I heard from Lin."

"What does she have to say?"

"You are not going to believe this." Rose says. She notices the dust on her dashboard and starts using her black leather glove as a duster.

"Believe what?"

"The guy who gave her the lottery ticket thinks that he is entitled to half."

"You're kidding me. Now that's audacious." Aris laughs. "Half?"

"Apparently Lin just laughed, but I think she is disappointed – disappointed in people." Rose looks at her now dirty glove and leans over the gear shift to wipe the glove on the carpet of the passenger side.

"Winning millions can bring out the worst."

"I can almost understand the guy though. He went and bought two lottery tickets and randomly chose to give away the winning ticket - that's gotta hurt. And if he didn't ask for half…"

"You don't really think that, Rose. If he said that to Lin in your presence you probably would have hit him."

Rose tries to envision the probability of such a scene in

Lin's store. "I probably would have just called him small," she answers.

"When does your flight leave?"

"5ish. Yours?"

"25 minutes."

"Well then, I really need to get going," Rose says as she notices the security guard returning. "I actually do have a flight to catch and I am a couple of hours from the airport. Thanks for calling."

"Thanks for answering. Hey, good luck nailing their expletive."

"You know that's a line from 'Intolerable Cruelty.'"

"I knew I heard it before. 'Intolerable Cruelty,' eh? You have put some thought into this. Intolerable Cruelty is a good phrase."

"Apt, under the circumstances."

"Did you find good tunes for the drive? Well, other than Billy Joel?"

"T'Pau spoke to me. Give a little bit of heart and soul. Give a little bit of love to grow," she recites.

"Ugh. Now that's intolerable cruelty," Aris says.

Rose laughs. "Ah, but my guess is that you are smiling. It's a really good song. Anyway, I really should go. Thanks Aris, thanks for being there. Talk to ya later." She slides her phone closed.

Rose flips the manila folder in her hand and opens it. She carefully re-reads the letter and leafs through the proposal she spent the past four days working on. She already sent an email containing this idea to Hershey. Yet she decided a personal delivery was necessary before taking the next step. It is easy to delete an email. Rose surmises that it must be slightly more difficult to slam the door on an actual person who cared enough to make a personal delivery. She hopes she is right.

***

As usual, Aris's prediction is correct. The folder was received with a warm, yet vacuous smile by a young brunette with metallic orange nail polish. Rose leaves the building minutes after entering, empty-handed and spurned.

"It is useless attacking the insensible. Can't say I wasn't warned. Right, Abdul?"

CHAPTER 3
THE HAWK AND THE NIGHTINGALE

A NIGHTINGALE, sitting aloft upon an oak and singing according to his wont, was seen by a Hawk who, being in need of food, swooped down and seized him. The Nightingale, about to lose his life, earnestly begged the Hawk to let him go, saying that he was not big enough to satisfy the hunger of a Hawk who, if he wanted food, ought to pursue the larger birds. The Hawk, interrupting him, said: "I should indeed have lost my senses if I should let go food ready in my hand, for the sake of pursuing birds which are not yet even within sight. –Aesop

Rose is not particularly thrilled by the sound of her alarm. She hates waking up every morning annoyed. She cannot use music or the sound of ocean waves to wake her – they will just be incorporated into her dreams. She has to wake up annoyed. She has no other choice.

Rose hits her alarm "snooze" because it is faster than finding the off button, a problem that she swears she will fix with her next purchase of an alarm clock. She pulls her down comforter up to her chin and tries to focus her eyes. She really dislikes the textured paint on her ceiling – if it were smooth she could paint it. She daydreams of Van Gogh skies. Van Gogh is her favorite artist and theologian.

After regaining control of her eyes, she throws her comforter to the left and rolls out of bed. She slides into her pastel yellow robe and black slippers and shuffles into her kitchen. *Dark Magic.* She listens for the fog horn sound of her Keurig and tries to reproduce the same sound. Her morning ritual continues when she lifts the lid to her laptop.

"What does Cookie have to say today?" she whispers out loud to herself. She opens her Hotmail account to find the message from her daily pen pal who lives in Arizona. Cookie, nee Lisbeth, is her confidant. They first met when Rose was seventeen. They lived together as easy roommates for a few years in their early twenties. Lisbeth became Cookie after she graduated from a culinary school in Baltimore. They have been exchanging daily emails for close to a decade. Their emails are generally about their plans for the day, including errands and dinner suggestions. They also write about yesterday's trials and today's dreams. These emails are as important and comfortable to Rose as her morning coffee. Her response email is usually written in the time it takes to finish her first cup. She tells Lisbeth her plan for the day. She is going to meet with Ms. Nightingale, the president of an enterprising chocolate company. She writes that her intention is to force Hershey's to keep their promise with her bird in hand. Her last sentence details that she will be having pierogi for dinner. Rose logs out of Hotmail and shuts down her laptop. She places her 16 oz. mug into the sink and shuffles to the shower.

    Rose cannot help but think that today is a day filled with promise – their promise. She recites from memory the first objective of the Harkin-Engel protocol: "Industry has publically acknowledged the problem of forced child labor and will continue to commit to significant resources to address it." She continues with a very angered, whispered tone, "…Industry will reiterate its acknowledgement…in a highly public way." Rose makes a habit of venting her more angry existential thoughts during her 20 minute shower. She thinks the water can clean the emotion. Clean anger, according to Rose, is a very good motivator.

    "Significant resources to address it," Rose continues to mutter as she looks to her closet. She chooses a dark brown tweed sleeveless dress with a silhouette reminiscent of late 40's to early 50's. Rose loves vintage fashion and is happy to live in a place with a significant older population. To suit her needs, she makes frequent stops at the Salvation Army and Lin's dry cleaning establishment. "Ah Lin, I hope you are doing alright." She matches the dress with a heeled Mary Jane with bold stitching. She wants to fully accessorize with gloves and pin curls, but she tempers her desire with an antique looking ladies watch that she purchased on a whim at Boscov's.

Her meeting is at 10 AM. She told her boss that she has a morning dental appointment to address a problem with sugar sensitivity. She smiles to herself because of her lie; she is almost clever in almost telling the truth.

Rose has a bowl of oatmeal to ease her stomach and uses the extra morning hour to practice behaving like a normal person. She mentally goes over her greeting, the handshake, and of course, the explanation of why she is so darned fidgety. She has been through many interviews and has often tried to explain that what may be perceived as interview nervousness is actually her normal energy level. Her explanation usually fails to gratify the interviewer. Yet there were a few times when her candor opened up the interview to a more effective and efficient conversation.

***

At 9:50, Rose arrives at the main offices. She sits in her car looking towards the door and takes a few moments to pray. She prays for humility, grace, charisma, thought clarity, and a recipient listener. She thanks God for the opportunity, grabs her black leather folder and then finishes her prayer while stepping out of her car. "Abdul, this one is for you."

She is excited to meet with Rebekah Nightingale, the person in charge of her family's favorite local chocolatier. She has been receiving Nightingale Chocolates for every major holiday, including her birthday, since she was seven. Her father still shows his love by stopping by the Second's store to pick up her current favorite – sea salted milk chocolate caramels. Rose always defends her current favorite by explaining that although the combination sounds wrong to the ear, the flavors are very gratifying to the taste buds.

Ms. Nightingale agreed to meet with her to discuss a book idea she had about a young woman who works in the chocolate industry. Rose uses this clever ploy to garner a bit more attention than she may have if she approached her in a more typical fashion. In a business letter, she wrote that she is writing a book and needs more information about the chocolate industry, information that she could not obtain from web searches. She recognizes that this little plot twist may hurt her chances for cooperation; yet she is confident that she would have been dismissed all together if she behaved otherwise. To cover her bases, she wrote her first chapter entitled "Just In Case."

At exactly 10 AM, Rose is led by Rebekah to her office. "I must admit that I found your letter to be a bit more interesting than my typical correspondence. Your letter found me particularly comical that day... I had a series of seriously boring meetings... paint drying would have been more exhilarating than those meetings. I must say that I've been looking forward to this meeting. I even told my husband about it," Rebekah says generously to the oddity in her office. She motions to the mission style table, a perfect complement to her desk. Her office is situated in the corner and has one window overlooking the lobby and another overlooking a production line.

"I'm very happy to be here and not to sound over-confident in my manipulation..." Rose stops herself and then mocks her host with an adaptation of a sinister character, "It is all part of my plan. Ha Ha Ha." Rose begins to second guess her small joke and attempts to recover by looking at her feet.

Realizing that a professional demeanor is essential, Rose awkwardly and abruptly shifts gears. "This is a very pleasant office space." She casually glances over the entire space and then takes her seat at the table with a bit of affected old-fashioned feminine maturity. She sets her purse under her chair, and places her leather folder on the table in front of her and gently folds her arms on the table. Dressed in a finely tailored women's suit, Rebekah sits across from her.

"So you are writing a book about the chocolate industry?"

Rebekah asks in a no-nonsense, yet casual way. She softly moves her caramel colored hair from her right shoulder and gently leans forward.

"Yes Ma'am, I am. And if I told you that you were chapter two, would you want to hear about chapter one?" Rose asks teasingly and quickly prays that Rebekah is still willing to continue with the conversation.

"You might as well start at the beginning," she says politely.

Rose takes a deep breath and starts to mentally run through her prepared starting sentences. She quickly wonders whether or not this would be a good opportunity to explain her mannerisms that tend to be awkward to those who do not know her. Should she tell her about her past work experience or education, even though both of these were somewhat covered by her initial request for a meeting? She worries that too many seconds have passed without her talking. *God please.*

"I am going to try to explain myself a bit before I explain my book," Rose finally says, her body starting to relax. "First, please forgive me - I suppose I am a little anxious. I have played out how this meeting will go in my head since the moment I started writing the letter you received." She smiles, hoping that this notion doesn't sound crazy and *is* actually normal.

"I think I explained a bit of my background in my letter. I am first and foremost a theologian. It's hard to find work as a theologian these days – and even harder to find people willing to even believe that theologians still exist." *Am I lying?*

She takes a breath and tilts her head to look at Ms. Nightingale. Rose actually thinks about mimicking a small bird. "My focus in graduate school was ethics. I am sure that it wouldn't shock you to learn that there were very few jobs in my field. Ethics in America – what was I thinking!? Anyway, the only gig I could get was using my bachelors in biology. I work in clinical research. I like the job. I am not a big fan of the industry. However, it pays the bills." Rose then humbly adds, "I hate working for money."

"I have decided to do my ancestry proud and actually be a professional theologian. And the only way to get paid as a theologian is to either get a Ph.D. and teach, or write a book. As a big fan of multi-tasking, I decided that I would write my dissertation and then go back to get my Ph.D. This book, the book that I am here to talk to you about, is essentially that dissertation. I want to write an insightful dissertation about ethics wrapped and bound in a narrative. What else should a descendant of Aesop do? Isope is an ancient spelling of Aesop."

"And now about the book..." Rose looks at Rebekah to size up her interest thus far. "Am I talking too much?"

"I understand."

She decides that now is a good time to make her apologies. She opens her folder and brings out her agenda. "I brought a meeting agenda. You are going to have to exercise good managerial skills and rein me in when necessary. I talk a lot and often my tangents are only interesting to me. It's a flaw in a person, yet it really isn't so bad in a writer. Fair?" Rose exhales through her nose and giggles. "Golly, I did not think I was going to be this nervous."

Rebekah shakes the agenda. "Gee, I thought this was supposed to be different from my regular meetings."

"I think agenda is a funny word."

"Never really thought about it."

"I think its Roman." Rose reaches over to her agenda and lightly touches it. "Roman numeral I: The Plot."

Rebekah shifts in her seat and folds her hands near the paper.

"I initially heard about the Harkin-Engel protocol in a news story on CNN.com. Have you heard of it?" She takes out a copy of the protocol from her folder and places it down next to the agenda.

Rebekah responds in the affirmative and glances through

White Lies and Dark Chocolate

the 16 pages. She notes that the majority of the pages are signatures.

"This is like gold to a student of ethics. A simple agreement signed by eight companies with six goals - sensationally simple." Rose takes a breath. "I am now going to tell you the sentence that I paid $30,000 dollars for – the cost of my degree - the definition of ethics. My ethics professor taught me everything I ever needed to know about ethics in the first five minutes of his introductory class. The definition of ethics is…" Rose pauses for dramatic effect and positions her arms as if to say *Tah Dah*. "Ethics is the creed that defines your deed. Your deed is your morality. And integrity is how well the creed and the deed reflect one another." In a very clear voice and a strong tone, Rose finally explains the purpose of this meeting. "Ma'am, those eight chocolate companies… those companies who signed the Harkin-Engel protocol on page 16 are seriously lacking in integrity. And I need your company to set things right."

Rebekah is startled for a moment. She did not expect this turn in the conversation, although she realizes that she probably should have. With her high coloring, her anger is not hard to read.

Rose immediately responds, "In my book, ma'am, in my work of fiction." Rose tries to convey calmness and continues, "A small yet substantial chocolate company, the company that employs my heroine, Amaran, decides to take these eight companies to task and change their way of doing business." Rose looks to Rebekah. "I need your help with the plausibility of the narrative."

"Well… I am not quite sure… I don't know if," Ms. Nightingale tries to get a word in edge wise.

"I know about ethics. I don't know anything about chocolate… well other than the fact that it is probably," she stops to consider her ranking, "…divine."

"I will agree with that," Rebekah says lightly. "DEEEVine."

"In my book, Amaran's boss becomes irate because they are unable to meet their high-end boutique customer requests for certified chocolate while remaining fiscally solvent. The problem falls on the idealistic shoulders of Amaran. She decides that because they are not big enough to change the world's cocoa processes – the only solution is to publically lead by example and force the larger chocolate corporations into a global movement. Sounds so 'Hollywood,' doesn't it?" Rose says with an amused smile.

Rose points to the second Roman numeral. "On page two, the first goal of the cocoa protocol is 'to publically acknowledge the problem of forced child labor and to commit to significant resources to address it.' It has been 11 years since these companies have signed and they have not done this – well not in the true spirit of the protocol. The public is really NOT aware."

Rose thinks for a moment. "It's like being an alcoholic and going to AA meetings without making the commitment to stop drinking. They are not really facing the problem." She realizes the analogy is weak after completing it. "I am sorry. I don't think that is a fair analogy. No. That's not fair at all." She looks down and shakes her head.

Rebekah helps her recover. "So in your story, you want a smaller company to call out a bigger company. A modern David-and-Goliath-type thing."

"Exactly." Rose pictures a handsome white robed brunette and a sling shot before revising her response. "Well, after a fashion. That's a popular interpretation. You have to remember that you are talking to a theologian." She smiles and almost winks. "Maybe it is like a Rebekah thing – bringing water to those in need?"

Rebekah smiles and asks, "What kind of business woman am I in your book?"

Slightly embarrassed and not quite sure how to respond, Rose looks out the window. "I am sure that I would use adjectives like strong, respected, kind and classic."

"Can I have jet black hair?" She smiles.

Rose laughs out loud. The two women start chatting about hair color preferences and styles. Rose tells Rebekah that she has always wanted dark hair as well - dark hair and blue eyes.

With several careful compliments and minimal effort, Rose successfully brings the conversation back to task. "Last week, I walked around downtown... this was probably the day after I read the news story on CNN. I was still pretty angry. I stepped into a few local chocolate shops. Anyway, at each place I went to the counter and asked whether or not they have heard of the protocol. They hadn't. Two out of three were, at the very least, moved by the information. I spoke to one shop owner and she was amenable to a small percentage, quite small, of their profits going towards a solution."

"There are a lot of good chocolatiers in this area," Rebekah says with sincerity.

"My ruse for those conversations was that I was preparing for an interview with Hershcy's."

"So you are not writing a book?" She asks astutely, while acting mildly confused.

"No. I mean, I am writing a book." Rose blushes.

Rose explains her actions with Hershey's and her plan to raise money to build schools using specially packaged Kisses. She told Rebekah about her ad campaign. She also explains how disappointed she was in their non-response. Rose asks, "Do you think public awareness is accomplished by putting a link to a press release on a web page that you have to be looking for to find? It just makes me want to melt their chocolate.... You know... mad." She stops to ask, "Is that a good industry joke?"

"Why are you hounding me?" Rebekah asks bluntly.

"Abdul and Aesop." Rose pulls up the inner flap of her folder and pulls out a copy of the original article. She points to the picture of Abdul and the caption below the picture. She then asks,

"Are you familiar with the Aesop fable, "The Hawk and the Nightingale"?

"I may have heard of it," Rebekah answers.

Rose reaches into her folder and pulls out a 3x5 notecard with one version of the fable and its moral printed on the front and another version printed on the back. She also included her contact information in small print on the notecard.

Rebekah accepts the notecard with an amused "huh."

"Ma'am, I am a descendant and have spent my life considering my ancestor's legacy. Now and again I have found my understandings of the classic fables discordant with the classic morals. In *my* book the Nightingale convinces the Hawk to make a different decision. The Nightingale is allowed to sing and helps the Hawk hunt and those that are not seen… the children become visible. I want people to see Abdul," Rose says softly while picturing Abdul and an amaranth.

"The Hawk and the Nightingale." Rebekah lifts her eye brows while simultaneously flipping through the protocol and says, "I am not sure I have time for this."

Relentlessly, Rose mimes the plucking of a string, "The plucky company forms a guild with the local chocolatiers called the 'Chocolatiers Initiative's Pen,' or 'ChIP' for short. My heroine starts by getting every chocolatier in the area, or maybe the state, to sign a petition to commit a small percentage of their profit to the cause –excluding that company in the capital. Then this *plucky* company… I like the word *plucky*… the *plucky* company, along with the support of the local, smaller chocolatiers, makes a formal public announcement and commitment with national coverage…local TV, local newspaper and CNN… and pledges that they will attempt to fulfill the promise that the larger companies have not been able to do in eleven years. The promise includes that the company will donate a percentage of proceeds from specially packaged chocolates to raise money to build schools for the children of the cocoa fields. The company also publically offers an invitation to all chocolate companies to join the Chocolatiers Initiative's Pen."

Rose finishes with one more statement, struggling to remember the ruse, "The publicity received from this initiative becomes very good for your company, I mean the company, and its chocolate sales. They gain the customers who knew about this issue. They also gain new customers who are just moved by the story and are just learning about the problem."

"Has anyone ever accused you of being subtle?" Rebekah laughs and flips the notecard in her hands.

Rose does her best impression of the Mona Lisa. "I want to give Abdul a chocolate bar."

"What happens if I justifiably kick you out of my office?" She asks, followed by a hardy laugh.

Rose smiles and twists in her chair to look at the door. She mimes a pluck again while fully extending her left arm. "Ma'am, there are two strings to my bow." Rose centers and gently places her hands back on the black leather folder in front of her. "I suppose I could base my work of fiction on a person named David Hawk. David Hawk willingly carries a giant CHIP on his shoulder," she says with a cool sarcastic tone, accompanied by a very large smile. "Do you think my narrative is plausible, possible, probable…dare I say… inevitable?"

"You are not asking for a job, are you?"

"No ma'am. I already have a job." Rose states the fact.

With a crooked smile, Rebecca recaps, "So, in your book, the company gets national attention for helping raise awareness of child labor in cocoa fields, spearheads a national and international chocolate guild and adds many new purchasing customers at extraordinarily little cost to me…" She smiles, "…I mean, the company."

Rose replies boldly, "Yep." She continues, "Well, I am here, after all, just looking for a reliable and professional source to test plausibility of this narrative."

"I see. You need to find out whether Amaran, is it?" Rebekah smiles. "You need to find out whether or not this is plausible fiction, and not fantasy."

"Exactly. Is this idea plausible or fantasy?"

"Well, let me think about it."

Rose smiles. "At least your answer is not 'No.'"

"'Roman numeral III. Plausability.' Interesting," Rebekah says while gently shuffling the papers.

"Remember when I asked in the beginning of this meeting that if you were chapter two, would you want to read chapter one?" Rose returns to her black folder and pulls out a printed version of chapter one and hands the copy to Rebekah. "Ms. Nightingale, it was a pleasure meeting you."

Rose collects her belongings and again thanks her host for the pleasant conversation. She quickly walks through the lobby as she wipes her very sweaty hands on the sides of her dress. She stops, presses the bar to exit and looks over her shoulder at the office where she just spent the last 55 minutes. She thinks of Aris and one of his favorite fables, "The Sick Lion." Her first breath of fresh air is close to perfect. Rose looks at her watch. *Time to go to work.*

CHAPTER 4
THE BUNDLE OF STICKS

AN OLD MAN on the point of death summoned his sons around him to give them some parting advice. He ordered his servants to bring in a faggot of sticks, and said to his eldest son: "Break it." The son strained and strained, but with all his efforts was unable to break the Bundle. The other sons also tried, but none of them was successful. "Untie the faggots," said the father, "and each of you take a stick." When they had done so, he called out to them: "Now, break," and each stick was easily broken. "You see my meaning," said their father. –Aesop

Rose sits very comfortably on her couch swaddled in her favorite fuzzy blanket with remote in hand. It's a Saturday and, of course, she is watching ingenious movies on SyFy. In truth, she is not really watching them. She can glean the most delicate and intricate plot points of these movies with minimal effort. The giant piranha, the movie's female lead, is really misunderstood - she is just trying to protect her children from the rare and miraculous giant double-headed fresh water shark. Should it be otherwise?

The phone rings. "Hello."

"Hi, Rose. It's Josephine. What are you doing?"

"Syfy on mute," Rose responds to one of her dearest friends, who happens to be newly engaged to one of her oldest friends, Augustine.

"Girl, you need to get out of the house."

"Actually, I need to spend some time in. I have been traveling way too much. I need some good quality time in the place that I spend a ridiculous chunk of my salary on."

"Augustine and I want to go out for a drink. Join us? A drink, coffee, whatever."

"Wanna hang here? I really don't want to put on shoes. I was thinking of baking brownies. Your visit would give the necessary incentive."

Rose listens as Josephine restates a possible plan to Augustine. Rose can then hear Augustine restating the plan back to Josephine to ensure he was able to process the change of plans to its greatest extent. Rose is amused by the tender reveal of their relationship communicare.

Josephine returns. "We'll be there in a few. Need anything?"

"Have you eaten? I don't have any alcohol in the house. You can bring wine or whatever. Kahlua and coffee go well with brownies," Rose suggests.

"You're not drinking, right?" Josephine asks.

"I was thinking about you."

"We'll be there soon with Angelo's pizza. 20 minutes tops."

"Great. Awesome. See you in a few." Rose ends the call.

"Brownies!" Rose says as she literally jumps up from the couch and runs to the kitchen as best she can in socks on a hardwood floor. She presses the bake toggle on her oven. She then, in all haste, grabs her yellow plastic bowl, aka the brownie bowl, and pours the contents of the mix. She quickly adds the oil, water and egg without needing to review the instructions. She then adds her handful of Tollhouse and another handful of special dark chips. She opens the refrigerator and contemplates raspberry jam. She grabs the bottle and heats a ½ cup in the microwave. She stirs the brownie mix, coats the brownie pan, pours the batter and then draws a line with the jam down the middle. She takes a butter knife and swirls. "Perfect. 28 minutes?" She reads the instructions. "39! So odd? I wonder why these brownies take so long?"

Rose quickly runs through her house making minor adjustments for her guests, including changing the towel in the bathroom. She returns to the kitchen and notices the clock, 7:43. Rose then stacks her notes and papers about chocolate in a pile and places them on top of December's Architectural Digest in the corner of her coffee table. She folds her fuzzy blanket and throws it over the top of her reading chair. She is turning up the heat on the gas fire just as she hears a soft knock at the door, accompanied by muffled voices of a very happy couple.

Rose unlocks the door and opens. "Hi, Guys."

"Hey, Rose. Angelo's!" Augustine announces, carrying a pizza box.

"Fabulous swirls of tomato-y goodness topped by the perfect nine cheese blend."

"Nine? Don't be ridiculous?"

"It may be less, but it sure tastes like more," Rose says taking the pizza from Augustine so he can remove his trench. "This pizza is magical."

"Hey, Josey. What's the word?"

"Mellifluence." Josephine lifts the bottle of Kahlua.

Rose smiles and sets the pizza on her kitchen island. "I have paper plates." She quickly retrieves three silver plates from her cupboard and turns to follow the gaze of her guests. She speaks as though she knows what they are thinking, "It's a two-headed fresh water shark, in case you were wondering. Its sorta like a chimera, only vastly different." Rose thinks of Lin.

"Obviously," Augustine confirms. "How's work?"

"I have root beer, ginger beer and blueberry juice." Rose grabs the pizza box topped with paper plates and napkins and carries it to the coffee table.

"Root beer," Josephine chimes.

"The same," Augustine answers.

Rose grabs three dark brown bottles from the refrigerator door. "Work is fine. I have been traveling a lot."

"So Josephine told me. Where to?"

"I was just in Milwaukee. Before that, Portland. And before that, Boston. I am usually in each city a bit less than 36 hours. Anyway, I don't want to talk about my work. How's life amongst the mentally sane?"

Josephine laughs. "You see Auggie, that's funny. It's funny because you work around psychologists and psychiatrists and by their professions alone, they must be sane."

"Very funny," Augustine humors his fiancé. "I guess the joke that I am supposed to say now is, 'I have heard it all before.'" Augustine stands on the left side of the coffee table and notices the prints of the vintage Hershey ads on top of the magazines. "I love old ad campaigns." He shows the ad to Josephine.

Josephine grabs the sheet. "Cool. What's this?"

"A Hershey ad. I am on this new kick," Rose says. "Did you hear about the child slavery issue in the chocolate industry."

Augustine nods. "I read something about it recently."

Rose quickly recaps the article she read, the trip to Hershey's and the conversation with Rebekah Nightingale to her friends while serving slices of scrumptious pizza. "So what do you think, doc? Is my mania rearing its ugly head?"

"What some may call mania others call initiative," Augustine notes.

"And you?" Rose asks.

"Well, you know my thoughts on this matter. I really do think you should reconsider your stance on antidepressants. I think you would feel a good deal better about the world."

"I've considered and reconsidered and then considered reconsidering my reconsideration. Anyway, after an obvious amount of… consideration…I really think life is supposed to be emotionally and intellectually taxing." Rose bites into her pizza.

"There is a point, Rose, when help is required." He hands out the napkins.

"Actually, I think the two of you could really help me with this little project." Rose briefly explains ChIP. "I would like to design a logo."

Augustine and Josephine look at each other and smile. "That's cool. We love graphic design."

"I know you do. And I could pay you, too."

"That's not necessary," Augustine says.

"A compromise, then. How about a dinner?"

"So what kind of logo are you looking for?" Josephine asks, looking more closely at the vintage Hershey ads. "I really like these, such bold color."

"I don't know. Something salient and provocative." Rose retells the idea of replacing the boy in the Hershey Kisses ad with Abdul.

"That's a little too provocative - maybe even off-putting," Augustine comments.

"I guess I want something simple, powerful that conveys strength and determination that is also mellifluent." Rose laughs as she shoots a kind look to Josephine. "I really like that image of the woman wearing the bandana flexing her bicep. Iconic."

"Sounds simple enough." Josephine heartily laughs. "So you want a logo that is both iconic and mellifluent and also conveys determination. Were you thinking two colors, or three?"

Rose laughs. "Three. And do you think you could include the continent of Africa?"

"Easy!" Augustine joins in on the laughter. "Hey, something just beeped."

"My brownies. I completely forgot about them. Thanks." Rose jumps and runs to the oven and opens the door.

"How could you forget about them? They smell delicious," Josephine says.

"I am sure they are." Rose tests their doneness with a cake stick. "They need at least 10 minutes to cool."

"What makes a good logo?" Rose asks, returning to her guests. "I've been thinking about it. I have been considering various forms of logos that have actually made an impact on me. I guess I've been trying to glean the difference between a significant logo versus a pedestrian tag."

"Hershey has its bar," Josephine says. "That's a pretty good logo."

"I was thinking that a chocolate chip could work, but I suppose other chocolate companies would have a problem using the Kiss," Rose says.

"Not necessarily, a chocolate chip is a chocolate chip is a chocolate chip," Augustine says.

"Sometimes a cigar is just a cigar," Rose teases. "Maybe you can combine a woman's bicep and draw in a chocolate chip in the negative space." Rose quickly jots down a doodle to explain what she means.

Josephine nods. "Why a woman?"

"Well, Rebekah Nightingale is a woman. I guess I am, too."

"You guess?" Augustine laughs. "I think you might need more help than previously thought. Anyway, I think you both might be confusing an iconic image with a logo."

"So what is ChIP again?" Josephine asks sincerely.

"Chocolatier's Initiative's Pen. It's a guild of chocolatiers that pledge a percentage of one of their chocolates to be given to the children who harvest cocoa for them. The money will be used to build schools - the best schools in the world. Wouldn't it be cool for the best schools in the world to be in Africa? I guess its sorta like, 'I have a dream.' It's a nice dream. Seems fitting, right?"

"Careful, Rose." Augustine says.

Rose furrows her brow and shoots a sharp look towards Augustine. "Aris has already warned me."

"And you are choosing not to listen," Augustine retorts.

"Extreme voices need to exist for people to find the common ground," Rose reposes. "And my voice is not extreme. Using trafficked children to harvest chocolate is wrong. Do you think that is an extreme stance?"

"Whoa," Augustine says.

"Mania, initiative, passion... same, same," Rose says softly. "Thanks for your concern, but the deep end is pretty far from here. Brownies?" Rose abruptly stands from her reading chair.

Josephine stands and walks with Rose to the kitchen. "Are you Okay?"

"I am fine." Rose laughs lightly. "Really, I am." Rose turns to Augustine. "Do you want ice cream on your brownie? I have black cherry and coffee with toffee."

"I didn't mean to upset you," Augustine says as he walks towards the kitchen.

"You didn't. I'm sorry I made you think that you did. I'm just a bit defensive, I guess. I guess I am emotionally involved. Sometimes my voice and my body and my thoughts are - misinterpreted. Discordant might be the better word."

"It's good to care about things," Josephine defends Rose.

Augustine nods. "Within reason, within bounds. And to answer your question, a small brownie with one scoop of coffee, please."

Rose smiles at her friend. "Chocolate syrup?" Rose lifts the Hershey's syrup from her refrigerator door.

"I'll have the cherry ice cream with the chocolate syrup, please!" Josephine yelps.

"Me too," Rose says as she lifts the lid of the cherry ice cream.

The three walk back to the couches and watch the school of baby piranha swim behind the credits. "The piranha won? I didn't see that one. I guess I was secretly rooting for the shark," Rose comments.

"Do you watch SYFY all the time?" Josephine asks.

"I liked it better when it was spelled 'SciFi.' And yes, especially on Saturdays. I watch much more often then I listen," Rose remarks.

"Text messaging has pretty much turned the world into lousy spellers." Augustine adds. "SYFY?"

"Don't get me started," Rose says. "Aris and I almost had this argument this past Thursday."

"How is Aris?" Augustine asks.

"He's good. I haven't seen much of him lately," Rose says somewhat despondently.

Augustine recognizes the look of loss in Rose's eyes and he takes the moment to recognize his own good fortune, "I love you, baby."

Josephine smiles. "Right back at ya." She thoughtfully transfers back to Rose, "Well, I want to meet this mystery friend of yours."

"That's right, you still have not met him," Rose says. "Huh."

"Why is that?" Augustine asks.

Rose looks at Augustine. "Some people say I like to compartmentalize."

"Do you?"

"I protect myself and others," Rose says. "Good brownie?"

Augustine looks at Rose inquisitively. "We are all friends here."

"And some of us are shrinks," Rose jabs and follows the verbal sparring with a toothy grin.

Josephine interjects, "Well, I do want to meet him. You seem to think very highly of him."

"He's a great guy," Rose attests. "He makes me laugh."

"He certainly made you cry," Augustine adds, remembering the break-up.

"Yeah, I suppose he did. I guess I needed to. Anyway, we're just really good friends now."

Rose looks at the single slice of pizza in the box. "He's like my sounding board. I tend to bounce my ideas off of him. He keeps me grounded, not caged." She picks up the box and walks to the kitchen.

Josephine looks at Augustine in an obvious way, and then turns. "Do you have a timeline set up of when you would like this logo?"

"I don't know, not really, sorta... well, how about – soon,"

Rose answers. "Hey look, another piranha movie. Coffee?"

"Yes, please." Josephine gets up and walks to the kitchen. "I love coffee and Kahlua."

"I have several varieties of coffee to choose from. 'Dark Magic' is my favorite." Rose spins the coffee carousel.

"Mud slide." Josephine makes her selection. "And look, there are two."

Rose grabs two large glass mugs from her collection. "I do not know what it is, but alcoholic coffee needs to be served in a glass mug."

"I agree. There must be some unwritten rule somewhere," Josephine says, watching the coffee fall from the Keurig.

"Thanks for your support."

"No problem."

"Do you think it's hot in here?"

"Maybe a little," Josephine answers.

Rose walks to the fireplace and lowers the temperature and notices Augustine flipping through December's magazine. "I love Architectural Digest."

"There is not much architecture here."

"No, but it provides plenty of fodder for the building of a dream home. And mentally building a dream home helps when one travels for a living," Rose mutters as she returns to the kitchen to brew her own cup.

"Augustine found my Architectural Digest," she utters quietly.

"My mother reads Veranda," Josephine says.

"I may prefer that magazine, but cannot justify the price. It's actually quite expensive."

Josephine shrugs. "I wouldn't mind an apartment with two bathrooms."

Rose smiles at her friend and laughs as she looks up. "God, why do I feel like I am learning a lesson in humility?"

Augustine turns in the couch. "It's amazing what people

can do. Did you see this bronze statue?"

"Thanks, God," Rose whispers.

Josephine carries a coffee beverage to her fiancé and sits down very close to him. She whispers something that is followed by gentle kisses and nuzzles. Rose watches from the kitchen with a quiet envy. She misses contact. She misses Aris. Rose tidies up the kitchen and takes the trash and the pizza box to the garbage chute in the hallway.

Returning, Rose says, "I was thinking of getting 1000 piece puzzles made out of those vintage ads. Christmas is coming up and I was wondering if that sounded like a good gift idea for someone you know. The more puzzles I order, the better the price."

"That's a good idea. Can you get anything made into a puzzle?" Augustine asks.

"Any picture. No babies," Rose jokes. "Maybe we can use a puzzle piece as part of the logo?"

Augustine and Josephine look at each other. She kisses his nose. "Puzzle pieces in logos are a bit overdone."

"Sometimes it really works though. I love puzzles."

At 11:25, Josephine and Augustine begin to take their leave. "Hey guys, thanks for the pizza and the conversation. I had a really nice evening."

"It's good to see you, Rose. You do need to get out a bit more often," Josephine says, issuing a hug to her friend.

"I wish I were home more often. I should really quit my job."

"You are doing good work," Augustine says in support of Rose and her career.

"Yeah, I guess. Drive safe and enjoy the rest of your weekend."

"You too, Rose. Good night."

Rose listens for the parking garage door to open before locking her door. She readies herself for bed, conducting her normal evening rituals. She climbs under her covers and stares at the moving tree shadows on her ceiling. Unable to sleep, she replays the evening in her head and tries to create a logo on her own.

"Me and my stupid artistic temperament named Bipolar. It's just a logo." She rolls to her right side. She begins to re-imagine her visits to the local chocolatiers, including Rebekah Nightingale. She thinks of handing them a perfectly executed and laminated logo. She sees the logo on a tray of chocolate placed prominently by the cash register. She turns to her left side as she struggles with the thought of her puppeteer fantasies. "This is stupid Rose, they aren't going to help. You cannot make them do it. You're wasting your time."

Rose starts to accept these dark thoughts as true. She starts to envision robots behind the counters, at the cash registers. The robots become dolls. Her mind then jumps to a grotesque image - a broken-faced porcelain doll resting on a shoulder with a tag line that says, 'ChIP. These are Real Children.' Lying on her back, she makes two fists and slams them down on the mattress. "Do you dream in chocolate?" She screams at the ceiling, "God, do the piranhas always win?"

I am sorry, Abdul. Rose tries to recapture the images of chocolatiers helping and Abdul smiling. *Maybe they don't always win.* She reaches over to open the window before turning back to her right side. "I just need a little help." She finds sleep in nineteen minutes.

CHAPTER 5
THE SICK LION

A LION, unable from old age and infirmities to provide himself with food by force, resolved to do so by artifice. He returned to his den, and lying down there, pretended to be sick, taking care that his sickness should be publicly known. The beasts expressed their sorrow, and came one by one to his den, where the Lion devoured them. After many of the beasts had thus disappeared, the Fox discovered the trick and presenting himself to the Lion, stood on the outside of the cave, at a respectful distance, and asked him how he was. "I am very middling," replied the Lion, "but why do you stand without? Pray enter within to talk with me." "No, thank you," said the Fox. "I notice that there are many prints of feet entering your cave, but I see no trace of any returning." – Aesop

It is a Tuesday night and Rose arrives at the coffee shop an hour early. She has a few items that she needs to work on prior to socializing. If she stayed at home she would have spent the hour either web surfing or watching TV. Although the coffee shop is loud and often disruptive, it often provides the necessary background noise to aid in concentration. She has work to do - work related to her actual job. She must write a report of a clinical visit for her employers as per regulation. These reports were often more cut and paste than actual depiction of events of the visit. Federal regulations provide such rigid format that the obvious can often be overlooked in order to find the time to satisfy the minutia expected. It is a frustrating duty that often requires complicity and a superiorly brewed cappuccino.

"Complicity and the Cappuccino," Rose mutters as she opens the report program on her company-issued computer. She is very often burdened by the word complicit. It is a sentiment that she combats daily in her career. In the pharmaceutical industry, medicine is considered a science. Yet, in her philosophy, medicine should be considered an art. She witnesses those who practice the science much more often than those who practice the art. The difference is stark – treating the symptoms versus treating the patient. Clinical trials do not leave room for art. And in so doing, often the adverse events of the experimental medicines are overlooked or unseen. Rose finishes her report and forwards the file to her boss with a simple line acknowledging completion. She sighs as she shuts down the laptop. She grabs her left wrist with her right hand and tries to feel the golden handcuff. She knows that it is there, but alas she only feels her eternally cold hands on her bony wrist. Her heart stings a bit as her mind starts to coil around her nine to five efforts. Her mind cannot help pairing the word complicit with contrition. *Complicit contrition.* She knows she should quit. Instead, she stands to stretch her legs and seek a refill of her coffee.

    It has been several weeks since the last time she met with Aris. They both travel with their jobs and making special efforts to meet is getting more difficult as they phase through adulthood. She still feels a bit guilty for monopolizing the conversation the last time they met. She is hoping this time to be a friend to him. She looks at her cell phone to learn the time. Aris arrives one minute early.

    The coffee house is quieter than usual. Rose assumes that the holiday might have something to do with it. Her family is local. Luckily she does not have to travel this week. Aris's family lives outside of Baltimore. He and Nora will be leaving tomorrow morning. Rose suspects that Aris will only be able to stay about an hour. Her throat tightens with this thought. She does realize that these meetings will end, probably sooner than she would like. She knows she is on borrowed time and fears she is experiencing this fear mostly because he is actually early by an entire minute. She acknowledges his personal feat and sends a very wry smile to Aris.

    Aris takes a seat at the small table. He adjusts the chair so his back is not to the door, but rather to the wall. She gets to look at his left profile tonight. He is happy. She can tell that he is looking forward to spending time with his family.

Aris starts. "What is your plan for the holiday weekend?"

"Dinner on Thursday with the folks. My brother and sisters will be there with their spouses. A day and night filled with tryptophan and pumpkin pie. Other than that, I suppose I may do a bit of shopping and possibly make it to the gym a few days in a row. You are leaving tomorrow morning, right?"

"Yes. I am really looking forward to going home. It's been awhile." Aris looks down at the table with a simple smile of contentment.

"You really look happy," Rose observes with a tear almost reaching into the left corner of her eye. With a bit of a quiver in her voice, almost undetectable, she repeats, "You really do look happy."

"Thanks. I think I am," Aris responds. "It's been a couple of weeks, anything interesting to report?"

Rose responds with an expressive shrug. The shrug suggests to Aris that Rose is trying to be conversational.

"I told Nora more about your chocolate campaign. She also told me that there is a similar thing going on a bit south of Ghana in the Tungsten mines. Apparently, in order to make our shiny IPods, they need tungsten. And there are children mining the tungsten," Aris says while gently tapping his fingers on the table, similar to how a hand moves on a keyboard.

"There is a joke to make here about apples falling from trees, maybe something to do with Gravity and Gilbert Newton Lewis's photons and dot structures, covalent bonds and frequent visits to the periodic table... yet I am too tired to make it funny," Rose says with a self-satisfied look.

"The Molecule and the Adam? I know the story all too well," Aris adds, content with his superior summation.

Rose starts singing Afro Celt Sound System lyrics, "Cause

when you're falling, I can't tell which way is down. And when you are screaming, somehow I don't hear a sound."

"Peter Gabriel, still?" Aris asks.

"Peter Gabriel always," Rose replies. "I guess I will never grow up."

"Peter Gabriel has always been a bit too pop for me," Aris says while hurriedly stepping out of his seat into the recently vacant line in front of the barista. "Can I get you something?" he asks in a clearly audible tone.

"Yes. Apple tea. Thanks."

Rose slips her purse under her coat and steps quietly to the loo. Walking back to the table she notices the chess board stashed in the cupboard below the condiment station. She quickly grabs the folded board and the box of pieces. She flashes both before Aris with raised eyebrows. "Got time for a quick game?"

"Chess. The quick game." Aris acquiesces by lifting his cup to make room for the board. Rose skips the remaining two feet to her chair. She grabs a white and black piece and shows her fists. Aris punches her right fist with his. She reveals white. Together they speedily set up the board.

"Remember when you told me that you wanted to marry the man who would be happy to play a game of chess with each visit to your shared bathroom," Aris asks. "Have you met him yet?"

"Ah yes, my dream man…" Rose almost dares herself to look directly at him. She turns her body slightly to move her computer case strap from one corner of the chair to the other, believing this gesture is enough to ensure safety. "What do you think? Do you think there is such a man? I think he is probably married to someone else." She moves her pawn to match his opening.

"You are still looking, aren't you?" Aris moves his bishop.

"For my knight?" Rose moves her knight, yet still holds the piece. "I am not sure if I should." She lifts her hand and moves for her tea and takes a sip. She nearly spits and then laughs out loud. "It's orange spice."

"There is no comparison," he says, actually laughing at his joke. "I'm sorry. I could not resist."

"I know you could have... resisted. I like orange tea and it's seasonally festive." She smiles because at this moment she is happy. She wonders if she ordered orange tea whether she would have received apple. *Not so quick brown fox.*

Aris pulls out his knight and his phone. It is Nora. Rose begins to feel guilty as she tries to pretend she is concentrating on the board. "Where are the tungsten mines?" he asks the receiver. "Rwanda and Uganda," he utters while looking at Rose.

Rose decides that she should get a glass of water. She wanders over to the house pitcher and takes her time while attempting small talk with Chloe, the barista. She finds out that Chloe is flying out tomorrow morning at 6 AM. She is spending five days in the Florida Keys. Although she is looking forward to the sun and surf, she is not a big fan of her father's new wife, Victoria, who chose the location. Rose notices Aris putting his phone back into his coat pocket. She wishes her barista a pleasant holiday. She refills her water glass and returns to the table.

"Is Nora excited about tomorrow?" Rose asks while clearing room for her glass.

"She only had a few questions about the particulars. And yes, I think she is excited," Aris replies. "You moved your pawn to protect your knight?"

Rose nods and wonders whether she should ask about Nora. "You could say that."

Aris smiles as he castles. "So have you thought more about those Kisses?"

"A little," Rose answers with a hint of anger wrapped in confusion. "I have spent more time thinking about boys." She moves another pawn.

"Boys who play chess?" he asks while staring at the board.

He takes his first piece while contemplating his next three moves.

"You're acting strange," Rose observes as she plays the traditional trades and then casually returns to the conversation, "I bet there is a patch for that."

Aris looks to Rose with his own confusion. "What?"

"Do you think you can earn a Boy Scout merit badge in chess?" Rose asks. She realizes she is unsure if Aris was ever a boy scout.

"I am a little old for earning merit badges," he says with a simple smile. "Of course, a boy can earn a merit badge in chess. It's a checkered board with a knight on it. It was just announced, actually."

Rose's unasked question is answered. "I think a system of merit badges could work as part of a plan to help protect children in the cocoa fields - Field Scouts of the Ivory Coast. I think this could also help in the mines in Uganda and Rwanda."

"Thorn, you are over simplifying things," Aris says with a tone of dissatisfaction. "You have never even been to Africa. And you think you can show up with a badge and call it a solution. It's not that easy."

"I see. You never got your chess merit badge. You're bitter," Rose says as she castles, queen side. With a tone of her own dissatisfaction, she adds, "Maybe the solution is that easy."

Aris smiles at her green move. "I think they call that a long castle. It leaves your king more vulnerable."

"I have trained my guardsmen well. My king has nothing to worry about," she says with vulnerability weighing heavy behind her eyes. "Chess does seem to carry a strange sense of complicity. The queen should be the one being protected; she seems to be the most powerful piece. Yet she is out there taking all of the risks," Rose sighs. "I guess the truth of the game is that a queen is replaceable and the truth of this conversation is that I am mishandling the word complicity. I wish I knew how to say 'C'est la vie' in Farsi."

Aris moves to threaten both her queen and her rook. "Thorn, you do realize that this is a game of strategy; not a game of courtship."

Rose protects her rook. "It can't be a game of courtship. There is only one woman on the board and she is married. Well, actually, to be fair, I suppose a couple of foot soldiers could become queens - probably already have their outfits picked out." Rose attempts humor with an exaggerated flutter of her lashes.

"You play chess with an impalpable and shadowy understanding. You never play to win," Aris says with an air of frustration as he forks her knight and bishop.

Rose protects her knight and threatens his bishop. "The queen never wins. On the other hand, she doesn't always lose."

Aris moves for the check and smiles. She moves her pawn one block and looks at Aris as he considers his options for mate. His eyebrows make a perfect arch while the wrinkles on his forehead sink a bit deeper. She knows she lost this game. She wants to kiss him.

"Check," Aris says. "Mate in three."

"I can pretend that I can follow how it is that you are going to…" Rose makes air quotes "…mate me." She twists the right side of her mouth. "Not much between despair and ecstasy."

"That is not the kind of mate I am contemplating," Aris says coldly.

"Guess I wasn't careful." Rose nervously giggles then exhales. "Grand Master, where do you want me to move?" She gently kicks his calf with her boot, accidentally on purpose.

"You could slide your piece over here - for mate in two," Aris says while sipping the last of his cool Turkish tea.

Rose does what she is told to do. Aris makes his last move and then stretches his hand above the board. "Good game, Thorn."

With a gentle mock reserved for him, Rose takes the tip of his fingers and shakes his hand like a lady of an English court. "Good Game, Good Sir."

"One knight in Bangkok." Aris looks to his watch and notices the time. "I am curious, have you heard more from Lin?"

"I know she got herself a lawyer and a pair of diamond earrings. They're pretty."

Aris smiles. "I suppose you harped on her about where the diamonds come from?"

"There was no harp." Rose reposts, "Maybe a touch of hostility? Golly, Aris!"

Aris lifts the right side of his mouth. "I really need to get going. I have a long drive tomorrow."

"Four hours is not a long drive," Rose adds haughtily. "Do drive safely. Precious cargo."

"Will do, Thorn," Aris says with a gentle, prodding tone.

"Have music for the road?" she asks with a suggestive glance.

"Nothing like the Cranberries." Aris grabs his cup and saucer and places them in the bin nearest their table. "Probably something less nostalgic."

"Smashing Pumpkins," Rose says with a smile. "Have a good night, Aris."

Aris nods while checking for his keys. "Good night, Rose."

While trying to appear gratified, Rose smiles and just mouths the word "bye." She starts to look at the ground for her purse and her coat. She looks up and watches Aris leave the building.

"Does he know that you are in love with him?" Chloe asks without even the slightest hesitation about such a personal question.

"He's not a fool," Rose counters as she lobs her computer bag over her right shoulder. "Does that answer your question?" She shoots Chloe a sharp look and punctiliously continues, "Enjoy the sunshine and wear sunscreen. Can't be too careful." She quickly escapes before she hears another question she cannot answer.

CHAPTER 6
THE TREE AND THE REED

"Well, little one," said a Tree to a Reed that was growing at its foot, "why do you not plant your feet deeply in the ground, and raise your head boldly in the air as I do?"

"I am contented with my lot," said the Reed "I may not be so grand, but I think I am safer."

"Safe," sneered the Tree. "Who shall pluck me up by the roots or bow my head to the ground?" But it soon had to repent of its boasting, for a hurricane arose which tore it up from its roots, and cast it a useless log on the ground, while the little Reed, bending to the force of the wind, soon stood upright again when the storm had passed over. –Aesop

At 11:45 AM on Sunday morning, Rose enters the Pet Palace with a deli bag in her left hand and a pair of charming dark brown, bold-stitched Mary Jane heels in her right. Her computer satchel hangs across her back. The small corner pet shop is empty except for Josephine and her co-worker, Abigail. Rose is prepared to wait for at least an hour for Josephine's lunch break. She is hoping to spend a little time with the shop's birds. Rose counts the caged bird amongst her greatest muses. To her, it is an excellent example of societal constraints placed upon colorful imaginings. Rose thinks she knows why *the caged bird sings* and likes to be reminded as often as possible.

"All I have to do is clean the cricket case, and I'll be able to take lunch," Josephine says while pushing the plastic bin of wood chips to the back storage area. She screams to the front, "I really hate cleaning up the cricket case. I feel like my skin is crawling for the rest of the day."

Rose waves to Abigail through the kennel glass and then walks over to the cricket terrarium that sits on a wooden cabinet in the front left corner of the shop. Looking over the hundreds of small crickets jumping and walking all over each other, Rose understands Josephine's stated dislike for the task. "Do they stink?"

"Do they stink? You realize you are asking a person who works at a pet store about offensive pongs," Josephine says with a super quick cadence.

Rose laughs. "I guess you are right. My father always returns with 'Is the Pope Catholic?' when I ask stupid questions." Rose squats and looks again at the crickets from a lower vantage point. "I don't envy this part of your job."

"Ah. So you *do* envy the cleaning of the mice's cage, the kennel, the bird cage, and the fish tanks?" Josephine replies with a bit of exasperation. "I have no idea why I continue to work here."

"You love animals. And because you are an idiot," Rose says with a simple smile.

"Oh yeah, that's it."

"You two." Abigail smirks while carrying a very tiny and undeniably cute Shih Tzu puppy to the sink for its bath.

"It's too early for dark 80s comedy... nah scratch that... it's too late for dark 80s comedy," Josephine yells to Abigail from the cricket's cage to the back room's large basin sink.

"Heathers and the Crickets," Rose says while holding back her laughter.

"What's for lunch?" Josephine asks.

"Tuna on 12 grain, of course. I also bought you a small Greek salad. The salad looked very good to me." Rose lifts the bag and rocks it left to right. "And the shoes, per your request."

"I am trying to cut back on my vegetables," Josephine declares. "Hey Abs, you want a Greek Salad?"

Abigail leans away from her sink and peers toward her interrogator to answer, "Fancy free food with feta is fabulous."

"Always awesome, Abigail," Josephine articulates, while dropping the last of the new paper towel cardboard pieces into the terrarium. Turning to Rose, she says, "I have three versions of the logo ready to show you. I am not sure if you are going to like them. I tried to incorporate Africa and cocoa and a woman's shoulder. Augustine added the detailing. He has such fine pencil work." She puts the lid back on the cricket cage.

"How was your holiday with his folks?" Rose asks.

"We had a very nice time. His parents like me and I like them," Josephine answers. "They are older than my parents, so our conversations are weighty, yet not heavy. I guess they want to get to know me quickly."

Rose looks to Josephine and tries to empathize, but she is unsure of whether she can. She smiles at her friend and then looks to the ground. Rose realizes that she has a morsel of envy about her friend's situation. She has never had a boyfriend's parents actually like her. She has also never had a fiancé.

"Did you have wedding talks?" Rose asks. "Is the date set?"

"No. It's definitely going to be a small wedding. We may elope," Josephine says with a gentle quality and a far off stare.

Rose smiles and nods her head.

"Lunch?" Josephine asks. "I need to stay here to help with the adoption pick-ups. We're losing three puppies today to proud parents. And although we make appointments, they're usually inconveniently early."

"I don't envy *that* part of your job," Rose says with a manner of understanding.

The two women enter the break room and quickly close the door behind them. It is a very small room with white walls. There is an appropriate cute kitten poster on the wall opposite the door that says something close to "hang in there." The room contains a small, round table with two orange chairs made of a durable plastic. A gray plastic cart holds a small Mr. Coffee maker and a microwave on its top shelf, with mugs, napkins, and sugar stored on the bottom. There is also a vanilla soy candle sitting in the middle of the table.

"I suppose you want coffee." Josephine steps to the condiment table and places the pre-portioned filter in the coffee maker. She hands a long barreled lighter to Rose while simultaneously motioning to the candle.

After handing Rose a coffee, Josephine reaches into her large leather purse and pulls out her sketch book and three separate pages of computer rendered versions of the logo. She sits down and scoots her chair a bit closer to Rose to show her the preliminary sketches and the three designs for the logo for ChIP. Josephine tells of the difficulty of the assignment and why it took a few more days than she expected. She points out features in each that she really likes.

Rose takes all three versions and explains that she is not quite sure which one she will use. She realizes as she accepts these logos that she is about to pass a point of no return. A startled Rose looks to Josephine and says, "I am 'crossing the Rubicon.'"

An anchor bend knot starts to develop in her stomach. To calm her seas, Rose shores the conversation by changing the subject. She invites Josephine and Augustine to her apartment for a small dinner party to properly thank them. She explains that she will send an invitation via email after her work travel schedule is set in stone.

"Rose, I hope you don't mind me saying so... yet this cocoa thing, you seem almost manic about it," Josephine says while implying that it is something that she did not want to say and is in fact trying to be courageous. "I just think you are looking for control of a completely uncontrollable situation – and you are going to get hurt."

"You sound like Augustine," Rose says with a laugh. "Manic? I am bi-polar. No worries. My mom says that I am often like a dog with a bone," she says with her chin nearly to her chest. Rose looks up at Josephine and acknowledges her concern, "I think that I would prefer to fail at something to doing nothing. Besides, Caesar was successful."

"Huh?"

"Uh – Crossing the Rubicon," Rose says while lifting both eyebrows and utilizing a tone of "didn't I already say this."

"Am I supposed to know what 'crossing the Rubicon' means? Something requiring a Jeep?" Josephine asks defensively.

Rose nervously giggles. "Sorry, Josey. I forget that not everyone shares my love of idioms." Rose considers how her friend may have heard her and becomes somewhat embarrassed. "I wasn't trying to… I am sorry." Rose looks down and then at Josephine and exhales. "'Crossing the Rubicon' is an idiom that dates back to Julius Caesar. Caesar's army crossed the Rubicon River in 49 BC and made armed conflict in the regions of the Roman republic inevitable – Caesar's civil war."

Josephine reacts with a wry grin as she says, "History lessons by Rose Isope."

"It's interesting, no?" Rose says, catching her eye. "The Roman republic became the Roman Empire with Julius Caesar at the helm. The phrase 'crossing the Rubicon' refers to any person or group pledging itself irrevocably to a revolutionary cause. Incidentally, apparently Caesar also uttered 'The die has been cast' at this famed river."

"So you are full-on serious about this, aren't you?" Josephine asks while looking in the bag for her pickle without actually looking in the bag. She finds the deli delight and waves it at Rose. "Don't you just love them pickles?"

"Pickles and coffee. Yum. Two great tastes that go great together," Rose says, smiling as she takes the last few gulps of her coffee.

"Hey, I wonder what would have happened if ole Julius didn't cross the Rubicon," Josephine says.

"I am pretty sure he was running from his creditors – he had to go somewhere," Rose responds while laughing at herself. "And besides, Rome was not built in a day."

"Ha," Josephine exclaims. "Very funny."

"And to answer your earlier question...about me being serious...I did my own little art work for you. I made a short video for you to watch." Rose removes her computer and starts it up. "I made this over the past two days. I lifted some pretty serious news clips about child slavery in the cocoa fields from CNN Freedom Project and tempered... ha ha... and tempered the chocolate slaves with PETA pictures." Rose gives a cynical laugh. "It is soooo funny." She starts up the three minute video and watches Josephine take in the terrible images set to Phil Collins's "Against all odds."

"Oh my God. You are so mean," Josephine says, wiping the tears falling from her eyes and laughing it off. "Alright Rose, you can be serious about this. I give you permission."

"Pleasant viewing experience, right?" Rose responds. "Reel chocolate children. It is so funny," Rose says under her breath with a palpable weight. "Yep, I am pretty serious. And on that note, I should get going. I want to go to the gym to exercise my vanity and am pretty sure that they close early on Sundays. I also need to stop by Lin's to pick up a suit."

"The gym? You are like a fitness freak."

"Imagine what my energy would be like if I didn't exercise."

Josephine laughs. "Scary thought." She tosses her empty lunch bag at the trash can in the corner. She raises both of her arms in celebration as she makes the basket. "Thanks for the lunch, and the shoes – I am supposed to have dinner with Augustine's fellowship director. I have the dress, I just needed these shoes. And Rose...You are right. After a day like that, Abdul needs a piece of chocolate."

"Hey, thanks for the art. I cannot tell you how much I appreciate your help with this. I hope you will see these logos over and over again." Rose rolls the three pages together into a tight cylinder and places them in her purse. "Tell Augustine I said thanks and I will send him this video via email for kicks and giggles."

"Um, Rose. Augustine and I had another idea. We were thinking of making chips into cute little cartoons - like little smurfy characters. Like Sneezy Chip or Grumpy Chip? You could tell cute little stories using Brainy Chip and Chipette? I know it is not what you asked for, or were looking for, but it might work... you know, to help get the point across."

"Wow. That's a really good idea." Rose quickly adjusts her mindset to this new artistic take. "Cute little chips talking about child slavery is awesome."

A lightness appears on Josephine's face. "We actually drew up a whole slew of them. It was fun." Josephine opens her plain notebook to show her the five rows of ChIP characters, including "Body-Builder ChIP" who was actually just a chip upside-down with googly eyes. "Body-Builder ChIP is my personal favorite."

"These are great." Rose laughs at each and every one. "Were you afraid to show me these?"

"No. It's not like that. I was just thinking you wanted something more serious. Nightingale Chocolates is huge." She flips the page to show Rose a few more. "We were just doodling these for fun."

"I love them. They are perfect," Rose says, laughing. "Can I have this? Or do you want to make a copy and send it to me?"

"Sure," Josephine says. "I actually think that Auggie already scanned them in. He scans everything."

"I don't know. I think I could probably use both. Give the chocolatiers the option. This is awesome. Thanks. Cool." Rose smiles. "I am so happy. Cool." Rose looks into the corner of the room. "You know, I could probably make a pretty cool brochure for ChIP using these."

Josephine just smiles at her friend.

"I really need to get going." Rose grabs her coat and turns to open the door. Turning back to look at Josephine, she asks, "Do you like mole sauce?"

"I have a couple in the cage over there... they'll cost ya,"

Josephine says with a smile as she approaches levity. "I think you mean Mo-lay sauce."

"You hope I mean Mo-lay sauce." Rose returns the smile as she steps past the door. "There are actually people here. You should probably get out here. Abigail looks a bit harried."

Abigail's expressions intensify as she sees Josephine emerge from the back room. "Mr. and Mrs. Wilkins are here for Fjord an hour early. I will need you to help me with their paper work as I get him ready."

Rose watches Mr. and Mrs. Wilkins playing with their Alaskan Husky puppy while glancing over to Abigail to see if she can actually see steam scream from her ears. Her red complexion, reminiscent of a steam train cartoon, makes Rose think it is almost possible.

"I'll take Fjord. It's my turn anyway." Josephine grabs the black and white fur ball and takes him to the back room for his final grooming. "I am going to miss you, Fjord," Josephine says in a whisper to Fjord's ear.

A tear starts to form in Rose's left eye as she grabs the puppy's paw. "Good luck, Fjord." Rose looks to Josephine. "Have fun." She waves to Abigail as she exits.

"Caesar at the Pet Palace. It is just so close to irony," Rose mutters to herself in amusement as she clutches her purse a bit tighter and steps out into a very cold and windy November afternoon. *Body-builder ChIP.* Rose takes notice of the black skies in the west. She takes a moment to notice the feel and smell of the air. *Cool.* She reaches into her purse and retrieves her cell phone. "Call Mom."

"Hi, Rosy."

"Hi, Mom. It's going to snow." Rose sings, "It's beginning to look a lot like Christmas."

"Let's decorate!" Her mother answers.

"Exactly. I just have to get a few things from my place. I will be there in an hour. Do you need anything? Milk, bread, coffee, water… the usual first snow arsenal stocking items…"

"I think we have everything we need. Your father brought home salt and tested the generator. We are ready to go. You are staying the night, right?"

"That's why I am stopping at my place first."

"It has already started snowing here. So take your time. No need to rush. And I love you."

"I love you too, Mom. I'll see ya in a bit."

CHAPTER 7
THE YOUNG THIEF AND HIS MOTHER

A young Man had been caught in a daring act of theft and had been condemned to be executed for it. He expressed his desire to see his Mother, and to speak with her before he said: "I want to whisper to you," and when she brought her ear near him, he nearly bit it off. All the bystanders were horrified, and asked him what he could mean by such brutal and inhuman conduct. "It is to punish her," he said. "When I was young I began with stealing little things, and brought them home to Mother. Instead of rebuking and punishing me, she laughed and said: 'It will not be noticed.' It is because of her that I am here to-day."

"He is right, woman," said the Priest; "the Lord hath said: 'Train up a child in the way he should go; and when he is old he will not depart therefrom.' –Aesop

Rose arrives at her childhood home with her computer, a suitcase and a dry-cleaned suit. The suitcase is filled with clothes: clothes for lounging in front of a ridiculously large TV, clothes for decorating both inside and out, and clothes for walking in the freshly fallen snow. She also packed a few other items.

Her father, Joseph, meets her in the driveway as Rose tries to lift her suitcase from the trunk. "Your mom told me that you were staying the night, not the week. What do you got in here?"

"I'm prepared. You're the one who told me the importance of being…" Rose nearly drops the suitcase onto the driveway. "I did bring a DVD box set of 'Planet Earth' for your viewing pleasure. Let's see, I also packed a couple of books, hand weights and a 30 minute exercise DVD, my winter ducks, and…"

"Your mom is making meatloaf and mashed potatoes for dinner."

"Yippee Skippee."

"And she had me bring up all of the Christmas boxes from

under the stairs. You do realize that you are decorating."

"Actually, it was kinda my idea. Mom asked on Thanksgiving for help. She wants to decorate the parsonage, too. And you know I have a rule about Christmas decorating."

"It has to be snowing." Joseph takes her suitcase from her.

"It certainly helps. If no snow, then snowball cookies."

"Well, we are going to get plenty of snow – twenty-four inches here. I heard down where you are they are expecting sixteen inches," Joseph says, slightly winded himself from her heavy luggage. "Anyway, now that you are here, I need to get back to my feetsball. I'll take this up to your room."

"Thanks, Dad."

Rose follows her father into the house, through the foyer, and they part at the stairway. Her father climbs the stairs and Rose enters the kitchen.

"Hi, Mom."

"Hi, Baby."

"You're making snowballs?" Rose asks.

"Of course I am. You cannot decorate for Christmas without snowballs."

Rose beams. "It's good to be home." She immediately walks to the refrigerator and grabs a Snapple peach tea. "You got eggnog?"

"It was on sale. You know your father and sales…"

"I love eggnog."

"You know your father…" Grace smiles.

Rose returns the Snapple and grabs the eggnog. "Dad bought this for me?"

"He heard you were going to be here." Grace rolls the last of the dough and carries the sheet of snowballs to the oven and sets the timer.

"Good, good, good to be home."

"Well, I was thinking this year we would put up a tree in the living room and the den, but that we would take the one that usually sits in the sun room to the parsonage. The tree they have there is… well, it is on its last legs, and we really do not need three Christmas trees."

"Are we putting the garland on the stair railing this year? Or are we going to put it on the mantle?"

"I like it better on the mantle. I bought two wreaths from the UMW this year and I thought that we could dangle them from the bannister."

Rose nods in agreement and takes a small sip of the eggnog. "What about the windows? Wreaths or candles?"

"Just candles I think."

"And outside?"

"The deer, of course. I was also thinking about the two cherry trees."

"Have you seen those giant outside tree ornaments?"

Grace smiles. "Let's not get too carried away."

"I love me some Christmas decorations."

"How is work?"

"Ugh. I should really quit. However, the cocoa thing is moving right along. We'll talk about that later." Rose finishes her eggnog and reaches into her pocket. "I got coupons for free dry cleaning from Lin today. I was thinking you could use them, or maybe you could gift someone at your church. Free dry cleaning is a pretty good gift." Rose slides two folded coupons on the counter. "I will set up the trees." Rose kisses her mother on the cheek and sets off to set up the two pre-lit fake trees in the living room and the den. Twenty minutes later she returns to the kitchen and eats cookies and drinks coffee with her mother.

"I have been reading the original 1908 edition of Robert Baden-Powell's *Scouting for Boys*," Rose tells her mother.

"It's pronounced Pole, Baden-Pole. I met his wife once, the leader of girl-scouts. She made a very careful effort to pronounce the name correctly."

"Huh. Anyway, I am enjoying the book. I had no idea about

the history of scouting."

"The Defense of Mafeking in the Second Boer War in 1899," Joseph interjects. "Any cookies left or did you eat them all already?"

"According to the book, the men were being killed left, right and center, so I guess you can say that they were short staffed. So Baden-Powell got together the boys from the town, ages 12 to 15, and made them into a cadet corps." Rose looks to her mom as she quotes from the book, "And 'a jolly smart and useful lot they were.'" Rose laughs. "Jolly smart. I love that phrase."

"I remember learning about the Mafeking war when I was about 12. I cannot believe I still remember this stuff," says Joseph.

"Why 'cause you are old?"

"I have never been older than I am right now."

"He was a national hero because of what he did there," Grace adds. "Scouting was very popular when we were children."

"Have you ever read the book?"

"Of course, we actually have it in our library."

"Really? I'm sorry. Why did you let me prattle on and on?"

"It's been awhile. I know you know that your father was an eagle scout. Did you know that I am pretty much the equivalent for girl scouts? I received the curved bar. I guess that is, or was, the top honor."

"I am pretty sure I didn't. Wait, the curved bar? Seriously? Scouting for a curved bar? Compared to an eagle, seriously?"

"I don't think that they have that award anymore." Grace pulls a sheet of cookies from the oven. "These have to cool for a few minutes," she says as she puts the cookies from a previous batch into the bowl of powdered sugar. "I see your point, but it is not worth pointing out. The Girl Scouts are very different today."

"I hope so. Anyway, there is something else I found terribly interesting, almost ironic. In addition to commanding a boy brigade to help save the town, he also armed 300 African Natives with rifles, even though it was supposed to be a 'white man's war.' These soldiers were nicknamed the 'Black Watch' and used to guard the perimeter."

Grace shakes her head and adds, "In those days, things were different."

"No they weren't," Rose says. "Things are still very much black and white – like this cocoa thing with Hershey, M&M/Mars, and Nestle taking advantage."

"Rose, it's not all bad," Grace says.

"No mom, it isn't ALL bad. However there are large sections of pretty damn awful."

"So what, no cookies?" Joseph says pushing himself from his typical spectating position in an attempt to lighten the mood.

Grace puts her hand on her right hip, "Don't you have a game to watch?"

"They are in the tin, Dad. Right next to the coffee maker – exactly where they belong."

"How many of those have you had, Joseph?" Grace asks.

"A girl scout touting a curved bar is asking me about the number of cookies I have eaten?" Joseph says while adding two more just for spite.

Rose is quietly amused by the exchange between her parents, yet returns to the conversation she wants to have. "The other thing that I found absolutely fascinating is that the motto, Be Prepared, is from his initials, Baden-Powell, B-P, Be Prepared."

"I forgot about that," Grace admits.

"I'm not sure I ever knew it," Joseph says.

"Interesting, right? Good Jeopardy tidbit."

"So anyway, Mom, I was thinking that this Boy Scout thing is sorta like… well, it's sorta like a revelation." Rose addresses her mother because the conversation is moving more toward her mother's expertise.

"And on that note…" Joseph pours eggnog into a glass, leaving a bit of room. "Did you see? We have eggnog. There is also some spiced rum in the other room."

"Joseph, you know Rose doesn't drink."

"Nonsense." Joseph grabs a few more cookies and a napkin and returns to his man-cave.

"So you were saying..." Grace returns to her daughter.

"It is like MLK, Jr. and the civil rights movement, well sorta..." Rose takes a long swill of her coffee to organize her thoughts, and then continues, "He was compelled to create and train a youth brigade of boys, ready to be called to action to defend, in both war and peace. I think this was done as a response, or possibly a reaction to his nation's inappropriate interactions in Africa and their quest for other colonial holdings."

"You think he was called by God?"

"I think it's possible – that he might have been a prophet."

"A prophet?" Grace smiles. "My daughter... ever the theologian."

"Well, okay then, he didn't exactly write the Bible or the Koran... alright maybe he was just a small-time prophet with a seriously huge influence. The Boy Scouts, now that's huge. Okay, so maybe he's not a prophet – maybe just a prophetic teacher – issuing a warning?"

"I understand what you are saying," Grace says. "I need to peel potatoes, wanna help?"

"Sure," Rose says as she walks to retrieve two vegetable peelers. "It's just such a clean idea. So what he needed to do was to mesh a training program of good, respectful and thoughtful personality skills to supplement and enhance good soldier skills provided by standard military training. The result is Ethics Supreme with an oath, a law, a motto, and a slogan. It's actually pretty impressive when you think about it."

"I'll say it again, in those days, things were different," Grace says.

"You mean it wouldn't fly today."

Grace nods.

"Remember Zeke as a scout? I think I remember the Scout oath and law from him. I remember him trying to learn them."

"Your brother didn't like to memorize things."

"I remember sitting next to him in our van on the way to a scout meeting practicing reciting the oath. 'On my honor, I will do my best - To do my duty to God and my country and to obey the Scout Law; to help other people at all times; to keep myself physically strong, mentally awake and morally straight.'"

"A scout is: trustworthy, loyal, helpful, friendly, courteous, kind, obedient, cheerful, thrifty, brave, clean, and reverent," her father recites the law as he enters the kitchen. "That eggnog is delicious. And so are the cookies. I think I am going to have seconds of both."

Grace looks at the clock. "Dinner in 1 hour, maybe you should wait."

"I'll wait," Joseph says. "Don't forget to do a good turn daily."

"You mean the neckerchief thing," Rose says.

"The neckerchief thing?" Grace asks.

"You are supposed to do a good deed daily, and if you did it you can put a small knot in your neckerchief. And if you didn't you will have to do two deeds the next day," Joseph answers.

"It's the scout slogan," Rose tells her mother, "but I am not sure if that makes sense. How are you supposed to determine whether your deed was actually good? One man's treasure and all that…"

"The Eagles are up by ten," Joseph reports. "Dinner in one hour?"

Grace nods.

"Anyway, about this cocoa thing," Rose says, after her father retreats once more. "I was thinking that I'm going to ask the Boy Scouts of America for help. I mean, who better to fight child labor abuses than the Boy Scouts. Fight Fire with Fire!"

"I see your collection of idioms is coming in handy," Grace

mocks. "You are being a little Pollyanna-ish, aren't you honey?"

"Pollyanna on a high horse. No, Mom, I am trying to be serious." Rose takes a breath to steel herself before explaining, "Serious about the motto- Be Prepared. I went online to look at the current merit badges for scouts. I think I could submit this idea to the Boy Scouts with the suggestion of a merit badge."

"I don't understand."

"Well, in order to receive a merit badge in 'Citizenship of the World,' for instance, you have to do a number of things… eight, I think. Most merit badges have about eight steps.

"Rose, you can't just walk in and change the Boy Scouts of America to suit your whim. It's disrespectful." Grace places the peeled and cut potatoes on the stove and lowers the temperature of the oven.

"Well they already have 126 badges, what is 127?"

"Rose," her mother says sternly.

"I hear ya."

"Do you?"

"Yes. I'm not saying that I'm going to listen." Rose smiles at her mother. "I hear you, though. Aris reminds me almost daily that I should be more humble in my arrogance."

"He wants you to be humble?" Grace laughs. "How arrogant!"

Rose laughs. "We are very similar in quite a few ways."

"How is he doing?"

"He is visiting his parents with Nora. He should be home soon."

"Hmm."

"Anyway, I am going to write the local Scout Master and request a meeting to talk about adding a new merit badge – a merit badge in 'Civil Action.' Maybe his troop might be interested. It cannot hurt to ask, right? I was thinking that I would complete a similar outline to the other badges and submit it to him in our meeting. I will do this before I send the letter so that I will…"

Rose drum rolls as she continues, "…so that I will 'Be Prepared' when he agrees to the meeting."

"Very funny, Rose."

"I thought so."

"Honey, would you please set the table?"

"Sure."

"I think we could probably decorate the trees after dinner."

CHAPTER 8
THE DOG IN THE MANGER

A DOG lay in a manger, and by his growling and snapping prevented the oxen from eating the hay which had been placed for them. "What a selfish Dog!" said one of them to his companions; "he cannot eat the hay himself, and yet refuses to allow those to eat who can."

-Aesop

Rose stands in front of the fully decorated Christmas tree. "It sure is a pretty tree."

"I saw an ugly Christmas tree the other day," Grace says as she places the last of her favorite ornaments. "I did not think they could make an ugly Christmas tree. It was decorated in red lights with red bulbs, red bows, red birds and a red spear tree-topper. It was really ugly."

"Remember that house down the road from your church in Orwell? They decorated for Christmas using red lights. I swear it looked like the devil lived there," Rose says.

"This tree was like that, but much, much worse. It was honestly ugly."

"I like red," Joseph adds.

"The color-blind do not get to participate in this conversation," Rose jokes.

"I am not color blind."

"What color is this?" Rose holds up a purple glass ball ornament.

"Blue," Joseph answers.

"Fine, Dad. You have color astigmatism. I am white-washing your color blindness. And speaking of white washing, the snow is really falling now. There is already a foot out there." Rose runs to the window to peer out with a familiar enthusiasm. Turning back to her dad, she says, "It is not the red that mom found so disturbing, it was the fact that the entire tree was in red. Right?"

"So what is your favorite decoration this year?" Joseph asks.

"I guess I like the poinsettias, garland, candles and stockings - the fireplace," Rose admits. "What is yours?"

"The tree, of course," Joseph answers.

"What's yours, Mom?"

"The Nativity. When I was a child we had a set where the baby Jesus could be removed. On Christmas Eve, my mom gave me the task of putting the baby Jesus in the manger. The nativity is always my favorite. It just means Christmas to me. It's a good memory."

"And a good story," Rose says, smiling at her mom in earnest. "I wish I could have met your mom."

"I suppose you are raring to go for your walk," Joseph comments. He knows how Rose feels about walking in the snow, especially the first snow.

"I am excited. I packed my ducks, my Mp3 player...I also packed my spelunking helmet that you gave me for Christmas last year."

"I really hate it when you walk at night," Grace says.

"I'll bring my cell phone."

"You know we don't always get reception out here."

"You'll be able to follow my footprints," Rose says. "Like Woodcraft. I'll be fine. I will stay on the roads. Mom, I am 32 years old. I can walk on country roads at night. I'll go now, and will be back before you go to sleep. Okay?"

"I'll go with her," Joseph announces.

"No offense, Dad. I kinda wanted to make this walk myself and I wanted to listen to music. I guess if you had a dog..."

"Honestly Rose, how old are you? We know you want a dog. You are just going to have to stop traveling and live in a place where you can have one."

Rose laughs playfully. "But don't you want a cute little puppy?"

"Rose," Grace says.

"A cute little 110 pound chocolate Labrador? You know you do." Rose lifts her eyebrows with exaggeration. She smiles at both of her parents and then leaves the den and makes her way to the staircase.

Rose enters her room. Inspired by Van Gogh, a twin bed rests in the corner with a chair placed next to it. There is a reproduction of her room in a Van Gogh print over the bed. "Hi, Vincent. It's been a while." She puts on her flannel lined jeans, a ribbed turtle neck, knee high woolen socks and her mid-calf rubber ducks. She completes the look with her favorite pink gloves and hat set she received for Christmas last year and her white parka trimmed with white fur. She sets the tone for her walk with classical music and exits the house wearing her ear buds.

Inspired by her latest interest, she begins to think like a trail scout. She shuffles down Blue Spruce Road in a snaking pattern. Rose stops at the corner to estimate the size of her "Narrow Fellow" in the snow, and quietly speaks a few stanzas:

> *Several of Nature's People*
> *I know, and they know me*
> *I feel for them a transport*
> *Of cordiality*

> *But never met this Fellow,*
> *Attended, or alone*
> *Without a tighter breathing*
> *And Zero at the Bone*

Rose decides that Emily would have been an excellent boy scout as she considers the famous poet's words. Baden-Powell called the skill Woodcraft. Woodcraft is the art of knowing animals. According to the original scout master, this skill is gained by following up their foot-tracks and sneaking up to them so that you can observe them in their natural state. It is not possible to shadow an animal without understanding your body's response to it.

She squats at the corner of Blue Spruce and Vine and with her index finger draws a wolf's head with an arrow above it. She realizes that the scout who would recognize her signal is probably not out walking at this time of night, looking for scout signals. She does this to honor the memory of Robert Baden-Powell, and for his sake, considers the time it would take for her tracks and patrol signal to be erased by nature.

She reaches Truman Park, a small park situated between the elementary school and the middle school. The gate is closed with a sign of park hours located on a metal post to the right. She considers her tracks by lightly wiping those closest to her with her right foot while eyeing the fence. She decides to walk to the right and follow the slight slope to look for another entrance, one that is less obvious. "Park Hours?"

She walks along the border landscaping until she reaches the swing set. It is a classic swing set with rubber seats that bend with the body. She has sat in many swings on many sets; this set is special. It accommodates an adult hip width. She brushes the heavy snow off the seat and attempts to dry the seat with her glove. Recognizing the futility of her attempt at wiping a wet seat with a wet glove, she sits, tip toes her way back and swings forward. "Abdul, have you ever been on one of these?" Rose asks the sky. "I wonder," she stops the swing to adjust her hat to completely cover her ears and continues to swing for another 10 minutes.

Rose rejoices in this first snow. She is sure that she will be working from home tomorrow and is exceedingly grateful. Although she does not particularly dislike her office mates, she prefers to work alone. She is more productive and less inclined to practice her comparable neonatal skills of nattering. Even after many years in a corporate environment, she is still adroitly inept at playing the game. While participating in their social rites on the surface, the core of her being envisions a huge black man smashing the backboard, sound and all. These thoughts inevitably lead to social withdrawal and the desire to practice martial arts. In order to reincorporate, Rose must interminably convince herself that everyone recognizes this type of interaction is superficial and somewhat cruel – a vestigial reminder of conquering elementary playgrounds. "Elementary Playgrounds... I will bet you do not know what these are either." Rose twists and spins on the swing for the remainder of her time, thinking only of the snow and Abdul.

Beginning to feel the cold and the hour, and with her Mom's interest at heart, she gets up and puts her own body in a forward motion and jogs back to her home.

***

She quietly enters her house and locks the side door, "I am home. It's beautiful out there."

"You see anybody?" Grace asks meeting her in the hall. "I was passed by one car. I think it was Mr. Montgomery – the baby doctor."

"It's time for me to go to bed. We'll decorate the parsonage tomorrow?"

"Maybe in Red? Or how about black and white?" Rose jibes. "Hey what is your password to your wireless? I have a bit of work to do. I would rather get it done tonight."

"Password." Joseph says.

"Yeah, the password?"

"Password."

"Secure."

"Good night, Rose. Don't work too hard. And there are lots of cookies."

"Thanks guys, Good night."

"Dad? Can I talk to you for a second?"

Her mother ascends the stairs. "What do you need?" Her father asks.

Rose whispers. "We should get mom a Nativity with a removable Baby Jesus for Christmas this year."

"I actually already got her something."

"Really? What is it?"

"A Christmas gift," Joseph jokes. "You'll find out. I think the Nativity is a good idea. I think she has been asking for one for several years now. I don't know... I don't speak MOM."

"It is a language that requires listening skills that we don't quite have." Rose laughs, "Good night, Dad."

Rose sits comfortably in the den admiring the tree for a few minutes before she opens her laptop. Her first task is office related. She sends a few emails to her work colleagues explaining the parts of the project she will be working on and that she will forward her reports before traveling to DC on Wednesday. Rose moves on to her second task – the civil action of bringing Abdul a piece of his chocolate.

She opens Word and then the document aptly named mymeritbadge.doc and begins to work on the requirement specifics of her Civil Action merit badge. "Civil or Civic?" Rose answers, *"Civil." Let's replace the word "Action" with "Response."* In a *Eureka* moment, she again renames the badge to the "Mafeking Response." She pats herself on the back.

Who couldn't use a boy army? Rose asks herself as she thinks of a dozen situations that call for one. *With a little repurposing...* She decides that she is ironically seeking a merit badge in Entrepreneurship and decides to follow the achievement requirements for it. She thinks if she does this well, she could score major "brownie" points with the Scout Master.

"Cookies and Brownie points!" Rose gets up from her computer and walks to her kitchen with the intention of getting a glass of eggnog and a couple of snowballs. She takes a moment to look at the hand-painted pictures hung on the refrigerator by her niece and nephews, hanging next to Lin's coupons. Upon finally opening her refrigerator, she rejoices at the sandwich fixings.

"Guacamole, sprouts, roast beef, horseradish, tomatoes, and cucumbers…It's good to be home. I can build a Dagwood."

She begins to consider one of her favored idioms "biting off more than you can chew." Rose wants this tattooed somewhere on her body - represented symbolically by a cartoon Dagwood sandwich on her right hip. It would be as apt of a description of her as the rose tattooed on the top of her left foot. She loves the challenge of layering different things that one might not necessarily put together. She loves the idiom, yet never really considers it true.

"Biting off more than you can chew…let's see. I am going to deliver an idea of a new merit badge to the Boy Scouts – the meat." Rose grabs the package of roast beef and 2 slices of 12-grain bread. *What's next?* Rose looks at condiments – brown mustard, guacamole and horseradish. *Combine the horseradish and mustard on one slice and put the guacamole on the other –bread and butter. I will use the merit badge requirements for Entrepreneurship to organize the proposal.* Rose completes her sandwich with two slices of provolone, bean sprouts and two thin slices of cucumber and tomato. She puts the enormous sandwich on a salad plate and adorns it with two snowballs.

Rose reads aloud, "The first step is for the Scout to define entrepreneurship and the role of the entrepreneur in the economy. The second step is to identify and interview an individual who has started his or her own business and find out how the entrepreneur got the idea for the business as well as how the entrepreneur recognized it as a market opportunity. Easy."

"Step One." Rose, trained in the fine art of nouveau philosophy, recognizes the *semantics* of this undertaking and redefines entrepreneurship in the context of social movements. In her definition of the word, Robert Baden-Powell was an entrepreneur; his business was the Boy Scouts. Martin Luther King

Jr. was an entrepreneur; his business was the civil rights movement. She uses one of her favorite quotes to help define economy. Calvin Coolidge said "economy is the method by which we prepare today to afford the improvements of tomorrow."

"Step two, how the entrepreneur got the idea," Rose quietly speaks to her computer screen.

Rose says quietly to herself, "if Robert Baden-Powell is the entrepreneur then obviously the Siege of Mafeking was the impetus for the idea for the business. He recognized the need in the market and fulfilled the need. The crunch of the bean sprouts!"

She continues completing the tasks for the merit badge by retrieving *Scouting for Boys* from her computer satchel. "How did he get the capital?" After perusing the book for five minutes, she finds the answer to her question. "Huh, it's the book!" Rose is taken aback by the irony, "Behold the power of cheese."

Rose reads that the book was ingeniously marketed and sold at a very affordable cost. The book's publishing from 1908 until World War II was second only to the Bible in the English-speaking world. The book, as well as the Boy Scout movement, is actually esteemed as Britain's most successful recreational export of the 20th century.

"Baden-Powell is an entrepreneur," exclaims Rose, "just *Like* that Facebook guy."

"How's business?" She discovers after a brief internet search that in the past decade, enrollment numbers have fallen. The current published membership numbers are about 2.7 million; scouting is half of what it was in 1972 when enrollment was at its highest. Rose notes that these drops in membership can easily be attributed to more program choices for kids and tougher work schedules for parents. The Boy Scouts of America have also been battered by accusations of discrimination – mainly in cases brought by gays and atheists. Rose recognizes the symptoms of the familiar albeit trite Darwinian argument – adapt or die.

Some things are just black and white. Rose says as she

considers Darwin's black and white moths, the symbols of the 'adapt or die' argument. The Scouting Movement – its history, its present and its potential – its evolution – is located within this superficial black and white satire. Rose sniggers at the irony of the silver wolf, the highest honor of Baden-Powell's organization being ensnared by its own dogma. *A wolf trapped by dogma.*

Rose takes some time to appreciate the Christmas tree in front of her and notices the absence of black ornaments. "I wonder if *they* even make black ornaments."

Rose continues her search regarding the current business practices of the Scout Movement and is delighted to find the kente cloth neckerchief. The kente cloth neckerchief is an accepted uniform adjustment for the African American community recommended in 1996 by the Boy Scout of America Urban Scouting Task Force. "A good deed."

Rose's heart starts jumping in her chest as she recognizes the classic spin of the kente yarn. "Correction, a good deed revealed."

According to the legend, a man named Ota Kraban and his friend Kwaku Ameyaw learned the art of weaving by spotting a spider weaving its web. Taking a cue from the spider, they wove a strip of natural raffia fabric and thus began a process refined by centuries. She spends the next thirty minutes looking at various kente cloth patterns with names like 'God's Richness' and 'Unity is Strength'. *Woodcraft woven into the neckerchief, that's as cool as a cucumber.*

"God, is this more than I can chew?" Rose laughs at herself and her attempt of building a cocoa-Boy Scout sandwich. *Yuck.*

Rose takes the last bite of her actual sandwich and returns her attention back to the merit badge requirements and reviews her notes. She thinks of both her mom and Aris who have both warned her about overstepping. She prepares a quiet argument for them; *Hershey cannot make something publically known in the time of Twitter. And the boy scouts need new skies for their eagles.* "They obviously need my help."

The Entrepreneur and the Economy. Rose is always amused by her classic Aesop pairings. She is confident that with a few more hours of tweaking, she will be able to make a powerful and emotional argument to the Boy Scouts for the market of the "Mafeking Response." She saves the document under a new name, 'browniepoints.doc'.

"Hey Aesop, how about the Sandwich and the Christmas tree?"

CHAPTER 9
THE VIXEN AND THE LIONESS

A Vixen who was taking her babies out for an airing one balmy morning, came across a Lioness, with her cub in arms. "Why such airs, haughty dame, over one solitary cub?" sneered the Vixen. "Look at my healthy and numerous litter here, and imagine, if you are able, how a proud mother should feel." The Lioness gave her a squelching look, and lifting up her nose, walked away, saying calmly, "Yes, just look at that beautiful collection. What are they? Foxes! I've only one, but remember that one is a Lion." - Aesop

There is an exquisite modern pendulum clock hanging on the wall behind the espresso bar at the café. The clock frame and its pendulum are made of a very shiny copper alloy surrounding what appears to be an aqua mother of pearl face. The numbers on the clock are made of a copper, yet the metal has an antique patina, as if only the numbers have aged. Rose has had many conversations with the owner of the café about the possibility of acquiring this clock. As an ex-professional boxer, Oscar tends to practice his verbal sparring with Rose mostly because she is often the only opponent he can find on short notice. In one of his more hard core verbal jabs, he explains to Rose that she will receive the clock on her wedding day. With every repeat of this conversational promise, say three or four times a year for the past seven years, Rose acts out a knock-out scene for his benefit. On his warmer days, he often stops and asks her whether he is at risk of losing his clock. He likes Rose because she respects his establishment and shows her support daily. The striking aged copper reads 5:30.

After spending two days with her parents, Rose is very anxious for social interaction of an unfamilial sort. *Unfamilial? Is that a word?* Rose has, over the years, actually met a good deal of her social network with one shoulder to the brick wall of this café.

White Lies and Dark Chocolate

Like so many cafes in university towns, there is good lighting to be found and intelligent conversation to be had. She orders a cappuccino from Chloe and while waiting she interrogates the foam artist about her Florida visit. Chloe recounts a weekend spent pretending to be much more adult than she should be at her age. Apparently, her father's new wife enjoys wine tastings, pottery galleries, and sea food brunches. Chloe says she feels like she aged a decade and is hoping to go to the local bar after her shift to kill those mature brain cells before they take root. Rose laughs and is honestly entertained by the details of Chloe's new family dynamics. She takes her cappuccino to the condiment station and grabs her single packet of raw sugar and wooden stir stick. She finds her favorite corner table.

Shying away from striking up a conversation with a stranger, Rose decides to open her laptop to review her plan of attack. She is very pleased with her merit badge work in Entrepreneurship. She is also pleased with the letter that she wrote to the Scout Master, Nicolas Grey. "Brownie points, I am so funny."

Rose closes her laptop while finishing the last of her cappuccino. She heads to the barista counter to purchase a dark chocolate brownie with a cream cheese swirl and asks for a large steamed milk with a half shot of white chocolate syrup. Rose displays and slaps down her fully stamped card; much like someone might display the last card in a royal flush, to let Chloe know that this drink selection is on the house.

"Free drink, eh?" Chloe affirms. "How many years have you been coming here?" She staples the card to Rose's would be receipt. "If I were the owner I would have you on some sort of platinum credit where you get one free for every three. I think you may single-handedly keep this café in business. I mean, like you are here every day. I think you drink my rent in coffee."

"Ah shucks. I cannot tell if you are paying me a compliment or whether you are delicately reminding me that I really should get a life, or at the very least my own espresso machine," Rose says with a kind smile. "I suppose you could pitch the idea to Oscar and see if he hits. He seems to be the kind of guy who is willing to listen anyway." Rose takes her steamed milk and brownie back to her table and turns to Chloe. "I suppose it wouldn't hurt to try. I guess you could call them Manager's choice VIP coffee drinker's not-so-anonymous cards." Rose giggles and takes her seat, and with a pretty loud tone adds, "On second thought … maybe something shorter…Oscar's Uppercuts?" Rose is pleased with her suggestion and now quietly wishes Chloe follows her advice so she can save a few dollars on coffee. Although Rose does very little other than work and drink coffee, a few dollars saved would be helpful.

Rose takes the corner of her brownie without looking and mindfully enjoys the miracle of chocolate. Rose whispers with a satisfied and then aggrieved sigh, "Abdul has got to try one of these." She takes a casual look around the café to see if she recognizes anyone. Oscar steps out of the office and walks towards Rose. He takes the seat reserved for Aris. "How is the brownie?" he asks, looking at the trapezoid shaped piece on the plate.

"Delicious. Would you like a piece?" Rose answers without hesitation.

"Can't. I'm in training for an Ironman. Sure does look good," Oscar says with an easy to spot hunger in his eyes. "It is close to dinner. My blood sugar must be low."

"Ironman? That is running, swimming and biking, right?" Rose asks earnestly.

"Close. It's swimming, biking and running. Ya swim for 2.4 miles, then ya bike for 112 miles and then ya run a marathon," Oscar responds.

"And when you say 'ya' you really mean 'you' and definitely not me?"

"Ya seem fit enough. Ah the feeling is great. It's like man and machine become one – like how a lion would feel right when he finds his prey – strong, powerful, and natural," Oscar says with a hint of his boyhood Scottish accent jumbled with a Chicago dialect. "Ah, da training is fun. I ran 22 miles this morning. I feel pretty good."

Rose starts imagining Oscar on a road bike pedaling away from a ferocious lion in the untamed African wilderness. "When is the race?"

"It's in May – 6 months from now in Texas," Oscar explains. "I have given myself plenty of time this year. Last year I only trained for a couple of months and it was no good. Anyway I was waiting for you to put down the computer, I did not want to disturb ya. I heard yar into yoga. I heard it helps with endurance."

Rose furrows her brow. "I don't know much about endurance, so I may not be the best person to ask about this. My sister who lives in Colorado practices Bikram yoga. It's something like 25 poses performed three times in a row in a $100°F$ room. It's also called Hot Yoga. I took one class here and decided it is for rich white kids into extreme sports." Rose shifts a bit in her chair. "Although I may have just knocked it – you may want to try it. It might be very good for extreme sport athletic training. There is a studio on Carter. I think they have 3 classes a day and it's about $15 for 90 minutes."

"Yeah, I know the place. Hey thanks. I gotta get something to eat – have ya had dinner yet?" Oscar asks.

"Yesterday my mom sent me home with a huge amount of homemade New England clam chowder. So yes, I've already eaten." Rose pauses, "Have you seen Lindo?"

"Yeah, I saw her early this morning. I think she's in hiding."

"Like 'Where's Waldo?'" Rose laughs at her own joke.

Oscar looks puzzled and then says, "I'll tell her you are asking 'bout her."

"I guess I am a little worried that it's all a bit too much." Rose notices Aris walking in the parking lot and leans to the left to get a full view. She looks to Oscar and smiles with her lips pressed together.

Oscar notices her noticing Aris. "Is he the clock man?"

"I fear he belongs to another," Rose says with a sincere look. "Your clock is safe, for now."

"Belongs to another… lemme know if he needs his clock cleaned," Oscar says while standing and rapping his knuckles on the table twice.

Rose is not quite sure how she should interpret his threat; he may be serious. She decides to spar on the side of humor and immediately responds with, "Oh that was pretty bad. Cleaning his clock…Ha." Rose emphatically restates her sentiment, "Ha."

Oscar sizes Aris up as he approaches the table. He looks back at Rose and cracks his knuckles with an affected grimace on his face - a scene stolen from one of the many mafia-esque movies. He twists his neck to look at the clock. "Well, I better get me some vittles. Rose, take care. Have a good night now."

"Hi, Thorn, sorry I am late. Need something?" He looks a bit anxious as he steps in a short line to get his Turkish tea.

Rose stands to greet him and walks toward him. "Are you late? Can you be late?" She hugs him very gently, with a good deal of space between them. "Hi Aris, it is good to see you. I actually missed you." Noticing his body language, she immediately and possibly inappropriately asks, "Are you doing alright?"

"I'm fine. I guess I'm a little angry. I had a bad day at work and…." Aris orders his tea from Chloe and starts to check his pockets. After paying, he moves his wallet from his coat to his back pocket.

Rose marvels at the sight. She has only seen him out of sorts once, maybe twice. She decides to put away her computer and papers and set them down on the ground between her chair and the brick wall. She rushes to clear the table to make room for him. She places her milk glass in the bin a few steps away and places a napkin over the remaining brownie.

Aris sets his tea on the table and removes his black woolen pea coat. He is wearing a black fitted sweater and Levis. Rose is sure that he has a Hanes undershirt on under his sweater – to Rose it is the most amatory piece of clothing a man can have in his wardrobe. His skin is the color of skim milk in a golden peach glass and his black hair is perfectly out of place. She really has missed him.

Rose gives him about thirty seconds to situate himself before asking, "Is it from the past, or for the future?" She brushes a few crumbs of brownie from the table onto the dark mahogany below.

Aris repeats, "Is it from the past, or for the future? Huh." He looks directly into Rose's eyes inquisitively. "I suppose that is a good question. I am not sure if I understand it." He finally settles in his chair.

"I know that there are two things that 'get my Irish up' and they are memories of past mistakes incessantly haunting my present, or my present not allowing, or not understanding, my plan for the future," Rose says with a bit of a shake to her voice as if she is sharing a deep vulnerability. She pictures a fully committed fencing pose and wonders if the image would help Aris. She decides against talking any further.

"So in your ideal present you are not disturbed by either?" He immediately serves the thought back to Rose.

"I am here," she says with posture that suggests both fight and flight. "Yep. That's me… Always in the moment."

He huffs, "I believe you."

"So do you want to answer my question and talk about what made you," she pauses to look at the copper and subtracts five "…eleven minutes late?"

Aris adjusts his chair and intertwines his fingers behind his neck and stretches his chest as he leans against the wall. "I guess today's problem is for, or is it against, the future."

"So it is the past," Rose says with a gentle, receptive smile.

Aris laughs through his nose. "Yeah, the past is in the way of the future. I guess that is always true."

"You'd be guessing wrong," Rose says while revealing the brownie underneath the napkin. "Would you like a corner? A brownie point?"

Aris brings his arms down and picks up the brownie, breaking the trapezoid using both of his hands. He sets the larger right side back onto the dessert plate. He stands and walks a few paces to pick up a drink napkin. He falls back into his chair and lifts his eyes to Rose. "Thanks. I needed this."

Rose is happy she is able to help. She looks at the remaining piece of brownie and decides that the rest is for him if he wants it. She pushes the plate to his place setting lifting both of her hands, indicating that she is relinquishing the entire brownie to her friend. She sing-speaks, "these are a few of my favorite things."

"Hey, was Oscar finally asking you out?" Aris asks while lifting his appropriately steeped tea to his lips.

"Did you know that he's training for an Iron Man?"

"I think I remember him training for one last year."

She takes a small piece of the plated brownie. "He was asking a question about yoga. I told him about the Bikram place on Carter."

"I thought you hated that place and that practice."

"It isn't for me. However it may be good and helpful for someone training for an Iron Man. I think his personality would probably like it - extreme yoga." She shakes her head and furrows her brow. "In spite of what you may think – I am capable of being open-minded."

Aris accepts the statement. "No doubt."

She reaches over and touches the band of his watch with her index finger to indicate that if she could she would have grabbed his hand. "I want to hear more about your day. Talk."

"My day? Funny. It definitely hasn't been my day." Aris

says with a tone of frustration.

Rose tilts her head to the right to watch him talk.

"Work. So yeah, I have been working with multiple groups, including the EPA, to try to get more result-oriented project goals for wind farm development. It seems to me that they seem less interested in having wind farms than they are in talking about having wind farms. They prefer bluster to wind power."

"Idiocy is not economical," Rose declares.

Aris continues, "The thing is, good wind resources are often found in remote, economically disadvantaged areas. Wind power can provide steady and significant revenue to rural farmers and their communities. It is almost a perfect match because the wind turbines occupy little surface area, leaving land open for other things. And you'd be surprised by how many farmers would prefer to be energy self-sufficient. There are some farms out in those mountains that are literally running on cow methane. That's a whole other wind farm, yet I digress." Aris stops himself to take the last of his tea. "The problem is fat cats."

"Politics, or have the cats been particularly feral this year?" Rose says looking for a smile. "Did you know that the term "fat cats" used to be a good thing - I mean originally. It's sort of like the swastika. Now, *I* digress."

"Huh." Aris acknowledges that he did not know. "Anyway, these guys are smart, educated people, but rather than working together – like forming an alliance between the wind and natural gas industries – they get in each other's way and stop both from progressing. It's very frustrating."

"Sounds like a problem for the GLAAD lobby," Rose says facetiously. "If we could get that group interested in alternative energy resources, rather than gay marriage – solar, wind and natural gas industries would be the subject of every tweet, news reel and every dinner table conversation in America."

"They are an impressive force in American politics," Aris acquiesces with a sort of edge, somewhat taxed.

Rose looks to her computer bag and then at Aris. "I've been thinking about 'economy of method' for the past few days. Calvin Coolidge said that 'economy is the method by which we prepare today to afford the improvements of tomorrow.'" Rose processes what she has heard from Aris. "So your frustration is that you are working with groups that are not even prepared to talk today about tomorrow."

"We are definitely prepared for tomorrow," Aris says agreeably. "I think we spent about an hour today talking about the fact that we will be bringing in chicken salad from the deli on Jefferson tomorrow." He stands up suddenly. "I need to... I will be right back." He grabs his coat and exits the building.

Rose watches Aris walk to his car. She watches him open the driver side door and lean in. She takes the opportunity to use the loo. She returns to find Aris in his chair. Slightly puzzled, Rose walks to the house water pitcher and pours two glasses and brings them to the table.

"I am sorry about work. I suppose they wouldn't call it work if dot-dot-dot," Rose says while taking her seat and catching a glimpse of his white undershirt. "How was your holiday?"

"Good. Interesting and informative," Aris responds with a simple lightness.

"Happy to hear. Did you drive in the snow?" Rose asks.

"We left a bit early to beat the storm. We pulled in about 2:00 PM on Sunday. I tried calling your cell phone..."

"I was at my parents - Christmas decorating. I turned off my cell phone. They really don't get reception there. It is spotty anyway."

"You like to decorate for Christmas when it is snowing."

"You remember?"

"I don't forget much," Aris explains. "I think we may go skiing this weekend. All of the slopes are open."

"I am having a small dinner party this weekend. I am cooking a mole sauce for Augustine and Josephine. They are helping me with this cocoa craze of mine. I was wondering if you and Nora would like to join me, I mean us? " Rose breaks one of her essential rules of never asking a question where she doesn't want to know the answer. She asks because she is actually not quite sure what answer she wants.

Aris pauses for a moment with his jaw dropped. "About that…"

"About what?"

"My weekend was interesting and informative and um, well, Nora and I have hit a rough patch."

Rose shifts uncomfortably in her chair trying to balance her personal emotions with her friendship duties. "Wanna talk about it?"

"I am just trying to figure out whether our miscommunications are about us or maybe she is going through something because of her father."

"Wow," Rose whispers her understanding.

"I am trying to sort it out, I mean, we are trying to sort it out."

"Good," Rose says softly. "Have you talked with Mina? Her husband's mother died when he was young, right?"

Aris looks directly at Rose, "Yeah."

"Maybe he can help?" Rose suggests.

"Good advice," he says with a gentle directness. "Thanks, Rose."

"So maybe dinner is not such a good idea right now."

"I don't know. I'll ask Nora and email after. What time?"

"Around 7ish," she says with her right hand pitching from right to left and back. "I think I am also making fried ice cream with fried pineapple, if that helps."

"Like I said, I will ask," Aris responds almost abruptly.

Rose physically responds to his hurried response by hugging herself as if she is cold. She looks to the barista counter and wonders whether she needs another cup of warm liquid. She turns to look over her shoulder to find her scarf. She wraps her neck with the piece of colorful comfort. "Did you head out for Black Friday? She says trying to awkwardly change the conversation."

Aris laughs. "Actually, I did. I mean, we did. Mina and her husband wanted to go so we decided to embrace the madness," Aris says, smiling. "We went to an all-night diner and were outside of Macy's at 5AM."

"Yikes," Rose says while picturing herself at a mall at 5AM.

"Funny you should ask. I bought you something. I saw this and decided you would probably never buy this for yourself because you never seem to buy music other than the occasional Mp3." Aris looks to Rose.

Rose, hopping in and out of her seat much like a baby, reaches to Aris. "Yay, a present."

"I hope you like it." Aris hands a thin brown paper bag shielding a jewel case. Rose tries to grab the bag as Aris jokingly pulls it away. Rose brings her hands to her chin and almost mimics a dog begging, yet straightens both her fingers and her thumbs to create an image-perfect CD slot. Amused, Aris slides the CD into her hands.

Rose opens the bag and reads "So Beautiful or So What" by Paul Simon. Both of Rose's eyes well up, yet at this point she is capable of restraining her tears. "Thanks. This is perfect." Rose lowers her head and closes her eyes and continues to fight her natural response. She tries hard not to think *he is perfect*.

"I know you really like Paul Simon," Aris says sensing her true sincerity.

"Yeah, I am the first to admit it," Rose says with a clear amount of tears in her eyes. "Thanks, Aris. I love it." She uses the jewel case to fan her tears and then sets the case on her lap and uses her fingers to catch the ones that fell. "Thanks."

"Whoa, emotion," he says trying to help her recover.

"Don't let my ice cold exterior fool you," Rose says with a titter, followed by a deep breath in and out. "Did you get your Christmas shopping done?" She asks while achieving composure and simultaneously slipping the CD into her computer satchel.

"I think my sisters and I are going to send my parents on a cruise," Aris says while taking a small bit of the brownie.

Rose mocks Aris by taking an equally small piece from the brownie. "From Baltimore? Where are you thinking of sending them?"

"Monte Carlo, I think. We would have to fly them to Florida first."

"Sounds like a nice gift. Your parents like to cruise, right?"

"They have been on three, I think," Aris answers.

"I can ask my travel agent at work for help if you want."

"Nice. Mina is in charge of this. I will let you know if we need help. Thanks." Aris takes the last bit of brownie from the plate and takes his final sip of tea. "I probably should be getting home. I still have not quite recuperated from Friday's madness. I would like to get to sleep a little early tonight."

"Maybe you should tell your work buddies about Calvin Coolidge to set the mood for the meeting."

"Was he Republican?"

"I am not sure if that is the right question for your purposes. Was he pro-gay marriage?" she says. She wonders if she should re-word that. "I guess I am not being politically correct."

"No, I think you're on the right track. Maybe we could merge the natural gas lobby and the wind farm lobby and the gay rights lobby into the 'Alternatives' lobby, maybe they would be GLAAD they did it."

"I certainly would not mind a different conversation," Rose says with a tonal quality that is neither leading nor misleading. "Thanks for the CD. I will give you a review of it next Tuesday?"

"Next Tuesday?" Aris gets out of his chair and puts on his coat. "I will ask Nora about dinner."

"Yeah, dinner is Saturday at 7." Rose looks up at her departing companion, "Well, alright then. Drive safe - precious cargo."

"Good night, Rose." Aris puts his hands in his coat pockets as he leaves.

Rose notices the clock - 9:19. She decides to follow Aris's lead and try to get to bed a bit early. She quickly gathers her belongings, thanks Chloe and walks briskly to her car. She starts her car and catches the end of the classic "Love Me Do" and notices that she is happy for the moment and the present.

CHAPTER 10
THE STAG AT THE POOL

A Stag overpowered by heat came to a spring to drink. Seeing his own shadow reflected in the water, he greatly admired the size and variety of his horns, but felt angry with himself for having such slender and weak feet. While he was thus contemplating himself, a Lion appeared at the pool and crouched to spring upon him. The Stag immediately took to flight, and exerting his utmost speed, as long as the plain was smooth and open, kept himself easily at a safe distance from the Lion. But entering a wood he became entangled by his horns, and the Lion quickly came up to him and caught him. When too late, he thus reproached himself: "Woe is me! How I have deceived myself! These feet which would have saved me I despised, and I gloried in these antlers which have proved my destruction." - Aesop

 Rose throws her car into first and turns off the engine. She stares over her dashboard at the familiar patch of wilderness, now covered in snow, in front of her parking space at work. It really is not her parking space; it is the space she parks in day after day - the farthest away from the entrance to her office building. Every day she counts the paces it takes to reach the front door as a form of mental cleansing to prepare her mind for the office. Today it is 126. Strangely, it is never the same number twice.

 According to her desktop, Rose arrives at her cubicle at 9:03. She switches on her classic green library lamp that she brought from home to decorate her space. Spending time at a library cubicle is infinitely more desirable than a modular one created in an old main frame space with white concrete walls now used to house six cubicles. She is happier here than she would be on the other side of the door where there are close to fifty cubicles in a single large room. She fully realizes that this location is a privilege and reminds herself of this luxury every time she enters the main room to use the copier. After logging on to her computer and checking her schedule, she grabs two quarters and her stained mug and heads to the break room. She places her quarters in the tin and pours herself a cup of City Roast. Although she prefers a darker and bolder roast, she is happy to get a decent cup of coffee at the office, another amenity that helps her through her day.

Rose leaves the break room and immediately heads to Diane's office. It is her custom to check in with Diane early in the day to see if priorities have changed, and they often did. Diane is Rose's favorite manager thus far. She does not micromanage. In fact, their relationship is more personal than professional. Diane trusts that Rose will do her job and do her job well as long as she is emotionally balanced. Diane finds this personality type very easy to manage. Rose only requires "management" when experiencing a personal crisis, and luckily these are rare. Diane recognizes Rose's professional talents and abilities and does her best to ensure proper advancement within the company even if it means losing her as a member of her team.

"Are you enjoying the snow?"

"I always love the snow in November. Ask me in February," Diane replies.

"Thanks again for telling me to cancel my trip. I should have thought ahead. I guess that is why you sit in your chair and I..." Rose sits in the chair opposite Diane. "So I called them on Monday afternoon to cancel my visit for Wednesday. Genevieve was grateful. Actually I think I am understating the sentiment - she was ecstatic. She should be ready regardless; the site has not had a subject for over three weeks. The paper work should have been done...I don't know..."

"I know that it is not one of your favorite sites to visit, but they are an important one. They conduct lots of trials there and they have a good reputation."

"Well-oiled machines are greasy," Rose replies while

rubbing her neck.

"Listen Rose, if you have a gut feeling about this site, pay attention to it. I trust your instincts, especially after that debacle in Dallas," Diane says while signing papers related to another project. "I read over your report and as usual, just a few minor grammatical errors. I am beginning to think you put those typos in just to check if I am reading your reports." Diane smiles with a look that suggests she is not kidding.

"I can assure you that I would never do that. You know how important those reports are to me," Rose says with a look that suggests she is kidding. "I don't have much to do today because I was scheduled out of the office. Do you need help with anything?"

"Actually we are getting ready for a client audit on the Summit project. Want to help with in-house file audits?" Diane asks.

"Sure. Can I work at my desk?" Rose asks, assuming that a conference room has been set aside.

"I think it might be good for you to work with this group. I would not be surprised if you get placed with them after this study is complete," Diane says with a hint of managerial authority.

"If that is what you want," Rose complies.

"Give me three hours and then you can go home."

"Aw. You're the best manager ever." Rose accepts her conditions and quickly leaves the office before Diane changes her mind. She goes back to her cubicle to change her voice mail and to update her time sheet to reflect the day's plans. She locks up her purse, grabs her ID badge and heads to the conference room on the second floor. Upon entering she notices that there are three women and two men around her age sitting at the conference table. All five have placed their cell phones within reach of their file folders. She laughs to herself as she grabs the back of a chair two spaces away from the group. "Diane Carrington sent me to help. I am yours until 1:00," Rose declares as she pulls the chair from the table. "File Audits - I love them."

Charlie, the manager of the project, lifts his head and motions to the loaded cart in the corner. "Great. We could use the help. We are attacking them alphabetically rather than chronologically. The source documentation checklist is here. Any questions?"

"Alphabetically. Funny. No. I am good." Rose takes the next folder and the source documentation checklist and sits down taking up as little room as possible. She feels the quiet tension in the room and hopes that it is due to office drama rather than difficulty with the task. She quickly learns that it must be office drama. She conducts five audits in the time she promised to the Summit group. She hands her checklists to Charlie and quietly and discreetly leaves the room. She walks to her desk, turns off her library lamp, unlocks her purse and quickly leaves her cubicle's cubicle. She rapidly walks to Diane's office to peek her head in. Diane, on the phone, waves in a sweeping motion.

Rose runs down the stairs and forcibly pushes the push bar to exit. The door swings 15-20° beyond its usual 90° opening and stirs up a bit of the awning protected, dyed pine bark landscaping located between the building and its parking lot. Rose walks over the threshold and with a skip starts a light jog to her car, hopping when necessary as she moves in between cars. The clock on her car stereo reads 1:11. She speaks to her car, "Take me home, Percy. I have a party to plan."

She enters her apartment at 1:45 and bee lines directly to the refrigerator to make a small sandwich for lunch. Just as she takes her first bite, still standing, the phone rings. "Hello?" Rose speaks into the receiver before noticing who is calling.

"Hey, what are you doing home? I thought I was going to leave a message. Did you turn your cell phone off?" Aris asks.

"I got out of work early."

"Do you ever work?" he says.

"Nah, I just collect pay checks."

"Nora and I would like to accept your invitation to dinner.

That is, if your plans have not changed."

"Great, good news." Rose breathes a sigh of relief as she considers that her friend must have begun to work out his difficulties. "I will be pulling the first appetizer out at 7:00. I suppose dinner will be served around 8:00. And one more thing... semi-fancy dress please."

"Need a reason to wear those gold wire shoes?" Aris asks.

"It is kind of sickening how well you know me."

"Sickening," Aris replies.

"I bought a dress to go with those shoes," Rose says with a child-like brattiness.

"Nora will be happy. She likes to dress up."

"Good. Augustine and Josephine like to dress as well. I think this will be fun. I am thinking that maybe I should invite Lin, yet I am pretty sure that she is kinda busy."

"You should ask."

"She is probably being bombarded with invitations. I would hate to be grouped in with those kinds of people."

"Nonetheless Rose, I know you are honestly concerned. You should ask."

"I think I will. Anyway, would you like to produce the music for the evening? It is a Spanish-Mexican fusion meal in honor of the birth place of cocoa."

"Spanish-Mexican fusion – I got it," Aris says with very little hesitation as it is a task with which he is comfortable and capable.

"So I will see you and Nora at 7:00 at my place. Apartment 7, in case you've forgotten," Rose says and then wishes she had not made that last comment.

"Rose, I have not forgotten," Aris says sharply.

"Perfectomundo," Rose replies. "I better get going I have a shopping list to adjust."

"See you Saturday. Until then keep your feet on the ground and keep reaching for the stars." Aris hangs up before Rose can make the sound effects that usually follow his verbal cheese.

"Reaching for the stars..." Rose thinks about the entrepreneur merit badge that shows a hand reaching for a star. "I hate how well he knows me."

She finally hangs up and walks to the living room and looks at her dining room table. "Spanish-Mexican Fusion." She remembers that she has a bright Aztec print linen table runner. She walks to her grandmother's hutch and pulls out the table runner from near the bottom of the linen drawer.

I wonder if there is a spider behind this print, too. She sets the table runner down the middle of her rectangle dining room table that she found and refinished this past September. Pleased with the look, she spends a few moments in view of the seating – she is one chair short. The discovery puts a smile on her face. Rose prefers her dining chairs to not match – each individual deserves his or her own individualized chair. She hopes this will become a tradition that the family she plans to have will one day carry. She usually purchases a single chair, from places like the Salvation Army, and then paints it with various colors and stencils. She also secretly puts a staff and a different musical note on the front left underside corner of each seat hoping for one dreamy day when someone will suggest musical chairs.

Now that she just added another two and a half hours to her dinner prep with the task of painting another chair, Rose starts to get nervous about the dinner party. She walks over to her computer to print the menu that Cookie suggested. After printing the email, Rose recognizes that her friend is online on Yahoo Messenger.

Roseisope: COOOOOOOKKKKKKIIIEEEEE

Cookiebits123: Hey Rosie.

Roseisope: I am making my grocery list right now and have a few questions. Gotta minute or maybe 30?

Cookiebits123: Yeppers.

Rose finds a more suitable position on her couch where she can chat while looking at the printed menu.

Roseisope: I love the mini green corn tamale idea. The dough though… masa harina, LARD, broth, and salt… People still use lard?

Cookiebits123: Duh.

Rose has an image of her friend rolling her eyes like a teenage girl and flipping her thick blond hair. She laughs out loud.

Cookiebits123: Lard is used in quite a few Mexican recipes. I guess you can use Crisco. Lard is better.

Roseisope: I'm looking at the recipe you sent for the champagne margaritas... what is Cointreau?

Cookiebits123: It is an orange liqueur.

Roseisope: Yum.

Cookiebits123: It will go really well with the ceviche.

Roseisope: You also listed Horchata. What is that?

Cookiebits123: It is a very popular non-alcoholic Mexican rice drink. The 'H' is silent.

Roseisope: Darn those silent H's. ORchAaaTaaah.

Roseisope: About the raspado palate cleanser... Necessary?

Cookiebits123: You will not regret it.

Roseisope: For dessert, I think I am going to try the flan.

Roseisope: The evening's menu: Pre-dinner drinks will be champagne margarita with a virgin variation; appetizers are mini green corn tamales followed by a shrimp ceviche; Main course is a Pollo en Mole and/or a sweet potato, pinto bean Mole served with brown rice and a Syrah. And Choco flan for desert with Mexican spiced coffee. Am I forgetting anything?

Cookiebits123: You forgot the raspberry raspado.

Roseisope: Raspberries!

Cookiebits123: Are you nervous about Nora?

Roseisope: Totally. She is always a bit "testy" around me.

Cookiebits123: Does she know?

Roseisope: How I feel about her boyfriend?

Cookiebits123: Yeah

Roseisope: Yeah, maybe, I don't know.

Roseisope: I think that there will be enough food and conversational topics that I won't have time to get all wrapped up

Cookiebits123: I kind of hope, for your sake, they are a little off.

Roseisope: Off?

Cookiebits123: Not all smoochy and stuff

Roseisope: Me too

Cookiebits123: Hey, lunch is calling me

Cookiebits123: black bean salad and couscous

Roseisope: Sounds good. Have a good day.

Cookiebits123: Get back to work!

Roseisope: I'm not at work. I got out early.

Cookiebits123: Me too. But I have to go back later. Christmas party catering bites.

Roseisope: Is there a joke in there? Good luck Lizzie.

Cookiebits123: You too.

Rose closes her laptop. She folds her grocery list and places it in the back pocket of her woolen skinny cargo pants. "I can do this," she says out loud as if she were trying to convince herself. Rose glances at her kitchen clock and notices that it is 3:28. With a renewed energy and an internal promise to be back at her apartment by 6:00, Rose grabs her winter white suede hooded coat, her pink gloves and her vintage 40's purse and quickly exits her apartment for International Eats.

CHAPTER 11
THE BOWMAN AND THE LION

A VERY SKILLFUL BOWMAN went to the mountains in search of game, but all the beasts of the forest fled at his approach. The Lion alone challenged him to combat. The Bowman immediately shot out an arrow and said to the Lion: "I send thee my messenger, that from him thou mayest learn what I myself shall be when I assail thee." The wounded Lion rushed away in great fear, and when a Fox who had seen it all happen told him to be of good courage and not to back off at the first attack he replied: "You counsel me in vain; for if he sends so fearful a messenger, how shall I abide the attack of the man himself?'- Aesop

    Rose wakes three minutes prior to her alarm. She considers this a good omen as it rarely occurs. She cat stretches, sits up, toggles off her alarm and then turns to close her window. The chill in the air feels and smells good. Anxious about the remaining tasks to do prior to her dinner party, she has very little trouble getting out of bed. Having seemingly misplaced her slippers she grabs pink and yellow striped fuzzy socks from the top drawer of her dresser and quickly puts them on. She takes a moment to look down and appreciate her decorated feet. She wiggles her toes and then wraps herself in her robe and saunters to the kitchen.

    While waiting for her Keurig to warm, she looks at her new chair on the drop cloth in front of her picture window. She is pleased with the stencil work she did last night. She chose an elaborate fleur-de-lis stencil flanked by scrolling leaves. She used brick colored acrylic paint and a copper metallic acrylic for highlights on the dark mahogany stained chair she found at the Salvation Army for twelve dollars. The stenciling is subtle and matches the wood quite nicely. Rose moves the chair to her dining area and consequently moves her carved, rose backed chair to the head of the table. Rose recognizes the emotion – contentment.

She brews her coffee, grabs her laptop and writes Lisbeth of her progress –the beans are soaking, the chicken is marinating, the shrimp is cooking in the lime juice. She tells Lisbeth that she learned that flan is easily the favorite dessert of both Josephine and Augustine. She confesses that she is still very nervous about Nora, yet feels that the idea to invite her is a good one – they should be friends. She concludes her email and finishes her first cup of the day. Rose eats a small breakfast of vanilla Greek yogurt and three large strawberries.

Whilst brewing her second cup, she reviews the flan recipe and with a deep inhale accompanied by a simple prayer, Rose starts her final dish with the recognizable ritual of lightly greasing the pan. "My Bundt is buttered."

Rose spends the better part of the hour assembling the layers of her chocolate flan, making a meticulous effort to precisely follow the recipe. She consults online recipes to find a recipe for Lisbeth's suggested garnish, chocolate covered strawberries. Rose is pleased to find the recipe that offers an up-side down colander as a drying rack. After staking the last strawberry with a tooth-pick, she brews another cup of coffee.

Time to set the table. Rose grabs five black stoneware plates and sets them down near the center of her dining room table. She pauses to enjoy the sun warming her cheek. She turns her head to look toward the light source and in that very simple, quiet and precious moment it dawns on her that she will be the fifth wheel at her own dinner party. *How did I not think of that?*

Rose looks up toward the ceiling and speaks, "God, are you laughing?" She walks back to the kitchen, grabs her coffee from the platform and counts her steps back to the table –six.

Holding the side posts of her chair, she considers the seating of her guests. She would love to put Aris at the other head of the table – he calms her. "Sir Arthur – my kingdom for a round table. A fifth wheel at my own party!" Rose decides to put Nora on her left with Aris next to her and Josephine on her right with

Augustine next to her. Her attentions shift to the building across the street and its Christmas decorations, including lighted wreaths, angels, and bells. There is one lone plastic Santa hanging from a balcony two levels down. "Are you lonesome tonight…"

Rose remembers the two pound chocolate Santa she has in her guest room. She purchased it from Nightingale's for her project team's excessively early Christmas party next week. She shuffles in her fuzzy socks to the room and grabs him. "…And each must play a part." She stands him up at the opposite end of the table. She walks back to her own chair and looks directly at her date for the evening.

"Your job is to field the more difficult questions and conversations and to tell me I am pretty when I am feeling insecure. Understood?" Rose raises her mug to her evening's date and then takes the last gulp of coffee. "Fifth wheel? Can't you see my Claus?"

She fetches her grandmother's silver and places them according to the rules of table etiquette learned in fifth grade Home Economics class. Rose looks to Santa. "Any suggestions for a centerpiece? Put the red drip candles in my jade candle holders. Have you done this before?" Rose finds the drip candles in the hutch and retrieves the jade holders from her bedroom and places three assembled pieces along the center of the table. "Muy bueno."

The timer sounds and Rose runs to the kitchen. She pulls open the oven door and carefully slides the rack out. She inserts a cake testing stick and it comes out clean. She carefully lifts the Bundt pan from the roasting pan and puts it on the top shelf of her kitchen's island to cool. Rose looks at her kitchen clock – 10:47. She now has approximately five hours to relax and begins by actually patting herself on the back.

***

"Bubble bath, hair masque, and a nap."

She fills the bath. She prefers to take baths at night and takes necessary steps to recreate the atmosphere. She lowers her roman blinds to darken the room and even tucks a towel around the frame of the window to minimize the light even further. Satisfied with the results she lights her banana bread scented candle and closes the bathroom door. Rose smiles as she notices the raspberry sorbet bath gel. *Of course, I forgot the raspberry raspado.* Rose pours the bath gel into the tap's stream while leaning over the rim to test the temperature and watch the bubbles multiply. By candlelight she applies her Alterna hair masque and slowly lowers her body into the tub.

    A heavy knock on her front door shocks her. A bit confused and possibly even frightened, Rose jumps out of the bath and quickly grabs her robe and towel. She carefully walks to her front door leaving wet footprints in her wake.

    "Who is it?" Rose asks as she looks out the frosted windows of her front door.

    "Hi, Rose," Aris answers through the door. "I have your music."

    Rose partially opens the door. "Ah shucks. You did not have to bring this by early. You could have brought it with you tonight." She pinches the top of her robe together with her right hand and checks the twist of the towel on her head with her left.

    "I had to pick up my pants at the dry cleaner and was just two blocks away. I thought it would be nice to give you a preview. I guess I should have called," Aris says apologetically.

    "It's fine. Well, I was enjoying my bath… No worries. You *are* going to be here tonight, right?" Rose asks while simultaneously recognizing the awkward attempt at small chat.

    "About that, I actually was wondering if we could talk. I could come back in an hour so you can finish your bath," Aris says. He nudges the door open.

    Rose looks down upon her wet robed covered body before answering, "I guess I can always use another cup of coffee. Come in." She steps aside and motions for his entry.

    "Smells good in here, chocolate and raspberries."

Rose lets out an embarrassed chuckle. "There is banana bread in the bathroom." She tightens the towel around her head. "Coffee and conversation. I'll make the coffee, you make the conversation."

Aris opens quickly, "It's Nora. She's feeling insecure. And I am not sure why."

"Do you think it has something to do with her father?"

"If it does, she is not saying so. I have actually asked her point blank about him."

"Are you different?" Rose asks. "Work has been a bit difficult for you, are you behaving more distant or something?" Rose turns her back and busies herself with a mug and the Keurig. She turns back around. "I'm listening."

Aris furrows his brow. "Distant? No, I do not think so. Anyway, a lot of her anger seems to be related to you. I think she is jealous."

"Jealous of me? That's ironic." Rose mutters to the Keurig.

"Why is it that girls can have guy friends, but guys cannot have girl friends?"

"Does Nora have a good guy friend?"

"No. Not exactly. Not like we are."

"Well, then, I think you have your answer. You're not cancelling on tonight, are you?" she asks with a tone that is both annoyed and desperate. She hands him his coffee.

"No. She doesn't even know I am here."

"Are you going to tell her?" Rose asks straightforwardly.

"Probably. Anyway, I am just concerned that she, well... She has a hard time keeping things to herself. What I mean is, she is not like you. I, and everyone around her, knows exactly how she is thinking and feeling."

"That's a very good quality." After a moment of processing what Aris is trying to say, Rose is slightly offended. But she *is* able to keep her feelings to herself – too many of them. "I don't want to sound... Are you thinking that she might say something to me, and you are here to warn me?"

"Maybe, but really I haven't got a clue why I am here." Aris says as he looks at his iPod. "My legs just brought me here."

"So how did you do?" Rose asks attempting to lighten the conversation as she reaches out to almost touch the iPod.

"I had lots of time to do it. I am pretty happy with the compilation. There are a few surprises." He slides the iPod a foot to his right so she can reach it. "Anyway, Nora has been pushing me away and I really have no idea why. I am beginning to think that maybe there is someone else."

"Really?" Rose asks with a tone of pure disbelief.

"You know how some people will accuse someone of something because they are the ones guilty of it?" Aris says.

"I guess I have seen it. But do you really think she is cheating on you?"

"No," Aris says. "But maybe there is someone else, real or imagined."

"Wow," Rose says quietly. "You guys really need to talk. Have you told her about this fear of yours?"

"No."

Rose leans on the counter with her elbows. "I think you have a place to start." She turns her head to look at the iPod.

"I should really get going. I suppose your bath is p'rolly pretty cold by now."

"Luckily, water is plentiful in these parts. If want to talk more..." Rose offers.

"Is Lin going to be here?" Aris asks.

"No, I did ask. She was gracious in her decline. She already had plans with her cousin's family."

Aris notices the large, yet grainy black and white photo on the refrigerator. "Is that Abdul?"

"Actually, it is. I printed out the picture last night. I think I'm kinda crushing on him," Rose admits lightheartedly. "I should get a better printer – one that prints in color."

"Crushing on him? He's like ten," Aris jabs.

"I was in love with Calvin for fifteen years and he's only six," Rose says as she moves a laminated clip-out of her favorite Calvin and Hobbes cartoons to frame the picture of Abdul. "Abdul inspires me."

"Inspiring and a dry sense of humor are two of your required traits in a mate," Aris says, remembering an old conversation. "And let's not forget the willingness to play bathroom chess."

"Is it too much to ask?" Rose says, laughing lightly. "Anyway, I think about Abdul when I feel sad or defeated, and I seem to perk right up. I guess I used to think of…" Rose catches herself and looks down at her bare feet.

"I should really get going. Do you need anything for tonight?"

"I think I have everything. Yet don't be surprised if I call at 5:55 with a request," she says, smiling gently as she walks him to the door. "Josephine is going to be here an hour early to help with the final touches."

"You *do* smell really good, like raspberries."

"Raspberry sorbet to be exact. You can smell that?" Rose asks. She lifts her eyes directly to his as she brings her left arm to her nose.

"Uh hum."

Rose looks nervously behind her. "I don't think I could live without my Mp3 player for seven hours."

"I couldn't either. It's my back-up," Aris responds as he steps over the threshold back into the hallway.

"Appetizers are at 7:00. See ya later alligator," Rose says with a child-like quality and closes the door. She realizes her mistake and re-opens the door to yell down the hall, "Hey, Aris – thanks for the music." She quickly closes the door and locks it.

Friends? Rose looks at the white iPod, sighs and gently hits the back of her head against the back of the door. "Just friends."

She pushes her body off the door and snatches the iPod and her ear buds and walks to the bathroom. "Good friends." She warms the water for a minute and is able to relax into the bath in two. "Best friends."

Rose places the ear buds in her ears as she reads the iPod, *The Roses Border Mix*.

"Well, what do we have here?" The mix starts with Spanish Guitar's *Suite Espanola*. Rose closes her eyes and listens. "Beautiful." She opens her eyes to watch the seconds rise with each strum of the guitar. *This will be a good night.*

CHAPTER 12
THE WIND AND THE SUN

The Wind and the Sun were disputing which was the stronger. Suddenly they saw a traveler coming down the road, and the Sun said: "I see a way to decide our dispute. Whichever of us can cause that traveler to take off his cloak shall be regarded as the stronger. You begin." So the Sun retired behind a cloud, and the Wind began to blow as hard as it could upon the traveler. But the harder he blew the more closely did the traveler wrap his cloak round him, till at last the Wind had to give up in despair. Then the Sun came out and shone in all his glory upon the traveler, who soon found it too hot to walk with his cloak on. –Aesop

"We'll need the pitcher and the champagne from the freezer," Rose says to Josephine while setting up the blender.

The doorbell rings. Rose looks at the clock, and it is precisely 7:00.

"Wanna get the door? I need to pull out the tamales," Rose says.

Josephine looks a bit confused yet follows the order. "You're sure about this?"

"Yeah, I'm sure. It's a little joke," Rose says.

Josephine opens the door. "Hola. I'm Josephine." Josephine looks back and forth between Rose and the two strangers and shrugs her shoulders. She steps back and continues to hold the door. "Adelante! Pase!"

"Hola, Josephine," Aris responds. "We finally meet. This is Nora, my girlfriend." Aris looks over to Rose who is taking the tamales out of the oven with a very large, toothy grin. She nudges the top of her head toward the clock.

"Hi, Nora," Josephine says with a gentle nod. "Let me take your coats?"

"I got it," Aris says loudly for Rose's benefit and then looks kindly at Josephine and steps towards the closet. He takes his coat off and then helps Nora with hers.

Rose walks over to greet her guests. "Hi, Aris. Hi, Nora. I am glad you're here."

"Hi, Rose. The place looks great and dinner smells really good. Thanks for inviting us," Nora says graciously. She reaches her right hand out for Aris.

Stepping from the closet, Aris takes the offering. "She's right," Aris says while gently lifting their hands and looking at Nora.

Rose somewhat awkwardly interprets the overt hand signals and casually turns her back and walks over to the stereo. She lifts the volume a few notches. "Thanks for the music – Suite Espanola. Hey, can I get anyone a drink? Champagne margarita?"

"We'll have one," Nora says while smoothing the skirt of her plum, spaghetti strapped column sheath dress to sit. "I had one of those a couple of years ago. They are delicious."

Rose notices Nora hug herself as if she might be chilly. "Am I making two or three?" Rose looks to Josephine who is handling a small wooden table puzzle.

"Three."

Rose acknowledges the order and steps over to her gas fireplace and presses the remote up a few degrees. She looks at the clock 7:05. "Be right back. And Josey, Aris is really good at those puzzles." Rose casually glances between them as she leaves the living room area. As she begins to lift the blender pitcher onto its base, the doorbell rings. "Ha. Augustine."

"I'll get it, Rose." Josephine nearly skips to the door and throws it open. "Hi, Honey."

Augustine slips his right hand around her waist and gently kisses her. "Wow. You look beautiful." He turns to Rose, who is peering around the portioned wall watching them. "Hi, Rose. Sorry I am a bit late. I left the house without the wine and had to go back."

"I'm making champagne margaritas, would you like one?" Rose asks stepping back into her kitchen. "I have it on pretty good authority that they are delicious," she says with a bit of extra volume to her voice.

"I would love a glass. Thank you," Augustine says as he takes his coat off.

Rose gets the tamale appetizers and champagne margaritas out to her guests. With a deep exhale, she turns and sits in her reading chair.

"Aren't you having a margarita?" Nora asks.

"Ah...um... I don't drink. I have a bit of an addictive personality and find that alcohol and I, although once upon a time were close acquaintances, should not be friends. I will taste an occasional drink, if it is new or seems unusual, yet, for the most part prefer non-alcoholic beverages." Rose says while rubbing her right calf with her right palm and with quite a bit of shake in her voice.

"The tamales are really good. You made these?" Aris asks. He leans forward to retrieve a bit more guacamole on his plate.

Rose nods her head. "The recipe Lisbeth gave me actually had lard. Lard! I used Crisco. They were a bit of work. I think next time I will buy them in the frozen food section of my local grocer."

"Hey, don't forget me. I helped," Josephine chimes in. "I stacked them in the steamer."

"Could not have done it without you," Rose says. Unable to relax, she fidgets a bit more before standing and picking up a single plain tamale to nibble. She looks to the iPod to watch the display switch from Acoustic Alchemy to Tom Waits. "Wow. You even got Tom Waits for the evening," Rose says as she casually glances at Aris.

"Odd choice, I know. There is something about the gruff of his voice that made me want to hear him among Spanish guitars. Paul Simon would have been too predictable," Aris says while staring into his champagne.

"Although a dinner party with both Tom Waits and Paul Simon would be interesting, don't you think?" Rose surmises as she sits back into her chair.

"Years ago you told me you wanted to host Bjork, Abe Lincoln and Chevy Chase's Fletch for your fantasy dinner party," Augustine says.

Aris laughs out loud. Nora places her right hand on his thigh and he quiets his chuckles. Still amused, he continues, "And what would you cook for them?"

"Mutton," Rose says as she pushes herself to standing with a super sharp look aimed directly at Aris. She walks toward the kitchen and then turns to broadcast, "On second thought – I think Bjork is probably a vegetarian."

"Speaking of vegetarian..." Rose says, turning to Augustine, "I did make a vegetarian dish for you, Augustine, and made enough for others as well. Anyway, now, I need to get grilling for those who still eat meat."

Rose looks down at her dress and then opens her dish towel drawer. *Apron? I need more.* Rose leaves the kitchen and goes to her room. She returns wearing her long, black bubble coat and her teal and black boot slippers.

Nora smiles. "Going somewhere?"

"The architecture along this road forms something like a wind tunnel - and it's cold out there," Rose says in an attempt to explain her costume change. Rose steps to the right and drops her arm down in the patented game-show model move. "This is my winter season grilling coat." She grabs the plate of marinated chicken and her barbeque tongs. "Josephine, I am leaving you in charge." She winks and steps out onto the patio, quickly closing the door behind her.

Josephine, taking her charge seriously, stands and asks if anyone would like another drink. She takes an order from two and heads to the kitchen.

Aris stands and walks over to the stereo to adjust the amplifier. He notices Rose, through the window, leaning over the railing. Slightly worried, he decides to step out to the patio. "What's stirring up in that little mind of yours?"

Rose looks to Aris with a bit of hurt in her eyes. "No mystery here, eh. Just a cookbook – a really boring cookbook. Actually, I am thinking of writing a cookbook."

"It is not so cold out here. I was bracing myself for an ice age." Aris takes a similar stance on the railing.

"So long?" Rose mutters inaudibly as she kicks the wrought iron railing. "Yeah, the wind is not blowing – for now. By the way, you look good. Those pants are perfection. Someday you will have to reveal the *mystery* of where you shop. I am sure one cannot find camel hair pin striped slacks at the Macy's men's department."

"I bought the shirt at Macy's," Aris says, looking down at his brown polished ankle boots. "You look beautiful too. The bubble coat suits you quite well." He takes one small step away from Rose. "You look very pretty."

"Yeah, I can wear the heck out of a bubble coat and it goes great with the shoes," Rose says as she kicks up her left slipper boot to show him the sole. The wind starts down the corridor.

Aris acknowledges the truth of her earlier statement and grips the railing and simultaneously pushes his body back. "It is cold. I should head back inside." Aris looks through the window at the rest of the party standing around the island. He places his hand on the door knob and turns to look at Rose, who is already watching him. "Thanks for doing this Rose. FYI, we talked this afternoon. I think your advice helped. I guess I have been a bit distant. She wants us to spend more time together doing things. She might join my gym."

"Sounds good. Sounds like a good place to start," Rose says, inadvertently furrowing her brow. "I am happy for you."

"Anyway, thanks for the advice. You are a really good

friend."

"I try." Rose quickly changes the subject, "I am glad that you finally got to meet Josephine. I think you guys will really get along." Rose looks down at the grill.

"Are you alright?" Aris asks. "I guess it's been awhile since you have cooked and hosted, hasn't it? Too much?"

"I'm a bit moody, pensive, perhaps.. I like to cook when I have problems-slash-questions, like this cocoa thing. Cooking gives me clarity. Just like a good idea – a good recipe can always be improved, like you and Nora." Rose hides her disappointment behind a smile. She wants to keep on talking so that he doesn't leave. "Anyway, it is too cold to be out here without a coat. Go on. The chicken will be done in about ten minutes, if you wouldn't mind informing the others."

She watches him walk toward the island and put both of his arms around Nora for warmth. Nora smiles and is very happy to oblige. With both warm and sorrowful feelings, Rose continues to watch the two couples interact. She takes a few moments to thank God as well as to request a renewed tensile strength for the remainder of the evening.

***

After the entree dishes are all served, Rose takes her seat at the head of the table opposite Santa, who has a full place setting. She takes her wine glass filled with Horchata and raises it to her guests. "To God and for Abdul." The rest of the table awkwardly looks at each other and then Rose points to the picture on her refrigerator. "Abdul." She sips her drink and then takes a bite of her chicken and is pleased.

The table sends both general and specific praise to their hostess by complimenting her on the grilled chicken and the flavorful sauce. The conversation is free-flowing and comfortable. Nora offers a story about the first time she had a champagne margarita. She was visiting a relative in Texas and was staying at the River Walk in San Antonio.

"I used to travel to Dallas for work – yet the site was closed down. Other than Dallas - I have not seen much of Texas," Rose responds.

"The River Walk is very nice," Nora says and takes another bite of her meal.

"Linde Sendero," Rose says quietly while gently adjusting the table runner.

"I am sorry. I didn't hear you. What did you say?" Nora asks.

"I said Linde Sendero, sort of like a river walk." Rose responds with an inflection in her voice that implies that she is not exactly sure what she is saying. "I guess I am thinking out loud."

"Sendero means path, right?" asks Aris. He repeats the word, "'sen-day'-ro' – it means footpath, right?"

Rose looks and speaks to Aris as if he is the only person in the room. "I only took a semester of Spanish in the seventh grade so needless to say my Spanish is… I can count to ten on a good day. Anyway, I spent this past week thinking about recipes, ingredients, boy scouts and, of course, Mexico, and I had this idea form in my head. The whole mess of issues related to the US Mexican border, illegal immigrants and their families, drugs, gun violence… blah blah blah… I was thinking about all of that and at the same time I was stenciling the leaf scrolls on the back of Josephine's chair and started to think about the garden path stones that I used to paint for my mother's garden. Anyway, I looked up the Spanish words for boundary and path – Leen-day Sen-day'ro." Rose finally takes a breath.

"Boundary Path," Aris says while using his knife to place extra sauce on his last bite of grilled chicken. He turns to look at Nora as he says, "This is one of those Rose storms I was telling you about."

"It is just an idea that I thought you might find interesting." Rose smirks and turns her body to speak directly to Nora. "Ya see, Nora, I have this tendency, let's call it a 'habit' for obvious reasons," Rose says, looking to Aris and raising the right corner of her mouth before continuing, "...to oversimplify huge problems and provide what I think are simple solutions."

"Well, Rose, don't leave us hanging. What's the idea?" Augustine eggs her on.

Rose centers in her chair and looks around the table and settles on Aris and asks him with her eyes, *Should I?*

Aris shrugs.

Rose takes a deep breath before responding, "I am just going to spit it out. In short, America would give up 5 miles of territory and so would Mexico. In that span of 10 miles the two governments and the Catholic Church could create a new Mexican Vatican; I have decided to call it the 'Linde Sendero.' This would be a country in and of itself. It would be set up with supremely significant tax breaks for manufacturing businesses. Both America and Mexico can attempt to steal manufacturing businesses back from China. Anyway we would have major factories in this area as well as catholic social services and schools. The factories would sign a charter contract for monies to support the Catholic schools and services. Most of Mexico is Catholic, and I think this may even be true for the drug dealers, and this alone may curtail violence. Anyway we create a place, a space, to increase honest work and beneficial revenue for both countries. The reason people come to America is because they are looking for things that the Mexican government does not yet supply. Maybe we can help Mexico's government create more social services with the help of the Catholic Church, whose organization and mission could also seriously benefit in this arrangement. Anyway, the separation of church and state would take on a new meaning at our border. Mexico has a lot of beautiful land and beaches. The music and food are obviously fabulous - in spite of the lard. Other than the amazing amounts of money that their people can make from American drug addicts - I am not sure why people would want to come here. Medicine and education - I guess. Both of those things the Catholic Church can offer better than almost any organization in the world. So yeah, Linde Sendero."

"Can anyone say tornado in Spanish?" Nora asks as she looks around the table.

"Sustantivo. Although, I am not sure if you can make a tornado without wind. You really should learn to breathe, Rose," Aris says. He follows his admonition with a simple demonstration of how to breathe both in and out.

"I like the stenciling," Augustine abruptly adds. "Did you do all of these chairs?"

"Yeah. I like Aris's chair the best. I think I must have been channeling Van Gogh when I painted those flowers." She audibly breathes for his benefit.

"I like your idea," Josephine says. "I think it sounds like an actual plan."

"Thanks!" Rose says emphatically. She stands and begins to clear the table. "I guess the major shortcoming is assuming that the drug dealers are Catholic."

"Huh. Curious. Members of the Mexican cartel are Catholic." Aris narrows his eyes acknowledging the strange irony. "I guess you could ask them? The ones already in jail. Ask them if they are Catholic. My guess – just on Sundays."

"Rose, you do know that people aren't really looking for solutions to problems. It costs too much," Augustine notes while helping to clear the table.

"No. I guess I really don't know that," Rose responds and lowers her head to look at her hands. "I am still learning, I suppose. I am not quite mature enough to learn that yet." She changes her demeanor again and chirps, "I think it would be interesting to find out whether or not the Mexican cartel is afraid of holy ground."

"Chocolate Industries and drug smugglers beware," Augustine says. "I think your mania is cute," Augustine jabs as he returns to the table to collect more dishes.

Rose turns to Josephine standing on the other side of the dishwasher, "I am going to have to cook another dinner to thank you for helping me with this one."

"The dinner was fantastic and I can see why you like Aris. And Rose, you did make flan. I absolutely love flan. How about this? Can I keep the shoes? I got so many compliments."

"They are great shoes." The two women finish loading the dishwasher and then return to the table carrying the next course. "Raspberry raspado – palate cleanser."

A few minutes later, the tea kettle sounds and Rose excuses herself. She takes the kettle off the burner and then takes a minute to relax and gently wash her hands. She fills her pressed pot with the espresso, cinnamon sticks, nutmeg, brown sugar, vanilla and cloves. Rose turns from the sink and is happy to see everyone is just sitting down on the living room couches. Both Augustine and Nora have picked up one of the brain teaser puzzles.

"There are more of those in the cabinet under the stereo. I kind of collect them," Rose says across the room.

"Are you any good?" Nora asks.

"No, actually. I think I have only solved one. Yet, I do like them," Rose responds. "Aris?"

"Yes," Aris responds.

"I made Mexican coffee. It is a sweetened coffee with cinnamon, cloves, vanilla, and a wee bit of cocoa." Rose holds up a box of black tea. "I also have tea."

"Tea, please." Aris stands and walks towards the kitchen. "Can I help?"

"I need to set up this tray," Rose sets up her ceramic tea set as Aris watches.

"This serving tray is your grandmother's, right?" Aris asks as he moves to stand next to her.

"True. I inherited quite a bit from her. I really do wish you could have met her." Rose looks into his eyes.

"So you keep telling me," Aris says. He holds her gaze

briefly before giving her a gentle elbow to her side.

"Are you saying that I repeat myself?" Rose huffs.

"Yes, you usually do. Yet with each telling, I swear there is greater intonation," Aris articulates as he lifts the tray and timidly walks into the living area.

God, he is so cute. Rose's eyes nervously and lovingly follow him into the living room. She grabs the silver spoons and a handful of napkins and tries to mimic his stride. Rose is thankful to notice that no one noticed.

"What, no flan?" Josephine asks with a sense of urgency.

Rose immediately remedies the flan-less and serves the flan. Still not quite ready for dessert herself, Rose takes her coffee to her reading chair and attempts small talk. "Have you scheduled the cruise yet?"

"Not yet. Well, actually I have not spoken to Mina this week," Aris replies.

"Let me know," Rose says. "How is the flan, Nora?"

"Very guud. It tastes quite a bit different. Tha cake is eckcellent." Nora offers a bite to Aris, who also declined the initial offering.

"No thanks. I will get a slice in a bit. I am still full from dinner," Aris says to Nora, brushing his chin on the top of her hair. She is clearly starting to feel the effects of the alcohol, food and sugar.

"Me too," Rose comments and then sits back in her chair and quietly observes the couples for a few minutes, trying not to eavesdrop on their tender conversations. *I could certainly drink more coffee.* Rose gets up and asks, "Would you like another cup of tea?"

Aris looks into his cup and at the woman nearly sleeping in his wing. "If you don't mind?" He hands her his cup.

Rose stops at the island on her way back to the kitchen to hear praise of the flan. She listens with her ears as her eyes watch the couple on the couch. *They seem happy.* She sets the cup down on the counter and looks to her friends. "So when is the date?"

"Actually, we are thinking the last weekend of May," Josephine states. "It is going to be small with just two attendants, my sister and his brother. I am always happiest in the spring." Josephine runs her arm up and down Augustine's back.

"Finally. I am happy for the both of you. I really am. I am glad you set the date," Rose says as she grabs Aris's cup and takes it to her Keurig.

"You'll have to bring a date, you realize?" Josephine says to Rose.

"I don't think tonight's date is going to last until May," Rose says.

Josephine delivers a very confused look to Rose as she slowly turns her eyes to Aris. Rose immediately intervenes. "What? You did not notice my date?" Rose walks over to the table and lifts the Santa.

"Rose, you can do better than that," Augustine says.

"What an Angel, perhaps." Rose expounds, "A wise man once told me that 'we don't get to choose who we fall in love with.'" Rose looks at her wire shoes. "Although I like the idea of falling for an angel."

Aris lifts his head and looks fixedly at Rose. She notices him in her periphery and without looking at him steps to the Keurig to retrieve his tea. "I am really not interested in dating anyone," she tells them. She takes the cup to Aris with a heavy stride. She touches the back of her bun and pushes in a pin with her thumb and her index finger as she walks back to the island.

"I do hope you realize how lucky you both are," Rose says as she cuts a piece of cake for herself.

Rose looks at Aris and lifts her plate. Aris nods in the affirmative. She slices a slender piece and places it on a caramel laced plate. She places two strawberries at ten o'clock. Grabbing a dessert fork and another napkin, she walks her plate and his over to him. She hands him his dessert and then falls back in her chair.

"She really liked the champagne, I think," Aris says.

"She looks very peaceful," Rose says while looking at the petite beauty. She grabs her enormous dictionary and sets it on the couch next to him.

Aris smiles and nods his head. "Thanks." Aris places his mug between his legs and his plate on the dictionary. He twists very gently to find the posture that will enable him to gain access to the cake without disturbing his date. "Cocoa flan?"

"Choco-flan," Rose corrects. "Hey, thanks for the music tonight."

"No problem, I enjoyed the task," Aris says.

"And thanks for being here," Rose says with an expressive tone.

Nora opens her eyes and angrily leers at Rose. "Honey, let's go home."

"Power nap?" Aris asks.

"My dad sometimes falls asleep sitting up after a big meal. He usually denies the fact and says that he was merely looking at the back of his eyelids," Rose imparts.

"I was sleeping. Sugar sometimes does that to me," Nora responds sitting up while placing a kiss on Aris' lips. "I want to go home."

"I am getting pretty tired," Aris admits as he lifts his arms up to relinquish his partner for a moment.

Rose stands and picks up the desert plates and takes them to her sink. "Aris and Nora are leaving."

"We were thinking of calling it a night, as well," Augustine says in a louder than usual tone. "Champagne and wine can make one a tad bit sleepy."

Rose opens her junk drawer in her kitchen and pulls out coupons from Lin. "Everyone is alright to drive, right?" Rose asks with a sincere concern as she hands out the coupons. "Free dry cleaning. A party favor, compliments of Lindo."

"Auggie, do you want to drive?" Josephine looks at

Augustine and then at Rose. "Is it alright if I leave my car here in your parking deck all night?"

Rose nods.

"Thanks for the dinner. I will be back for another piece of flan tomorrow, after work." Josephine turns to meet Augustine, who is holding open her coat. "Thanks, Sweetness."

"Thanks, Rose," Augustine says with a gentle nod.

Rose's attention turns to Aris as he puts on his coat. "Thanks, Thorn."

"Thorn?" Nora asks as she reaches her hand up to his. Aris takes her hand and gives it a gentle squeeze.

"Good night, Aris. Good night, Nora." Rose turns and tries to busy herself as her guests make their way to the door. "Please drive safe. Precious cargo."

The door closes and the room finds the music once again. "Further to Fly."

"Predictable," Rose says as she shakes her head. She leans her forehead against the center of the door and locks. *Thanks, God. Too much food?* She looks at her reflection in the living area window and notices Abdul on her refrigerator. "To God, and for Abdul. Thanks to the both of you." She looks at her clock - 10:47.

CHAPTER 13
THE THRUSH AND THE FOWLER

A THRUSH was feeding on a myrtle-tree and did not move from it because its berries were so delicious. A Fowler observed her staying so long in one spot, and having well bird-limed his reeds, caught her. The Thrush, being at the point of death, exclaimed, "O foolish creature that I am! For the sake of a little pleasant food I have deprived myself of my life." -Aesop

Rose pulls into the parking lot of the Maplewood United Methodist Church fellowship hall one-half hour early. She was told by the Scout Master, Nicolas Grey, that the meetings typically let out about fifteen minutes early. He requested that she wait to see members of the troop leaving before entering. She drives into a parking space illuminated by one of two lamps in the parking lot. She places her car in neutral, lifts the hand brake and lowers her headlights.

"A boy army and a children's crusade," she mutters as she reviews her agenda and notes she prepared. Twenty-three minutes later, she lifts her head from her notes to witness the first set of boys walk out of the fellowship hall. The four boys huddle for a minute and then disperse to their respective mothers, who are each practicing their own waiting rituals. She delays until she sees two more boys leaving the building before she gathers her items and exits her very warm car.

Just as she reaches for the handle to one of the heavy wooden double doors, it swings inwardly revealing four more boys dressed in their green scout uniforms. A bit startled and then amused, Rose says "hello" to the boys as they scurry past. She takes a moment to remember the lessons of Baden-Powell and tries to make a mental note of their approximate heights and weights as well as other features including hair color and eye color. She is even able to determine that two of the boys probably have semiregular visits to the orthodontist. She smiles then turns to ask, "Nicolas Grey? Is he at the end of this hall?"

"Yes, Ma'am, the last door on the right," the tallest of the boys answers just as the door closes behind them.

"Thanks," Rose replies, although she is sure that they cannot hear her. She continues down the hall, as per their instructions, and finds a room fit with a giant white board and multiple book shelves. A quite handsome Nicolas Grey stands in the middle, straightening the chairs around the conference table. "Nicolas Grey? Hi. I'm Rose Isope."

"Hi, Rose. Good timing, we just finished. And it is Nick, please," Nicolas says, reaching his right hand out in a customary greeting. "Any trouble finding the place?"

Rose shakes his hand. "Nick. No problem at all. Your directions were very good. I've been here approximately half an hour experiencing quiet solidarity with the mothers of your troop." She awkwardly looks around the room, removes her coat and places it over her arm. She stands behind the second seat on the right side of the conference table.

"So you have a scouting idea?"

"Actually, I have more of a problem that I think scouting might be able to help," Rose says while taking her seat and placing her black leather folder on the table. "Actually, I'm looking for Baden-Powell's cadet army."

"Okay," Nicolas says with a somewhat cautious tone.

"I decided that if I was going to talk to a Scout Master then I should 'Be Prepared,'" she says with a simple smile while opening her black folder. She slides Nicolas a Reese's Peanut Butter Cup. "Nourishment. Two great tastes that go great together." She looks for a response to her gift. Re-energized by his apparent satisfaction, she continues to pull items from her folder. With each item – first the newspaper article, then the Protocol, then the ChIP's brochure, and finally her merit badge paperwork – Nicolas's face takes on a heavier appearance.

"What is all of this?" Nicolas asks bewildered.

"Have you ever seen that commercial where there is a person holding a jar of peanut butter yelling, 'Who put their chocolate in my peanut butter?'"

"Yes...I have," Nicolas responds uneasily.

"Sometimes it takes pure genius to put two things together – two things like chocolate and peanut butter. I have been trying to solve a social problem and think I may have the beginning of a solution, and I am wondering if you and your troop would not mind testing my hypothesis. The problem is chocolate and the solution is a boy army."

Nicolas starts to attack the wrapping of his peanut butter cup. "How can you have a problem with chocolate?"

Rose smiles. "How many people in America know that all this chocolate they are eating is being produced by child labor, or worse, child slaves?"

"Gulp." Nicolas stops eating. "I see, it's a trap. Giving me candy... I should have seen it."

"No trap. It's the problem of chocolate."

"I fall for it every time."

"Really, there is no trap, I have a problem and need your boy army," Rose responds. "Alright - the problem is – Abdul has never had chocolate." Rose explains the ten-year-old's situation to the Scout Master.

"The problem is that the public ought to know about it and then ought to take action to stop it," she continues. "The public is waiting for the chocolate companies, like Hershey's and Nestle, to stop child labor in its industry, yet, really, they don't have the incentive to do so."

"They need incentive?" Nicolas tries to understand the conversation of which he is supposed to be the second half. "They need incentive to stop using child slaves."

Rose's eyes light up as she recognizes that she is actually being heard. "Apparently, they do."

"Out of sight, out of mind, right? It's not their children, therefore it is not their problem," Nicolas summarizes.

"Here is the scoop. After a series of news reports surfaced about the problem in 2001, a few lawmakers, namely Senator Harkin and Representative Engel, try to force the industry to do something about it – to change. I guess prior to that day, no one really knew about it. Or at least they weren't talking. The incentive – well, to cover their ass, I guess. Excuse my language. Anyway, they got caught. Truth be told, UNICEF estimates that nearly a half-million trafficked children work on farms across Ivory Coast. FYI, the Ivory Coast produces nearly 40% of the world's supply of cocoa. The Ivory Coast and Ghana produce nearly 70% of the world's supply."

"So, after intense lobbying by the cocoa industry, these fine men weren't able to push through a law despite their best efforts. I know shocking!" Rose lightly touches the article and continues, "What they got was a voluntary protocol, signed by the heads of the chocolate industry, Hershey, M&M/Mars, Nestle… to stop the worst forms of child labor as a matter of urgency.

"A matter of urgency? I suppose I do not know what urgency means, because a month ago, I found this," She separates the article from her and spins it on the table. "Eleven years later, David McKenzie and Brent Swails of CNN report that the chocolate industries decision to implement a solution of cocoa certification – a way to prove that children were not being used to harvest the cocoa – is not working. I understand that these things take time, but eleven years? Obviously their plan is not working. They are trying to fit a square peg through a round hole." Rose pauses for a brief second, "Do you remember that plastic red and blue decagon thing where you had to put the plastic yellow star through the star hole, the circle through the circle, etcetera?

Nicolas smiles looking down at the table, "I know exactly what you are talking about." He demonstrates his understanding by miming pulling the two pieces apart.

"In my humble opinion – they are going about it the wrong way. They are breaking off the points of the star by trying to get the star to fit into their way-too-narrow box." She takes a breath and tries to find the light in her poor, unsuspecting prey. "Now, I know I just threw a lot of information at you. My intention is not to scare you or burden you – I just think that the Boy Scouts of America or heck, Boy Scouts International can do more to fix this than any other organization. Fight fire with fire."

Nicolas sits back in his chair and pops the last of his candy into his mouth. Still chewing, he says, "You seem like you are mad at me."

"I am sorry. I guess I care… and I want someone else to," Rose admits.

"So, you are having a hard time finding someone to care about children being used as slaves. And so you thought that maybe you could convince a child organization to care." Nicolas smiles knowingly. "Your logic seems sound. What do you want the Boy Scouts to do?"

"I want the boy scouts to help raise awareness using already established channels."

"I'm listening."

"I was looking at the merit badges and all that these boys must do to earn one. There is a lot of work that goes into earning these badges," Rose says. "I kind of want to make a new badge – a badge called the Mafeking Challenge."

"Robert Baden-Powell's cadet army." Nicolas nods his head in understanding, "Now we are getting somewhere."

"I have been reading about the Boy Scouts, after I read Baden-Powell's original book, *Scouting for Boys*, and although the Boy Scouts of America are doing alright – I think they could use a little push - a national call to action," Rose says with a tone of authority.

"Rally the troops, eh. Interesting. No, I mean it –

Interesting."

"To earn the Mafeking Challenge badge – I'm thinking that they could talk to their schools in an assembly of sorts. You know, hand out flyers detailing the problem. Talk to them about kids their age working in cocoa fields without ever having chocolate. Talk to them about kids their age working in the cocoa fields without ever having gone to school. And tell them about ChIP."

"ChIP?" Nicolas asks. "What is ChIP?"

"The proverbial peanut butter – the beginning of the solution. This analogy is getting a bit goofy. The gift, the peanut butter cups, they were supposed to give you enough of a sugar rush to not kick me out…"

"So what is ChIP?" Nicolas asks, amused. He notices the energy level of this complete stranger dwindling. "I think you need one of these. You got any more candy shoved in that folder?"

"Nope. I am afraid you got the last of it," Rose says smiling, trying not to laugh.

"I heard breathing helps," Nicolas suggests

Rose inhales. "So what was I saying…? Ah yes – ChIP! The Chocolatiers Initiative's Pen…" Rose exhales loudly. "I like coffee more than I like air. I'm guessing you do not serve coffee at troop meetings?"

"No. We are a bit old school here - we don't serve coffee to the boys. However, this is a church and the kitchen usually does have instant coffee and water. Let's go get some."

"Really? I can get a cup of coffee?" Rose lights up as she leaps to her feet. "I've had a really long day."

"Wednesdays are always long days," Nicolas says as he holds the door to the kitchen. "I really like these guys. I really do. Yet, two or three tend to require a bit more patience than I typically have at this time of day. I wish we could have lunch meetings. I could handle them at 1:00 in the afternoon much easier than 6:00 at night."

"Coffee!" Rose immediately locates the hot water urn next

to the sink. She finds coffee crystals in the cupboard directly above the urn. "Coffee. Coffee. Coffee." Rose retrieves two mugs located in the same cabinet and sets them down on the counter. "You would like a cup, right?"

"Yes, Ma'am. Although coffee crystals reminds me of camping in college – very few of my friends in college were scouts and they had no idea how to make coffee. Coffee crystals – bad."

"I would imagine that meeting fellow Boy Scouts in college was rare."

"You'd be surprised. I met quite a few," Nicolas acknowledges. "I think that many of them would be surprised to hear I have my own troop."

"A happy surprise?" Rose asks as she stirs both cups with the plastic spoon she found in the cabinet. "Sugar?"

"No thanks. Just black," Nicolas answers.

Rose hands Nicolas his cup and nods her appreciation as she takes her first sip. "It is not so bad," she says and laughs.

"Taster's Choice! It's delicious."

The two head back to the conference room discussing camping in college. "Camping is probably still my favorite thing to do. I even like to camp in the winter," Nicolas adds.

"Yeah – I prefer solitude, too," Rose adds, hoping that he hears her sense of humor.

"So about ChIP?" Nicolas asks as he arrives at his chair.

"The brochure sums it all up – well, pretty much," Rose comments as she points to the brochure in front of him and then takes her seat. "It is something to help raise money to build schools in the cocoa fields for the children and their future. Look, there is Brainy ChIP. Isn't he cute?" Rose glances at Nicolas. "I am hoping to get Nightingale Chocolates to help me, too! I think that the 100 billion dollar industry could probably afford a few schools.

"This is the logo – I was hoping to get it made into a 1.5 inch circle badge for this meeting. But, I suppose that is a long way to go to find out the diner is closed?"

"What?" Nicolas asks.

"Ah, never mind. It's my college story. One night my brother and I decided that we wanted to go to a diner; we both wanted meatloaf. You know the kind of meatloaf you could only find at home or at a 24-hour diner. Anyway, we drove about three hours to find out that the 24-hour diner of our youth, the 24-hour diner that never closed, happened to be closed that particular night for their annual cleaning. On our drive back we joked back and forth about driving for hours and still not getting our meatloaf. It has turned into a private joke between the two of us – and I guess, now you." Rose smiles as she reminisces of the particularly odd night spent with her brother. "I was thinking of turning this into a merit badge to help make my case – yet did not do it because I thought that the likelihood of being asked to leave was as probable as ever having this conversation."

"So the Mafeking challenge – this is the logo?" Nicolas asked.

"No. Gosh, I was hoping the coffee was going to help clear things up." Rose starts jumping in childlike frustration. "This is the logo for ChIP," Rose proclaims. "I actually thought that the cover art on his book would look great on the Mafeking Challenge merit badge. You have seen it, I am sure."

"I have the book," Nicolas immediately responds.

"I was thinking of that and the merit badge for 'Entrepreneurship' – the hand reaching for the star. Huh, like the yellow plastic star…" Rose smiles at the sky. "I was thinking maybe a star in the place of the rock, or maybe on his walking stick? I completed the requirements for the 'Entrepreneurship' merit badge to prepare for this meeting, thinking that creating a 'Mafeking Challenge' merit badge was an act of entrepreneurship."

"You did what? Really?" Nicolas asks while picking up the 24 pages of typed information Rose completed.

"It was fun," Rose adds with a very toothy smile.

"Fun. I actually have this badge, and I am pretty sure that I did not think it was fun."

"I am not fifteen," Rose says.

"I was fourteen." Nicolas flips through the pages. "Just so you don't feel as if you wasted your time, I will read it."

"I hope you do. I wrote it just in case you did not have time to meet. I spelled out the particulars and thought that if you found this introductory meeting interesting enough – you would have something written to refer to when speaking with other Scout Masters. You know, *be prepared.* I guess I am glad I wrote it down. Apparently I am not being as clear as I…" Rose takes a sip of her coffee.

"I can't believe you did this. I am assuming you were a girl scout," Nicolas observes.

"Actually, no. I was a brownie. I flew up to be a girl scout – we cross a bridge… Well, in our first meeting, we sat around a table and made instant pudding. Instant Pudding! We poured two cups of skim milk into a round plastic jug, added pudding mix, put on the lid, and shook. I waited two years to become a girl scout – I walked across a bridge to make instant pudding." Rose shakes her head while forcing air out of her nose. "Even at that age, I knew better. I quit that day."

"My sister did not like the girl scouts either. She wanted to be a boy scout," Nicolas says.

"Apparently, that was not an all-too-unfamiliar sentiment for girls my age," Rose comments. "I have met over a dozen young women who had a very similar experience to mine and quit the girl scouts. I hope it is different now. I am pretty sure it is."

"Are you going to go to them with this idea?" Nicolas asks honestly.

"No. I really think that this is a job for the boy scouts," Rose responds concisely. "I think the Boy Scouts are in trouble and I hate to see it. Uh…um, I hope you don't mind that I just said that to a person who spends every Wednesday night with a troop of twelve, is it twelve? I think this is a beautiful organization – a diamond in the rough…rough times, that is – and needs a polish. I am mixing metaphors… How about fresh air; we could bring fresh air to Baden-Powell's dream… I really do admire him. I would like to revive his cadet army for a good cause." Rose looks up and to the left, puzzled by her random thought, "I think it is strange…that the girl scouts aren't suffering as much as the boy scouts. The press does not seem to be targeting them. I wonder why…" Rose looks down into her lap and quietly utters her own answer, "It must have something to do with those darn tasty thin mints."

"I like the Tagalongs, no – Samoas," Nicolas acknowledges the double standard with a light laugh. "Listen, once a month, on the third Thursday, all of the local Scout leaders get together for a meeting at the Scout center and then go for a single beer at Charlie's. It is almost my old Cub Scout pack, three of my original Cub Scout pack are still active in scouting. Anyway, we have been talking about stirring things up for a while. We are a bit frustrated fighting the kids and the parents. I don't know. However, this – this idea of yours might help."

Rose closes her eyes and says a quick prayer of thanks.

Nicolas continues, "I think it is a good thing to bring up the past – remembering our forefathers and the like. So thanks for the reminder. I remember learning about him from my Scout Master when I was about thirteen – I mean really learning about him and his life. We spent a month talking about the history of Scouting. It was important to my Scout Master."

"Did you tell your guys about the history of scouting? I thought it was fascinating."

"Things are different now." He looks at his reflection in the window. "We spend a lot of time talking about merit badges and putting forth the effort to get them. We don't spend much time talking about the reason they exist. I have not thought about him and the battle of Mafeking in years. Anyway, I think I could probably shoot an email to the guys and you could probably speak to them – next Thursday night."

He lifts the merit badge packet in the air. "It may be a bit short notice - yet you seem to 'be prepared.'" He sets the packet back down on the table. "And I think you are right, I think he would find this cause worthy of attention. Not only did he hate uselessness – he really loved Africa."

"Do you happen to know whether or not he liked chocolate?"

"I am pretty sure he liked peanut butter."

"Have you ever heard of the Aesop fable of the 'Thrush and the Fowler?'"

"No. I don't think I know any Aesop fables," Nicolas responds.

Rose looks down at the table and presses her right fingers back. "I like Aesop fables. Anyway, in the fable, a thrush finds delicious berries to eat and stays in the one spot and eats and eats and eats. The Fowler snags the thrush for his own meal. Anyway, the moral of the story is – repetition leads to demise."

"The Boy Scouts need to shake things up. I get you," Nicolas says succinctly and understandingly.

"Yes – exactly. I usually have to explain myself more. And I am usually much clearer. This is nice." Rose lowers her head and looks at the table. "I think I could be ready to give a speech by next Thursday. My mom says that I am like a dog with a bone, and well, I am not exactly sure if my…" Rose makes air quotes as she continues "'speech' will not alienate the audience. I mean, I am not a scout, a boy scout or a girl scout. I am an outsider thinking I can walk into a room full of Scout Masters and tell them what to do. Again with the mixing of the metaphors but… well, I am not exactly the easiest pill to swallow. I am open-minded, it's just… Well, my mom is right…I am kind of like a dog with a bone."

"I hear ya. The guys, well, I don't think I am wrong saying that we think there is a problem and who knows, maybe we need to remember exactly what it means to be a Scout. Scouts are supposed to go out ahead of the war and report back what we see. Right? I think I remember learning that when I was thirteen." Nicolas looks at Rose. "Yeah, I think you are right. Let me talk to the guys and I will get back to you about next week. No time like the present, right?"

"I have to admit I actually thought ... well, I was *prepared* to be dismissed, a polite dismissal, but a dismissal nonetheless. That is kinda what happened at Nightingale's," Rose says somewhat defeated, yet quickly changes her demeanor to reflect her current satisfaction. "I hope you know that I really and sincerely appreciate the consideration. If you please, read over my merit badge work. It will probably give you enough of a heads-up of what my talk would be like and will present things to you with a greater clarity than I have." Rose looks directly at Nicolas. "Not to make excuses, but I have had a really difficult day - stupid job stuff. Anyway, if you don't mind, I would really like to hear what you think. My email and phone number are located on the brochure for ChIP," Rose says while standing and slipping her right arm into her coat.

Nicolas stands and smiles at Rose. "I really think that this is interesting and really want to thank you for thinking of us, Rose. I will read this and get back to you ASAP. This is a cool thing you want to do. I hope we can help."

"Cool? I think so and hope so. My passion burns pretty hot on this one. Abdul has never had chocolate. Argh! Seriously, Argh!" Rose says with her hands gripping the air and then immediately changes her body language to a completely relaxed manner. "Thanks for thinking it is cool and not a waste of time. I have to admit most people I have talked to about this think it's a pipe dream.

"Most people don't think," Nicolas responds. "Rose, it was a pleasure."

"Hey, thanks, Nick." Rose nods as she lifts her coat over

both of her shoulders and grabs her black folder from the table. "Let me take your mug to the kitchen."

"Nice. Strange, but nice. No, thanks. I got it. I have to lock up anyway. Have a good night, Rose," Nicolas says.

"Hey, do you dry clean your clothes?"

"I have a wool coat that I take every year." Nicolas responds puzzled by such a random question

Rose hands him a coupon from Lin. "My friend has been handing these out like candy. They are not as tasty as a peanut butter cup, however. Thanks again for meeting with me, Nick. And for being so patient. I am normally sane and methodical, I swear it. Anyway, thanks. Have a good night." After a brief pause at the door as she debates whether she should apologize again for being so flaky, she steps into the hallway. She walks past five doors, two on the left and three on the right, before reaching the double doors. "Get a grip."

She steps into the very cold December night and walks very quickly to her car. She sinks into the bucket seat and says a small prayer. "Thanks, God. He is nice. I think he might be one of yours. I guess I should have probably prayed for clarity. My mistake. He is cute, too." Rose starts her car and pushes the gear shift into reverse, mimicking the tight whine of the car. She presses the 'On' of her car stereo. "Shadows of the Night."

CHAPTER 14
THE FOX AND THE WOODCUTTER

THE FOX having been hunted hard and run a long chase saw a Woodcutter at work, and begged him to help him to some hiding-place. The Man said he might go into his cottage, which was close by. He was no sooner in, than the Huntsmen came up. "Have you seen a Fox pass this way?" said they. The woodcutter said "No," but pointed at the same time towards the place where the Fox lay. The Hunstmen did not take the hint, however, and made off again at full speed. The Fox, who had seen all that took place through a chink in the wall, thereupon came out, and was walking away without a word. "Why, how now?" said the Man "Haven't you the manners to thank your host before you go?" "Yes, yes," said the Fox; "if your deeds had been as honest as your words, I would have given you thanks." – Aesop

  Rose walks into her bedroom to find her phone lighting up, signaling to her that she had a message. Anxious because only her closest of friends and family call her on her land line, she hurriedly picks up the receiver and presses the combination of numbers necessary to retrieve the message. The message is from Aris. "Rose, we need to talk."

  "We need to talk? Why didn't you call my cell phone?" Rose talks into the air and realizes that she should probably be saying the exact same thing to him. She dials Aris's cell phone and repeats the same two sentences into his message recorder. She places the phone back into its cradle and inadvertently stares at the bed side table for a long thirty seconds.

  She leaves her bedroom and decides upon shredded wheat for dinner; bite-size frosted shredded wheat and a cup of cherry orchard yogurt, to be precise. "The dinner of champions," Rose utters as she lifts her spoon above her head and mimics the roar of a crowd. She walks over to her calendar and places a note under the date. She likes to keep track of the number of times she eats cereal for dinner hoping to one day either pioneer a dinner cereal or keep the number below ten per month. She has been keeping the calendar for over two years and has yet to accomplish either goal. She takes a bite of her cereal and speaks a possible name for the dinner cereal, "Bowl Vittles?" She keeps a list of possible names on a pad in the drawer of her coffee table; 'bowl vittles' will make the list.

She takes her bowl to the coffee table and sets it down on the table while conducting a search for her note pad. She taps her pen on the table as she reads down the list and laughs at "Kat-tees." Rose's purse begins to ring. She chugs the remaining milk in her bowl before rushing to answer the call. "Hi, Aris."

"Hey, Rose. I have been trying to reach you all night. Where have you been?" Aris asks with a rushed tone to his voice.

"Uh... did we have plans?"

"No. I guess I assume that you will always take my call," Aris says with a hint of vulnerability.

"I met with the Scout Master tonight – Nick. He is cute, cute, cute and very helpful. I wonder if he plays chess," Rose says while pouring a few biscuits of shredded wheat into her bowl. "Why? What is going on? Are you okay?" She considers the crunchiness of her dinner as she awaits his answer. There is none. "Aris? Are you there?"

"Sorry. I guess those are difficult questions to answer. Have you had dinner?"

"Just," Rose explains.

"Cereal?" Aris asks. "Chicken chips?"

"It just so happens that you are correct, my fine-feathered friend – bite-sized frosted shredded wheat. What do you think of Bowl Vittles?" Rose asks as she tries to envision her friend's face.

"Wagon Wheels sound so much tastier."

"Yum - wagon wheels. Do you remember 'gravy train'? Gravy. Gravy, Gravy – New Chuck wagon gravy is here," Rose sings and awaits a witty retort. Instead she receives silence.

"Seriously, Aris, what is wrong?"

Aris gives another long pause before answering, "Can I come over?"

"Uh, sure, of course you can," Rose answers tentatively with an audible twist of alarm in her voice.

"I am fine, Rose. We do need to talk and I would prefer a more private setting, and the phone... the phone is not going to work this time. I will be there in ten." Aris quickly drops the line and Rose is left listening to electrons.

"Weird." Rose quickly scans the room and pops one dry biscuit into her mouth, leaving three in her cereal bowl. Her stomach begins to knot as she grinds her teeth into a dry biscuit. She starts to pace nervously. *I hope he is okay.* She puts another biscuit into her mouth and throws the remaining two into the trash. *I hope his parents are okay?* She places the bowl and the spoon into the dishwasher and puts the cereal box back in its cupboard. She walks to the bathroom and cups a few handfuls of water into her mouth, swishes and spits before picking up her toothbrush. She finishes by checking the remnants of her eye make-up. She picks up her morning's towel from the floor and puts it back onto its rack. She shuts off the light to the bathroom and then walks to her bedroom to make the bed. Just as she finishes smoothing the comforter she hears a quiet knock at her door. Rose takes a deep breath and catches her reflection in her full length mirror before exhaling. She runs to the door.

Rose yanks the door open with her left hand and keeps her right hand on her hip. "Entre vous."

"Hi, Rose," Aris says as he steps past her. "Sorry about this." Aris takes off his coat and carries it in his left palm toward the couches.

Rose follows him with a deep wrinkle setting in her forehead. "Sorry about what? You are actually beginning to scare me. Are you in trouble?"

"Funny. I guess I am," Aris says with his own look of

concern and a lowered chin. "We need to talk."

"Yeah. You keep on saying that. Can I get you something to drink? Orange juice?" Rose asks.

"Orange juice sounds perfect, thanks." Aris finally sits down in the same spot he sat a few nights earlier.

Rose pours a glass of orange juice for Aris and fills her own water glass before returning to the couches. "So talk," she says. She lifts the top of her left ear with her fingers to signify that she is listening.

"Nora and I have had a huge fight," Aris begins, "and this time it was all about you." He lifts his eyes and looks right into Rose's.

"Does this have something to do with the other night? I couldn't sleep because I realized I brought up my father in conversation twice with Nora. I thought that maybe she would think I was insensitive or something?"

"She didn't mention it."

"Do you think I should apologize? I am not exactly sure what I would say," Rose says sincerely, yet does not wait for a reply. "Anyway, I am sorry you are fighting," she utters with an almost sincere tone. "So what, you cannot go home right now?"

"No, that's not it. It's not that kind of fight," Aris says. "You're being evasive."

"I am not. How am I being evasive?" Rose asks while forcibly pushing her hands from her hips to her knees. "Pesky crumbs." She lets out a nervous giggle before locking her eyes on his.

"Stop it. I told you. The fight was about you. You are supposed to ask what we were fighting about," Aris states strongly. Aris knows that Rose never asks a question unless she wants to know the answer.

"Fine." Rose stares at Aris.

"Ask!" Aris yells.

Rose squints her eyes and twists her mouth before

complying with his request. "Aris, what were you and Nora fighting about?"

"Are you in love with me?" Aris answers.

"You always answer my questions with another question," Rose says trying to lighten the conversation, or possibly concoct an overt ploy to distract him.

"Are you in love with me?" Aris asks again, quietly, straightforwardly.

"Who wants to know, you or Nora?" Rose responds with a palpable irritation that could probably be felt in Texas.

"She says she already knows," Aris replies.

Rose takes a sip of water while looking at Aris. She notices the color of his jeans and his army green argyle socks peering over his brown loafers. She notices his white oxford and his perfect white undershirt. She notices his Italian brown belt. She also notices the coloring or reddening of his skin. He is angry at her. She wants to walk over to him and climb in his lap so he could hold her. He is supposed to be holding her. She has pictured this moment hundreds of times. Every time she tells him exactly how she feels – he is always holding her in his lap – every time except this one. "Aris, what do you want me to say?"

"See, evasive! You mean she is right?" Aris asks in disbelief.

"I don't know. What did she say?" Rose asks sincerely.

"She said that… she said that you were waiting for us to break up," Aris restates the sentiment of his mate, matter-of-factly.

"Then no, she is not right. You seem really happy with her," Rose says. She tries to appear non-plussed, yet her voice indicates otherwise.

Aris looks around the room and forcibly stands to walk towards the stereo. "I am sorry Rose …" Aris opens the CD player and inserts his selection "… I really had no idea." He takes a step back to look at Rose. *Piano Concerto No. 23.*

"Mozart? You are really beginning to freak me out," Rose

says standing in a nervous fit. "What do you want from me? Mozart is way too heavy for this." Rose walks over to the stereo and almost presses eject before Aris grabs her wrist and throws it away from the stereo.

"Just listen," he says, "the song is really beautiful. Sit down. Listen. It almost says it all."

Rose turns her back. "I have heard it before, friend. Why do you think you can show up here and boss me around?" She busies herself by stacking her *Architectural Digest* issues on her coffee table with her nervous energy as she tries to think of following his command and just listening.

"Sit down! Listen!" Rose says, mocking Aris. She picks up the stack and slams them down and yells, "What are you doing here?"

"What am I doing here?" Aris laughs and shakes his head in incredulity. "Rose, you don't have the right to be mad. I just found out that my best friend is in love with me. YOU don't have the right to be mad at ME!"

Rose quiets to an almost eerie decibel as she says, "You sit."

Aris sits.

"Now that's better," Rose says with a smirk. "And Aris, how I feel about you doesn't matter." Rose speaks through her teeth with a loud nine-year old repressed truth aimed at deflecting her exposed vulnerability. "It really doesn't matter. If you had any of the same feelings for me you would have recognized mine by now. So it really doesn't matter."

"How can you say that?" Aris asks purposefully.

"It doesn't," Rose says. "Over the past nine years, I've watched you fall in and out of love – what five times? And never with me." Rose starts to relax as she speaks her nearly decade long thought process. "And I have never said or did anything to interfere with your relationships. And have done everything to be a good friend to you."

Aris continues to just stare at her.

Rose continues, "Well, I guess there was Naomi – I really did not like her. I may have used a few manipulative tactics with her – yeah, maybe just a few... Yet, I *really* did not like her."

"Nine years? We were dating nine years ago," Aris says.

"Duh. For such a smart guy..." Rose shrugs her shoulders and sits down to pick up her water glass. With an over the top, affected calmness she says, "If you must know, I realized I was in love the day after you broke up with me." She sips from her glass and swallows while holding the glass in its tipped position, intentionally blocking her face. "I wish I had some scotch."

Mozart finishes and Aris presses eject. "Why didn't you say anything?" Aris asks calmly as he pulls another jewel case from her bookshelf. "How about 'Dream of the Blue Turtles'?"

"If you love somebody... if you love someone," Rose sings in an attempt to ruin his calm.

"Too heavy, then?" Aris infers. "Florence and the Machine – Ceremonials?"

Rose laughs. "Too many words. Vivaldi."

"Perhaps silence." Aris turns off the stereo and sits.

"Ahh, the sound of silence." Rose rolls her eyes and tries to breathe.

"Let me get this straight. You were in love with me when I was dating Jennifer, too?" Aris asks. "I had no idea. I wasn't even sure if you liked me when I was dating Jennifer."

"Naomi, Jennifer, Joanna and Celeste," she responds while forcefully flipping through November's issue, stopping only to pretend-look at the photographs. "I like Nora the best. She makes sense. She is pretty, smart, confident ... employed." Rose slaps the magazine back down on the stack she had just formed minutes prior. "Don't be obnoxious, Aris."

"So you love me," Aris says obnoxiously with an affected toothy smile he is sure Rose will interpret favorably. "It is because I have dry humor and also like chess."

"What were you like in high school? Were you a prick then, too?"

"I was shy in high school. And on the chess team," Aris admits.

"Of course you were. And yes, I love you," Rose says flatly while shaking her head No.

"I thought we were friends," Aris says plainly.

"We are - best friends. Your opinion matters to me more than any other ever has. I'm not even understating the fact."

"Why didn't you tell me?" Aris asks.

"Tell you what? Tell you I was in love with you? I did. I told you nine years ago. I was sitting on the stairs in your foyer. I was touching the bannister. I told you then. I guess I meant it. Whatever, Aris, the truth is… the truth is we would not be here today, having this conversation, if I told you every day."

"There is something very sad about that," Aris replies, changing his stance to express himself fully.

"Pitiful," Rose agrees. "I am right though."

Aris just stares at Rose. And Rose allows it.

"Rose, I have pretty much thought of you as my best friend for seven years now. And to be perfectly honest, there have been plenty of times that I was very attracted to you... painfully attracted to you," Aris says. "In fact, the entire conversation I had with Nora last night is because I mentioned that I thought you looked gorgeous on Saturday. Nora did not like that…"

"I'd imagine not. Why did you say something like that?"

"It did not mean anything at the time."

"Telling your girlfriend of two years that you think your best friend, who happens to be a girl, is gorgeous…How should she have reacted?" Rose asks with Nora in mind. "She'd be a fool to not feel somewhat threatened."

"I thought she understood about you. Yet, it turns out that she was right and I was the fool."

"You are not a fool, Aris," Rose says quietly as she gently

fans out the magazines on her coffee table. "I love *Architectural Digest*."

"Incidentally, she really didn't like my pet name for you – Thorn. She's jealous because I don't have a pet name for her and she thinks... she thinks that means something."

"Incidentally?" Rose laughs at his word choice. "She realizes that you call me that when I'm being prickly, right?" Rose asks.

"Not always. I call you that because you get under my skin," Aris says while looking to the far left wall and then back at Rose. "You always have."

"If I said, I know, would that piss you off?"

"I don't understand you," Aris admits.

"Actually Aris, you are really the only one who does – understand me." Rose looks down at the floor. "Although the scout master I met tonight..."

"You met someone?"

"Yeah, well, sorta... maybe?"

"Figures," Aris says.

"What is that supposed to mean?" Rose asks with a shadow of anger.

"I don't know...You have had nine years to process this. I have had less than 24 hours. And now you might have met someone."

"You're kidding me. You did not just..." Rose begins to reach a new level of anger.

"You don't get to be mad at me – or think that my feelings, or my understandings are belittling yours. I will say this again, I had no idea you had these feelings for me," Aris says, responding to her anger. "I feel betrayed, or something. I feel like I have to question every conversation we have ever had."

"Fine. I will try to be a bit fairer, yet no promises." Rose looks at her feet. "I tried very hard to be the person you needed, being that I was not the person you wanted."

Aris stares at her. "I thought I knew you. I thought I understood you."

"You do. I do have a nine year old process of suppression. I'll admit that denying my feelings for you is second nature to me now. And well, my primary nature – my primary nature calls bull dung on your 'I had no idea' argument. You may not have wanted to admit it – yet seriously, Aris, I am not exactly the most subtle of God's creatures."

"What about…" He asks exasperatedly, "What about when I talked to you as a friend about Nora, or Celeste, what were you thinking?"

"I was thinking about you," Rose admits. "I was only thinking of you."

"Celeste and Naomi, they thought you were…"

Rose stands again. "And about those times…" Rose makes air quotes "…those 'times' that you were attracted to me. I felt them. Every once in a while you would look at me – like a man looks at a woman. You actually know the look and, boy, do you know how to deliver it... Anyway, just so you know, I never attributed those glances as you, Aris, being attracted to me, Rose. I just thought it was a man being attracted to a woman – a pheromone thing – not a deep connection." She tries to hide a hot flush to her face.

"Rose, you are beautiful," Aris says simply. "You are even more beautiful when you are vulnerable."

"You like me when I am vulnerable. You did not just say that. What the hell!" Rose pleads, "I can't believe you just said that!"

"Wait a minute. Whoa. That did not come out right. What I mean is…Rose, you are scary. Both Naomi and Celeste said that you were the scariest person they ever met. The thing is, you do not seem to need anything or anyone. It's true. You never have. I am just admitting that it is kind of nice when you are vulnerable. I remember being really attracted to you when you actually needed me. Do you know what I mean?"

"Stop it. Maybe you don't understand me. Don't you understand how much that hurts?" Rose puts her hand over her heart and hunches forward and rests on her thighs to protect and shield her most valuable possession.

"I'm sorry. I'm just really mixed up and well, angry. Can't you understand why I am angry? How could you hide this from me for so many years?"

"I think you know how," Rose says quietly. "You do."

"Explain it to me."

"Do you remember what you said to me the night *we* broke up?" Rose asks.

"I think I said something close to... close to...I said that you were cold," Aris says with a hint of regret.

"You thought *I* was cold. I guess if I could have responded immediately... if I could have responded to your allegation and told you that I was not cold, that I was guarded then... well, then... maybe" Rose tries to recollect her feelings from that night. "I understood what you were saying and feeling. I always have."

"I am sorry I called you cold," Aris says nodding his head while looking at his feet. "I guess I was big into irony back then." He gives a light laugh.

"I don't know – I am not sure if any other word choice would have made the same impact on me. I took your adjective to heart. I knew I wasn't. Yet you perceived me to be and the fact that you, of all people, you thought I was cold - well that, *that* really bothered me. I have tried to change, but to no avail. I am still guarded, yet I have lowered my guard in your presence more than anyone else. And I am sure you have felt this...to be true." Rose says in an attempt to lift Aris's chin.

She succeeds and Aris raises his head to look at Rose. "I suppose you do share quite a bit with me – yeah, you pretty much have shared everything except this one little fact."

"Exactly," Rose says smugly.

"You still have problems with irony, don't you?" Aris responds with a huff.

"No. I think I have problems with insincerity," Rose barks back. "I've loved you every day and you are mad at me for not proclaiming it from the mountain top? Whether I tell you or don't tell you doesn't change anything."

"You are a fool. It changes everything," Aris says with a quiet frustration.

"What is it that Daisy says – Daisy Buchanan? Pretty little fool? God, you arrogant…" Rose throws her arms up and paces in a complete circle – twice, and then throws herself back onto the couch.

"Daisy? Rose, what are you talking about? Are you…I mean we, are we still talking about irony?" Aris asks.

"I've had nine years; obviously I did not spend them trying to make sense." Rose laughs at herself.

"Do you really think that we can just be friends after this?" Aris asks. "You lied to me. Or I can take one of your theological offhand apples and say you tricked me."

"I did no such thing. I just did not tell you everything. There is a difference. Listen, I was hoping it would just go away – that you'd be none the wiser." She pauses. "I really thought that my love would grow into something else… something that I would not have to bother you with - eventually it would just be something else, a different word… not love, something else. Dammit Aris, I wish I had lied to you or even tricked you – then at least my feelings would be adulterated. I could have, you know – lied. I could have just lied to you twenty minutes ago when you asked that stupid question. It was a stupid question. I considered it. I considered lying. If you did not ask your stupid question so clearly, I probably would have, or could have – lied. I *don't* understand you – *You* came over here with the intention of destroying nine years of friendship." Rose looks directly at Aris, "What answer were you expecting?"

"I didn't know. I really thought that Nora was just looking for a fight. I guess I came over here to make her angry," Aris says.

"Liar. I think you underestimate me. I actually do know when you are lying. I have made a pretty careful study of you," Rose states her case convincingly. "You knew how I felt on your way over here. You knew as soon as you hung up that phone."

"Yeah, well… I said something else to you that night we broke up. I remember very clearly saying that you scared the hell out of me. And that is something about you that will probably never change."

"I remember. I remember because I really thought that was the most romantic thing anyone ever said to me. I thought it was a good thing. I thought it was good to have the Hell scared out of you. I thought that with Hell gone – there was only heaven left." Rose pensively looks around at the trappings of her apartment as she avoids Aris's eyes. "I didn't know that there was another way to interpret it. I suppose you taught me that there was."

"There is that Milton guy again, Can make a heav'n of hell, a hell of heav'n?"

Rose smiles as her heart drops a few inches. "Still teaching me, eh?"

"I think I am a very different person today."

"Sorry? I see very little difference. The color of your neck is a little darker. Other than that, you are pretty much the same. You are the best and worst of men. You're my David," Rose says coldly.

"Your David?" Aris says while wiping his hands on his thighs. "What do you want me to do?"

"That is not exactly a fair question, and I know you do not want me to answer," Rose says, leaning forward with a very stiff neck and back. "I can say that I have only ever wanted for you to be satisfied – more than happy, more than content. I think Nora makes you happy. And I make you…let's face it, I make you look for someone else." Rose finally drops a tear which she immediately wipes away with all four of her fingers.

"Rose?" Aris says with an audible shake to his voice. "Rose."

"Aristotle," Rose counters.

"I am sorry I hurt you," Aris replies.

"You didn't hurt me. Don't you understand? I grew up because of you."

"I don't understand how you kept this from me," Aris says looking straight into her eyes.

"I could be cruel right now and ask, how is it that you did not notice?"

"I am not sure," Aris says quietly.

"Because you didn't want to," Rose responds while choking on emotion lodged in her throat.

"I am not sure if that is the truth. Maybe I was afraid to?" Aris suggests.

Rose tries to escape his eyes. "I can't breathe."

Aris looks at her in a way she has never seen. "I feel like I just started."

"Breathing?" Rose asks, mystified.

"What do you want me to tell Nora?" Aris asks.

"The truth," Rose responds. "You have always been honest with her. There is no reason to change. You guys will never get past this unless you are honest with each other."

"Honest with her, just not honest with myself," Aris says under his breath. "I guess I should go."

"Do you want me to give you a long account of the history that brought you to Nora? I can, if that helps," Rose says.

"All starting with Naomi?" Aris asks.

"No. All starting with me," Rose answers.

Aris sighs. "For a pair that is not a couple, we sure do fight well."

"Get out of here. Go home. Sleep." Rose uses the top of her head to motion towards the door. "I have had a day. I am tired and have to travel to Seattle tomorrow."

"When are you coming back?"

"Early Saturday. I am taking the red-eye out of SEA-TAC. Heck, I might even get a red-eye in SEA-TAC," she says somewhat flippantly. "Seattle has a couple of great coffee houses."

"Rose? Is it my wit?" Aris asks with his humor intact.

"Well, it is certainly not your taste in women," Rose says chewing on her lower lip while looking at his feet.

Aris takes the hint and steps toward the door. He pauses after he opens the door and turns to look over his shoulder. "Rose, thanks for the orange juice."

"Aris?"

"Yeah?"

"We are friends. We can always be friends. No matter what, okay?"

"Rose, I think the truth is we have always been more than friends."

Rose pulls on her remaining strength. "I want to help in any way I can. I will be happy to talk to Nora if that is what she wants or needs. And I will stay away, too."

Aris nods. "Hopefully it won't come to that."

With tears in her eyes, Rose says, "I don't want to lose you because I love you. Better yet, I don't want to lose you *because* I love you."

"I am so...I wasn't expecting this," Aris says with a defeated tone.

"Come on now, there are worse predicaments to be in," Rose jokes.

"Two beautiful women... yeah, I suppose you are right. Poor me."

Rose looks at her refrigerator. "Think of Abdul. He helps me every day, giving me perspective and stuff."

Aris looks at his feet, as he stands with his hand on the door knob.

"Or Lin, for that matter. Her place got egged the other night. She thinks it was someone who stopped by earlier asking for money."

"Rose, I just wish you told me," Aris says as he shakes his head.

"I am sorry. I didn't mean to hurt you."

"Do you want to know what I was thinking on my drive over here? I was thinking that Tuesday is my favorite day of the week, and has been for a long time."

"Gulp." Rose says under her breath, and then gulps.

Aris looks toward the kitchen. "Still crushing on Abdul, eh?"

"Crushing? I am pretty sure I love him, too."

"Thanks for the perspective and the orange juice. Good night, Thorn," Aris says as he closes the door behind him.

Rose stands and takes two breaths in and out, in and out. "Good night, Eyre." She walks towards the door and lifts the end of the chain with her finger tips and moves to fit it into its metal track. She swings the chain just to listen to the sound of metal scratching on the door. Rose utters an "I love you" as she drops her hand from the chain to the dead bolt and turns.

"God, he was supposed to hold me." Rose turns off the lights to her kitchen and living area and then drags her body into her bedroom. She strips to her underwear and crawls into her bed. "What was his name...Rochester Fairfax?" She collapses onto her pillow and starts to cry. She doesn't know where the tears are coming from. Rose finds sleep in twenty-five minutes.

CHAPTER 15
THE ANT AND THE COCOON

An Ant, while searching for food, came across a Cocoon. The Cocoon was at its stage of transformation and moved its tail, catching the attention of the Ant. The boastful Ant looked at the Cocoon and shouted rudely, "I feel sorry for you! While I can run and move about as much as I like, and if I want to, climb even to the top of the tallest tree, you lie there in your shell, with power only to move your scaly tail." The Cocoon heard the Ant but did not answer. A few days later, the Ant came back. He saw only the shell of the Cocoon. He wondered what had happened when he saw a shadow cast by the wings of a butterfly. "Look at me," said the Butterfly, "your much-pitied friend! Tell me again of your power to run and climb, if you can even come near me and get me to listen." After saying this, the Butterfly suddenly flew away, up into the morning breeze towards the sun, leaving the Ant behind forever. –Aesop

Rose walks into the empty conference room at the Scout Center. She admires the view of the sun setting behind the mountain from the long windows. She is about an hour early for the meeting that Nicolas scheduled with the area's Scout Masters. Nicolas informed Rose that there will be six Scout Masters and six den mothers attending. Rose walks over to the end of the table and takes her seat behind the table-top podium. She notes that the room is quite large and that the table seats twenty. She takes her note cards from her computer satchel and places them on top of the podium on the left. She begins to link up her laptop and the center's projector. It has been several years since she has given a talk and, although nervous, she is actually almost comfortable speaking in public.

Rose spent the majority of Saturday and Sunday alone, isolated in her apartment working on this PowerPoint presentation. She needed the solitude; she needed the distraction. She actually determined that the activity and the weekend was easily the most gratifying weekend she had spent in months. She just finishes a quick visual run through of the projected slides as Nicolas walks into the conference room.

"Wow. You are a bit early," Nicolas states bluntly.

"Yeah, I tend to run early. I left work and did not have quite enough time to go home – so I picked up a cup of coffee and arrived here about ten minutes ago. You said it would not be a problem if I got here early. You are here early, too."

"I, too, tend to be early for appointments. Punctuality was very important to my parents. I took it to the next level. I am usually fifteen to twenty minutes early for appointments – even to the dentist," Nicolas responds. "It drives my girlfriend crazy."

Rose laughs as she hears Aris's voice in her head, *It figures*. Rose pushes the thought away and returns, "I am usually ten minutes early to my dental appointments. Fifteen minutes early to my hair dresser."

"I tell people that it is important to get to your doc's office early because it is essential to read six month old *Time Magazine* articles – it helps navigate pre-determined pitfalls six months later. I hope that I just made sense to you. It is weird though. Right? It has been my experience, and therefore fact, that every doctor's office seems to have one six-month old issue of Time Magazine and no current issue? It is weird, right?"

"I have to admit that I have never noticed the six-month old Time Magazine. I will make an effort."

"So how are you feeling? You get nervous about these kinds of things?" Nicolas asks sincerely.

"I am a little nervous and thought that acclimating would help a bit. I am generally able to relax after the first few sentences. Starting is always a bit rough."

"I am sure you will do fine. I will leave you to it. I need to set up the coffee and cookies. I see you got the projector working. You need anything else?" Nicolas says. He taps on the door frame as he steps out of the room.

"Thanks. I think I am good to go. Wait, uh, Nick? Nick?" Rose says with a raised volume.

Nick re-enters with a quirk of an eyebrow. "Yeah?"

"Yeah... um... you know these people... how are their senses of humor?" Rose asks tentatively.

"Michael, Eric, Heath and Ian... they are pretty sharp and appreciate all kinds of humor. I think you guys will get along quite well. The den moms, I don't know them so well, although they seem nice. But they don't mess around. I could have said that a bit better. Sorry. I don't like to throw around gender politics, but the women seem to actually want to get stuff done."

Nicolas looks out the window and points, "Hey, great sky. I like this building – great windows." He looks back at Rose. "Daniel, he's like our leader; he has been here the longest. He is a straight shooter. He will probably ask a few really tough questions. He likes straight forward answers. Don't bullshit him and you will be fine. What I mean is, if you don't know the answer, say you don't know. When you find the answer then do a follow-up."

"Wow. You are really helpful." Rose laughs. "I guess a career in politics is out of the question for a guy like you."

"Yeah, I am honest. You'd be surprised at how many ridiculously awful situations my honesty has gotten me into. Anything else?" Nicolas inquires.

"Coffee and cookies, please." Rose smiles and winks.

Rose spends the next twenty minutes quietly reviewing her notes. At 5:30, she starts to hear female voices in the hall. She turns off her cell phone and places it in her purse. She takes the opportunity to use the loo and brush her teeth. She looks at herself in the mirror and pinches her cheeks and puts on a bit of lip gloss. Rose knows she looks good. She admires her perfectly fitting chocolate tweed-patterned, herringbone belted pant suit she found at an antique boutique in Seattle. She bought it specifically for tonight. She also found a glorious English pink shell top and a stunning pair of square toe, open back English pink sling backs. Sometimes she likes her job – shopping in Seattle is almost always pleasant. She smiles, checking her teeth in her reflection. *God help me. I am prepared – and a little bit vain.*

Rose reenters the conference room and finds the majority of the attendees are present. She meekly smiles as she walks toward her computer. She nods at two of the mothers who are sitting on her right. "Hi. I am Rose. I'd shake your hand, but mine are kind of sweaty."

"I am Julia, and this is Rachel. We heard that there was going to be a woman speaker tonight. I take it that you are her?" Julia asks with a gentle smile. "Great suit. Where did you get it?"

"Seattle," Rose says. "I travel with my job and get to a lot of great vintage stores. Seattle vintage rocks! Although the Sally's right down the road is pretty choice."

"I don't like to wear other people's clothes," Rachel says.

"Dry cleaning at Lin's," Rose responds and grabs two coupons from her purse and hands one to both Julia and Rachel.

"Thanks," Julia says.

"Don't mention it. I am just glad you are here - the women of the Boy Scouts."

"We are den mothers – Cub Scouts!" Julia softly corrects Rose.

"My mistake. My mom was a den mother twenty years ago." Rose smiles. "When I told my mother I was speaking here tonight, she reminded me that she was a den mother for three years. She said she liked the job."

"Here? What troop?" Rachel asks.

"The Mountain Spring area? She told me the troop number last night… it is not that I wasn't listening… it is just, well…" Rose clears her throat.

"Troop 520 – that's Sarah's troop now. And there she is. Sarah, this girl's mother was a den mother for your troop twenty years ago," Julia yells to the woman as she enters.

"Really? Small world," Sarah says while pulling out the chair next to Rachel. "Hello, Bitches."

"That is an inside joke – we *are* den mothers after all," Julia shares while fluffing her hair. She follows with an impression of a sardonic laugh.

"Nice." Rose laughs. "Any of your boys ever catch you calling each other that?"

"Nah. That would mean that they were actually listening," Rachel says while laughing. The other two women join her in the laugh.

"Rose, I think we are all here. Let me start with an introduction," Nicolas says while standing mid-table on the left. "Rose came to me last week with an idea for our Scouts. It is a bit unconventional – but I think it is kind of what we are looking for. Ya ready?" Nicolas looks to Rose and nods as he sits.

"Thanks, Nick. Thanks for giving me this opportunity," Rose says directly to Nicolas and then looks to the faces of the 12 people sitting around the table. The men are all sitting to the left. The women are in two clusters of three each on the right. Rose inhales and exhales. "Can you hear me?" Rose asks and again scans the faces of those sitting at the table. "There are two things that brought me here tonight – chocolate and Baden-Powell." She turns on the projector to a slide showing the cover art to *Scouting for Boys* with a chocolate bar Photoshopped onto the side of his hat. "I love chocolate and although I have never met Baden-Powell, as a student of ethics and a descendant of Aesop, I am *prepared* to think that I would have liked him very much. About a month ago I was reading an article on CNN and learned about the worst forms of child abuse taking place in the cocoa fields of the Ivory Coast and Ghana. As a student of ethics, this caught my attention. My mind started to picture the scene – children working in the cocoa fields – and oddly enough, they were wearing uniforms. I am not exactly sure why my mind saw uniforms, but it did. I immediately thought of the Boy Scouts – children in uniform. Following the proverbial white rabbit – I ended up at the library checking out *Scouting for Boys*. I have since purchased a copy. Chocolate and Baden-Powell."

Rose takes a breath and moves to the next slide - an image of a camp fire linked to an animation of a plus sign followed by a ball of yarn. "Baden-Powell loved to spin camp fire yarns. My favorite is "The Diamond Thief" – a play, best performed in the open and in *dumbshow*. I am not exactly sure what dumbshow means. Yet I am going to do my best to retell the play yarn with a spin of my own." She turns to the next slide and shows a pencil drawing of "The Diamond Thief" scanned from the book.

Rose begins telling the tale verbatim from the book. "A party of prospectors has been out in the country of South Africa, and has found a magnificent diamond. They are now making their way back to civilization with it. Horse-sickness has killed off their horses, and so they are doing the journey on foot, carrying blankets, food and cooking pots."

Rose's posture changes as she begins to relax in her speech. "You can see it right? Fine British gentlemen circa 1900 making their way through the country of South Africa. The men stop to set up camp and have placed the magnificent gem in a sardine can that they have placed in the center of the camp site. They have assigned guard duty so that each man can sleep for a few hours.

"In the wee hours of the morning, one of the guards on his shift begins to close his eyes. He hears something in the woods, only to discover it is a rabbit. He continues to drift and accidentally falls asleep. Meanwhile, a diamond thief has been following the men through the country and has been slowly creeping into the camp site for several hours. When he watches the guard finally fall into a deep slumber, the thief takes his opportunity to steal the diamond." Rose breaths as she scans the room. She finds she has a captive audience.

"So the story goes, the thief takes a few precautions to cover his tracks and disappears into the wilderness. Of course, moments later, the leader of the camp mysteriously awakens and notices that there is no one standing guard. He yells and wakes the camp. He runs over to the guard that is supposed to be at his post and shakes him awake. 'What happened? Where is the diamond?' The startled and confused guard cannot answer the simple questions. The other officers scurry around the site and discover tracks to be followed. Three of the gentlemen go into the wilderness to try to catch the diamond thief.

"Meanwhile, back at the campsite, the chief hands the guilty sentry his pistol and hints to him that having ruined his friends by his faithlessness, he may as well shoot himself." Rose interjects a "dun dun daaahh."

"Just in the nick of time," Rose winks at Nick as she continues, "a shout is heard from the gentlemen – they have found the diamond and caught the thief. Woo Hoo.

"The men return with the thief bound. They try the sentry and collectively condemn him to shoot the thief as his punishment.

"They dig a grave. The thief is made to stand up, wearing a blindfold. The sentry shoots him. The men then bring a blanket and lift the dead man into it and carry him to the grave. They lower the body into the grave and cover it with dirt. All the men shake hands with the sentry to show that they forgive him. They pack up their camp, put out the fire, and continue their journey with the diamond."

Rose pauses to take a breath to let the story sink in. "This entire exercise," she continues, "this play, is to be done for an audience to raise money for a troop. The instruction Baden-Powell provides for the grave is ridiculously specific and entertaining. He says 'The whole thing wants careful rehearsing beforehand, but is most effective when well done, especially when accompanied by sympathetic music.'

"Sympathetic music," Rose repeats after a deep breath. "I have sympathy for the thief. Where is the one good turn? The sentry's life is spared just in the nick of time – yet the thief? Funny thing about imperialism, we are not even sure if the five gentlemen did not steal the diamond first, right? Is this what ethical powerhouse Baden-Powell meant when he said 'dumbshow'?

"For those who are still with me, a dumbshow is a form of pantomime that went out of fashion in England in the seventeenth century. So this play is supposed to be pantomimed. Actions without words. Words without actions." Rose breaths. "Chocolate and Baden-Powell. Just words? Just actions."

Rose briefly tells her audience about the cocoa protocol. She explains that the first primary goal of the cocoa protocol is to publically declare that there is a problem - and those who signed the protocol have failed the first order. She provides a slide with web sites to go to for those who are more interested in the particulars of the protocol. She explains that she has a brochure that contains some of the facts along with website addresses that contain all of the particulars. She completes this two minute section with a simple statement. Rose asks, "Who better to fight on the behalf of children – than children?" Rose flips to the next slide – "The Mafeking Challenge."

"Did I bury the lead?" Rose asks. "As I am sure that all of you know – the inspiration for the Boy Scouts was the battle of Mafeking. A cadet army was assembled to help alleviate the men from duties such as messengers and ammunition supply. Baden-Powell talks about Cadet Goodyear...." Rose sings, "he was a very good year." She smiles at her little joke and continues, "Cadet Goodyear, when given the task to carry a letter across the camp undergoing gun fire said, 'I will pedal so quick, sir, they'd never catch me.' Rose smiles at Nicolas and moves to the next slide of the penny stamp with a featured cadet on a bicycle. "The messenger service only cost a penny. These boys risked life and limb to carry out their orders. Crazy? Or inspired?"

Rose moves to the next slide, a combination of the original cover artwork of a Boy Scout standing on a mound and a penny stamp seemingly buried. "Did you know that the Boy Scout movement across many continents each donated a penny to Baden-Powell to purchase him a wedding gift – a Rolls Royce. The power of a penny." Rose moves to a slide of a photograph of the car being presented to the newlyweds. "A penny today... well I heard it costs more to make a penny than an actual penny."

Rose flips to her next slide, a coin animation she lifted from Youtube and then quickly moves to her next slide – a cartoon of a woman holding two cents. "What could two cents do?" Rose flips to a copy of the "Mafeking Challenge" slide. "I would like the Boy Scouts of America to take on this challenge. I want to start here with our local troops and then take the idea nationally. I want our boys to talk to their schools about these children and collect two pennies from their classmates. I want our boys to talk to their churches and get two cents from each member of their congregation. I want our boys to learn about piece-time." Rose turns to another animation slide of pennies adding up and then to a slide of a fleet of large vans. "I want to boys to help pay for transportation. I want the boys to help get these kids to school."

"Chocolate and Baden-Powell." Rose moves to another animation slide. "Chocolate and ... chocolate and ... chocolate and..." Rose smiles and asks her audience. "What goes with chocolate?" Rose looks at her audience and moves to the next animation slide of B.P. "Chocolate and Baden-Powell."

Rose turns in her seat and grabs a basket of peanut butter cups and walks around the table to place a peanut butter cup down in front of each person. She walks around the table again and places a brochure of ChIP in front of each person and then returns to the podium. "One good turn deserves another."

She turns to her next slide, a page of directions of the neck tie she lifted from *Scouting for Boys*. "Baden-Powell suggested that each boy tie a small knot in their necktie after their deed is done for the day. And if they forgot that day, they should do two deeds the next.

"I am trying to get Nightingale Chocolates interested in

helping. I have spoken with Rebekah Nightingale about ChIP." Rose lifts her brochure. "I am hoping we can work in combination... a good combination... like chocolate and ... like chocolate and Baden-Powell."

Rose wraps up by thanking them for their time. "I hope this 36 minute presentation was at least somewhat interesting to you. I would love, and I mean love, to answer any of your questions about this idea. If you want to think about this and ask questions later, my email and phone number are located on the brochure. Again, I would like to thank you all, and in particular Nick, for helping me try to do my good deed." Rose smiles at Nick and wipes an unseen tear from her eye. "Thanks."

"Again Rose, I think this is a really interesting idea," Nicolas concedes. "What do you say guys? Any questions?"

"You want to use the Boy Scouts to raise money for your charity?" Daniel asks bluntly.

"Yes, sir. That is one way to put it. Yet I would add that I would like to challenge the Boy Scouts to take on this issue in the spirit of Mafeking." Rose swallows a few of her nerves and says, "It's not raising my charity, it is raising their cause." Rose looks down at the podium. *God please.* She lifts her eyes and then her chin and says with a challenging look aimed directly at Daniel, "I want to get these kids to school. I want the Boy Scouts to help." Rose starts to feel a bit of anger in her stomach, yet is able to rein in her passion by lowering her head.

"This is a big project," Julia says. "I would not even know how to start."

"I guess if you are interested in the effort, we would start by talking to the boys," Rose says, hoping that she does not sound condescending. "It is a big idea for children – not unlike the Boy Scouts themselves."

"I don't think my boys are mature enough for this," Ian says.

Nicolas responds, "Yeah, but would you like them to be? I

mean, we are supposed to be guiding them to manhood, right? Although the skills of fishing, archery and first aid are extremely important to their development – the purpose of the merit badge is not the badge itself – it is to build men of worthy character, right? Kids interested in real issues in the world make men interested in real issues in the world. Well that is my two cents." Nicolas winks at Rose.

Rose blushes and mouths the words "thank you."

"I don't know about you, but I have this feeling in my stomach – excitement. I think it is worth thinking about. I want to talk to my son about it. I am actually kind of excited to talk to my son about it," Heather says as she looks to Rose. "You got my vote."

Rose nods. "Thanks."

"I like the two cents and all that. But, let's be serious. Two cents? I think we should change it to two quarters, or 50 cents." Julia adds.

Rose smiles and nods. "Even better."

"We got a lot of information here," Daniel says. "I say we call it a night and take the time over the next few days to think about this. This would be a pretty serious commitment. I am not sure if we really have the time for this. We all know how to email. Nick, why don't you try to see if you can organize a discussion group about this? You seem kind of fired up about it."

"I am. I think it is a good idea - a movement for boys within a movement for boys. It is kinda cool," Nicolas says.

"Yeah, but can we get them to care?" Sarah asks.

"Who knows? I was trying to ask myself whether or not I would be interested in something like this when I was fourteen. I am not sure," Eric says honestly. "I think that the Boy Scouts are in a rut and this might help. Or we could fail miserably."

"I think Rose is right – we need to ask the boys," Rachel adds. "I keep on seeing my son with a machete in a cocoa field. It is horrifying."

"The strange thing is – the concept of merit badges – it would not be so frightening if your son had learned the skill under adult supervision," Rose admits. "I really think that the Boy Scout Movement itself would really help the situation there. The same thing is going on a bit south of Ghana and the Ivory Coast at the tungsten mines. Our cell phones and hand held devices require tungsten and it's being mined by children, too. The Mafeking Challenge could help way beyond the cocoa fields. Raising awareness and providing transportation to get these children to school – although each year they can select a new cause."

"Social responsibility," Michael says. "It is part of our oath and as the world becomes more globally connected – if we really want the Scout Movement to continue - I think we need to 'think locally and act globally.' I loved that bumper sticker."

"We could make bumper stickers. Two cents? Ask a Boy Scout?" Heath says. "Or something like it."

"What did the preacher say… words and actions? Actions and words," Joan says.

"Did I sound preachy?" Rose asks to the woman at the end of the table.

"Yeah, but in a good way. I was thinking that it was a good talk. Inspiring – like a sermon should be," Joan answers.

"My mom is a United Methodist Minister. She would probably be amused to hear that her daughter was a preacher."

"Your mother is Grace," Sarah proclaims.

Rose nods. "Yep."

"She is the minister of Mountain Lake, right?" Julia asks.

Rose nods as she speaks quietly to Julia. "She has been there for four years now. She likes it there. They have a big youth group."

The rest of the table begins to collect their things. Nicolas stands. "Rose, thanks again. I will be contacting you. And guys, I think we know what we need to do, right? Think about it. I think we can do this. We can start with bumper stickers." Nicolas pantomimes a heavy punch into Heath's shoulder.

Nicolas walks over to Rose and shakes her hand. "You did a good job. The slides were good and the speech was…memorable."

"Wow," Rose says. "Thanks. I was afraid I was a bit too heavy handed – one of my many flaws."

"There were some pretty good light touches," Nicolas says. "So the guys and I are heading to Charlie's for a beer? Wanna join us?"

"I really would like to but I did not sleep very well last night because I was pretty nervous and was running through this speech over and over," Rose says.

"Say no more, I hate public speaking. Maybe next time. It might be better for us to talk about this without you being there anyway."

"Man – that honesty of yours. Yikes," Rose says with a nervous laugh.

"So what's next?" Nicolas asks.

"I think that if you want to do this – I mean, well you know what I mean – I will need your help with Rebekah Nightingale. I think that if I show up with the Boy Scouts, she might take me a bit more seriously," Rose says commandingly.

"I think we – all of us – could probably help," Nicolas says. "I mean me and the guys."

"Nick, I am glad I met you," Rose says meekly. "I feel like I can save my breath."

Nicolas looks at Rose with a puzzling look and then says, "Some people require a bit more instruction. I understand."

"You really seem to. Thanks," Rose says. "I need to get home. I have not eaten anything today – nervous stomach. I am starting to get woozy."

"Alright Rose. Have a good one and I will be sending you an email soon. Going anywhere for your Christmas vacation?"

Rose smiles. "I'm a local. My parents live about forty

minutes away. And I still go home for the holidays. I travel for a living and staying home is the best sort of vacation."

"Merry Christmas," Nicolas says.

Rose puts her coat on and swings her computer bag over her shoulder. "Have a great night and super holiday. Thanks again, Nick."

Nicolas smiles and walks her to the door and opens it. "Good night, Rose. Drive carefully."

CHAPTER 16
THE FOX AND THE CROW

A CROW having stolen a bit of meat, perched in a tree and held it in her beak. A Fox, seeing this, longed to possess the meat himself, and by a wily stratagem succeeded. "How handsome is the Crow," he exclaimed, "in the beauty of her shape and in the fairness of her complexion! Oh, if her voice were only equal to her beauty, she would deservedly be considered the Queen of Birds!" This he said deceitfully; but the Crow, anxious to refute the reflection cast upon her voice, set up a loud caw and dropped the flesh. The Fox quickly picked it up, and thus addressed the Crow: "My good Crow, your voice is right enough, but your wit is wanting." -Aesop

Rose, sitting under her blanket with a novel in her lap, lifts her mug to take the first sip of her homemade hot cocoa, complete with actual marshmallows. She hears a knock at the door and turns to look at her kitchen clock to note the time - 10:32. For a moment, she is marginally frightened. With a well-rehearsed ability to muster courage, Rose sets her mug down and walks to the door and unlocks the deadbolt. She opens the door with its chain still attached.

"Aris? What are you doing here?" Rose quickly closes the door and unlatches the chain and reopens. She repeats, "What are you doing here?"

"Hi, Rose. Umm… I need a place to stay for the next four days," Aris says bluntly.

"And you want to stay here? You're joking, right? I could have sworn that you were smarter than that. In front of a judge and everything…" Rose steps aside to let Aris enter the apartment with his computer over his left shoulder and a medium-sized wheeled suitcase attached to his right hand. "So I guess you are not perfect. Good to know."

Aris whirls his suitcase around and stands in front of Rose. "Nora's sister is arriving tonight – around midnight – and she just decided, like a half hour ago, that it would be better if I wasn't there. I know its short notice, she told me I could stay with you."

"And you believed her?" Rose says with a genuine fear in her eyes. "Seriously man, what are you thinking?"

"I am thinking that you are my best friend. I am thinking that you are the only one of my friends that actually has a spare room – a bed rather than a couch. I am thinking that I really cannot afford to stay in a hotel right now. I'm thinking I am really tired. I'm thinking I need a place to sleep. Please, Rose," Aris says with an exhausted tone.

"And you said that Nora knows you are here?" Rose asks with concern.

"Yes," Aris says.

"Alright then, my naïve and/or stupid friend, you can stay as long as you'd like," Rose says looking over her shoulder as she locks the front door and slips on the chain. "I wonder if I should baby proof the apartment? You know you shouldn't stick your tongue in outlets, right? And that toilet water is not for drinking…"

"Thanks, Rose. Thanks for the reminder about that other stuff. I only need four days – only four days. I am going home for Christmas," an exhausted Aris says with an attempt at lightheartedness. "Let me put this in the spare room. What are you listening to?"

"Gregorian chants. I thought it would make good reading music. It's surprisingly disruptive," Rose responds. "I was just having a cup of cocoa – hoping that it would help me sleep. There is another mug full left on the stove, if you're interested."

Aris looks to the stove and then back at Rose. "Thanks. Let me get these things into the room and I'll think about it."

Rose watches Aris enter her guest room. She walks back to her couch and lights the vanilla candle on her coffee table and lifts her blanket around her shoulders before sitting back down on her couch. She leans forward to pick up her cocoa and then returns to a reclining position. Three minutes later, Aris returns to the living room.

"Rose, I am sorry about this. I know this is probably a bit awkward," Aris says as he sits next to her on the couch and puts his feet up on the table. He mimics her. He looks at Rose with the left corner of his mouth slightly lifted.

Rose looks to her right and leans her head against the cushion of her couch. "Want to talk, or are you all talked out?"

"I do want to talk, but not tonight. I think I will take that cup of cocoa and hopefully just go to sleep," Aris says as he slaps his hands on his thighs and pushes into them to help him stand. He walks over to the stove and grabs a humorous mug from Rose's collection and fills it near the top with the remaining cocoa. He returns to the couch and smiles. "This mug seems appropriate."

"The shotgun mug. I have never used that one. I guess I bought it for this occasion. Perfect, is it?" Rose says as she looks at the mug that has a gun for a handle pointing to the mug.

"I don't know if I would say perfect. The cocoa is very good though," Aris says.

"Did you add marshmallows?" Rose asks.

"I thought about it. I figured they would get in the way of the consumption of the beverage," Aris says conversationally.

"Yeah, they kinda do. I should get the mini ones rather than the large ones," Rose states. "Yet, I like to toast marshmallows over candles." Rose points to the lit candle on her coffee table. "Help yourself. But be careful, fire burns."

Aris smirks. "How did your talk go – it was tonight, right?"

"I think it went well. I am tired and wired at the same time," Rose says. "And now, here you are. Another day."

"Another four days," Aris says reclining back into the couch and putting his feet back up on the coffee table. "Good cocoa."

"Thanks. Are you working tomorrow?"

"Yes. Well, I was planning on it. I could work from home, that is, I don't have to go into the office," Aris replies. "How about you?"

"I have to go into the office – meetings. You could stay here. I don't mind," Rose says as she tries to scoop up the melted marshmallow with her index finger. "Marshmallows are so odd."

"I like the taste of cereal marshmallows. Yet, I am not quite sure if they are marshmallows. I am pretty sure that they are something else masquerading as marshmallows."

"Green clovers, pink hearts, yellow moons, and blue diamonds," Rose says with a gentle yawn. "Well, Lucky, I really need to get some sleep. Do you need anything? You sure you don't need to talk?"

"I think I will work from here tomorrow, that is, if you are sure you don't mind. I really cannot handle the office - not right now anyway."

"Mi casa es su casa," Rose says as she stands from the couch and shakes the blanket from her shoulders. "Can I ask? Are you guys okay?"

"We broke up. Her sister is here to help her get her things."

"Wow. Merry Christmas," Rose says in a hardened whisper.

"You ain't kidding," Aris says, matching her tone.

"I'm sorry. I really am. I hope I didn't mess things up for you."

"No, I think I pretty much did all of the messing up. I hope you understand that I really don't want to talk about this now."

"You sure?" Rose looks down on her companion. In a maternal impulse, she touches the top of his head and smooths his soft, dark hair. "Good night. I hope you sleep well. We can talk tomorrow, or whenever."

"Good night, Rose. Thanks for this." Aris stands and takes the mug from her hand. "I will take care of this and the stereo, the fire and the lights. I'm probably going to be up a little while longer. And don't worry, I will be careful. You look like you really need to go to sleep."

"I *am* very sleepy." Rose walks to the bathroom to perform her evening ritual. Stepping from the bathroom, she sees Aris sitting on the couch staring at the candle. "Good knight." Rose closes her bedroom door, drops her robe onto the floor, opens her window, and climbs into bed. Rose finds sleep in seven minutes.

DAY ONE

Refusing to open her eyes, Rose fumbles for the alarm clock – it is 6:40. She exhales deeply the second she is finally able to stop the dreadful noise that the small box produces. She opens her eyes and then retrains them by focusing on the overhead light fixture. *Aris is across the hall.* She immediately gets out of bed and throws on her robe. She locates her slippers and is forced to look in the mirror. She cleans away the residual mascara and pinches her cheeks for color. She shakes out her hair. *Regardless of what he said, he has a girlfriend. Stop.* She stops and jabs her fledgling nails into the palms of her hands. *This is a normal morning… just like any other.* She leaves her bedroom and shuffles to the kitchen. She takes out her mug from the dishwasher and places it on her Keurig. *A normal morning.*

"Good morning, Rose." Aris steps out into view from *his* room.

Rose grabs her heart. "You scared me. I wasn't expecting you to be awake this early."

"I am always up this early. Remember?" Aris says, walking into the kitchen wearing his white t-shirt and blue and green flannel pajama pants. "I like the morning."

"You also drink coffee in the morning, right?" She grabs the shot gun mug from the dishwasher. "Would you like a cup?"

"I'd love one. How'd you sleep?" Aris asks, walking closer to the coffee machine and Rose. His left triceps brushes the edge of her shoulder. "I hope well."

"I did. I think I was asleep as soon as my head hit the pillow," she says nervously as she takes her cup from the platform and places his onto the platform. She takes a step away from him. "I have several varieties of coffee to choose from," she tells him and points to the carousel of coffee.

"I'll have what you are having."

Rose steps in front of the machine and feels his arm on her shoulder again. "Alright." She makes Aris a cup of coffee, taking a sip of hers at every step of the process. Rose hands Aris his coffee and steps toward the island and tentatively grabs her laptop. She takes it to the couch and sits. *Just like every other morning.* She opens her personal email and tries to conduct her *normal* morning ritual of writing Lisbeth.

"Aris is here," she writes. "I am not sure why. Cannot write – nervous. Write from work. Who the hell knows what is for dinner!!! Rose." She sends the email and quickly closes the lid to her laptop and turns in her couch to locate Aris. He is reading the cartoon clippings on her refrigerator. "I miss Calvin," Rose says. "Do you like the coffee?"

"Bold. So this is what bold tastes like."

"Bold, you say," Rose huffs. "So Aris, what are you doing here? I mean besides drinking coffee and reading comic strips on my refrigerator."

"I am supposed to be figuring stuff out." Aris takes a seat at the island as well as a sip of his coffee. "So far I have figured out that I really like your laundry detergent. The sheets smell great. Oh, and that candle wax can really hamper one's enjoyment of a toasted marshmallow."

"Live and learn. And as far as the sheets – it's probably the Downy. I actually just changed those sheets on Monday. I must have been expecting you – even though I have not heard from you in like a week," Rose says with a subdued anger.

"Did you miss me?" Aris asks teasingly and then quickly changes his demeanor. "Sorry about that, Nora requested that I not talk to you for a week."

"I suppose you could not write and tell me that you were

not talking to me?"

"So you did miss me."

"Super. Full-on obnoxious and smug at 7 AM," Rose says lifting her coffee to her lips. "Impressive, as it is extra bold." Rose lifts her coffee to salute and then drinks.

"Seriously, did you miss me? I actually missed you. I really did not like not talking," Aris says sincerely.

Rose thinks about the agonizing nights she spent not talking to Aris. She immediately squelches the emotion and springs up to standing. "I am going to take a shower. Want to make cinnamon rolls? They are in the refrigerator door – second shelf. It's a morning, just like any other," she says scratching her scalp as she walks to the bathroom. She closes the door and locks it and whispers, "What, God, what is going on?"

She emerges from the shower and can smell the cinnamon in the air. "Thanks for making breakfast. I'll be out in a minute." She enters her room and quickly puts on her undergarments, hose, a navy pin stripe sheath dress with a three-quarter sleeve and collar, and adds a bone pump with navy stitching. Rose towel dries her hair before putting it up in a tight bun. She walks out of her room four and a half minutes later.

Aris looks at Rose and smiles. "You look nice. They're not going to be ready for two more minutes."

"Time for make-up." Rose skips to the bathroom and brushes on mascara and dots blush on her cheeks and eyelids. She walks into the kitchen and notices the clock – 7:28.

"It really doesn't take you long to get ready in the morning," Aris says somewhat amazed.

Rose motions to her hair. "Sometimes it takes longer. Are they ready? They smell good."

"Yeah – they need to cool for another minute," Aris says. "Then I need to frost." Aris waves the packet of frosting like a pendulum of a clock.

Rose grabs her mug from the coffee table and walks over to

the Keurig. "Coffee. Coffee. Coffee."

"So Rose – would you like to have dinner with me tonight? I could cook."

She looks at Aris and furrows her brow. "Aris? I don't quite... um... I am not quite sure if... well..."

"It is the least I can do. Let me cook you dinner," Aris says while looking in the utensil drawer. "Where is the flipper? Oh, here it is." He grabs two salad plates from the cupboard and places a frosted cinnamon roll on each and then hands one plate to Rose. "Let me cook you dinner."

"Dinner," Rose says sitting down heavily at the island. "Just a day like any other. Aris is cooking me dinner." She picks up the cinnamon bun and starts to carefully unwind the dough. "Yep. Just a day like any other."

"What time do you need to leave, and what time will you be back?" Aris asks and then takes a bite of the warm pastry.

With her hand covering her mouth Rose answers, "I need to leave here in about twenty minutes and I guess I will be back around 5ish. Work is slow now – everyone has pretty much already checked out for Christmas. And it is Friday. The holidays – I don't even have to travel until possibly mid-January. Yay for me!"

"Want to go Christmas shopping tomorrow?" Aris asks. "I need to get Mina and her husband something."

"Christmas shopping?" Rose utters with a delicate, feminine voice, "Aris, are you okay? I don't know, yet it seems that you are acting a bit strange. I mean, you really don't like to shop – well not at actual stores. Are you just trying to stay busy? Seriously, Christmas shopping? A week before Christmas?"

"Rose, I want to go Christmas shopping with you."

"You want to go Christmas shopping with me," Rose repeats with a confused tone. "Okay, then, you want to go Christmas shopping with me. Perfectly normal day." She smiles and pops the last of her sugared dough into her mouth. "I think I just remembered that I am supposed to be at work early."

Gripped by the ironic madness, Rose begins to laugh. "Good Morning, Aris. Thanks for the cinnamon roll." She grabs the pad of paper and pen located in the middle of the island and writes the password to her wireless network. "Although you know me better than anyone else, you might not be able to guess my password –Iftahyasimsim." She slides the pad over to Aris and turns to walk to the bathroom. She begins to brush her teeth with the door open and watches as Aris walks into view of the mirror. "Ya er goin ta wash mi brahsh ma teef?" she says with foam falling from her mouth.

"Yes. Yes, I am," Aris says.

She spits. "Am I going to have to lay some ground rules?" She puts her hands on his hips and gently pushes him out the bathroom door and into the hall. She feels the fabric of his pajamas under her palms; her entire body reacts. She immediately removes her hands and drops them to her side. "I have to go to work." She wipes her mouth with the back of her hand as she walks past Aris, who is smiling in the hall. She reaches her coat closet and retrieves her black woolen trench. She checks her coat pockets and finds her gloves. "Have a good day, Aris. There is an extra set of keys in the coffee table. If you need to leave, please lock." She quickly opens and closes the door behind her and makes her escape. She is all the way to the stairs when she hears her apartment door open.

"I missed you," Aris says and then closes the door.

"It had to be the shotgun," Rose says before taking the first stair.

NIGHT ONE

At 5:02, Rose opens her unlocked apartment door. She immediately notices Aris standing at the railing on her patio. She sets her purse and keys down on the foyer table and walks to the patio. She opens the door and steps out. "It is cold out here. Want me to get you your coat?"

"The cold feels good. I just heard we are supposed to get

snow tonight – ten inches," Aris says as he looks down onto the side walk below. "I like your apartment. I am very comfortable here and it is surprisingly quiet."

"You did say that you were staying just four days, right?" Rose jokes. "Actually I don't have neighbors so you are right – this place is pretty quiet," Rose says while studying Aris's profile.

"You are staring at me," Aris says without moving.

"Yes. Yes, I am. I am going to change into something a little more comfortable," she says with a shake of her left shoulder attempting a Mae West impression.

Aris grins without moving his head. Rose walks back to her coat closet and hangs up her coat. She stops to lock and chain the front door. She then walks to her bedroom and changes into her favorite Levi's and a t-shirt. She takes her hair down completely and runs a brush before putting it back up into a high pony tail. She grabs a pair of light pink fuzzy socks and puts them on while standing. *Balance.* She opens her door to see Aris enter *his* room. To avoid prying, she quickly walks to the kitchen to grab a glass of water. As she finishes the first glass, Aris walks into the kitchen.

"Get any work done today?" he asks.

"Actually, no, I guess I was a bit preoccupied," Rose concedes. "I have been thinking about you and your pajamas all day. Ya see, you were in my kitchen this morning – in your pajamas. It wasn't a normal day. I normally don't see you in the morning, in my kitchen, in your pajamas. We had coffee and cinnamon rolls and you were in pajamas."

"You were in pajamas, too," Aris proclaims.

"It is normal for me to be in my kitchen in my pajamas."

"Would you rather that I wasn't in my pajamas?" Aris asks.

With an exceedingly loud exhale, Rose turns to fill her water glass. With her back turned she says, "So you are going to make me dinner tonight, right?"

"I did. It is in the oven. I thought we would eat early, watch a movie and then go to bed," Aris says as he reaches for the oven door. "I am going to set the table."

"It is a big table for just the two of us," Rose comments. "How about we eat at the coffee table and sit on the floor." She walks to the living room and performs a game show hostess movement standing over the coffee table.

"It's a big meal. We need the table," Aris says convincingly. "Occupy yourself please. Dinner in fifteen."

Rose obeys his orders and takes in the smells as well as the opportunity to check her personal email. She reads an email from Lisbeth telling her to be careful and cautious. She sends a quick email thanking her for the two words – careful and cautious – and that she would try to be both. Rose shuts her laptop and turns to watch Aris work. *God, I love him.*

The two friends sit down to dinner across from one another, utilizing the width rather than length of the dining room table. Aris presents Lobster Thermidor cakes served over roasted asparagus with a side of garlic and thyme roasted red potatoes.

Rose giggles as she looks down at her plate. "Did you get any work done today? I cannot believe this. I suppose you went to the grocery store."

"I did. I noticed you were running low on cereal." Aris smiles as he lifts his water glass. "To God."

"To God." Rose meets his water glass with hers. "Thanks, Aris. This is really beautiful."

The two share the incidentals of their day as they eat their meal. The conversation remains light and easy through dessert – lemon chiffon coffee cake he bought at the bakery across the street. The two finish their dinner and clear the plates together.

"Would you like to watch the movie now?" Aris asks as he places the last dish into the dishwasher. "I think you are going to like my selection."

"Aris – dinner was delicious, truly delicious. Are you sure that you don't want to talk?" Rose asks as she grabs a new dish towel from the drawer. "I like pink elephants as much as the next girl…I really do. "I don't want to force the conversation, yet I am concerned…cautious, careful and concerned."

"I am communicating… give me a chance," Aris says, gently tugging on her pony tail. "I like your hair like this."

Rose does a helicopter with her pony tail and then stops to look at Aris. "I like you – in my kitchen." Immediately overcome with feelings of both confusion and guilt, she excuses herself and walks to the bathroom. She looks into her vanity mirror. "God, let me be his friend. I need to be his friend." She washes her face and hands. She returns to the living room with her nails digging into her palms.

"Do you still have that giant floor pillow?" Aris asks standing with remote in hand as he pushes in the DVD tray.

"I do. It is in your room." Rose quickly turns and walks to the guest room. She walks to the far left corner and grabs the steel blue suede floor cushion. Aris meets her at the door. His hands are gripping each side of the door frame. Rose's eyes make a sharp connection. "Hey, look at that, you are making like a door."

Aris lifts his elbow to let Rose slip under his arm. He gently grabs her wrist and frees the pillow from her. "I could have done this, you know."

Rose looks at her wrist in his hand and feels a warming sensation under her rib cage just above her stomach. "Sometimes it is just …easier," Rose says restraining her gaze as she tries to regain her composure. "So what is the movie?"

"You'll see momentarily," Aris says as he gently lets her arm fall. "I am quite satisfied with my selection."

Rose walks to the living area and takes her seat on the left side of her couch. Aris walks around the back of the couch and places the floor cushion down and leans his back against the right side of the couch. "You don't mind that I have the remote, do you?"

Rose's face starts to flush and she starts to get a bit dizzy. "No, Aris, not at this moment. Thanks for asking though – I really appreciate the consideration."

The movie starts up. "*Arabian Nights*," Aris says with a very pleased tone.

"I see. You figured out my password. I guess I have to change it now," Rose says lovingly.

"I am not interested in abusing privilege," Aris says. "Open Sesame. Have you ever seen this movie?"

"No. However, it has been on my list of classics for many, many years. Nine, I think," Rose says with a shake to her voice that she attempts to cover by fidgeting her blanket up over her body.

Aris looks at Rose with a gently forming furrow. "Are you comfortable?"

Rose sighs. "Arabian Nights and snowfall. I'm close to heaven." Rose lifts her chin to inform Aris that the snow has begun. "I'm happy."

"Good." Aris turns his head to the screen and the two watch the movie without conversation.

When the movie ends, Aris presses the mute as the credits roll. "Would you like another piece of cake? I would."

"I am fine. I should probably drink a few more glasses of water. Since you are up…?"

"Sure." Aris walks to the kitchen and turns on the light.

"I love the architecture. I cannot even imagine the amount of time and energy that went into those waves," Rose comments.

"I have the distinct feeling that time moves very differently in that part of the world," Aris says as he delivers Rose a wine glass filled with ice water.

"I would love to visit Iran, Iraq, Lebanon, Egypt and Turkey," Rose says while looking at herself in the reflection of the window. She leans forward and lights the candle on the coffee table. "Would you mind turning off the lights in the kitchen. My vanity… I always end up looking at myself in the window's reflection and it makes me feel… vain."

Aris looks mystified as he looks at Rose's reflection. He immediately complies and is back on the couch with his cake in his lap within 7 seconds.

"It is not easy to travel to the Mideast right now or otherwise I'd say that we should go."

"Traveling is never easy. Yet, you would go? Everyone always looks at me like I am crazy when I share this little dream," she says while running the palm of her hand up and down on her blanket, creating the appearance of light and dark.

"Dream a little dream," Aris responds, setting his plate of crumbs on the coffee table. "Rose – I think we should go to bed."

Rose's face ignites. "I am not quite sure if I can fall asleep yet."

"I have a book to read." Aris stands and picks up *One Hundred Years of Solitude*. "I want to go to a clock store in Connecticut for my sister's gift. I think we should leave here around 8 AM. I mean if… if you would like to go shopping with me."

"8 AM on a Saturday?" Rose exclaims. "I was born in Connecticut. Did you know that?"

"I did. So…I will drive?" Aris prods.

"I'll go. Can we leave at 9? It *is* Saturday."

"Nine o'clock is fine. Good night, Rose. Sleep tight." Aris grips the book with his left hand and walks into *his* room.

Rose pops out the DVD and turns off the TV. She then turns off the fireplace and blows out the candle. She walks to the bathroom and performs her evening ritual. She enters her room and steps out of her clothes, and slips on a burgundy satin spaghetti-strapped nightgown and climbs into bed.

Rose turns to her right. *He is across the hall.* She turns to her left. *He is reading a book in the room across the hall.* She looks at the ceiling. *He was in my kitchen wearing pajamas.* She lies on her back and stares at the ceiling for a torturous two hours and fifteen minutes trying to think of something, anything other than Aris's presence in the room across the hall.

Just as her body begins to overheat and she starts to feel sweat drip down her sternum, Rose throws off her comforter to the right and swings her body out of bed. She furiously grabs her robe and slippers and then, reining in her fervor, quietly opens her bedroom door. She immediately walks to her patio door and steps outside, leaning her hips into the railing as she looks at the white street below. *Silence.* Rose unties her robe and lets the wind remove her perspiration. She finally starts to relax.

Just as Rose starts to feel the cold air and is ready to re-enter her apartment, the kitchen light turns on. Rose watches a shirtless Aris get a glass from the cupboard and water from the refrigerator. She puts her hand on the door's handle and briefly contemplates whether she should remain outside until he returns to *his* room. He sees her and starts walking to the door. Rose enters and quickly closes the door.

"You are not exactly dressed for the patio," Rose says as she looks upon Aris standing in the shadow of the dining room.

"Neither are you. What were you doing out there?" Aris asks.

"I was hot," Rose says unapologetically, gripping the lapel of her robe with her right fist.

Aris lifts the right corner of his mouth. "And now?"

"I wish I was thinking… I cannot think about anything… except…" Rose's eyes follow the lines of his clavicle and her mind wishes she had a tape measure so that she could scientifically record the perfect shoulder width for future posterity. "Listen, I cannot talk about this now. I'm still hot." Rose drops her robe to the floor and walks to her mantle and adjusts the position of small pink elephant figurine for his pleasure. "Pink elephants." She quickly walks toward her room and closes the door without making a sound. She locks and steps backwards to her rocking chair. She lifts her knees to her chin, hugs her shins, and stares at the door knob. Five minutes later, she crawls into her bed. Rose finds sleep in nineteen minutes.

DAY TWO

Rose opens her door and finds her robe folded into a perfect cube at her feet. *Mercy, mercy me. Things aren't what they used to be.* Rose picks up the robe and darts into the bathroom to shower. She enters the kitchen fully dressed and ready to leave at 8:56. "Good Morning, Aris. I just need to get some coffee. I have a travel mug around here somewhere." Rose starts to open and close cabinets with a bit too much energy. "Ah, here it is." She places the silver travel mug on the platform of her Keurig, which starts to brew. "Sleep well?"

"Yes. Once I fell asleep, I slept very well. I really like those sheets," Aris says from the reading chair.

"Ready?" Rose says lifting her full travel mug to Aris. "It is nine o'clock."

He lifts the right corner of his mouth and sets the book down on the side table. "I am."

"Let's go. A clock store, eh. Sounds like a good time." Rose celebrates her line with a little tap dance. "Are we looking for anything in particular?"

"My sister and her husband are habitually late to almost everything," Aris says while helping Rose with her coat and then putting on his. "I have decided that I want to get them a clock every year – starting with this one." Aris opens the door with her apartment keys in his hand. "I was going to buy online, yet I found this one website that had really nice looking clocks and they have an actual store in Norwalk."

"I wonder if all of the clocks are all set for the same time," Rose interrupts.

"Precisely," Aris agrees. "I immediately thought of you when I decided to check the place out."

"Ooh ooh ooh… maybe they have separate rooms with clocks set to different times… like time zones?" She continues to try to picture the magical clock store.

Aris laughs. "I am wondering if they provide ear plugs. Can you imagine two hundred ticking clocks? It would be maddening."

Aris opens the car door for Rose and then quickly walks to his. He sits down and turns the key. He squirms out of his coat and places it on the back seat. He looks to Rose. "You ready?"

"I've got like four hours to prepare myself for this magical place full of ticking clocks." Rose smiles. "I am having a good time already."

The two pull out of the parking deck at 9:05 AM. Rose watches Aris watch the road as they drive through town onto the interstate. "It has been a long time since I have been in a car with you."

"I guess we do always drive separately," he says looking at her.

Rose smiles and points at the road ahead. "How are the roads?"

"They are fine. I think it stopped snowing four hours ago. I checked the weather in Connecticut – we should not have any problems." Aris relaxes in the driver's seat. "Want to tell me about the meeting with the Boy Scouts."

"I think it went really well. Of the twelve, I think that seven were honestly... um, what is the word – motivated, maybe... to at least think about taking the next step," Rose summarizes. "I am trying not to get my hopes up too much. You know how fragile I can be," she says with a childlike tone. "Nick, the Scout Master I spoke to initially, the super cute one, he seems to be really interested and he is probably my strongest advocate. He might even help me meet with Rebekah Nightingale again. I do not want to get my hopes up. Can we talk about something else?" she asks getting slightly jittery. "I know – we can talk about you. So Aris, what is new with you?"

"Ah... would you look at the time?" Aris snaps the digital display in the middle of his dash. "Think we need a little music? I do." Aris pulls a CD case from the center console and drops it in Rose's lap. "We have access to all of this." Rose opens the CD case to find pages and pages of jacket covers.

"I heard from Lin. She is giving her shop to her cousin. He just moved to the area about six months ago and is having trouble finding acceptable work. So anyway, Lin is going on a long vacation back home – to Beijing, I think. Her son is a freshman at Columbia. He is going to finish school and get his own apartment in the city." Rose beams. "I am really happy for her. Oh and by the way, she gave me free dry-cleaning forever. How perfect is that?"

"Free dry cleaning –awesome gift. Man, it must feel like you actually won the lottery."

"It kinda does." Rose sighs and presses the back of her head against the headrest. She crosses her arms and holds on to her shoulders. With a temperate voice she changes the subject. "Hey did you see that – I think it was a pink elephant." She points out the window into the valley.

"Rose, have you dated anyone in the past nine years?"

"I'd rather we talk about you. I am tired of talking about me."

"I need to know. Have you? Dated anyone?"

"I am not sure if I can answer that question, and I know I don't want to. Are you in love with Nora?"

"She thinks I am in love with you," Aris answers simply.

Rose fans her face. "Is it hot in here?"

Aris looks at the console. "71 degrees."

"It feels hotter," Rose says with a smile.

"Am I in love with Nora?" Aris checks his blind spot. "I am not exactly sure if that is a fair question. There is a recognizable trick to that question – or more precisely, a deliberate trap." He looks over into Rose's lap as she flips through the leather jukebox. "If I said that I was pretty confident that I was in love with Nora four weeks ago and am no longer then… what does that say about me? And how does that make you feel? I think that information might actually hurt you." Aris speeds up and changes lanes. "Your opinion of me is important and ..." he checks his speed again and moves back into the right lane.

"I think you know that I know that your feelings don't run shallow. I mean, if that is your concern."

"Thorn."

"Aristotle." After selecting a CD, she says conversationally, "I was thinking of nicknaming you Eyre. E-Y-R-E."

"From the Brontë novel? Strange. Why?"

"Do you need to know? Ha. Ha," Rose jokes.

Aris laughs. "Rose, you're funny. This conversation isn't. This conversation is serious." He reflects again on what she said. "Do you need to know? Very funny. I wish I could run off to some relative's estate to figure things out like they do in a Brontë novel, or is it Jane Austen?"

"If you don't know the difference, I am pretty sure that this relationship is doomed from the very start."

Aris taunts her with his arrogance. "But I have a dry sense of humor and I like chess."

"Alright, Eyre."

"I don't want to make a mistake that would jeopardize our friendship and whatever else this is. You are just going to have to be patient with me. Do you think you can do that?"

Rose reaches her left hand and gently rubs the lobe of Aris's right ear with her thumb and index finger. "I would put all of the waterproof sport watches in a blue room with a giant fish tank in the middle. I need more coffee. There is a donut shop at the next exit." Rose removes her hand from his ear and points across her body to the highway sign.

"So I need time and you need coffee," Aris says with a soft chuckle.

Two hours later the pair enters the Ye Olde Clock Shoppe. "This is not quite what I had envisioned," Rose says with a smile while overtly scanning the main room of the clock shop.

"Just because they don't have an Australian room with all of the clocks hanging upside-down?" Aris asks understatedly.

"Just because," Rose says as she kisses his cheek while striking a low arabesque.

Aris purchases an antique bronze "time zones" clock featuring a central clock flanked by four smaller clocks for a cool $269. "I am pleased. I am sure that we will have a year's worth of jokes of why they are late this time."

"Who knows, maybe they will surprise you and be hours early," Rose says as she holds the door for an encumbered Aris carrying a large box. "Your keys are in your coat pocket, right?" Rose reaches into his pocket and locates the keys and unlocks the trunk. "Can I drive?"

"I would let you – yet your comments about the passing scenery are the best part of having you in my car," Aris mocks, gently taking the keys from her hand.

"You're going to follow that with salt, right?"

"How about falafel?" Aris points to the Mediterranean deli across the street. "We got time," he says with a wry smile, trying not to laugh out loud.

Rose jumps up in the air and flaps her hands. "Are you kidding?" She pivots on the balls of her feet and runs across the street, leaping over the snow bank. She abruptly stops by the door and looks to see Aris still standing at his car.

"Are you sure about this?" he yells across the parking lot and the street, looking at Rose and then at the keys in his hand.

"Ha."

The pair enjoys a leisurely and flavorful lunch before boarding the silver BMW 3-series to make the return trip. The drive time of three hours and fifty-seven minutes is spent discussing the difference between 80's punk and 80's alternative rock music. The car pulls into the parking deck at Rose's apartment at 7:15PM.

NIGHT TWO

Rose enters her apartment and immediately runs to the loo. Aris knocks, saying, "Please take your time."

Rose laughs. "I am going as fast as I can – give me a second, or two." Rose flushes and swings open the door. "Your turn."

Aris kisses her forehead and then rushes past her. Rose watches the door close before she raises her left hand to touch the place he did. *God, help me.* She walks to her kitchen and opens the refrigerator. She stands there for a few minutes scanning the smorgasbord of various items purchased by Aris. *Sun dried tomatoes and garlic stuffed olives.* "Hey Aris, are you hungry yet?" she yells as she hears the bathroom door open.

"I could be," Aris replies as he steps behind her and places his hands on her hips to gently move her aside. He grabs a Corona from the refrigerator door. "I bought sun dried tomatoes – I am not sure what to do with them – yet they did call to me."

"I noticed them and the olives. I suppose we could make a pizza. My sister gave me a great recipe for pizza dough. I have feta and white cheddar. We could make a white pizza with Roma tomatoes, a smattering of sundried tomatoes and garlic stuffed olives." She looks over her right shoulder to try to look at his eyes. She can only see his mouth. She could almost fall into him. She quickly turns her focus back to the open refrigerator. "I also think I have fresh parsley, although it is probably wilted by now. I made chicken ravioli the other day. They are in the freezer."

Aris, again, puts his hands on her hips as he steps to the other side of her. "Homemade pizza sounds really good to me."

"Okay then. I need flour." She lets go of the refrigerator door and spins around to the island cabinet where she keeps her baking items. "I need flour and yeast and… the recipe." She walks to the other side of the island and slides up a bar stool. "I have been putting all of my tested recipes into a database."

"Do you follow them? I distinctly remembering cooking

with you once or twice and you used the recipe more as a guideline."

"I've learned to recognize my weaknesses."

"Care to share. I would not mind knowing a few of your weaknesses," Aris says humorously flirting.

"Cheese... and apparently handsome men in pajamas," Rose says as she puts the right side of her hair behind her ear and serves a flirt of eye contact.

"Ya got hot peppers?" Aris asks grinning.

"Yes, there is a jar of sliced banana peppers in the door, are they hot enough?" Rose replies with a new found serious tone. She is ashamed of her flirting. "I can make the pizza if you want to read, or relax, or whatever."

"I could help," Aris offers as he secretes a subtle air of disappointment. He walks into the living room and comments, "It just started snowing again."

"I could probably go out there and change it to rain," Rose pronounces inaudibly. She turns to wash her hands and responds to Aris over the sound of the running water, "I could use a bit of time. I am used to being alone."

Rose spends thirty minutes preparing the pizza and collecting her thoughts - for him, on him. She places the pizza into the oven. "Pizza should be ready in eighteen minutes. I have wrapping to do. I'm wondering if you have unwrapped gifts in your car. It is an activity anyway."

"Actually, I do. Do you have enough paper? If not, I could go get some." Aris says in an attempt to soothe her tense energy.

"I actually got gift wrapping as a Christmas present this year, oddly enough," Rose proclaims. "Jennifer, at work, bundled a bunch of wrapping paper and accoutrements to give as a Christmas gift at our dangerously early Christmas party." Rose runs to her room and brings the bundle to demonstrate. "It was presented in the shape of a Christmas tree – pretty clever, actually. There are gift boxes, tissue paper, bows and ribbons, obviously paper, tape, and there is even a box of three different types of confetti."

"Huh. I'll go get my gifts from my car." Aris immediately leaves to retrieve the gifts.

Content with the evening's plan, Rose lights several candles around the living room and retrieves two pairs of scissors and places them on the coffee table. A few minutes later, Aris gently kicks the door. Rose rushes to open to witness Aris carrying the clock on the top of his head held in place by his right hand and two large paper gift bags in his left. "Probably should have used a little forethought." Aris smiles at Rose's astonishment.

"Long walk, dear." She grabs the two paper bags from him just as the oven timer sounds. "Good timing, clock man. Pizza! Pizza! Would you like another beer? I am drinking ginger beer – possibly the most wonderful beverage on God's earth."

"I'll have what you are having."

Rose cuts the pizza and delivers the slices and drinks to the table. Aris sits down on *his* cushion and Rose sits on the floor next to him, Indian style. Rose lifts her green bottle. "To God."

Aris clinks hers. "To God."

Aris takes a bite off his pizza. "Alright Rose – why haven't you dated much in the past nine years?"

"Yikes." She listens to the question and then thinks about her answer over two bites of pizza, enduring his stare. "I think you mean to ask… of all the jinn joints in all the world… why did she have to walk…" Rose sets her pizza down and wipes her mouth and then her hands. "Remember the first night you walked me to my car outside of the Saloon, where we just met two weeks earlier? We stood on the stairway of the building, a school I think. You told me, and I quote, 'We don't get to choose who we fall in love with.'" Rose lifts her pizza to her mouth. "The thought, the sentence… it resonated… and I suppose it still does. I am not sure if it is resonating because I think you are right, or completely and totally wrong." She takes another bite and then changes her seating position from the floor to the couch.

"Did you answer my question?" Aris asks before drinking from his ginger beer.

"I did," Rose responds while tracing his left hand with her right index finger, completely unaware of what she is doing. She abruptly takes her hand back to her lap and says, "However, if I say much more you might want to leave the comfort of the mountain and head for the hills."

"I remember the night. And it was a Catholic school. You were wearing a fashionable coat – yet not very practical for the actual weather. Why do girls do that?"

"So maybe six weeks later when you told me that I was cold – you were really referring to my lack of proper dress."

"You scared the hell out of me."

"Iron…ICK," she says, nervously wiping her hands on her thighs. "Anyway, Aris, that sentence launched this theologian into a fantastic 'tale' spin. The tale is about the nature of revelation, the dichotomy of love, and the absolute essence of faith – a theological dreamboat… and I suppose… and I suppose I'm Noah, or maybe *his* wife. It is my true Master's effort." Rose smiles and lifts her green bottle and finishes the deliciously strong ginger ale. She stands and walks to the kitchen to get another piece of pizza and water. "So that is why I don't date. I think I found what I was looking for on those stairs, standing next to you, kicking the snow in-between the cast iron railing."

"A dreamboat?" Aris says with an awkward chuckle.

"You do understand that it isn't all about you," Rose says dismissively.

"So what other earth shattering truths did I say?" he asks flippantly.

"Something to the effect, or is it affect, of 'What's up with that?'" Rose stands and looks to the kitchen.

"What?" Aris says looking up.

Rose looks down at him. "You said that too." She walks to the kitchen while remembering a conglomeration of nights. "I still don't understand..."

"You don't understand what?" Aris asks as he watches her movements in the kitchen.

Rose pauses and looks at him. "And Aris, I am not cold." She starts to slam cabinet doors and drawers. "I can't find the…the…why do you have to make me feel so … so utterly and completely …vulnerable." Rose looks up at the ceiling and whispers, "Focus Rose. You are looking for the ice cream scoop." With an audible tone she speaks, "Dessert? Warm lemon cake with French vanilla?"

"I guess I am not quite ready for dessert," Aris says watching her scurry and scamper in the kitchen. "I am sorry, Rose. I guess, no, I think you are much more like an extremely hot ball of fire. Right now, at this very moment, you seem…"

Rose smiles and puts her right hand on her right hip, she flips the back of her hair with her left arm and says, "Thanks for noticing and then forgetting what you notice…" She walks over to her hallway closet and pulls out three bags of gifts and walks them over to the scissors.

"In my kitchen wearing pajamas," Rose whispers her own emotional summation as she surveys the gifts in front of her. She finds herself again. "This is my favorite purchase of the season thus far. I actually found my brother three bookends depicting the Brontë sisters. I found this clay artist in Portland. Super cool, right?"

"A fine present," Aris hears the conversation and is contented. He walks over to his gifts and looks down. "I think I like the clock the best. So, what do you think, music?"

Rose moves the floor cushion to the back side of the couch. "We will have more room," Rose says as she looks to Aris, who is now looking out the window. "Your choice."

"You do stick out your neck for me a lot, don't you?" Aris says while still watching the snow. He turns to look at Rose. "And your neck…is…"

"I love gift tape," Rose quickly interrupts, catching his eyes with an understated, steadfast glance. "There is a huge difference between regular scotch tape and gift tape."

"Simon and Garfunkel, it is." Aris makes his selection. "They remind me of...old friends."

"Bookends," Rose affirms. "Perfect."

Together Rose and Aris wrap fourteen gifts of various shapes and sizes. They exchange stories of Christmas mornings and the proverbial wrapping of the frying pan. Rose explains that frying pans make excellent dinosaurs. Aris contends that there is always a big enough box. The two finish their wrapping session with cake sans the vanilla ice cream. They say good night to each other from the patio.

"Aris, I plan on sleeping in as late as possible tomorrow."

"I plan on enjoying the sound of silence." Aris puts his left arm around her waist and with a chaste hug, kisses the top of her forehead. "Good night. I will see you in the morning."

"I think you mean afternoon. Afternoon... delight...full." Rose opens the patio door and leaves Aris to watch the snow. *Good knight.*

CHAPTER 17
THE THIEF AND THE HOUSEDOG

A THIEF came in the night to break into a house. He brought with him several slices of meat in order to pacify the Housedog, so that he would not alarm his master by barking. As the Thief threw him the pieces of meat, the Dog said, "If you think to stop my mouth, you will be greatly mistaken. This sudden kindness at your hands will only make me more watchful, lest under these unexpected favors to myself, you have some private ends to accomplish for your own benefit, and for my master's injury." –Aesop

At 11:20, Rose opens her eyes and rolls them up to look out the window without lifting her head. The skies are still grey and contain gusts of wind. A very light snow enters through the mesh of the window's screen. Rose celebrates the ten hours of sleep. She sits up and decides to put on last night's jumper. She fluffs her hair and puts on her slippers. *Coffee with Aris.*

DAY THREE

Rose walks into the kitchen and sees Aris sleeping on the couch. She quietly walks over and leans over the back of the couch, catching a glimpse of her love sleeping. Rose stays for about thirty seconds before deciding to return to her room. *Coffee can wait.* Rose retrieves a book from her nightstand and opens to her bookmark. Thirty two minutes later, Rose hears Aris's footsteps. She leaps from her bed and walks to the kitchen. "Good morning."

"Good Afternoon," Aris says as he pours a glass of water. "Sit, I will get your coffee."

Rose obeys. "Have you had a nice morning?"

"I have. I went to the gym and got a haircut," Aris

summarizes.

"I did not even notice. Sorry." Rose says, looking at his hair. "It almost looks the same."

"The mark of a good cut, I can assure you. Besides, you have yet to have your first cup of coffee."

"I should go to the gym today. I should go to the gym and write another letter to Rebekah Nightingale," Rose thinks aloud. "I am not exactly sure how to do that though. My first letter was clever. I can't hide this time."

"Drink." Aris puts a mug of coffee in front of Rose. "Can I cook you breakfast – an egg sandwich, perhaps? I bought bagels."

"Are you hungry?"

"I am," Aris says while opening the oven drawer and pulling out the omelet pan. "So how 'bout it?"

"An egg sandwich sounds good. I have sliced cheddar in the fridge." Rose picks up her laptop and walks to the couch. "I should check my email." She can hear Aris work in the background with an occasional string of lyrics being sung. In an email to Lisbeth, she apologizes for not writing yesterday and explains how she spent her day. She also reports that Aris will be leaving tomorrow, mid-afternoon. She writes that she hopes that they might be going to a restaurant for dinner this evening, yet would not mind if they cooked instead. She also sends short emails to her mother and father confirming their plans on Christmas Eve and Christmas day. She does not tell them about Aris. She closes her laptop as Aris appears in front of her with a salad plate.

"Oooh, orange slices." She happily accepts and slides over to the left side of the couch with plate in hand to give Aris space on the right.

"I was thinking that maybe we could go for a walk to the park at the end of the road," Aris says, pointing out the window, "yet, it is downright blustery out there." Aris eyes his sandwich before taking a bite. "Any suggestions?"

"Why do today what you can put off until tomorrow?"

Rose pauses. "If I cannot make it to the gym, I could do a class of yoga here. Yet I would prefer privacy."

"I can read – I am really enjoying the novel," Aris looks over at the reading chair. "I am pretty sure that I cannot help you with your letter; or rather, I believe that you will figure it out."

"Okay then... do you like puzzles?"

"I like to start in the middle and work out," Aris says dryly.

"See that is why we weren't able to stay together – I like to start from the outside," Rose says wishing she could kiss him while touching his ears. However, every part of her knows that once she starts kissing him, she would never want to stop. "C'est la vie."

"I thought it was because you scared the hell out of me," Aris replies, standing and requesting her empty plate.

Rose stands and walks with Aris into the kitchen to brew another cup of coffee. "I have several puzzles on the shelf of the closet in your room. There are even a few winter scenes if you are feeling festive." Rose leans against the pantry as she watches Aris stare into the refrigerator. "How did you sleep?"

Aris pulls out a pitcher of orange juice. "I spent most of the night and even the morning wanting to wake you up."

"So you weren't sleeping?"

"I couldn't."

Rose walks toward Aris and gently tugs on his black V-neck sweater near his waist. She rises to the balls of her feet and kisses him on the cheek and then falls flat on her heels. She raises herself again. "Tall." She places a kiss again and drops to her heels. "Short."

"Do you ever stop talking?" Aris says with his right hand wrapping the width of her left hip.

Rose swallows hard. "Go. Choose a puzzle. There is something very ordering about puzzles. I know when I am truly discombobulated – puzzles with the sorting – and then the finding – and then the re-learning that everything has its place is very gratifying."

"Satisfying," Aris says at the same time looking at his hand on her hip. He looks into her eyes. "Where are the puzzles again?"

"I will keep talking as long as you are actually listening. They are in your room, on the shelf, in the closet." She grabs her coffee from the counter and starts to clear the coffee table.

"I thought you wanted to do yoga?" Aris returns with a 1000 piece photomosaic of 'The Starry Night.'

"I just ate. Let's work on this for a couple of hours and then take a break. You can take a nap or read and I will do my yoga... and then maybe... would you like to go out to dinner?"

"It is really cold out there – and so very warm in here. Chicken ravioli sounds really good to me," Aris suggests.

"I could make some fresh bread," Rose says, looking over her shoulder to the kitchen. She quickly walks to the kitchen and pulls her kitchen aid. "This will only take me about ten minutes."

While Rose makes her dough Aris peruses her CD collection. He selects the Beatles "White" two-disc set. The pair sorts the puzzle pieces effortlessly – the whites, the blues, the greys, the yellows and the edges and each are satisfied to work on their sections with minimal conversation. They work on the puzzle for the duration of the album. Aris takes his nap. Rose completes her yoga at 5:23 and takes her shower. She meets Aris in the hallway while toweling her hair. "Good nap?"

"Good nap. Good stretch?" he returns.

"Good stretch," Rose replies with a gentle smile before entering her room and closing the door.

NIGHT THREE

Rose stands in front of her mirror admiring her clothing choices of a particularly flattering English pink hugging sweater and dark low-riding jeans. "Tight." She combs her wet hair with a center part and gently wrings. She walks to the bathroom and applies mascara to her top lashes only. She dabs on moisturizer and lip gloss.

"For me?" Aris asks standing in the doorway.

Rose puckers. "Pineapple."

"You should see your mile high bread twists. Want me to put them in the oven?"

"A pre-heated oven?"

"My sleep schedule is totally messed up – I am raring right now," Aris says with a bit of a hop.

"Follow me." Rose walks him to the space between the living area and the dining room. "Lie down on your stomach."

Aris complies. "Are you going to give me a massage?"

"You'll see." Rose lies down on top of him, with the back of her skull nestled right below the base of his. "Now, do ten push-ups."

"I guess I should say now that I have a better idea." Aris says, laughing through his seventh.

"Hush before I give you twenty," Rose says. "I think I will paint the ceiling beige."

Aris continues to conduct push-ups, laughing at the top of each. "This is pretty good exercise. And I suppose I could tell my locker room buddies that we did lie together." Aris does five more and then asks with restrained breath, "Are you impressed?"

"I could ask for more," she says as she rolls to the left onto to her back from his down position.

Aris rests his heated cheek on the cool floor and looks over her face. "Thorn, you are very pretty."

"Stop. You are making me blush," she says looking at the top of his hair. She performs a Pilates roll-up and then hugs her knees and looks at him over her shoulder. "Better, Beautiful?"

"God – where did my energy go?" Aris replies flipping his body to lie on his back.

Rose stands and leaves him on the floor and walks to the kitchen. "You did say you pre-heated the oven, right?"

"I did." Aris sits up and exhales.

"I wish I had some vodka. I'd like to make a vodka sauce

for the ravioli."

Aris stands and quickly walks to *his* room. "You are not going to believe this..." He returns with two airplane bottles of Smirnoff in his hands. "I was flying with Charlie, my alcoholic co-worker..." Aris places the bottles on the counter. "He kept on buying me drinks on our flight to Atlanta. I accepted and put them in my coat pocket and just drank the tomato juice. They have been in my suitcase for six months."

"I fell asleep last night thinking about the word 'extraordinary,'" she says with a look of absolute wonderment. "I think this classifies as extraordinary." Rose lifts the bottles as if to make sure that they are real.

"Extraordinary," Aris walks into the kitchen and chooses a beer from the refrigerator. "I should probably drink these," Aris says as he twists the top and drinks. "Need any help?"

"I'm thinking about Rebekah Nightingale. In our first meeting I told her the fable, 'The Hawk and the Nightingale.' I even gave her a copy of it," she says as she uses the can opener on the Carnation and then pours its contents into the sauce pan. "Maybe in my next letter I could use another fable. How 'bout... 'The Thief and the Housedog?'" Rose then opens the crushed tomatoes. "It's a bit of a stretch, and albeit, a bit heavy handed. I may only succeed in making her angry."

"I could set the table," Aris says entering in to the kitchen and opening the cabinet with the dishes. "Keep talking. I am listening."

Rose sighs as she watches Aris move throughout her kitchen. "I like having a roommate." She continues, "The moral of the fable is..." Rose turns and puts her back against the counter. "The moral is that a bribe in hand betrays mischief at heart." Rose looks to Aris as he places the plates and silverware at the dining room table. "I could liken the chocolate companies to the thief and her company to the housedog."

"And who is the Master?" Aris asks with a piercing look

affirming that he actually knows the fable.

"I want to cite the movie, 'The Last Dragon.' And say I am the Master," Rose says smiling. "I loved that movie." She turns back to the stove and places scallions into a small frying pan. "Anyway, the bribe is the PR she could get from organizing with the Boy Scouts. In that sense, she might be offended." Rose fills the pasta pot with water and places it on the stove and turns the dial to 'Hi'.

"Rose, I think you often have too much faith in people. And well, most people don't read into things that far," Aris states as he walks back into the kitchen to watch her fry the onions.

"I could maybe go a step further and, in my letter, suggest that the thief actually listens and learns from the housedog. I did something similar when I re-directed the fable to reflect the Hawk actually listening to the Nightingale." Rose stops and looks at Aris inquisitively. "So, what do you think?"

"I think I will slice the garlic, my little amaranth," Aris jests while taking the cutting board to the other side of the island.

Rose nods with a huff. "Thanks." She opens the oven and notes that the bread is just about done. She toggles the oven and closes the door. She looks over her shoulder at Aris as he stands over the cutting board. "I am not sure if I have too much faith in people. I think I have a talent for recognizing potential," Rose says with a sweet tone. She continues while gently pushing the onions with a wooden spoon, "Some people require a different incentive to do the right thing. Social and professional accolades may prove to be a pretty powerful incentive." She places the onions into the sauce and stirs. "I am ready for the garlic." Rose spins the little fryer in her right hand.

Aris walks over and slides the slices into the pan. "How much do you really need her? I mean, if the point is to bring the issue to light. Do you really need her to do that?"

"Are the boy scouts enough? I don't know. I guess I could get the other chocolatiers... Really, though, I think she,

Nightingale Chocolates, is pretty integral to the ultimate success of my plan."

"Well then, I would suggest a different kind of bribe: 'The Silkworm and the Spider?'" Aris suggests.

"True art is thoughtful, delights and endures." Rose rises to the balls of her feet and kisses him on his left cheek, close to his lips. "I am not sure if I have ever appreciated you as much as I do right now." Rose lowers her body and looks up to him. *God, this is love.* Rose looks at the oven and then back at Aris. "Light the fire, but don't burn the bridge." She removes the bread from the oven and brushes the twists with a combination of melted butter and olive oil. She sprinkles them with coarse garlic salt and parmesan cheese. She opens the freezer and pulls out the bag full of chicken, mushroom, and ricotta ravioli. "These will be ready in about three minutes. What would you like to drink? I need to drink water."

"Water is good." Aris walks over to the stereo and after two minutes of searching, selects Peter Gabriel for Rose. He grabs the bread and the mixed green salad and brings it over to the table and stands behind his chair as he watches her collect the ravioli in a serving bowl.

She ladles the sauce over the ravioli and carries it to the table. She stands behind her chair and looks at her dinner companion. "Aris, I think I should probably warn you, these ravioli are so good that you may want to scoop me up and carry me to your bed." She acquires eye contact then gently averts her eyes before taking her seat at the table.

"I am not exactly sure if I need the ravioli. I have pretty much wanted to since… since the hot cocoa," Aris articulates with a straightforward intensity that softens as he looks to the couch to reveal the time and place.

"Now, we are talking," Rose says with a coy monotone. "All part of my plan and well… these ravioli will just add to my allure." She picks up the bread plate and offers Aris a twist. He accepts and sits down with her.

"I am looking forward to it," he says as he reaches over to place salad onto her plate. "I do love… ravioli."

Rose finds her wine glass and lifts it. "To God."

Aris's wine glass meets hers. "To God." Aris drinks and places his glass down on the table. "Your economy of words at grace is endearing," he says as he lifts his napkin and places it on his lap. "I would imagine that your real prayer goes on and on and on and on."

Rose inhales and exhales a good deal of her nervousness, even the exhaling carbon dioxide has a shake to it. "Ha… and you think you know me. Rambling?" Rose rips into her bread.

"I think I want to know you for the rest of my life," Aris says. "I think you need a job in a think tank. A job where you can work with a bunch of people that actually want to proffer solutions rather than … rather than…what is it that most people do? And besides, I know that you are not a big fan of Big Pharma. I really thought that you would have the courage to quit by now."

"Do you think there is a website for those kinds of jobs? An international think tank application form? And in this extraordinary application, do you think that they would have a section where I can place my Middle East peace plan? In earnest, about five years ago, I really wanted to apply to the League of Arab Nations. I wanted to give them my peace plan. I never did. I am pretty sure that I am not quite… I am not sure if they are looking for a girl like me."

"The Peace Plan? You mean the garden idea?" Aris says while trying to place lettuce, tomato, black olives and banana peppers on four slender prongs. "Making the entire Tigris Euphrates region into the world's garden filled with museums, art galleries, medical research labs, libraries, space exploration facilities… mankind's greatest accomplishments to serve as a reflection of the Garden of Eden idea?" Aris smiles, "That idea? Lame. A Garden of Eden – it's been done before."

"Lame duck," Rose says ironically picturing a ballet move.

"True. And you are right, sending 100,000 intellectual gardeners to the Middle East, rather than 100,000 gun-toting soldiers is definitely sending the wrong message.

"If I can find a way to build these schools in the cocoa fields... that would be one of my garden gates," Rose says straightforwardly.

Aris serves the ravioli to Rose and then himself. He takes his fork and splits his first in half, pierces the piece and lifts it to his mouth. "You weren't exactly kidding about these were you?"

"I am almost always serious," Rose says with a smile of gratitude. "I can make righteous chicken ravioli." Rose tries to fit a whole piece in her mouth before deciding to nibble instead. "I make pretty good popcorn, too." Rose watches Aris return for a few more ravioli.

"I should visit more often. These..." Aris points to the ravioli with his fork "...these are much better conceived than your 'Chicken Chips.'"

"How about them 'Wagon Wheels'... they sound so... pioneering," Rose says trying not to laugh. She quiets down with the memory of that night and finishes her ravioli.

After placing the empty salad bowl on top of her two dinner plates, Rose says, "So for my garden, I suppose all I really need to do is learn how to tame the snake." She carries the haphazard stack to the sink.

"Hot, hot, hot." Aris says following her with his dishes. "Time, time, time."

"Did you say something?" Rose looks to Aris.

"You said something about a snake?" Aris says with a sharp tone. "I really don't think you need to worry about that. Rose, thanks for a wonderful meal. The bread was delicious. The salad was good and the ravioli... I really would like the recipe to give to my mom and Mina," he says as he steps in to help load the dishwasher.

"I cannot give all of my secrets away," Rose admits. "I

want you to still find me attractive, and without my captivating chicken ravioli... didn't I already mention my plan?"

"What do you want to do?" Aris asks.

Rose looks over to the coffee table. "Do you paint?"

"I do. Why? Do you have paints?" Aris asks with a bit of excitement in his voice. "I have not painted in years."

"No. Painting is something I would like to do. I want to go to a nice, cozy, woodsy cabin and paint," Rose says still looking over at the puzzle.

"Can I be there?"

Rose looks up to him. "You are the person I most want to paint."

"I will not pose nude," Aris says.

"I won't paint nude," Rose says.

"Guess we will have to find something else to do nude," Aris suggests.

Rose starts walking over to the puzzle. "I guess between the two us we could probably find something to do. Aris, there are so many pieces here." Rose grabs the lighter and lights the candles on the mantle. She then walks over to her stereo and stares at her CD collection.

Aris walks up next and stands at her shoulder. He looks down and she looks up. "What do you want to hear?"

"The Radio," Rose turns on college radio. "Do you need to do laundry before your trip home? I really would not mind. And please don't say that your mom likes to do your laundry."

"Good idea." Aris kisses the top of her head and enters *his* room. Rose listens to his movements as he starts the washer at the end of the hall. Aris returns to Rose just wearing his pajama pants. "There is still a little room in the washer. I could wash those for you, if you would just take them off." He laughs at himself.

Rose stands up and walks to her room and narrowly closes the door. Five seconds later she drops her shirt, jeans and bra to the floor through the opening. "Warm or Cold?" She opens the door wearing a tank top and fuzzy short shorts.

"Cold, gentle cycle," Aris says looking at her strong ivory legs. "Is this part of your plan? Seriously, it is a pretty good plan."

"I guess I am going to have to turn the heat up in the other room," Rose says shaking out her hair. She walks directly to the fireplace to raise the temperature a few degrees.

"I will just put these in the wash, then," Aris yells with a hint of distraction and humor.

"Thanks. Would you like your dessert now?" Rose asks from the opposite end of the hall.

"Your choice," Aris replies.

"My choice," Rose whispers as she walks into the kitchen and pulls out a can of chunk pineapple, honey and then a frying pan. She delivers the ice cream to Aris, who has found his blue suede cushion in front of the fire. "Fried pineapple." Rose sits on the floor on the other side of the coffee table and wraps herself in her blanket.

He pushes the entire coffee table to the left and turns his body around to sit next to Rose. "I like watching fires, even fake ones."

Rose slouches a bit so she can rest her head on the couch cushion. She looks across the breadth of his chest to the downward arch of his right shoulder. "As inconvenient as the circumstances that brought you to my place are..." Rose looks into his eyes from this lower position, "...Aris, I am glad you are here sitting next to me."

"Thanks for taking me in," Aris says as he searches the top of her head. "Rose, what do you want?"

Rose offers a deep sigh. She looks to the fire and then to the coffee table and takes the opportunity to put a bit of space between them. She sits up and slides to the left and crosses her legs Indian style. She places her arm and the empty bowl on the couch cushion. "Now you have done it," Rose says with a devilish smile. "You have stepped into my Rubicon."

Aris wiggles his toes in his socks and then adjusts his position to turn his body towards her. "Caesar."

"Aww." Rose stretches out her left arm and places her hand on his sternum. "Please don't come any closer," Rose pleads. "I can't think…"

"Rose, what do you want? Tell me," Aris responds. He wraps his right hand around her wrist and moves her hand down one inch and a hair to the left.

Reds and pinks take over Rose's cheeks as she drops the tension in her arm. "I want you to know exactly how I feel," Rose says taking her arm back as she lifts her legs to shield her chest. She hugs her calves.

"Guarded," Aris responds very gently tugging on her forearm. He accepts her defense and attempts to soothe by moving back a few inches. He then extends his legs to lie on his back with his head in his hands, elbows up and his eyes on her. "I am not sure I can do that – know exactly how you feel."

"See, that is exactly why you have held on to me all of these years," Rose says exasperatedly. "I am so in love with you."

Aris eyes darken as his skin lightens. "You scare the hell out of me."

Rose adjusts her posture and sits Japanese style. "See this…." Rose points to herself and then him, "… this is what we have… this is who we are… this is our connection… this is our friendship."

Aris rises to a sitting position. "Feels like more."

"Fine concession, Eyre." Rose smiles as she shifts her weight onto her hands while still sitting on her heels. "If all goes according to my plan, you will know that this is more. Yet, therein lies the problem."

"The problem?" Aris says with a nearly audible heart beat in his throat.

"I have spent years thinking about this – you and me. I think a good deal of my energy comes from the fact that I had to find something to fill the void you left when we broke up. The energy you and I created had to go somewhere." Rose focuses on the arches of his eye brows. Her eyes follow the curves on the right and then on the left. "I am seriously afraid, dangerously afraid, that if this works out the way I want and you finally come to your senses and are actually mine ... well then, I would be satisfied."

Rose continues, "I don't think I have ever been satisfied. I like wanting things. I want lots of things," Rose adjusts her position and sits upright on her heels and speaks slowly and pensively. "I want to give Abdul a chocolate bar and a desk at school. I want a music collection that offers puzzle music. I want to sleep in beautiful things made in exquisite fabrics. I want a pool table. I want a workshop with every saw imaginable with blades that don't break. I want my mom and dad to be happy and proud of me. I want my sisters and my brothers to find the beginnings of pure contentment. I want to work with smart generous people. I want my house plants to thrive..." Rose stops and looks at Aris, sitting and listening. She looks at his hair, his nose, his mouth, his neck, his chest, his hands that have been recently crossed at his waist. "I want you."

Angry at herself for saying and feeling way too much, Rose stands. "Rubicon be damned. And now, I want to know what I am supposed to do with this energy?" Rose walks to the kitchen and throws the faucet up and drinks from it. Tears of inexplicable emotion start welling up in her eyes and Rose turns from the faucet to look at Aris, "I want... I want... I... I... My heartbreak is – I *don't* know what you want. I want to *know* what you want. Yet I *need* you to know that I *can't* ask. And now, well... Now, I can't think." Rose turns back to the sink and grips the width of the counter and sink with both hands. "I am going to take a shower." Rose abruptly leaves the room, enters the bathroom and closes the door.

Twenty-two minutes later she emerges from the bathroom to find Aris waiting for her in the hallway. He's dressed in his winter running clothes. He hands her sneakers. "Let's run."

Rose holds the white towel up with her right hand and takes the sneakers with her left. "Give me five." Rose enters her room and closes the door.

"How cold is it? I could put a swim cap on, under my ski cap." Rose asks for advice through the door.

"I think the wind has died down." Aris starts to open the door to find a fully dressed Rose in front of him. "You look beautiful. Got your Mp3?" Aris asks.

"Never leave home without it," Rose chimes as she turns off her bedroom light.

The pair run in the streets when possible, yet mostly stay on the sidewalks. They have similar running styles in that they both sprint for stretches. Forty minutes later the two enter the apartment and cool down in the kitchen on either side of the sink. "Thanks for this, Aris." Rose says as she removes her ski cap and gloves. "I needed this."

"Good to get out of the house," Aris responds. "Now, I think *I* need to shower." He lightly pulls on her matted hair and pinches the ends. He takes a deep breath as he looks at Rose who is watching his hand. He looks to the hallway and then looks back at her before he takes his leave.

She watches him turn the corner and looks down at her sneakers. "Happy feet." She walks into her room, closes the door and stands naked waiting for the cold sweat to stop. She locates her pajamas and watches herself dress in her mirror. She sits down on the edge of her bed and focuses on her own eyes. "The point of no return. It's my point, not his. My Eyre." She leaves her room and pours two glasses of ice water and brings them over to the coffee table. Setting the glasses on the floor, she pushes the coffee table back in front of the couch. She picks up the water and places them on the table. She moves the suede cushion back to his side of the puzzle. She sits down and starts sorting the pieces. She can hear Aris at the dryer. She drinks.

"I brought water for you," Rose says as he enters the living area.

Aris smiles and takes his seat. The two work on the puzzle in silence for one hour.

"Please work from home tomorrow," Aris says.

"All part of my plan," Rose responds.

"Good," Aris replies as he watches her locate another piece. "You are pretty good at this."

"I like puzzles. They are good time consumers." Rose lifts her eyes and smiles gently.

"I am going to miss you."

"I know." Rose responds with a flirt of eye contact. The two work in silence for a half-hour. "I think I am going to try to go to sleep now. I'll see you in the morning."

Aris nods. "Good night, Rose."

Rose stands and finishes the last gulp of her water. She sets the glass down on the island and starts to walk to her room. "Aris?"

"Yes." Aris lifts his face to meet hers.

"Have you talked to Nora?" Rose says hugging the outside corner wall of his room.

"Rose, I think…" Aris starts.

"Never mind, I really cannot talk about this right now. Good night, Beautiful." She leaves the room and enters hers. She opens the window and climbs into her bed. She finds sleep in nineteen minutes.

DAY FOUR

Rose wakes up at 7:35. She quickly closes the window and stands. *Coffee with Aris.* She puts on her slippers and shuffles to the kitchen. Aris is reading his computer screen at the island. "Good Morning, Rose. How did you sleep?"

Rose smiles. "Like a teenager. Good morning." Rose walks to the dishwasher and grabs her mug and places it on the platform.

She mimics the fog horn sound of the machine and then yawns. "How long have you been awake?"

"An hour or so. I really like your apartment. The sunrise through those windows was spectacular," Aris says. "I wish I could... I guess I am not looking forward to the long drive."

"Again, four hours is not a long drive." Rose lifts her coffee from the platform. "When are you thinking of leaving?" Rose unknowingly frowns.

"I am hoping to have lunch with you and then take off," Aris says while shutting down his computer. "We need to talk."

Rose does not want to talk; she just wants to kiss him. "About last night?" Rose asks nervously. "I hope I did not make you too uncomfortable. I am sorry... it is just..."

"You are fine. Actually, I guess there are some things I need to tell you," Aris says as he stands and lifts his computer to his hip. "I need to put this away." He leaves the room and enters *his*. He returns 90 seconds later. "Can we sit on the couch?"

Rose looks down at her mug – half empty and still very warm. "Yes, of course. Peculiar. Can we sit down on the couch?" Rose walks to her normal morning couch position, on the right and then quickly adjusts for an Aris morning. She turns around to see that he is watching her from the island. "We sit on the couch."

"I need to make another cup of coffee, and then I suppose you will need to make another cup of coffee." Aris stands to show her his empty mug. "I like the Dark Magic – extra bold and very intense."

"I think the name is a little frightening... sorta like this impending conversation with my beautiful saboteur," Rose admits as she watches his movements in front of the Keurig.

Aris walks to the back of the couch and tries to take Rose's mug. She disallows as she takes the last two gulps. "You are particularly feisty this morning." Aris stands and looks out the window with intent and Rose follows, he steals the mug from her hand. "Dark Magic? I don't think so."

"I wouldn't fall for that trick... well not after my second cup of coffee," she says with a bewildered smile as she watches Aris place her mug on the platform. "How did you sleep last night?"

"I almost didn't. That is kinda what I need to talk to you about," Aris says, turning his back to the falling liquid. "I was awake last night for most of the night... almost all of the night fighting the urge to enter your room and ask you to put your arms around my neck so I could carry you into mine. For no other reason than that I just wanted to hold you. I was sure I would have been able to fall asleep if you were with me," Aris says leaning forward from the chair.

Rose listens as her entire torso starts to fall. "And you didn't."

"No. I couldn't. With every rendition created in my mind, with every one, you wouldn't trust me. You would not let me carry you," Aris admits.

"Sounds like me. I am pretty much a trained fighter," Rose says looking down at the blanket keeping her ankles warm. "And for obvious reasons..."

"Anyway, I took a good deal away from your rant last night. You don't mind that I am calling it a rant, do you?"

Rose shakes her head.

"Anyway, I think I heard most, if not all, from the 'what you wanted' category. I know I definitely heard what you needed," Aris says. "Now I need you to listen to my need," Aris looks at Rose. "I need you to trust me. I think you do, I think you trust me as a friend; I need you to trust me more, much more. This is going to take time and..."

Rose tries to be silent as this information sinks in, yet she can't. "Aris, I am the one on the limb. I am not sure if I can have that kind of trust from here."

Aris leans forward and then stands. He walks toward Rose and with his right hand he requests hers. She stands as he lifts her hand in his. "This is where I start. Rose, I want to be worthy of your trust."

Rose averts her eyes to look at the ground illuminated by the sun. "Do you know what you are saying?" She tries to look directly at him, but can't.

"I know what I am doing," Aris says. "I need you to trust me."

Rose's eyes darken as she glares up at him. "Big promises?"

Aris kisses her middle knuckle and takes a step back. "Alright, what about a small promise. I want you to like me more every Monday. Can you promise to like me more every Monday?"

"That sounds like a line." Rose twists her lips. "Just another 'Man-I-See' Monday." Rose starts to panic. "It is still me on the limb."

"You are afraid of me," Aris says.

"You already had Tuesday, and now you are asking for Monday." Rose says looking toward the sunshine.

Aris huffs a small laugh. "I guess I am."

"You just broke up with Nora. And now you are here offering promises. I know you. You are not that simple. This thing with Nora is not that simple and it is definitely not over."

Aris exhales loudly and then chuckles a little. "This is going to be harder than I thought."

Rose looks at him. "You're laughing?"

"I guess I am nervous and tired and... I have been playing this conversation in my mind for a couple of hours."

Rose just looks at him, focusing on the three lines across his forehead.

"I think you are trying to approach this from an outsider's perspective. Yes, I did just break up with my girlfriend. And I do still have strong feelings for her. Of course I do. Yet, we are different. With Nora, I hit a wall. With you, I feel like I have opened a door. You see the difference. You know the difference."

Aris touches her chin to bring her eyes to his. "I think you are worried about what other people will think about us. My feelings for you are not fly-by-night. I don't know why it took me nine years to get here. I don't. You might. I just need your trust that I understand a bit better now. I think I understand how you feel. Do you know what I mean?"

"Well, we can't date now. There are rules for a reason. I am pretty sure that we should not date for at least three months."

"Nora is going to hate the both of us no matter what."

"Still. You said you broke up with her, but these things take time and..."

"You are afraid of me. You are afraid that I am an opportunist, or I am taking advantage of you. Knowing you, you probably have an argument around the word 'capitulate.'"

"You don't know me too well," Rose lies.

"Yet, you are afraid of me."

"Of course, I am! I know you are not that guy, but this situation... it's got all the markings of a love-gone-bad novel and the reader is screaming, 'Don't pick that guy. He's lying to you. He just doesn't want to be alone.'"

"You are my best friend. Seriously, my best. Every good love story starts with that."

Rose sighs. "I'm scared."

"Every good romance starts with that, too."

"What are you, an expert? Love story versus Romance? It still feels like I am the one who has to take all of the risks."

Aris is silent in his acknowledgement of her fear and then smiles. "Like the queen."

Rose smiles. "Did you hear those foot soldiers raided my closet?"

Aris laughs. "Your closet filled with beautiful night gowns?"

"You're impossible." Rose looks to her ceiling. "God, why do I love him?"

Aris smiles. "So stop fighting me and start trusting me."

Rose tries to still her heart muscles and ends the conversation abruptly, "Have you had breakfast? We have eggs, cheese and ..."

Aris accepts her stopping point. "No, I've not had breakfast. I can cook. Check your email," Aris says with a sigh of relief. "Trust is important."

"Fine. I will trust that you will put at least a couple slices of cheddar cheese in my omelet?"

"I think you can trust me a little more than that."

"So last night you wanted me in your bed."

"I still do."

"Do you trust *me*?"

"I do," Aris replies.

"A good start," Rose says as she turns and opens her laptop. Within seconds, she recognizes that she cannot write. "I can't write," she says aloud as she turns to watch Aris cook.

Aris turns from the frying pan to look at Rose. "I think I could hold you all night." Aris carries an omelet with half of a toasted bagel to Rose.

"I'd break fast," Rose says earnestly.

He exhales fully. "Feisty." Aris scans her face. "I need water." He walks back to the kitchen and flips his omelet. He opens the cabinet door and pulls out two wine glasses. "Water?"

"Yes, please," Rose answers.

The pair finishes breakfast and spends an hour on the puzzle. Aris gets up to take a shower and Rose checks in with the office. The two spend the rest of the morning talking about Christmas. Aris collects his things and packs his suitcase.

"When are you going to be back?"

"Sooner rather than later."

"That is some limb."

"Are you afraid?"

"Years of ballet have given me a good sense of balance. I

am afraid, yet recognize what a partner means when they ask for trust. I am afraid because… well, I guess I am a bit worried that you don't quite know what the word means to me. Trust, that is. I am faithful, and a faithful trust betrayed can be utterly devastating. I hope you know what you are doing. So says the ballerina… I am a lot heavier than I look."

"Rose, I really want to be worthy of your trust." He walks to his suitcase and pulls up the handle.

"Then be." Rose stands to walk Aris to the door.

He grabs her left hand and stretches each finger before intertwining his with hers. He lifts her hand in his and kisses the back. "This was fun and I'm sure I'm going to miss you." He leans forward and kisses the top of her head.

Rose closes her eyes and swallows hard. "All part of my plan to which I have added patience and trust." She holds on to the door knob for balance. "Drive safe. Precious cargo." Rose looks at his hand in hers and squeezes before letting go.

"Merry Christmas, Aris," she says slowly, closing the door.

"Merry Christmas, Rose." Aris says through the door.

Rose remains at the door until she hears the door to the parking deck. She rests the top of her forehead on the door, closes her eyes and says, "God, he wants my trust. So help me." She turns and slides her back down the door to her Filipino squat, "I love him."

CHAPTER 18
THE SILKWORM AND THE SPIDER

Having received an order for twenty yards of silk from Princess Lioness, the Silkworm sat down at her loom and worked away with zeal. A Spider soon came around and asked to hire a web-room nearby. The Silkworm acceded, and the Spider commenced her task and worked so rapidly that in a short time the web was finished. "Just look at it," she said, "and see how grand and delicate it is. You cannot but acknowledge that I'm a much better worker than you. See how quickly I perform my labors." "Yes," answered the Silkworm, "but hush up, for you bother me. Your labors are designed only as base traps, and are destroyed whenever they are seen, and brushed away as useless dirt; while mine are stored away, as ornaments of Royalty." –Aesop

"My neighbor, Henry, who lives at the end of the cul-de-sac, has this giant, and I mean giant, snowman. It is taller than his house. He drilled holes in plywood and put LED lights through the holes. It lights up the entire street," Mike tells Nicolas while they sit in Nightingale Chocolates' greeting foyer. "The local news reported on it and people have been doing drive-bys for weeks. I hate the end of the season when all the Christmas lights go; but I will have to admit that I am looking forward to a few dark nights. I really like the guy. He is fun. But I almost need one of those blindfolds my wife wears to sleep. It is so bright!"

"I love setting up Christmas lights. I like the cold and the danger. Hey, did you hear about Heath's brush with the law?" Nicolas asks.

"No, Man, I didn't," Mike answers.

"He decided to do a comical scene with his lights this year. First he took one of those angels… and twisted the detachable wings to make a rifle and set it up to shoot one of those lighted deer. He replaced just a section of the white bulbs on the deer with red ones. Amusing. However, the cops came to his house about the other scene. He made a dummy using his clothes, and you know what a big guy Heath is. Anyway, he made a dummy that was hanging from the ledge of a second story window. It was supposed to appear as though the guy was hanging his Christmas lights and fell off the ladder. The ladder was there…and a dropped string of lights. During the first week it was up, in early December, cars were stopping in the middle of the road to run and help the dummy. Apparently, a few people did not find it all that funny. He was asked to take them down." Nicolas shakes his head in disbelief. "I write messages on my roof to remind me of being a kid. I was always afraid that Santa would miss my house."

"So what do the messages say?" Rose asks.

"This year – 'No Gluten-free cookies,'" Nicolas responds.

Rose laughs. "That is one way to get Santa to your house, I suppose."

"Most people don't get the joke," Nicolas says.

"People," Mike says. "Hey, my mom is gluten-free."

"So is mine," Rose reports.

A very jolly brunette with exceedingly white teeth enters the foyer to welcome the three. "Hi guys, sorry to keep you waiting. I am Melissa, Manager of our Public Relations Department. Rebekah just called and told me that she is going to be a bit late. She told me to proceed without her. I think I will give her a few more minutes." Melissa stands before the three learning each of their names as she leads them to the conference room at the end of the hall. She enters the room and steps aside. "Make yourselves comfortable. Can I get anyone anything? Water?"

"Apples," Rose exclaims at the basket of apples in the center of the table.

"We try to keep fresh fruit in the office at all times," Melissa explains. "There are oranges and pears in the break room if you would prefer."

Mike's eyes light up. "I would love an orange. The break room? Where is that?"

"I'll get you one. Have a seat," Melissa responds.

"I will have a water," Nicolas says.

Melissa nods and leaves the three in the conference room. Rose grabs an apple and a napkin from the basket and reaches into her purse for her pocket knife before sitting in the burgundy fabric covered swivel chair. "Fuji apples. I love Fuji apples."

"Nice knife," Mike says. "The chick carries a Leatherman in her purse."

"My dad pretty much insisted on it. He has given me a pocket knife of sorts every year since I was like eleven. And yes, before you ask, I have a brother." Rose smiles as she shows off her blue metallic Leatherman.

The two scouts pull out their knives from their pockets and set them on the table. The three spend the next few minutes discussing the pros and cons of pocket knives. Rose tries to argue that her knife is better than their deluxe Swiss Army knives. They unrelentingly stand their ground.

"A chick with a pocket knife. Man, that is so hot," Mike says.

Rose blushes. "I like to think it practical. I have this bag I have to carry everywhere. What else am I supposed to carry in it?"

Rebekah and Melissa enter the room. Rose's posture immediately adjusts and reflects a little embarrassment at being caught off guard. "Hello, Rose. Nice to see you again," Rebekah says directly to Rose and then follows Melissa with her eyes as she delivers the orange and water to Mike and Nicolas respectively.

Rose smiles and admirably regains composure. "I am very happy to see you again, too. Rebekah, I would like to introduce Nicolas Grey, I am sorry, Nick Grey and Mike Zimmerman. Nick is the Scout Master of Troop 4648. And Mike is the Scout Master of ..."

"Troop 5280." Mike stands to extend his hand.

Nick also stands and walks around the table to meet Rebekah. "Pleasure to meet you, Ma'am."

Rebekah turns to Rose. "You are not kidding around, are you?"

"No Ma'am. I think I am Scouting," Rose says with a personal smile as she tries to convey her understanding of the subtly of Rebekah's question regarding the two very handsome men in her conference room.

The two women take their seats at the head of the table and hand out confidentiality agreements to the attendants. "We need you to sign these before we continue. This is a standard confidentiality agreement. It may be unnecessary for our conversation today; however our lawyer insists that any talks should be covered by this type of agreement," Melissa says with both of her hands flat on the table. All three take a few minutes to read the agreement before signing.

"I must admit, Rose, that I am impressed with the progress you have made on this idea," Rebekah says coolly. "I think when we originally spoke, you were considering a partnership with other chocolatiers."

"Yes, Ma'am." Rose nods her agreement and tries hard not to run at the mouth. "Two strings to my bow."

"I see," Rebekah says.

"If I may be so bold to say, I figured it would be easier for you to stand if you had an army behind you," Rose says nervously while fidgeting with the palms of her sweaty hands.

"We are in the beginning stages of talking about this plan amongst ourselves and with the kids. We do think that our organization can really be strengthened with this type of action," Nicolas adds.

"I think that most of this will be subject to good timing," Mike interjects. "And a feedback loop. I am not sure if we will need your company to motivate our kids; or whether your company will need our kids."

"What is the goal, for now?" Melissa asks. "What do you want us to do?"

Rose looks at Nicolas and then Mike before speaking. "Negotiate. Well, I think that maybe we should possibly start with setting up a meeting with the national headquarters of the Boy Scouts of America. I think your company, if interested, will provide the catalyst - give us the clout to make a plausible pitch to the national organization."

"Grass roots movements can work. However, they are typically more effective if they start from the top," Nicolas says. "I think if our Scouting contingent takes this idea to the national headquarters, with a good deal of the details ironed out, and from there make a national plea for help... then we can hit the ground running."

Rose quickly turns her head toward Nicolas and smiles. "Good idiom."

"Again, I think it has to do with timing," Mike adds, "and good public relation skills." He smiles at Melissa.

"Alright, so what are we negotiating?" Rebekah asks.

"A commitment," Rose says simply. "In my original idea, your company would set aside one product to mark with the ChIP's logo where a percentage of the proceeds would go to collect money to build schools in the Ivory Coast and Ghana. I suppose that now the idea may have been slightly altered in that we may wish to combine the effort to include the Boy Scout emblem to reflect a joint venture."

"We have a department here in charge of fund-raising, it is different from our public relations department. I suppose we should make them part of this meeting," Rebekah adds.

"I can talk to Brooke after this meeting. I'll let her in on the loop, so to speak," Melissa volunteers authoritatively. "For now, though, I think my department can cover this."

"Very good. So where were we? Joint venture?" Rebekah's eyes move starkly from Melissa to Rose.

Rose continues, "I would like for your company to be the flagship company of the movement. And as that flagship, I would like your company to make a public request that other major chocolate companies pledge a percentage of the proceeds from one of their products. An adult form of peer pressure, if you will."

"I wonder if we could use the concept of 'peer pressure' as part of our program's push," Mike adds disruptively and is immediately embarrassed. "I'm sorry, I didn't mean to interrupt. The thought just popped in there."

Rose smiles at Mike kindly. "Happens to me all of the time."

Nicolas issues a sharp look to his team and then takes the lead. "As we said in our email – we want to use our Scouts to help raise awareness nationwide about the exploitation of children in the cocoa fields and then maybe in the future – other areas like the tungsten mines. Our scouts will speak to schools and churches and local organizations about the problem and raise awareness and money to help fix the problem. Our scouts will be talking about ChIP and your flagship status as the prime mover of it."

Rose backs up Nicolas as she says, "Essentially, to start, we need three things. The first is a commitment of a product to carry the logo and the emblem. The second, we would need a representative, possibly yourself or Melissa, to travel to Irving to help pitch the idea to the Boy Scouts of America's national headquarters. And thirdly, we need the willingness to take this as far as we can carry."

"Do you have a timeline of how long you think these preliminary steps will take?" Rebekah asks. "I don't mean to sound callous; however, it does seem to be a pretty large undertaking. And you seem to be making grandiose movements. Most people don't work that way."

"Fair," Rose says as she lowers her head. She looks up, then at Nicolas and Mike and finally at Melissa and Rebekah. "Yet, why?" She swallows and tries not to continue and, of course, fails. "I keep on thinking about that Police song, 'Giant steps are what you take, walking on the moon.' I am a big fan of our nation's space program and we did not get there by thinking how most people work. We set a high goal and worked to achieve it. Is that spirit our past?"

"We had one den mother, a mother of an 11 year old boy," Mike says. "At our initial meeting about this project she said that she could not bear the thought of her child carrying a machete."

"I looked up your company online before this meeting," Nicolas picks up. "I learned that your mother founded this company because times were tough and she needed to bring money into the house. She started hand-dipping chocolate in her home kitchen. However, her company did not really start making money until she started making chocolates for church fund-raisers. She received the skill of hand-dipping chocolate because she had to quit school in the third grade to work because her father, your grandfather, had died and the family needed money to survive."

"You seem to have done your homework," Rebekah admits.

"So your mother, although things turned out well for her, I am sure that she would have rather stayed in school." Nicolas says. "This idea… is a natural step in your mom's legacy, don't you think?"

"Wow. These guys are heavy hitters." Melissa laughs an infectious laugh. "Like a tag team of hyenas, really."

"Carry on," Rose says laughing. "And thanks for noticing. Actually we just met a few weeks ago. Pretty impressive, eh?"

"Very impressive," Melissa says. She clears her throat as she looks to Rebekah and drops a little giggle.

Rebekah gently nods her head as she looks to Mike and Nicolas. "When Rose first pitched this idea, she pretty much had me on the hook. It was during the Christmas season and so, well, I had to set the idea on the back burner. I want you to know that I am interested and that I am impressed with your hard sell. I will need to talk to the CFO and a few of my lawyers. I also need to talk with Brooke about how this move might affect our fund-raising operations and market. However, I can say that I am interested for all of the reasons that you have provided in this meeting and the initial one. Did she tell you about her book, too?" She looks at Rose. "I am impressed."

Rose falls back into her chair at Rebekah's high praise – a reflex propelled by the odd formation of forward momentum coupled by a natural fear that inevitably occurs when things actually start to go well. She recognizes the emotion and calls upon her courage. "How about we meet in two weeks? We will draft our initial letter to the Boy Scouts of America and send our version to you, Melissa, for you and your team to look at and make your changes. I think that setting up the initial meeting will help establish a more true to scale timeline. It has been my experience that it may take several drafts and revisions and requests and pleads to get the letter answered." Rose winks at Rebekah.

"Nick, Rose and I can probably get the letter to you by Tuesday the 13th. Guys, what do you think? We can do it in 5 days," Mike suggests casually.

"Personally, I work better with a bit of deadline pressure. I am sure we can," Rose admits.

"Wanna meet tomorrow at the Lodge at Noon?" Nicolas asks.

Melissa asks and laughs a deep belly laugh. "Do we need to be here for this?"

Rose giggles and then smiles at Melissa and Rebekah. "Sorry. Did you know that it is a Boy Scout thing to do what you are told when you are told to do it? It is so refreshing and odd, almost peculiar. Most people I work with don't work like this. Anyway, I think that Mike is right. I think we can get a draft to you by the beginning of next week."

"I think this is off to a pretty good start. I think you are right that an initial letter will be a good way to set up a timeline for the project," Rebekah says as she looks at her watch. "It is late, 5:22 on a Friday. We should all get home and enjoy our weekend.

It was nice meeting you all, and please copy me on all major correspondence." Rebekah stands and leaves the room.

Melissa looks around the table. "My job here is public relations and I have worked with various types of groups of all sizes and shapes. I can safely say that I am looking forward to working with you guys."

Rose beams. "Thanks."

"Yeah, thanks," Nicolas says.

Mike stands and reaches his hand out to Melissa. "I am sure we will enjoy working with you, too."

The three pick up their things and their coats and exit the building and huddle in the parking lot. "Well that went well," Rose says with an overtly surprised tone. "Must be you guys – things never go so smoothly for me. Does anyone else get nervous when things are easy?"

"I don't, but my wife does," Mike says.

"So, tomorrow at noon at the Lodge – BYOL?" Nick asks.

"I will bring my computer. We can cut and paste a lot of information into the letter," Rose says. "We do have access to the internet from there, right?"

"Yep," Nicolas speedily replies. "I will have to figure out who it is that we should write to. I wonder if Daniel can help with that."

"I am meeting up with Heath for drinks tonight at Charlie's. Want to join us?" Mike says. "I'll tell him about the meeting tomorrow. Maybe he might want to help."

"I have a date tonight, but thanks anyway," Rose replies.

"Let me ask Christina. I think she actually wanted to go out for a bit tonight," Nicolas replies. "Hey, it is too cold to be standing around in a parking lot. Rose, I will see you tomorrow at noon."

"Good night, guys. Thanks again. Sincerely," Rose says as she turns and takes the opportunity to sprint out of the cold and into her car. Rose turns the engine and idles for about one minute as she shuffles through her Mp3 player and stops at Silversun Pickups.

CHAPTER 19
THE BAT AND THE WEASELS

A Weasel seized upon a Bat, who begged hard for her life. "No, no," said the Weasel; "I give no quarter to Birds." "Birds!" cried the Bat. "I am no Bird. I am a Mouse. Look at my body." And so she got off that time. A few days after she fell into the clutches of another Weasel. The Bat cried for mercy. "No," said the Weasel; "No mercy to a Mouse." "But," said the Bat, "you can see from my wings that I am a Bird." And she escaped that time as well. –Aesop

Rose rushes into her apartment at 6:20. Her date, Aris, will be picking her up at 7:00. She considers whether she should call and ask for more time. Instead she drops her coat on the floor and races to the shower. She showers, shaves, plucks and intensely moisturizes her body with cocoa butter and her face and hair with argan oil. She dries and straightens her hair. She chooses a brown cowl neck, body conscious fisher knit sweater dress that falls just above her knee. She accessorizes with tights and a knee high, brown leather boot. She enters the bathroom to put on make-up at 6:59 and puts on the last earring at 7:02. She hears a knock on the door at 7:05.

Rose opens the door to find Aris with an envelope pursed between his lips. She looks puzzled. She cautiously takes the envelope from his mouth and grabs his left hand and tugs his body through the door. "Hi."

Aris grabs her other hand and looks down upon the fact that they are holding hands. "Hi." He turns their hands up and down slowly. "Did you have a nice week?"

"How was California and the flight?" She asks trying hard to keep her balance. "I think your challenge of 'absence makes the heart grow fonder' is a bit… well… my heart is way past fawned." She wriggles out of his grasp to model her costume for the evening. "What do you think – fawn, dear?"

"Good God! She is hurting my eyes," Aris says.

"I think you are giving me a compliment." She rises to the balls of her feet and gently kisses his cheek a centimeter from his lips. "So, my dear, what do you have planned for me? Can I open this?" She looks to the envelope.

"Please do," he says excitedly.

She opens the envelope to find two tickets to a marionette production of H.P. Lovecraft short stories. "You're kidding me?"

"No, I don't think so. I am pretty sure this is not a production for children. I have known about this troupe doing this for about six months. I am happy that I get to take you; I was worried that I was not going to be able."

An image of Aris and Nora at a play passes through her mind. "I didn't even hear about this…"

"I was thinking of giving you these ticks as a Christmas present. I almost told you about it several times. It was a hard secret to keep." He smiles and puts his arm around her back and kisses the top of her head. "Ready?"

"Yes. I just need my coat." She looks behind her to the couch where her black woolen trench lies. She picks it up and walks to the coat closet. She hangs it on a hangar and chooses her brown, fur collared cape. "I never get to wear this coat. Save today." Rose looks at her date. "You have a new coat, too."

"Old one. I just picked it up at Lin's today. I used one of your coupons. She wasn't there. I think I met her cousin."

"Nice lines."

"It's a little scratchy. I guess that is the reason why I bought a new coat," Aris reports.

Rose follows the lines of his coat down his shoulders to his hands and grabs his right. "I'm ready. Marionettes and Lovecraft." She walks into the hall in an absolute daze. "Marionettes and Lovecraft." She lifts her arms in front of her, closes her eyes and continues to walk.

Aris laughs. "What are you doing?"

"Sleep walking – marionettes and Lovecraft. And Aris," Rose says dreamily.

"And dinner. I have reservations at the City Café. They have crab cakes and portabella risotto," he says as he helps his zombie actress through the doors to the parking deck.

The two arrive in high spirits at 7:28 for a 7:30 reservation. The hostess happily seats them in the front window. Rose orders the crab cakes and Aris orders the mushroom risotto with a Merlot. Although they have known each other for years, there is a new energy surrounding them, an animated, anxious energy.

"So you have not spoken of California. Did you have a nice time?" asks Rose.

"The weather was very nice. The traffic… what is it you say… yikes?! I had a nice time with Sam, the project manager. We have to go back there again on Monday for another full week."

"Sorry, I do not want to have this conversation. Marionettes and Lovecraft! Oh my goodness, oh my goodness," she says jumping up and down in her chair. She stops to reclaim maturity before asking, "You were going to take Nora?"

"Well, no. It's not exactly her kind of thing," he admits with a furrowed brow. He shifts in his chair and adroitly changes the topic of conversation. "You have a favorite Lovecraft story, right?"

"'The Outsider,' definitely," Rose complies.

"And why do you like Lovecraft so much?" Aris sips his wine.

"For starters, it is an awesome last name," Rose says simply. "However, I am pretty sure that doesn't answer your question. Well, his style, I guess. He has such a vivid descriptive style. My favorite turn of descriptive phrase is from 'The Outsider.' He wrote something to the effect of 'a ghoulish shade of antiquity and decay.' Is it effect or affect? Anyway, in my teenaged mind, I knew exactly what that looked like – a ghoulish shade… The other thing I like about him is how his life is so eerily parallel to Edgar Allen Poe. Like great codas in classical music, some minds bear repeating."

"I guess I read him as a teenager, too. Admittedly, I have not taken a look at him with my more adult-ish mind."

"It's the idea of delivering Lovecraft via marionettes that is so remarkable," she continues. "I've been thinking a lot about evil lately – just plain evil. Earlier this week, I was reading about the history of Ghana and the castles that all these different nations built to hold the slaves to be traded. Civilized nations. How did that kind of thing happen? How scary is that? It is just plain evil. Marionettes... they just start to form in your mind, don't they?" Rose looks up as the waitress delivers their meal.

Aris turns his plate and then places his napkin on his lap. He picks up his wine glass to Rose. "To God." Rose meets his glass and smiles. Aris continues, "Did you know that a marionette puppeteer is actually called a Manipulator? And one of the very first marionettes was of the Virgin Mary, and that marionette in French literally means 'little Mary'? Factoids that I thought would put my beautiful little theologian into a flap."

"Talk about suspending disbelief," Rose offers her joke as she places the white linen napkin on her lap.

Aris nods in agreement.

"Your theologian into a flap..." She raises her wrists to her shoulders and flaps her hands like little wings. She squints in thought as she says, "Actually, that is more than a little bit creepy, scary even – little Mary? Truly, I have always had a little problem with the story of Mary. I think that God could have given her - and let us be fair Eve, too - a bit more information. God could have told Adam and Eve that there was something other than perfect divinity present in the garden. He told them about the tree, but did not warn them about the snake. And then Mary, always depicted stomping on the snake, the angel could have warned her about how much her son would suffer. And now I will have to revisit the story with her 'strings' being pulled by the 'Manipulator.' Now your little flapping theologian wants to ask whether or not the angel who spoke with Mary was actually the snake? I think she should have said, 'No.' Or maybe she should have said, 'Let me think about it' and then asked a few more questions.'"

Rose lifts a bit of the very lightly breaded crab cake to her mouth and melts. "This is delicious." She pushes and turns her plate for Aris. "Please try this."

"Are you kidding me? After that exposition, you are going to turn your plate and offer me the proverbial apple; if so, wisdom dictates that I should decline." He smiles. "Right?"

"I think you are supposed to offer me a bite of yours," she says while covering her mouth with her napkin.

Aris serves a spoonful to her lips and steals a bit of her crab on the return. "Lovecraft and Marionettes."

"Have you seen Nora? Have you spoken to her? Does she pretty much hate me?" Rose asks quickly as if she was pulling of a Band-Aid.

"I have seen and spoken to her; and yes, she pretty much hates you," he states the matter-of-fact. "I saw her this afternoon, actually."

Rose's face flushes red. "This afternoon?"

"Yeah. She came by to pick up a few more things," Aris explains.

"How angry is she?" Rose asks as she looks down at her plate.

"She was yelling almost the entire time she was there."

"So, how are you? I mean, are you okay?"

"I'm fine. I feel... well, I hate the fact that I hurt her. I hate the fact that I let her down. But, I think I made the right decision for the both of us. And I think she knows it, too. I think she knows that I made the right decision." Aris grips his napkin with his right hand. "It's not like this break-up was out of the blue. We have been pulling away from each other for months."

"Still. I know this has got to be painful for you, and her,"

Rose says looking for his eyes. "I guess you probably should have stayed somewhere else," she says pushing her crab to the right with her fork.

"Rose, those four days were the easiest days I have spent in months, possibly years. And I need you to know that." He sets his spoon down into his risotto and then picks up his napkin to wipe his mouth. "Those four days – I felt like I was actually moving forward."

Rose stops breathing for thirty seconds and then breathes in and out through her nose producing a small bit of noise. "I want to say words like 'good' or 'I am glad,' yet somehow they don't relate to…" She starts to get a little flustered. She lifts a bit more crab into her mouth and watches Aris pensively stare at her dish. She continues, "I know this conversation is terribly awkward right now. Three weeks ago you could freely talk to me, if you wanted. I was your friend. Now things have changed and our equilibrium has shifted. I like Nora and pretty much always have and sincerely don't blame her if she needs to dramatize. Frankly, I know what it feels like to lose you. And I don't mind if you need to talk about her; and I would pretty much prefer it – given that the task you gave me is to trust you." She pushes the last bit of crab to the left. "So here I am on my limb again – my greatest fear, my fear about you and Nora, is that I am either 'the other woman' or 'the rebound.'" She stabs at the pile. "And I need you to know that I am neither – I am something else."

He raises his eyes. "Rose, I hope you can hear this well – but that kind of coolness, can easily be interpreted as cold. You sound scripted."

She reacts with a detached whisper. "The cold and the scripted." Rose engages, her voice louder, "Cold and scripted? Ouch! You really know how to… I just wanted to start the conversation."

"Sorry, residual stuff… I did not mean …If it makes you feel better, I defend you to her as well." Aris stabs his risotto with his spoon, breathes, and then regains control. "You said you wanted to talk about it. And some of it is not pretty and a lot of it is hard to hear."

Rose hears him. "You're right. Are you sure we should be doing this? Dating? Maybe we should wait."

"What is it about wisdom dictating..?" Aris asks with a smirk.

"You always seem to answer my questions with another question."

Aris smiles. "Do I?"

Rose laughs. "I guess wisdom dictates that there is no such thing as perfect divinity – even in the garden."

"I really think our friendship can withstand this," Aris says commandingly.

"Did you just answer my question?"

"I did."

Aris looks startled as the waitress tentatively approaches. "Can I get the two of you anything else?" The waitress starts to clear the table. "Coffee? Perhaps, dessert?"

"Coffee, perhaps dessert?" Rose smiles at her date. "What 'tis this thing of which thy speak. Would *I* want any of those?"

"Crème brulee?" Aris asks smiling.

Rose jumps in her chair. "Really, they have crème brulee?"

Even the waitress laughs at her excitement. "Two or one?"

"Two coffees and two crème brulees, please," Aris places the order.

The waitress quickly leaves the table and Rose recaps, "Let me get this straight. Lovecraft, Marionettes and Crème Brulee!"

"There is talk of a garden too," Aris responds.

"Dreamy."

"I heard that relationships are all about timing."

"You did not hear that from me."

"Really?" Aris says prodding one of their first date conversations years ago.

"No, relationships are all about value. You need to value the same things."

"Do you think we need to wait?" Aris asks.

"Do you?" Rose laughs. "See, I can answer questions with questions, too."

"Did you know that in Burma the term for marionette puppetry is called Yoke thé. Burmese marionettes are very intricate as they employ 18 wires for male characters and 19 wires for female characters. My question is – why does the female require one more string?"

She lifts her hair into a ponytail with both hands. "Good question – probably some nefarious reason – the swing of her hip, perhaps."

Their desserts and coffee arrive. They indulge in a comfortable silence. Aris mimes the request for the check.

"Thanks for dinner, Aris, excuse me." She quickly stands and turns from her chair and with a strong stride walks to the ladies restroom. She uses the facilities and then washes her hands while staring into her own eyes. She reaches into her purse and pulls out her toothbrush and paste. She finishes with raspberry lip gloss. "You are not cold, and neither is he. You need to wait," she says to the mirror as she purses her lips together. She walks back through the dining room and stands next to her seat. "Marionettes – I can almost see them."

The pair walks to the car. Aris actually uses his key to unlock the passenger side door. Rose starts to sit. With one foot in the wheel-well, she turns to Aris who is still holding the door. "Aris, I think we should…"

Aris lifts his left hand and grabs the back of her neck. He pulls her face toward his and powerfully kisses her. "Sorry, I couldn't wait."

Rose closes her eyes and shakes her head and immediately returns his action. The two stand and gently kiss until they hear the siren of the nearby firehouse.

Aris looks directly into her eyes. "Rose, I think I am ready." He kisses her lips once more and takes his hand from her. His eyes direct her to the seat. He closes the door as she places her hands in her lap. He opens his door and quickly takes his seat and starts the car in what would appear to be the same movement. He looks at her and shuts the door. "Lovecraft and marionettes."

"I am scared," Rose admits. "And a little bit dizzy."

Aris gloats, "All part of my plan." He guns his engine and starts the seven block trip to the playhouse.

When they reach, Rose pulls the tickets from her purse and hands them to Aris. "If you can handle me, you can certainly handle these." She lifts her finger tips to her cheeks. "I still can't feel my face."

Rose begins to open the car door as Aris darts around the front to help her. He takes her gloved hand and kisses the top. "First date etiquette – I will get the doors." He tries to catch her eyes as she tries to hide them.

The two enter the playhouse and take their seats in the center of the second row of eight. They describe to each other the things they find interesting as more of the audience arrives. The room darkens and the little theatre curtains open. The first story told is 'The Lurking Fear.' Aris spends a good deal of the first story watching Rose watch the marionettes. Halfway through, he reaches his right hand into her lap. She takes her eyes off the narrator and looks down upon his hand. She grabs the offering with both of her hands and holds it until Intermission.

"Would you like a fine concession?" Aris stands from his chair.

"Swedish fish?" She smiles hoping he remembers their *first* first date.

"Swedish fish, still? I will be right back." He inches past several people sitting on his left.

"Swedish fish always." Rose watches Aris walk through the double doors while flipping through the program in search of the promise for future marionette productions. She daydreams about driving with Aris to Cleveland to catch the May marionette production of *Romeo and Juliet*. Three minutes later, Aris returns shaking his head and showing he is empty handed. "Jujubes are not Swedish fish." He takes his seat just as the house lights start to drop and returns his hand to her lap.

The next story told is 'He.' The sets exquisitely portray the labyrinths and passages of time the story requires. Their use of lighting is ingenious and completely and essentially captures the dark magical feel of the short story. Rose is impressed into silence and can scarcely speak in the car ride back to her apartment. Aris pulls into the parking deck and into his recent usual space. He turns off the engine and smiles as he looks at his completely silent Rose. "Lovecraft and marionettes."

She awakens from her thoughts and recognizes where she is. "Aris…Thanks for thinking of me. Thanks for the Lovecraft and the totally inspired manipulators." She scans his face and then traces the perfect arch of his right eyebrow with her thumb, resting her hand at his ear.

Aris raises his hand to her cheek and gently kisses her. "So… stage three, I need to walk you to your door." He smooches her lips once more and then steps out into the parking deck. Rose is out of her seat and next to the car before he can reach her.

"Oops. I guess I'm too fast."

"It is probably the cape," he says as he, out of habit, checks to make sure the door is locked. Aris does reach the door to the building in time. The pair ascends the three flights of stairs and reaches her apartment door.

Rose reaches into her purse and collects her keys. "Do you have a plan for now?"

"So, that thing we did outside of my car around 8:32 and then again inside my car at 11:46. I would like to do that until 7:30 AM on Monday. My flight leaves at 10:15," Aris says while slipping off her left glove.

Rose feels static throughout her entire body. "Good God. Help."

Aris takes her verbal cue to push his art form a bit further, and he pulls her body to his. They kiss with Rose's back pressing against the door. He deftly takes the keys from Rose's hand. "We need to get this door open."

"Stop. Aris, we need to talk."

"No, Rose, we really don't." He starts kissing her neck.

"Good God. Aris, you have got to stop. I can't think."

"All part of my plan."

Rose starts to get angry. "Stop. We really need to talk."

"I'm sorry, you were saying..." He giggles as he moves to the other side of her neck. "I can talk with my lips on your skin."

"Listen, the last time we seriously talked is right beyond this door..." Rose feels his lips and starts to lose her concentration. She rallies by grabbing his jaw and holding it still at a slight distance so she can see his eyes. She is able to speak, "Before Christmas, before New Year's, before your weeks in California... you asked me to trust you."

Aris looks at her. "I remember." Aris starts kissing the inside of her wrist while tugging at the remaining glove. He pulls her arm around his neck as he brings his own around her waist and easily finds her lips. Static starts to fill her ears and the fighter stirs. "Stop."

Aris finally understands and looks directly into her eyes. "I'm sorry. I hear you."

Rose leans her back on the door and slides all the way down into her easy Filipino squat.

"Let's go inside," Aris says in a whisper.

"Aris, sit," Rose says authoritatively. "There is no easy way to say this, so I am just going to come right out and say it. And boy, because of the last few seconds, it is going to be super *awkward*."

"What do you need to say?" Aris says unsuspectingly as he

sits down next to her.

"I was raped about a year before I met you."

"I am sorry, what did you just say?"

"And now I am afraid to..." Rose sits on the ground and stretches her legs in front of her.

"What?" Aris says out of breath. "What?"

Rose looks at him with an apology in her eyes. "He said he was going to ruin me for other men." She continues to speak barely audibly, "And although many, and I mean many, fulfilling, or is it fool-filling years have passed I can still hear those words – echoing."

"How come you did not tell me about this? How could you keep *this* from me?" Aris asks trying to find his breath, his mind, and his control. He was losing all three.

She continues with an apologetic look, "A lot of it was my fault. I was there smoking pot and drinking alcohol – you know, feeling sexy. I was there in a large part due to the pot and the alcohol; I am an addict."

"Rose... I didn't..." Aris tries to speak.

She lifts her hand to mime stop. "A year later, I met you. I prayed to meet someone like you. I remember one night, our second night. It was my birthday and one of the last few times I got intoxicated. I stayed with you that night. And on the ride to your place, you explained to me that nothing was going to happen. The following morning I left and drove back. I climbed in bed and started to cry, bawl actually. I bawled for hours. You were the first in my entire life, other than my family, to demonstrably care about me, to want more for me than I wanted for myself. You changed my life irrevocably. I was in love the very next day. I fell in love and you found... a drunk. It was another two to three months before I gave up the drugs and alcohol. I did mostly because... mostly because of you, and for you."

"I really did not know how much you were hurting. I really didn't," Aris says scanning the profile of his date.

"He hurt me. I know you can probably easily understand that. He hurt me – bruised me." Rose lifts up her hands to massage her own shoulders. "Some pretty severe bruising."

"Rose, I need to know, how come you never told me about this?" Aris asks.

"This is where my brain gets in the way. I spent a lot of nights talking to God, asking for the strength I needed to understand why I had to be there that day. Every day I prayed for the understanding. And a few years later, I started to hear the response. I started to trust myself again and to listen to my mind – my body of work. God gave me a talent – to see movements in history. It is funny how much of historical moments could be characterized and understood as instances of rape." Rose smiles. "Funny."

"Funny does not seem to fit here," Aris says returning her lightness he perceives to be for his benefit.

"Ha Ha," Rose says dryly. She looks to Aris with the crown of her head rolling against the door. "Think about it, historical events that happen, like Ghana, or even this chocolate thing… these things happen and you cannot even begin to process what is happening until it is over. 'Till the deed is done." Rose exhales a laugh through her nose. "And the victors tell the story and the victims have to prove the wrong."

"I don't, I can't…" Aris says trying to listen through the static in his ears.

"I did not tell you about it… mostly because of the thread I used to sew up the rip in my soul." She looks down at her hands. "I find it interesting that the history of man's understanding of their place in history and their placement of women in their history – says more about them than it does about women. Seize them, rape them, tame them, and then blame them."

"I wish I could say that I understand what you just said. I don't. Maybe we could go inside and talk about this…"

"Not yet. There are some things I do not want to bring

inside. Understand?"

Aris nods. "I'm trying."

She picks up lint from the carpet and utters into the silent hallway, "It's like the Yoke thé and the one extra string. It's like my Eve and my Mary, and the things their taut strings have taught me." She piles the collected lint in her hand and balances the pile on Aris's bent knee.

Aris puts his left arm around her and holds her right hand in his and gently drops his head against the door to look at her.

Rose answers his question, "I guess another reason I did not tell you is because of the words that the garden variety snake said – 'I am going to ruin you for other men.'" She puts her crown to the door again to look at Aris, her eyes filled with water.

"I am sorry," Aris says sincerely as he lifts her hand to his mouth and holds it to his lips.

"I am not looking for an apology." Rose offers a wry, reflective smile. "You did nothing wrong. You saved me from utter annihilation with your simple inaction years ago. I guess what I need you to know is that at this point, I cannot forgive him. I am pretty sure God will not allow it. And that burden... well that burden can weigh pretty heavy on me."

"I don't understand," Aris says, and then awkwardly laughs. "I keep on saying that."

"I wouldn't be telling you this if I didn't know that you could understand. For now, it is enough for you to know that I have this issue and well, I may... I may accidentally take it out on you. You can't let me."

Aris looks at her hand in his as he leans his head on her shoulder.

"When you called me cold so many years ago...I guess I am a little worried that this is the cause of what you felt from me."

He abruptly lifts his head. "Rose, why didn't you tell me? I should have known before we..."

"It is not that easy. It's not exactly the kind thing you can easily talk about, no matter how much time passes. It is easier now because I understand a bit better. I gave it a reason for existing."

"It shouldn't have happened." Aris eyes shift right to left as he tries to process what he has heard tonight. "Instances of rape?" Aris closes his eyes and utters, "You said it was the thread you used? I don't understand." Aris stutters with a tone of desperation, "What can I do?"

"You already have done what I needed – years ago. I think I just needed time to separate love from sex."

Aris furrows his brow, looks at her finger nails and then releases an awkward giggle. "I want to inappropriately quote St. Elmos Fire right now."

Rose smiles. "Ally Sheedy's character telling Andrew McCarthy's character that 'sex isn't love.'"

"Wow, I am impressed." Aris kisses her fingertips.

"I have thought about telling you many times before. I just didn't want to look like a victim or a fool or whatever crazy thing my psychological-self predicted your reaction would be. Again, it's my thread; it is my soul."

"Rose, I really think we should go inside."

"So praying helped and so did the Quran, ironically enough. My innermost self remains intact and protected. God knows the secret of my heart."

Aris scans her face as her tears begin to dry in her eyes. "I can only imagine," Aris says, squeezing her hand, "that is some limb you are standing on."

"Well, at least you know what the ground looks like to a girl like me." She lifts his hand to her mouth and kisses it. "So, you see, I don't know what is behind this door. I do know that although I am pretty severely bruised, I am not broken. Yet Aris, the way I feel about you... if I let you through this door – the potential for complete and total devastation is imminent." She flexes her feet as she tries to stretch her legs. "In summation, I can trust blindly... yet you need to know that I am not and cannot be blindly obedient." With a weary sigh she asks, "What time is it?"

"12:20 – It is getting pretty late," Aris says. "How about I make you a cup of hot cocoa? Let's go inside."

Rose flutters her eyelashes and flashes a grin. "I am still pretty light, considering." She quickly stands by pulling her knees to her chest and then standing from a full squat. She watches Aris select the correct key to enter the apartment. She watches as he closes the door and locks it.

Rose looks up to Aris's tender bewilderment and touches his stomach through his sweater, inches above the belt. "I do not want to talk about this anymore."

"Are you sure?" Aris asks sensitively.

She flirts eye contact and turns away slowly. "Hot cocoa? I need a moment. I need to change. I need to put on fuzzy socks."

"Hot cocoa with toasted marshmallows." Aris watches her disappear from the hallway into her room.

Aris immediately begins his task by locating the cocoa and searching for the recipe ingredients. Using matching mugs he fills one with milk, twice, and dumps the milk into the small sauce pan. He finds a tiny whisk in the ceramic column on the counter. He is confident that she probably calls the curled spring her cocoa whisk. As he waits for the milk to warm, he lights candles on the mantle and the coffee table. He notices that the puzzle is no longer on the coffee table.

"Rose, did you finish the puzzle?" No answer. He lights the fire and walks back to return to his duties at the stove. Nearly ten minutes later, a fresh faced Rose appears in the kitchen wearing a hot pink velour jump suit.

"You found my cocoa whisk!"

Aris melts. "I did." He leans to kiss the top of her forehead. "You smell good. Clean."

"Thanks," she says as she walks to the other side of the island. "I know. We need skewers." She grabs two fondue skewers from the utility drawer and a bag of marshmallows and takes them over to the coffee table. She sits down on her side of the couch and watches as Aris pours the cocoa into the mugs. He turns off the kitchen light with his elbow and carries the two mugs to the table. He carefully passes the mug to Rose before sitting.

She takes a sip. "Good cocoa." She sets her mug down to place a marshmallow on each of the skewers. She hands one to Aris and grabs the two dinner candles from the mantle and places one in front of Aris. "You pretty much have to use dinner candles to toast marshmallows."

"I didn't know," he says smiling as he passes the marshmallow through the flame.

"Live and learn, my love," she says as she blows out her marshmallow. "I like burnt marshmallows." She sets the other side on fire and lets it burn for a few seconds before blowing it out. Finally, she pushes the marshmallow into her hot cocoa and sits back into the couch.

"I think people say they like their marshmallows burnt when really they don't want to take the time to properly toast them." Aris looks down his nose at her mug of cocoa. Rose points to the marshmallow he just dropped too close to the flame and laughs. He blows on the marshmallow. "I suppose the point is for me to learn what it is you like."

"We are toasting marshmallows, not cheese," she says with a bit too much volume while staring at the candle. "This is really good cocoa. I sometimes add a pinch of decaf crystals for a mocha-y cocoa. Yet, as always, the original recipe is always the best."

"I noticed the puzzle is not here. Did you finish it?"

"I did. I hope you don't mind. It is actually hanging on the wall in your room, if you want to see it."

"Maybe later," Aris says. "I almost forgot. How did your meeting go with Nightingale?"

"Pretty good. I am meeting at noon tomorrow at the Lodge to draft a letter to go to the Boy Scouts of America's corporate offices. I think she is on board."

"Congratulations, Rose. I am proud of you."

"Again, with the fragile, I do not want to get my hopes up. The letter could be ignored and…you know the rest. I dare say I am at the very least optimistic."

"You are not fragile," Aris states. "Would you like to see a movie with me tomorrow after your meeting?"

"I'd love to. We could catch a late matinee."

He finishes his cocoa. "I should really get going." Aris looks down the hall. "On second thought, if you don't mind, I guess I would rather stay here. I'd sleep in the other room."

"Okay," Rose offers a gentle smile. "I want to take a shower and go to sleep. I am tired."

"I'll take care of things here," Aris says touching her cheek with his thumb. "Rose, thanks for trusting me."

"In spite of my shape right now, I had a really nice time tonight. Thanks for dinner and thanks for Lovecraft and thanks for the Yoke thé," she says as she moves her body closer to his on the couch. "And thanks for the kiss at 8:22 and 11:46 and 11:52 and…" Rose looks at the clock and whispers, "and at 1:19."

He returns her kiss with his right hand on her cheek. "Thanks for… your trust." He kisses the tip of her nose twice. "I had a very good time tonight, too."

"Thanks for listening." She finds her breath and welcomes the oxygen. She stands and touches his hair. "Thanks for being here."

"I really couldn't be anywhere else. And if I were somewhere else, I probably couldn't sleep."

Rose leaves the living room and performs her evening rituals particularly slowly. She wishes Aris a good night before closing the door to her bedroom. She finds sleep in 22 minutes.

CHAPTER 20
THE LION THE TIGER AND THE FOX

A Lion and a Tiger jointly seized on a young fawn, which they immediately killed. A fierce battle ensued, and as each animal was in the prime of his age and strength, the combat was long and furious. At last they lay stretched on the ground panting, bleeding and exhausted, each unable to lift a paw against the other. An impudent Fox coming by at the time stepped in and carried off before their eyes the prey on account of which they had fought so savagely. "Woe betide us," said the Lion, "that we should suffer so much to serve a Fox!" – Aesop

Rose reaches into her purse resting on the seat of her grocery cart to locate her singing cell phone. She catches the name on the way up to her ear. "Hello, Nick."

"Hey, Rose, did I catch you at a bad time?" Nicolas asks.

"I am trying to figure out how to tell whether a spaghetti squash is ripe," Rose says as she shakes a medium sized squash in her opposite ear. "Apparently, you can smell a melon. Anyway, what's up?"

"They wrote back," Nicolas says expeditiously. "A letter arrived in the mail today, an actual letter."

"Quick snail mail." Rose puts down the squash. "My ancestor would probably have a joke for this occasion. Well, what does it say?"

"I hate reading aloud," Nicolas responds. "They would like for us to make a presentation at a planning committee meeting in three weeks. Apparently, they were already assembling to discuss next year's Jamboree. They apologized for the short notice."

"Jamboree?"

"Oh yeah, I forgot you were never a Scout – my compliments. Every year the entire national organization gets together for one giant camp out. I went the year before my Eagle – it was fun."

"I knew that. Well, I think I knew that. Three weeks? So soon?"

"Hey, no worries, I thought your first presentation was pretty awesome – we could tweak it," Nicolas says supportively. "We just need to get together and brain storm and well... try to figure out how to deliver this. I am going to call Mike and Heath and see about getting together tomorrow late afternoon, after work. Want to meet up tomorrow at 5:30 at the Lodge? We will order pizza and knock this thing out!"

"You want to give the presentation? It would probably sound better coming from you."

"I think Mike is our man," Nicolas responds. "He's very comfortable talking and also very good at giving speeches... I hate both. Although, I think you would be the best for the job, just maybe not quite appropriate."

"No deer in headlights, got ya. I respect the organization – I really do. And frankly, I am thankful that I will not have to deliver the speech. I can meet tomorrow night at 5:30. Hey, do you think we could take a few of your kids to Irving, maybe we can write a little yarn for them – to introduce the motion?"

"Tomorrow. Let's talk about it tomorrow. I got to call the guys. See you tomorrow. Have fun choosing that squash." The call drops.

Rose completes her shopping list before calling her mother first, and then Aris to share her success. She spends the remainder of her evening reviewing her slides and writing down her suggestions for how to proceed in an outline. She decides to do an hour of yoga in her living room and follows the stretch with a bath. She opens her window and climbs into bed. She finds sleep in 23 minutes.

***

At 5:21, Rose pulls into the parking lot of the Boy Scout

Lodge located on Mountain Trail Road. She enters the conference room and finds Heath and Nicolas tossing a beanbag back and forth across the table. "Hi, Nick. Hi, Heath."

Nicolas looks at his watch. "Eight minutes early. My guess is that Mike will be here in 5 minutes."

"I think I saw him pulling into the parking lot just as I entered. I guess he will be here in one," Rose says, smirking, as she sets her laptop satchel down on the table two seats to the left of Nicolas. She looks over her shoulder as Mike walks in. "Hi, Mike." A bean bag whizzes past her head and is caught with his right arm behind his back and returned with the same movement in reverse.

"Hi, Rose," Mike says. "Way to get the ball rolling. Hey guys, this is really happening." He lifts his hands in front of his face to mime a football's receiver and seconds later receives the bag. He whips it back to Heath before taking a seat. "Who ordered the pizza and when is it getting here?"

"I did," Heath says as he flings a five dollar bill into the middle of the table. "Two large pies – one with pepperoni. D'Angelos." Mike reaches into his wallet and also throws a fiver. Nicolas throws in five ones. Rose takes the fifteen and snaps a crisp $20 and walks to Heath to hand him the money. She pulls a few additional dollars from her right hand and sets them on top of the twenty.

"Thanks, Rose." Heath takes the money. "I'll go stand lookout."

"February 13th, guys. That does not give us a lot of time," Nicolas says, looking to Rose and then Mike. "Did you happen to actually write out that speech you gave us?"

"I did make pretty careful notes, yet I would not exactly say it is written out." Rose hands a printed copy of her presentation and the typed note pages to Mike. "Did you hear?" Rose asks with a smile.

Mike shows off his Cheshire. "I did. I love the spotlight.

Good practice for when I accept the nomination for President. This is an awesome resume builder – speaking at a national conference for the Boy Scouts of America - are you kidding me? And hey, it would be totally cool for our guys to actually proffer a merit badge like this – it will look really good on their college applications. I am pretty psyched and, well, proud of us right now."

"He's so pretty," Nicolas jests. "It does feel right."

Rose cannot hide her own prideful smile. She is happy to be here for this conversation. "Hey, no jinxing. We have a pretty hard speech to write and it is not like we are asking for an afternoon or a weekend. We are actually asking for a campaign – Mr. President." Rose looks to Mike. "President? Really?"

"I love politics. I love the law. I love the spotlight. And have you seen my teeth?" Mike smiles again.

Heath walks in with the pizzas and a cold 2-liter of Coke. "Hey, want to grab some paper towels from the supply room?" he asks Nicolas, who steps out to do just that. He then looks at Rose and Mike. "You want to be Senator by 40, right?"

Mike looks to Rose. "He's right. My plan is to run for Senator – I have eight years to hit my stride. Who knows, this might be my ticket – my first step."

Rose nods. "We could use a few more Boy Scouts in Senate seats."

Nick returns with paper cups, plates and towels. "Alright guys, we have pizza and work."

Nicolas authoritatively takes over the meeting. "Rose mentioned on the phone maybe taking a few of our guys with us to Irving – to introduce the project using their enthusiasm. I think that it is a very good idea. I'm thinking that maybe we could ask the Senior Patrol Leader from each troop and pull together an old-fashioned yarn to be performed in Irving."

"A reenactment of the Battle of Mafeking?" Heath asks.

"Maybe we could totally psyche them out. How about this - we use two people to stage a reenactment of the Battle of Mafeking and as an aside we could have two Scouts commenting about how they would want to do something like that," Rose suggests. "Wait, did that make sense?"

"You mean like those Muppet guys, Waldorf and Statler?" Heath says.

"I love those guys," Nicolas admits.

"Well, sorta. I guess I wasn't joking," Rose says laughing at herself. "Muppets." Rose is distracted by Aris for a brief moment. "At least you guys got stage direction. It's sorta like a canon... two scouts will talk about Mafeking... and then two Scouts could talk about how cool Mafeking must have been... and two Scouts talking about the risk... and the two Scouts talking about a different kind of risk..." Rose sighs. "Am I making sense? Or should I start looking up hearing aid jokes?"

"Any playwrights in the house? Kermit?" Nicolas asks. He gives Rose a smile.

Heath says, "We could ask the troops to write something up. Yet we are running pretty short on time. We have to actually get the guys to agree to it, and the parents, and the money... nobody is talking about the amount of money it is going to take to make this trip."

"Baden-Powell to the Rescue – 'Camp Fire Yarn #1,'" Nicolas interjects. "The Mafeking Boy Scouts' is already written by Baden-Powell. We could have one set of guys do the original production and then we can write our own Waldorf Statler yarn."

"He's right." Rose tugs at her computer satchel and pulls out her copy of *Scouting for Boys*. She opens the book to page 9 to show Mike and Heath. Rose slides the book into the middle of the table and grabs a second piece of plain pizza.

"How did you know that?" Heath looks at Nicolas.

"Rose completed the requirements for a merit badge in 'Entrepreneurship' to pitch this idea to me. So anyway, I promised her that I would at least read it. I ended up learning lots of stuff about Baden-Powell including the story of the battle of Mafeking."

Mike looks to Rose. "Seriously, you completed merit badge requirements? You are so odd." He shakes his head in disbelief and then turns to Heath. "I am pretty sure... just about positive ... I can get a couple of my guys to agree to do this. They are thinking about college applications already and really want early acceptance into an Ivy League school. If they cannot for whatever reason, there are three of us... we can somehow... Okay so we need at least two more guys." Mike then looks to Nicolas. "I think that the chocolate peanut butter thing from Rose's speech could make a pretty good Waldorf Statler yarn. If we time the two productions to be done within the speech... it would make pretty interesting viewing, right?"

"Mr. President, I think you are correct," Nicolas says smiling and grabbing another two pieces of pepperoni. He looks at Rose. "I really liked the one good turn deserves another bit. Very compelling."

Rose blushes. "Ahh, shucks."

"I really liked your speech too," Mike says, holding the speech in his hand. "I have Photoshop and I think I could make a few improvements. I think you did most of this in PowerPoint, right?"

"Yes, and I just used the Paint program to do the simple additions to the pictures," Rose admits. "They were a little rough – yet I thought they got the idea across."

"They did. Definitely," Mike says.

Rose pulls out a zip drive. "I could give you the presentation and you can take it home and work on it. Nick, how much time do we have? Did they include a meeting agenda?"

"Yes, we have 1 ½ hours." Nicolas responds. "It is almost too much time."

"Well, I am pretty sure that the speech is about 30 minutes – give or take. If we add the two yarns in – let's say that adds another 30 minutes... then that leaves 30 minutes for open discussion."

"You forgot about the chocolate," Health correctly points out while tossing the bean bag up into the air.

"Huh. I guess I did. Funny. I suppose we could give Rebekah the floor at the end of our presentation with her explaining her role to help support the program."

"We could flank her with two scouts holding Chips on their shoulders," Nicolas adds with a sardonic smile.

Rose pulls out her computer and turns it on. While waiting for the boot-up, she moves a chair closer to Nicolas. "I sent Melissa an email today explaining what we were doing. I asked her to join us, yet she replied that she couldn't make it. I would really like to keep her in the loop." She whispers, "I am worried that trying to hoist both these flags will… I don't know… sink the ship?"

"Space mission, Rose. Space mission." Nicolas gives a gentle punch to her shoulder.

Rose loads the slide presentation onto the key chain zip drive, stands and hands it across the table to Mike. "You can borrow my book, too; you might be able to scan a few more things into the presentation. He is actually a pretty darn good artist." She places her hand on the book and shoots it across the table, watching as it lands in his lap. She throws her hands up, making the manly gesture of a field goal. "Score."

Mike accepts with a soft grin. "Thanks." He flips through the book. "I am not sure if I ever read this."

"There are some pretty amusing sections. Like a section where he tries to explain that you can really tell a man's character by the wear of his soles." Rose smiles. "The British." Rose takes the last piece of cheese pizza and refills her paper cup.

"I think I need a recap," Heath says.

"I think I need a night-cap," Nicolas says.

"Beer at Charlie's? What do you say, Rose?" Heath asks.

"I say… well, I really like your bumper sticker idea and that we should get bumper stickers made. I have a friend that works at the local sign store and he can get me a discount. I think we should hand out bumper stickers at this meeting. And I actually don't drink... however, I would be happy to go to Charlie's. I have not been there in ages. I used to play pool there with a couple of friends." Rose looks at Nicolas and then adds, "I do think we need to recap and make sure we let Rebekah and Melissa know what needs doing."

"I'll come up with a bumper sticker – and send it to you by the end of the week – I mean weekend," Heath promises.

Rose smiles at Heath. "Thanks."

"Speaking of stickers... maybe it is sticker shock... I guess I should probably mention that I am a pretty serious Frequent Flyer, and I have amassed a lot of frequent flyer miles. I think I can use my miles for about four tickets, maybe five – so it could pay for the kids. I also collect Marriott points and can probably pay for a few rooms there – possibly three or four. I will have to make a few calls to see exactly what it is I can afford and let you guys know sometime this weekend. I am sure it would help, but I am not sure if it will help enough. Do you guys have a treasury or do you have to dip into your own pockets for this?" Rose asks earnestly.

"Cool and super generous - scratch that, almost ridiculously generous," Nicolas chimes. "I wanted to put off discussing the reality of the trip to our next meet. I am still awaiting information from various funds we have access to. I have already spoken to Daniel about this and he said that he would look into these details on our behalf. I am hoping that we can fund this project ourselves, our organization that is, yet knowing you are there to help is ... priceless." Nicolas looks kindly at Rose. "Just how much traveling do you do?"

"About ten days a month for about seven years. It is getting more and more difficult to do. In my twenties – it was kinda cool." Rose motions with her chin to her laptop. "I actually bought that with racked up frequent flyers."

"You're kidding me!" Nicolas says as he walks over to

look at her Sony Vaio.

"Yes, I am. I am actually kidding you. I cannot even imagine how many miles I would have to fly to make enough points to buy something actually worth having," Rose says. "Needless to say, I can pretty much fly anywhere in the world for free – and even take a few people with me. I went to Greenland via Paris on my last voyage. It is just that I don't want to travel on my free time. Anyway, I would be more than happy to donate my miles to your guys."

Heath and Mike are discussing the speech when Heath declares, "I think Sam's Club has huge plastic jars of peanut butter. I actually am a member, so I will check it out. It would be a good prop and probably cause a stink at baggage check."

"Sam's Club – can I go with you? I heard they have bags of frozen meatballs. My little brother loves meatballs. His birthday is next week," Nicolas explains his interest.

"Yeah, how about tomorrow?" Heath says. "I'll call when I get home from work."

Rose stands. "So I will write a letter to Rebekah and Melissa letting them know that we would like Rebekah to provide a fifteen minute presentation about her efforts to initiate the ChIP program utilizing the Boy Scout emblem on her chocolate peanut-butter car fleet. Incidentally, it is her 3rd highest grossing chocolate line."

"It might be pretty cool if I could introduce the idea for the Boy Scouts to produce the transportation to the schools, and then introduce her, or Melissa," Mike says. "I think I need to talk with Melissa about the speech. I am pretty sure that she will be the person attending the meeting and not Rebekah."

Rose sits and explains, "I am not so sure about that. I spoke with Melissa and she is thinking of contacting ABC News; she has a contact. This idea might get public attention pretty fast. I would not be surprised if Rebekah really does take the helm on this. I, for one, think she should. I think she will do this in honor of her mother."

"Mike, I think your idea is a good one. There should be a smooth transition between the two presentations," Nicolas interrupts. He whispers to Rose, "You're getting a bit ahead of yourself."

"Point taken." Rose looks down slightly embarrassed. "Killer honesty, man. Good call." Rose recovers. "Mike, I will draft a letter to both Rebekah and Melissa and then send it to you for revisions. And then you can pass it on to them – copying me and the rest of us. Agreed?"

"Sounds good," Mike replies. "Are we breaking at Charlie's? Nine ball?"

Rose nods. "I like nine ball."

"Beer and nine ball," Nicolas says. "I'll call Christina. You should call Meghan and see if she wants to join us. Hey, Heath, call Elle."

Rose opens her purse and pulls out her cell phone. "Hi, Aris. Want to meet me and Nick, Mike and Heath for a few games of pool at Charlie's on Eisenhower?" Rose listens for a few moments. "Great. We are leaving in five." Rose smiles as she looks around the room. *A job well... just starting.*

CHAPTER 21
THE WILD ASS AND THE LION

A WILD ASS and a Lion entered into an alliance so that they might capture the beasts of the forest with greater ease. The Lion agreed to assist the Wild Ass with his strength, while the Wild Ass gave the Lion the benefit of his greater speed. When they had taken as many beasts as their necessities required, the Lion undertook to distribute the prey, and for this purpose divided it into three shares. "I will take the first share," he said, "because I am King: and the second share, as a partner with you in the chase: and the third share (believe me) will be a source of great evil to you, unless you willingly resign it to me, and set off as fast as you can." –Aesop

Rose sets up her easel in preparation for Aris's arrival. Suffering under some serious emotional turmoil and exhaustion, she decides that a public date is out of the question and that she needs a setting to provide both distance and safety – a valentine portrait. She knows her body needs some distance and her mind needs some answers. She is sure she can get both; yet she is wary of the cost.

She is wearing a clingy ribbed white cotton tank dress that is undeniably flattering to her figure; it is her painting dress. The dress is wearing every color she has ever touched with a paint brush. Her hair is in a messy high pony-tail and she is wearing thin white ankle socks. She saunters to the kitchen to rinse and dry her paint palate as well as to pour water into two mason jars reserved for her brushes. She brings all three items back to the easel and sets them on the mantle to her left. Rose turns to her musical library and selects the Cranberries for nostalgic reasons.

She hears a quiet knock at the door and as she sock skates to the door, she whispers, "God give me strength and courage."

She unlocks the door and slides the chain. With a deep inhale, she opens the door. "Hi, Handsome."

"Hi, Gorgeous. I thought we were going out for dinner tonight. It's our Valentine's Day – or are you just running late?" Aris asks, still standing in the door determining with half of his mind just how long it will take him to get her out of that dress.

"Our Valentine's Day?" Rose says, forcing an unnecessary explanation.

"Yes, our Valentine's Day – six days early."

"Next weekend is actually closer… it's just after…"

"I suppose you're right. I could've gotten a discount on these…" He pulls a chocolate heart and a single rose from behind his back. "What was I thinking?"

"A chocolate heart. Wow. Just what I wanted!" Rose says with an unmistakable tone of indignation. "Thanks."

Aris looks confused. "I don't understand. Is something wrong? You realize there is actually chocolate in this heart, right?"

Rose ignores his questions. "I am ordering in." She grabs his hand and pulls him through the door. "I may let you choose between Chinese and Mexican. I also have a menu for Maria's." She watches him take off his coat to reveal a soft aqua color shirt tucked into black cords and then watches him turn to the closet to hang his coat. "Have I ever told you that you look great in blue?"

"Only every time I wear the color. Blue and black." Aris turns around from the closet and slides his right hand under one of the two three inches of fabric holding up her painter's dress and leans in to kiss her trapezoid. He moves to her neck and then finally her lips. "I missed you."

"You did? Really?" Rose asks, grabbing his hand and leading him to the couch. "How much?"

"I am not sure if I can quantify the emotion. Missing someone is an emotion, right?"

"I feel miss? Huh. I suppose it is. I think it is probably somewhere between hope and loss. I am familiar with those emotions – a bit too familiar." Rose wraps her fuzzy blanket around herself wishing it were armor. "How was your trip?"

"Good. Good and very informative," Aris responds unwittingly to her easy questions. "D.C. was fine. I tried calling several times last night. You didn't answer."

"I had a rough night. It wasn't pretty," Rose responds.

"Is something wrong? What happened?" Aris asks, grabbing her hand and intertwining his fingers in hers.

Rose abruptly takes her hand away and stands.

"Where are you going?" Aris asks, confused.

"I suppose the answer is - nowhere fast," Rose says walking toward the easel.

"Are you mad at me?" Aris asks.

"Why? Should I be?" Rose stares straight into his eyes. "So it's our Valentine's Day – and what's Valentine's without a little blood? I am drawing first and you need stay right there on the couch." She wipes what she thinks is an undetectable tear falling from her right eye. "And don't move," she says under her breath.

"What's wrong?" Aris asks with an unusually heightened volume particularly rare for him.

The dancer spots his eyes and then gently turns up the heat on the fire. She grabs the pencil tightly in her right hand and lifts it to the top of the canvas. "My Valentine," she says with doubt, "I would tell you to stay still, but…"

"I am almost afraid to move. I'd probably do that wrong, too. What did I do?" Aris asks.

"You don't know," Rose mutters quietly as she lets another discrete tear drop. She quickly wipes it with her thumb still clinging on to the pencil. "So tell me more about your trip."

"Good. I had dinner with my parents after the meeting. They are excited about their cruise," Aris adds conversationally.

"Cruisin' for a bruisin'," Rose says abruptly both smirking and glaring. "So what did you and your parents talk about?"

"Cruisin' for a what? We talked about… Alright, Rose,

why are you mad at me?" he asks with both genuine concern and quiet alarm in his eyes.

"I asked you a question. What did you and your parents talk about?" Rose slams down her pencil and then gently picks up her palate and brush.

"We talked about…" a dawning starts to appear on his face.

Rose says, "Ah, there it is." She picks up her arm and brush into the air to move the tank back onto her shoulder. "Pick a color – red, blue, yellow, black or white."

"Did you hear? How do you know?" Aris asks. "How could you have possibly heard that? It is not like it…" It finally occurs to him. "Facebook?"

"Aris, I asked you to pick a color – red, blue, yellow, black or white!" she exclaims with a bit of anger in her voice.

"Red," Aris says. "I was offered a promotion yesterday with a pretty hefty pay raise and definitely a more suitable set of duties. However, I am guessing that you already knew that."

"You chose red, yet you are in the black," Rose says peering over the easel. She forces a smile using the right corner of her mouth.

"I answered your question," Aris says rubbing the palms of his hands together. "Now you have to answer mine."

"Facebook. So, pray tell me, where is this job?"

"Rose." The color starts to leave his cheeks and he finally begins to recognize his place in her eyes. He stands and starts to walk towards her.

"Sit! Don't come anywhere near me," Rose barks as a few more quiet tears fall from her eyes.

"Rose, I did not tell you because I needed to think. I needed to…" Aris says as he decides that it is probably important, even strategic, that he follows her order. He returns to the couch.

"You needed to trust *me*," Rose says simply. "I thought we were friends. I thought you were my best friend. How could you keep this from me? When were you going to tell me?"

"This is a big deal – for me and my future," he says. "I guess that I thought that…well, I thought that…"

Rose sets the red brush in the water and picks up a finer point and dabs in the black. "Your future, a fine point," Rose says as she lets a few more tears drop, "and a big deal."

"The job is in D.C. and I am supposed to start mid-March," Aris continues. "It is a good job, Rose, a really good job."

"I do not doubt," she says quietly. "Well, then I am happy for you. Congratulations." Her hand trembles as she lines his eyebrows, yet regains composure as she places a tiny and early deliberate mole at the top of his nose, at the bridge. Rose musters courage and coldly asks, "So what about dinner? Italian?"

"You seemed more interested in Chinese fifteen minutes ago," he comments. He tries to catch her eyes with his.

"Paper versus Styrofoam. There is no difference," she responds coolly. "The menus are on the counter. You choose." She sets down her palate and walks to the bathroom. She closes the door and sinks to the floor. Trying hard to control the volume of her sobs, she muffles her face into the towel that was hanging on the back of the door before her fall. Three minutes later and after three deep inhales and exhales, she stands and walks to her sink and her mirror to see her eyes. *They are not there.* She grabs her Noxzema and cools her face and then rinses with cold water. *I am not really here.* She opens the bathroom door to find Aris standing outside holding his forearms gently in front of him.

"You moved," she says as she walks right past him and into the kitchen. She locates her water glass and fills it with ice from the refrigerator door. "So what did *you* decide?" She flips on the faucet for a quicker glass of water.

"Mexican," Aris responds from the other side of the island. "I know how much you like those sweet potato burritos. What do you call them – bourrée-toes?" He moves closer and with a gentle movement he tries to grab her right hand.

Rose reacts to his advance with a sharp retraction of her

arm and places her right hand within her left. "Something good for your résumé, I assume. Don't touch me…" Rose shifts to her distant foot "… you might get paint on you."

"Rose, I am sorry. I didn't mean to…" Aris says making another attempt to grab her hand.

Rose walks to the easel. "You are not giving me an apology – you are giving me an excuse. Yeah Rose, that is some freaking limb," she says very quietly, using her go-to dumb guy voice.

Aris actually does hear her. "You don't want an apology and you don't want an excuse. What do you want?" Aris asks tersely from across the room.

"How did you hear me?" Rose asks amazed.

"Answering my question with another question. The student becomes the master."

"No, I'm serious. How did you hear that?"

"Rose, what do you want?" Aris asks again, louder.

"Not the dream, I suppose." She pugnaciously grabs the small, wide, flat brush and dips in the blue. "I used to think I wanted to win the lottery."

"There is more news on Lin's tale of woe?" Aris asks trying to find the banter he loves.

"Actually, I have not talked to her in a while. I guess I have been busy. I haven't even had a chance to visit the café in over a week."

"You've called to let them know you are okay, right? They might file a missing person's report," Aris says jokingly.

"I have had an interesting couple of days. I spent them with Nick and Rebekah. I think that the 'Mafeking Challenge' is now in safe, trustworthy hands, and well, I guess it is pretty much out of mine."

"Good," Aris says too quickly. "Are you ready for Dallas?"

"It's weird. You'd think I'd be happy. I mean, I decided to do something and actually got it done - well, mostly done. You'd think I'd be happy, at least happier. I feel like I am losing something. I feel like I lost something... Like this project is my baby."

"You put a lot of work into it. I can understand what you are feeling."

"Really?" Rose says with an overt disbelief. "Really? You know what I am feeling? Right now? Seriously?"

"I'm in trouble, aren't I?"

"Not anything you can't get out of," she responds and starts making wider strokes with her brush. "I mean, you are moving to D.C...." She mixes to make orange, green and purple and starts adding them to the canvas. He stands in the kitchen leaning on the island and watches her in silence as she paints him in silence.

Ten minutes pass.

"I think I hear the delivery guy in the hallway." Seconds later, both hear a knock at the door. "I'll get it." Rose rushes to grab her wallet from her purse and then flings open the door.

"$14.98, Ma'am."

She grabs $20 from her wallet and places it in the delivery man's hands. "Thanks. Have a good night." She closes the door and looks to Aris, who is still standing in the kitchen. "Wanna get the plates?"

"I wanted to buy you dinner," he says as he retrieves two plates from the cupboard.

"I am not exactly sure if I care what you want," she says dryly as she places the two Styrofoam boxes on the counter. "Should I care what *you* want?"

"Ouch. Come on now, Rose, you know me. You are very important to me. Please, try to understand this from my perspective."

"Yeah, you are the 'trust me' guy. You are the guy who told *me* to trust *you*." She dishes her sweet potato burrito onto her plate and squeezes the plastic sour cream and guacamole cups on top of the tortilla wrap. She takes a fork and a knife from the drawer behind Aris and walks back to the easel.

Aris walks over to the couch and takes his seat. "I can see that I have hurt you, yet I am not sure there is anything I could have done about it."

"No. I suppose not," she says. "There was nothing you could have done, for sure." She cuts a slice of her burrito. "You obviously put a lot of thought into your actions... and your lies. So, I suppose a few weeks ago when you told me you felt like you were actually moving forward... well, now I guess you really are moving – forward." She swallows her emotion before taking another bite. "No need to worry. Like a cat, I always land on my feet – my martial felicity."

"You are lying," Aris says.

"I'm lying! No. I am relearning just how cold I really am. Let me reintroduce the three laws of thermodynamics. The first is I cannot win. The second is I cannot break even and the third is that I cannot get out of the game," Rose says jaggedly. "C.P. Snow. Cool, right? Or is it cold?"

"Rose, can't we talk about this?" he asks pushing his uneaten fish tacos to the left.

"What is there to talk about? You will keep your distance and I will do what I have always done – love you from afar. It is just farther this time." Rose has no idea how it is she can actually speak.

"It's not like there weren't major things you kept from me while you were processing... That's the right word, right? Processing?" Aris says sternly with a bit of choked anger.

"Nice. Yeah, so I guess I'm back on my limb leaning on my secure tree looking at the ground..." Rose calmly looks at her feet before glaring directly into his dark eyes. "And you, my friend, my love, you betrayed my trust at what, your earliest convenience," she says without a hint of sadness. "I thought you knew me better. Dammit, again, it is my fault – tame and blame. I shouldn't have trusted you. You took me for granted. You are no better than the rapist."

"What? That is not fair," Aris yells.

"You started it. You compared rape with a promotion – you God-damned, arrogant, son-of-a..." Rose stands with a cold intensity. She takes her half-eaten, yet thoroughly mangled burrito to the kitchen. She places it back into the Styrofoam container and places it on the middle shelf of her refrigerator. Rose looks at the easel and then at Aris while steadying herself against the door of the refrigerator. "I think I have captured enough of a sketch to finish the painting without you. Right now, I really would like to... no, I really need you to leave. I want to be alone. Go home."

"Why didn't you tell me you knew about my promotion?" Aris asks as he stands with his plate still full. He steps closer to her and with each step he takes forward, Rose adds equal distance in the opposite direction.

"Want to know what it feels like to be blind-sided?" Rose says. "You asked for my trust...my blind trust... my reaction, my reaction is Newtonian, Hypocrite."

"Rose, what can I say?" Aris asks. "I needed to think. I needed to make this decision..."

"Say good night, Gracie," Rose responds with an audible swallow, followed by a minute of stifling silence while Rose stares down the stranger in her apartment.

"I don't want to leave," Aris says in response to his stymied situational advances. "I want you to go with me."

"Which one is it? You are a thief offering a bribe and you want me, an Aesop, to take your bribe?" Rose barks. "Apologies and excuses – what is the difference? Trust and obedience. Tell me Aris, did you not tell me because you thought I would ... What? Give you bad advice? Manipulate you? Tell you what to do? Oooh, or how about this – I would have actually cared!"

"Know," Aris accurately responds to the question.

"Cool then. Super cool," Rose says slamming her glass down on the counter, causing a clean break two-thirds down the glass. "A clean break – super cool. Ouch!" Rose drops down into her squat and hugs her calves. She yells up and over the counter, "Aris, Leave! Get the fuck out of here."

He stands still. "Rose, you need to…Rose, you know me."

Demonstrating an eerie calmness, Rose walks to the stereo and finds the particular song that has been ringing in her ears for the past twenty-four hours since she learned about Aris's future plans from someone other than Aris. She finds it - Bonnie Raitt's 'I Can't Make You Love Me.' She places the CD in the tray and selects the track. She turns the volume up and without looking at Aris, she walks to the bathroom. While gripping the frame of the door, she yells down the hall, "You can let yourself out."

Rose closes the bathroom door and locks it. She turns on the shower and strips. She closes the door of the shower and sits down on the tile just above the drain with her back to the stream and her knees to her chin. She hugs her calves strongly and gently rocks her body back and forth on her bony sacrum. She hears her front door slam. A shock runs through her entire body. *God I am sorry. I am so very sorry. Please forgive me. I wasn't his choice. I really thought I was his.*

Thirty-five minutes later, an ostensibly emotionally empty Rose turns off the shower and her tears. *A broken promise. It is nothing.* She steps into a relatively cold yet steam-filled bathroom and quietly towels off and then walks to the sink to brush her teeth. "Ies jus a daa lock anee uder. No beeg deeyl."

Rose leaves the bathroom and enters the hall of a dark apartment with the lone light source of a lit candle on the coffee table. She turns the light on in her bedroom and discovers a box and a single rose on her pillow. She opens the box to find a red, silk negligee with a card attached saying, "I think I found your size. Happy Valentine's Day!"

She drops her towel on the floor and retrieves her navy blue nighty from her dresser. *My size?* She walks to her bed and, while staring at the rose, grabs the pillow from the other side. Hugging it, she walks into her living area. She puts the pillow on the couch and grabs her familiar blanket from the floor. She lies down and covers her body and more than half of her face with the blanket and watches the candle dance through her seemingly ceaseless tears.

Rose looks up and whispers in a childlike voice, "I am Okay, God. It is just one broken promise. It hurts a little - alright it hurts a lot. I am thankful for what I have – for a hot apartment shower, for this couch and this blanket and this candle. I will stop crying soon. I will be a better person tomorrow. I can dream a different dream. A bigger one. It's just one small promise. I love you and I'm sorry." Rose closes her eyes and lets the tears fall to her pillow. She touches the wet spots with the fingers of her right hand. Rose finds sleep in thirty-five minutes.

CHAPTER 22
THE SHEPARD AND THE SEA

A SHEPHERD, keeping watch over his sheep near the shore, saw the Sea very calm and smooth, and longed to make a voyage with a view to commerce. He sold all his flock, invested it in a cargo of dates, and set sail. But a very great tempest came on, and the ship being in danger of sinking, he threw all his merchandise overboard and barely escaped with his life in the empty ship. Not long afterwards when someone passed by and observed the unruffled calm of the Sea, he interrupted him and said, "It is again in want of dates, and therefore looks quiet." – Aesop

Rose takes her seat in First Class with virtually undetectable pangs of guilt. She slides her computer and purse under the seat in front of her and stares out the window. Although there are a few flurries she is confident that she and her companions in Coach will be arriving at the Dallas Fort-Worth airport on time. Just as her thumbs enter her book, she hears a voice.

"Hi, Rose." Rose looks up to discover Rebekah taking the seat next to her. "Small world."

"Hi, Rebekah. I don't know about a small world... it seems pretty big to me. I suppose there are a smaller number of planes flying to Dallas today," Rose says with a wink. She quickly looks at her book and moves the bookmark, a Lin coupon, to her page before closing.

"The Scouts, Mike and Nick, are they on this flight too?"

Rose turns her head to look through the curtain. "Yes, they are just a few seats behind the curtain. Nick, Mike, Heath and four senior Patrol Leaders – Ian, Caleb, Trevor and Matt."

Rebekah looks toward the curtain and then takes her seat. "Are you guys ready?"

"Strangely enough, I really don't even need to be on this

flight. I guess I am going for moral support. I guess you could say that I'm a Tagalong. Ha ha. You see, that is funny because a Tagalong is a Girl Scout cookie."

Rebekah rolls her eyes and grunts with a respectable grace.

Rose adjusts her demeanor. "To answer your question – I think that they are. Mike is ready, I know that. The guy must have rehearsed for 20 hours. I am not exaggerating. I'm sure he is going to be great." She starts to gently push at her computer satchel with her feet. "The boys, well, I think that three are ready and one is still pretty nervous. Yet, I am pretty sure that Nick will be able to give the kid good guidance. He's got a knack for that kind of thing."

"Seems to," Rebekah says. "You guys are dating, right?"

"Oh, no. No," Rose says hastily. "No, he is involved in a very serious relationship as am..." Rose catches herself before lying.

"I'm sorry. I did not mean to presume. I think Melissa said..." Rebekah starts to apologize.

"Don't worry. Melissa asked Nick how long we've been dating," Rose says. "He is like a brother to me. We understand each other. I guess that might appear somewhat intimate to someone on the outside. Nick is very much like my brother, Zeke. Zeke has a more wicked sense of humor, yet they are similar in that they are gentle and kind and… and keenly observant."

Rebekah nods. "You seem to work really well together."

"It was kind of strange. I told him about this idea and he simply said, 'okay.' Serendipity, I suppose. We seem to look at things similarly and not sweat the small stuff. Mike and Heath serve as great counter balances. They actually do sweat the small stuff, or at least remind us that 'small stuff' exists. We do work well as a team."

"I would definitely say so," Rebekah utters, "a pretty remarkable team."

"So, are you ready?" Rose asks wishing she rephrased the

question to sound less condescending. She almost says something to that effect, but stops herself.

Rebekah taps her gorgeous leather petite brief case. "My father told me to answer that question with, 'I was born ready.'" Rebekah hands the brief case to the steward and requests bottled water.

The captain's voice is heard over the loud speaker and Rose respectfully performs a simple tightening of her belt before turning her head to look out the window. In relative silence the two women and the entire plane taxi to the runway. Rose opens her book and starts to read. The two women exchange pleasant niceties in between chapters. Rebekah even requests a few pointers as she shares a few of her presentation slides with Rose.

"These are the models in our fleet – we have chocolate Stingray Corvettes, '67 Mustangs, '57 Ford Thunderbirds, Porsche 911s, Ferraris, Jaguar XKEs, Mercedes Gull Wings, and the classic VW bug," Rebekah says as she shows the profiles of the chocolates on a print out.

"Who selected the cars? I mean, that's a pretty interesting selection," Rose says out of curiosity.

"Each one of us – my brothers and sisters, and my mom's two brothers. The Mercedes Gull Wing was my choice."

Rose smiles. "Sounds like a fun evening spent."

"I guess you have never met my family – it wasn't one night – more like five years." She chuckles.

Rose tries to imagine what the job of creating a chocolate car fleet would entail and how it could possibly take five years. She returns from her thoughts, "I received a VW bug as a birthday gift a few years ago – the big version. It took me a few days to finish it and that is saying something."

"They are pretty popular gifts," Rebekah says flipping to the next page in her presentation review process. "The VW was my sister's suggestion. She wanted something obtainable. All of the other cars are pretty much dream cars. Anyway, my brother

Jonathan told me about the iconic Pinewood Derby in the Cub Scouts and that some older troops do Soap Box derby. That is why we chose this product line. The idea of raising money for school buses... well, it seemed appropriate."

"Like chocolate and peanut butter – a really good pairing," Rose says sincerely as she inadvertently looks over the pages in front of Rebekah. "I should let you get back to work." She smiles and bends the pages of her book in both of her hands.

Two hours and twenty minutes later the plane lands safely at Dallas Fort-Worth. Both Rebekah and Rose quietly collect their belongings with very limited conversation. Rose follows Rebekah down the jet way and stops just beyond the ropes to await her companions. "Have a good evening, Rebekah. I will see you tomorrow."

"Same to you," she says over her shoulder as she quickly steps down the terminal's thoroughfare to exit the airport.

Rose turns to watch the fellow passengers deplane. She can hear Mike and Heath before they are visible. Nicolas appears first.

"There you are. I tried to find you on the plane," he says.

"First Class," she says with a smile. "Another perk of clocking ridiculous amounts of air time."

"Hey, did you get to watch a good movie?" Heath asks.

"Funny. No, I just read," she responds as she looks over to the four fifteen-year-olds quietly assembling behind the three gentlemen. "The hotel is very close. We can catch a shuttle van." She points to the sign that points to the shuttle vans. "How was your flight?" Rose asks Nicolas.

"Fine. Good." Nicolas drags his carry-on. "You look terrible."

"Uh, thanks." Rose huffs and shakes her head white furrowing her brow. "I think I may start calling you Abe."

"No, seriously, is everything okay?" Nicolas asks with direct eye contact. He simultaneously points out the shuttle van sign to Mike and Heath, who are looking a bit misplaced.

Rose debates her answer as she watches the boys circle in front of them. "Aris and I... well, we broke up."

"You broke-up? Or are you fighting?" Nicolas asks. "It has been my experience, and therefore fact, that girls don't know the difference. Walking out on a fight, and taking time, does not necessarily mean you have broken-up."

Rose nods in understanding. "I feel like I am broken."

"Do you want to talk about it? Mike and Heath can take the boys out. And we can go somewhere else," Nicolas suggests.

"I am not sure. I mean I guess I am concerned that it would not be looked upon... People already think we are dating," Rose says. "How's that for honesty?"

"The trick to being honest is to not care how people see you," Nicolas says as they leave the airport. The group walks together to the curb and catches a shuttle to the airport Marriott. Rose uses her rewards to purchase two suites for the scouts and one single room for herself. After checking into their rooms and dropping off luggage, the group meets in the lobby 20 minutes later for dinner. Nicolas has already explained to both Mike and Heath that he and Rose will be going elsewhere for dinner. The two scout masters and the four boys head off to the local kid-friendly Tex-Mex restaurant recommended by the concierge and Rose and Nicolas stay and eat at the hotel restaurant.

Rose and Nicolas are directed to a cozy corner booth. After their orders are taken, Nicholas starts.

"You and Aris have been friends forever, right?"

"Friends forever? We have been friends for a decade. We dated years ago, but it didn't work out."

"Why?" Nicolas asks.

"Can I attribute it to being young? He says that I scared the hell out of him," Rose says with a light smile accompanied by a distant look. "He thinks I am scary."

"You are like 100 pounds. How is that scary?" Nicolas jokes.

"He is not physically afraid of me," Rose says.

"I was just kidding," Nicolas says. "Geez, lighten up."

Rose just stares blankly for a few long seconds. "I guess I am pretty intense."

"I think you are confusing being forthright with being intense. You are forthright."

Rose looks down at her place setting and touches the prongs of her fork as she tries to collect her thoughts. "I love him. I have loved him for years. And he, he is just learning. I am not sure if I have the patience to teach him."

"Teach him? Are you talking about the Aris I met? He is not a fly by night kind of guy. He struck me as a very careful and conscientious man. I meet very few of those. I really liked him. You guys seem really good together, almost perfect for each other."

"He lied to me – for weeks. He received a job promotion that involves relocation and he didn't mention it – not even in passing," Rose explains.

"I can understand why you would be upset. What was his reason? I am sure he had a good one."

"He said that I would influence him or something…I don't know…I don't remember." Rose smooths out her napkin. "And he really did not tell me about it. I found out about it from his sister's Facebook page. I guess he didn't know that we were 'friends.'"

"So you caught him lying to you," Nicolas says. "Well that is a different story, I suppose."

"Yeah," Rose says moving the salt to the left of the pepper.

"Has he ever lied to you before?" Nicolas asks.

"I don't think so," she answers. "His honesty isn't as brutal as yours. I guess it's as consistent."

"So I suppose he thought he had a reason to lie – a white lie."

Rose huffs. "A white lie? This chocolate issue – I have been calling *it* a white lie."

"Interesting. Must be that ethics education that allows you to make that kind of connection," Nicolas says while looking up as the waitress delivers their sweet teas.

"It is, right? Hershey and Nestle and Mars…their promise is a white lie. We are going to stop using children – eventually." Rose gulps half of her tea.

"Thirsty?" Nicolas asks. "Are you rushing things?"

"I don't know. I think I am being forthright," Rose says with a laugh. "I guess if I was trying to be honest – I could say that I am – rushing things. He just broke-up with someone. Nora. They were together for two years. I guess we figured out that we had feelings for each other and then…"

"Nora?" Nicolas asks.

"Mea culpa." Rose explains the decade long situation to Nicolas. She then explains the dynamics, the conversations, and the understandings that have taken place over the past three months. Their food arrives and each stops the serious conversation to enjoy their meals. "I think we should get dessert."

"Always," Rose replies.

"My girlfriend rarely gets dessert," Nicolas adds.

"How long have you guys been together?" Rose asks.

"Five years," Nicolas responds. "She knows that I'll ask when she finishes her Master's."

Rose smiles gently and looks to a distant point. "Lucky woman."

"Well, Rose, this is how I see it. Aris is trying to sort things out to his satisfaction so that he can offer the best package to you. It is sorta like cleaning your house before guests arrive. You know what I mean? He wants to offer a clear directive – he doesn't want you to be an add-on."

"A Tagalong…" Rose laughs. "What makes you so sure?"

"I met him," Nicolas declares. "It's a guy thing, I suppose."

"I wish you hadn't said that. I'm tired. I feel like my heart is going to give out, collapse…" she says quietly with a confused look in her eye.

"Set a time limit on it," Nicolas says. "I am not sure if that is good advice, but it helps carry the burden. You run right? Think about it when your body is just about to quit and you play games with yourself like… Like you will keep running through the end of the song, or to the next tree, or to the red mailbox in the distance…"

Rose huffs as she knows exactly what he means. "You are pretty good at this."

"Not to everyone. You are easier to talk to than most. You actually listen," Nicolas compliments. "What I am trying to say is that you will know when you have to give up and until that point – just keep running."

Rose starts to cry. "Thanks. Thanks for understanding."

"You deserve it. There needs to be more people like you. And there needs to be more people helping people like you. There needs to be more people who hope you never give up."

Rose laughs as more tears fall down her face. "We make a pretty good team."

"Like chocolate and peanut butter," Nicolas says. "For now, to get to the next mailbox, just think about what you have done here. Tomorrow we are presenting a really good idea, your idea, to The Boy Scouts of America. And that is a pretty big deal – one that would have never happened if you didn't take the risks necessary. We are going to get that piece of chocolate to Abdul and kids like Abdul."

"I hope so. I hope it's not a white lie."

"This effort?" Nicolas asks.

"Yeah," Rose says as she looks up to see the waitress delivering their desserts.

"Well, I will say this one more thing about your situation. If Aris doesn't figure out what he has with you, then…"

"Smack," Rose says. "I am surprised that Hershey doesn't make 'Smacks'. They have kisses, hugs and bliss…"

"I have to admit that after learning about this issue, their commercials really piss me off. Seriously - I get angry," Nicolas admits while taking a fork full of his Snickers pie.

"They are pretty much all guilty," Rose says picking out a piece of Snickers from her own pie. "Heck, we all are, I suppose. She says with a snicker."

"There are problems and there are solutions," Nicolas says. "I think we are part of the solution."

CHAPTER 23
THE TWO CRABS

ONE FINE DAY two Crabs came out from their home to take a stroll on the sand. "Child," said the mother, "you are walking very ungracefully. You should accustom yourself to walking straight forward without twisting from side to side." "Pray, mother," said the young one, "do but set the example yourself, and I will follow you." – Aesop

At 9:52, Rose, accompanied by three Scout Masters and four Senior Patrol Leaders in full uniform, stands under the bronze statue of Lord Baden-Powell outside of the Headquarters of the Boy Scouts of America. Nicolas says a few words of encouragement as well as a few words of disciplinary suggestions to the entire group before leading them through the glass doors and into the attractively landscaped building. He takes off his hat and walks directly to the receptionist.

"My name is Nicolas Grey, and we are here to meet with Deputy Chief Scout Cliff Mazeri and then speak to the planning committee at 1:00," Nicolas says succinctly to the well groomed elderly woman sitting at the circular desk.

"Yes, hello, gentlemen. We are very interested in your project and are looking forward to hearing more about it," she says. "Cliff will be down momentarily. Please take a seat."

Three minutes later, Cliff steps off the elevator and walks toward the group. Rose watches the seven scouts stand simultaneously.

"Scouts Salute," Nicolas says. "Two." The seven scouts perform their salute to a smiling Deputy Chief who returns their salute.

"Hello Nick, I'm Cliff. I'm glad you guys are here. Any trouble finding us?"

"No, Sir," Nicolas says. "Sir, I would like to introduce

Rose Isope. This young woman is the person who brought this idea to me and my troops in early December. Without her we would not be here today." Rose stands and takes three steps toward Cliff.

Cliff extends his hand. "Ma'am, a pleasure."

Rose, emotionally affected, smiles and lowers her head. "I am pleased to meet you, Sir, and am proud to be here." Rose looks at Nicolas and Mike and offers a nod.

Cliff looks to the senior Scouts and attempts small chat. "Hello. Have you ever been to Texas before?"

"I have, Sir. My Mom and Dad are big Cowboy fans," Ian volunteers. The remaining three Scouts non-verbally respond in the negative.

"Very good. I have set up the stage for you boys and thought you might want to take in a bit of practice time," Cliff says with individual and direct eye contact with each of the four boys. "We really are looking forward to this. Are you guys nervous?"

Caleb jumps in, "Matt is!"

"No. He is just hyper-vigilant," Rose says smiling at Matt.

Cliff looks at Rose with a peculiar glare, as if he doesn't quite understand her presence. Rose unknowingly responds to his glances by grabbing her left wrist with her right hand behind her back. The group follows Cliff into the lecture hall where there is a podium set down stage left, or house right. "You have about an hour before people start arriving." Cliff clears his throat and looks to Nicolas and Mike. "Do you need anything?"

Mike lifts his computer. "A projector?"

"Certainly," Cliff says. "Our AV man will be here in minutes. I told him 10:30." Just as he finishes his sentence the AV man, Mark enters the lecture hall.

"Never fear. The AV Man is here," Mark says as he walks in energetically. "Sorry, I heard my name. I am AV Man." He takes a profile stance reminiscent of Superman.

"Hi, AV Man. Thank God you are here. I need a projector and the people of Small-erving… I can't do it. Darn it. It must be

Jet Lag," Mike says as he gives up the scene and shakes the hand of Mark, the AV man.

Mark smiles at Mike and looks to both Nick and Rose as he tries to determine what needs to be done using his keen telepathic powers.

Rose smiles and lifts both her hands in surrender and then shrugs her shoulders. "I am just here to field the more difficult questions." Rose takes a step back from the group and circles to find a theatre seat near the middle of the lecture hall. She watches the stage as the boys try to intuitively figure out how to set up their blocking. A few minutes later Nick and Cliff sit down within earshot of her.

"I am really intrigued by this idea and am interested in hearing more of the details. Daniel told me that you have also created booklets and bumper stickers," Cliff says. "We are expecting about 250 people today, mostly national district chiefs. If all goes well, we will present this idea at the annual conference in May."

"We're thankful for the opportunity. Two of the scouts with us today are applying for early admission to the Ivy League and are really excited about being able to put this project on their applications," Nick responds. "We have tried to pull together and present the best program we could, given the time constraints and limited budget. I am proud of what we have accomplished over the past three weeks, and I am sure you will be duly impressed. It is a good idea, sir." Nick casually glances over at Rose before continuing, "And yes, we prepared about 200 booklets and 200 bumper stickers. So I suppose we will be a bit short. If we leave them for the end, rather than present them as programs, we might be able to determine actual interest."

"Efficient and economical," Cliff says.

Rose notices Rebekah standing at the door, watching the stage. "Nick. Nick," Rose interrupts and lifts her chin towards the door. She then smiles at Rebekah.

"Sir, the woman at the door is Rebekah Nightingale of Nightingale Chocolates. Please let me introduce her and I do think she may have a few questions for you." Nicolas and Cliff quickly make their way to the svelte woman standing in the doorway.

Rose returns her attention to the stage to watch the four boys handle their props, including a giant peanut butter jar, a giant chocolate bar, two giant coins, and a bicycle made of foam. Rose smiles as she notices that Matt is beginning to relax; he is all smiles. *Thanks, God, for this opportunity. I love you.*

Just as predicted by Cliff, a few of the attendees start to filter into the lecture hall. Rose decides to find the group to make her own encouraging speech and to relocate to the back row of the lecture hall.

Rose sees Nicolas standing against the wall in the hallway watching Mike pace with his notecards. "You'd think that the guy would relax a little. I had no idea that he put this much time into his speeches. I suppose if I were this committed I would be less nervous about giving them," Nicolas says to Rose as she approaches.

"He is good. I really think you guys are going to knock this out of the park, so to speak. I know I have said this before, but I am glad I met you. I am sure we would not be here today if it weren't for you," Rose says bashfully. "Thanks for helping me see this idea through. I am sincerely grateful. And thanks again for dinner last night."

"No problem. My pleasure. And Rose, we needed this. We really needed this," Nicolas says with a tucked chin, his eyes focusing just past his shoes.

Rose leaves Nick and walks into the classroom and wishes good luck to Mike and Heath individually and all four boys together. She gives a salute and smiles before exiting the room. "Good Luck, Nick. I trust you can field the tougher questions. If not, I will be in the last row." Rose lightly punches his right shoulder and continues down the hall.

The presentation meets with resounding applause. Mike makes a spectacular delivery of light-hearted comedic elements and serious digital facts. The boys are charming and entertaining and earn more than an equal share of the applause. The transition to introduce Rebekah is done by two Scouts carrying Boy Scout emblem flags and a rocking foam ship placed across the lower half of her body as she makes her way to the podium - a cheesy joke about her flagship status. Rebekah's portion is informative and personal. She speaks of her mother's efforts as a child laborer, as well as her mother's adult efforts in fund raising success for various organizations. She ties the two speeches together with the word "Legacy." The applause continues for just under a minute before Nicolas takes the stage and offers to answer any questions regarding their presentation and the concepts located within.

"Do you really want to make this idea into a merit badge?" asks a 50ish grey haired gentleman with a slight Texan accent.

"Sir, I think that question is for this committee to answer. We think that the 'Mafeking Challenge' badge could serve as a troop unifier, possibly a rank unifier. I personally think that any scout, cub through eagle, could earn the Mafeking Challenge patch by simply volunteering the hours toward the cause with the number of qualifying hours to be determined. However, it is our understanding that those details remain outside of our involvement and are appropriately assigned to you, the District Chiefs." Nicolas looks to Mike and Heath and then Rose in the back row.

"You mentioned that the 'Mafeking Challenge' could change from year to year. Do you have a suggestion of how it is chosen?" a young black man in his 20s asks.

"We were thinking that the 'Mafeking Challenge' would be announced at the Jamboree. I suppose a democratic system would work with Scouts writing in suggestions prior to the Jamboree, sending out ballots to troops across the nation, and then announcing the winner at the Jamboree. We do think that a two year commitment to each project is appropriate. 'One Goodyear turn deserves another," Nicolas answers crisply.

"How long have you been working on this idea?" asks a man from the back row in plain dress.

"About a month and half, sir. Not very long," Nicolas answers quickly.

"I am impressed young man," the man replies.

"Thank you, sir." Nicolas squeezes the podium and asks, "On a personal note, I would like to say… Obviously I have been thinking about promises and legacies over the past few weeks and months. I was talking to a friend last night about personal promises and how much it hurts when they are broken. Lord Baden-Powell's organization carries both promise and legacy. As we try to defend ourselves and our organization against attacks because of his promise and his legacy – it is important to realize our own promise and our own legacy as individuals. And that we should hold these to the highest of standards." Nicolas looks down at the podium and closes his eyes for a moment of silence. He returns to the audience, "I remember the oath I took as a boy – as a man, I should be able to do even better. We can do better."

The microphone squeals, and Nicolas jumps. "Geez…" He looks behind him at his fellow scout masters and senior patrol scouts and laughs before returning to the audience. "Any more questions?" Nicolas scans the room. "Well then, I and my fellow Scout Masters as well as Senior Patrol Leaders Ian, Caleb, Trevor and Matt would like to thank you for this opportunity. We really believe in this idea. We think it is a necessary step for our organization's future to become more internationally responsible. We could be doing more. We need to be doing more. In other words, we really should do this. Thank you for your time." Nicolas leads the group from the stage into the hall.

Additional applause continues as Rose escapes out of the back side door and peers into the hallway and overhears Nicolas. "Thanks, Mike. You were great. And guys…you guys were awesome. I have not laughed that hard in years." Nicolas shakes their hands and then shakes the hands of Mike and Health. "I am pretty proud of us right now."

"You are so pretty," Mike says, punching him hard in the shoulder.

Filled with a warm sense of pride, Rose starts to well up. She turns to sprint down the hall toward the front doors. Nicolas notices her as she turns the corner of the foyer and begins to follow, yet is stopped by Cliff.

"Very impressive. You guys did a really good job – very persuasive presentation. I think we will be talking about today for a while. Are you guys leaving today?" Cliff asks.

"We are staying the night, sir. We wanted to do something fun tonight to repay these guys for their hard work. We are taking them to a rodeo at the arena," Nicolas responds.

"Good," Cliff says as he looks over the boys. "Good job. Best presentation we have had in years, and I mean it." Cliff shakes the hands of the three Scout Masters and then the boys and asks, "Where did Ms. Nightingale disappear to?"

"I saw her in the lobby not two minutes ago, Sir," Heath responds.

Cliff walks in the direction of the lobby and finds Ms. Nightingale sitting on the reception sofa, talking on her cell phone. Rebekah ends the call and the two share a brief conversation regarding the presentation. He gently escorts Rebekah to the glass doors, telling her, "Geoffrey Michaels, our lawyer will be in touch within the next few days. I think we will have a good deal of details to iron out, however I think the overall project looks pretty darn good – thanks to your corporate sponsorship."

Rebekah graciously accepts his praise while offering mutual praises of their future partnership. She also explains that she must be on her way, "I have a family emergency that I must address." Rebekah eludes the specifics yet conveys sincere turmoil. "I do look forward to meeting with you again." Rebekah places her leather brief case over her shoulder and starts to exit the building.

Cliff opens the door and wishes her well.

Outside, Rose hears voices at the door and turns to locate the sources. She sees the simple exchange between Cliff and Rebekah from the base of the Lord Baden-Powell bronze statue. Rebekah sees Rose and shifts her stride to meet her. "Your Scouts did very well today, you must be pleased."

"They are not my Scouts, Ma'am." Rose says, lowering her head. "However, I am very proud." She lifts her right index finger to her eye. "Do I have mascara running down my face?"

"You look fine, Rose." Rebekah clicks her heels together. "Emotional day?"

"Yeah, I seem to do this thing… these tears… they just seem to fall." Rose stomps her foot. "I wish I could say I had control over them." She looks inquisitively to her confidant. "You're sure I do not have mascara running down my face?"

"I'm sure. I tend to tear up when I see a project come together," Rebekah says with a feminine understanding. "Listen Rose, I need to get going – my uncle is in the hospital; it is pretty serious. We did good work today and I think… well, we did good work today."

"I am sorry to hear about your uncle. So you are leaving for the airport now?"

"Yes, I am going to try to make the 4:20 flight." Rebekah looks at her watch.

"Well, if you miss it maybe we can continue our conversation on the 5:50 flight. Go on - get out of here." Rose smiles as she watches Rebekah climb into a burgundy Toyota Camry.

Having fully recovered from her prideful breakdown, Rose reenters the building and finds the loo. Rebekah was not lying and Rose's mascara appears suitable. She uses the facilities and then washes her hands for a full minute, brushes her teeth and reapplies lip gloss. She inhales and exhales deeply. "Much better." She exits the loo and finds the scouts still standing in the hall quietly talking to each other. Nicolas notices her approach.

"You alright?" he asks.

"Yes, of course. I am fine. Hey guys, you did great! Seriously, great!" Rose says beaming. "And your closing… what can I say?"

"Cliff said we were one of the best," Matt boasts.

"I do not doubt it. You guys were really, really good and very funny. How do you feel?"

"Hungry!" Ian admits.

"When do you need to be at the airport?" Nicolas asks Rose.

"I have about an hour and fifteen. Pizza?"

"Yeah, pizza," Trevor chimes.

"Cliff told me about this deep dish pizza and sub place half-way between here and the hotel that has outdoor seating. It's a shame to miss out on a 72 degree day in February," Mike notes.

"Agreed," Nicolas confers.

The group load into a seven passenger Dodge Grand Caravan and stop for pizza and subs on their way back to the hotel. Nicolas walks with Rose to the reception desk as Rose ensures the rooms will be charged to her rewards account. "We are a pretty good team. I hope you get some sleep tonight. You still look pretty tired," Nicolas says.

"Yikes. Maybe it is just my mascara," Rose says. "Have a good time at the rodeo tonight – sounds trying. And good luck with your traveling circus tomorrow." Rose swings her suitcase by the handle. "Shoot me an email if you find out anything interesting."

"Will do," Nicolas says with a gentle smile. "Tell Aris I said hello when you talk to him. I mean, it is Valentine's. You have plans, right?"

"No," Rose responds. "I think I will probably just go for a long run."

"Tell him I said hello when you talk to him." Nicolas says reassuringly as he opens the door for Rose. "Have a good flight."

Nicolas salutes his friend as she thanks him for holding the door. "Tell the guys I said thanks – again."

CHAPTER 24
THE ANT AND THE DOVE

AN ANT went to the bank of a river to quench its thirst, and being carried away by the rush of the stream, was on the point of drowning. A Dove sitting on a tree overhanging the water plucked a leaf and let it fall into the stream close to her. The Ant climbed onto it and floated in safety to the bank. Shortly afterwards a birdcatcher came and stood under the tree, and laid his lime-twigs for the Dove, which sat in the branches. The Ant, perceiving his design, stung him in the foot. In pain the birdcatcher threw down the twigs, and the noise made the Dove take wing. – Aesop

Rose is awakened out of a deep sleep by the phone. "Hello?" she says with half of her vocal cords still asleep.

"I am outside your front door. Let me in?" Aris says.

Rose stares at the red digits of her clock. "It's 5:55 in the morning," she says with a tone that is both sleepy and confused. She falls to her back and puts her hand on her forehead to push back her bangs. "I haven't heard from you in…"

"Eleven days. You haven't seen me either. Let me in," Aris says.

"Hold on," Rose says as she tries to remember how to hang up the phone and walk. After recalling exactly how to accomplish both tasks, she finds her robe and walks to the door. She unlocks the knob, the dead-bolt and, at last, the chain. "It's five o'clock in the morning. What are you doing here?"

"Come on now, it is much closer to six," Aris says with a grin. He is holding a brown paper bag full of groceries. "I'm here to cook you breakfast."

Rose furrows her brow. "Breakfast?"

"I figured you probably haven't eaten yet," Aris says jokingly as he scurries past her to put the bag on the counter.

"Well, no, of course I haven't eaten yet. I'm still sleeping."

He laughs at her. "How about a Greek salad breakfast sandwich?"

Rose closes the door and locks the knob. "Aris, I haven't seen or heard from you in..."

"Eleven days. Did you miss me?"

Rose looks down at her red negligee that she has worn every night since returning from Dallas and covers it completely with her robe.

"I went to see Mina," Aris says as he begins to unload the grocery bag. "She says hi."

"Hi, Mina." Rose says sitting one cheek down on the stool with the opposite foot planted firmly on the floor. "I saw Nick, he too says hi."

The color drains from his face. He sighs, "I guess I should start with coffee."

"You guess?" Rose huffs a small bit of her resentment.

Aris grabs her favorite mug from the dishwasher and places it on the platform. "I took a couple of days from work."

Rose starts to feel slightly uncomfortable about her appearance. She shakes out her hair and then check for mascara with her fingers. "How nice for you," she utters with a palpable hostility. "Aris, what are you doing here?"

"Making you breakfast, of course. What am I doing here? Dumb question. Isn't it obvious? Apparently you need some of this," he takes the mug from the platform and gently places the mug in front of her.

Rose squints in her confusion. "Uh, thanks?" She takes the coffee and warms her hands with it before lifting it to her lips.

Aris grabs the frying pan and easily locates the cooking spray. "Actually, I guess I should probably start with the salad and then cook the eggs. I guess I need some coffee too."

"Maybe you shouldn't. You seem kind of wired," Rose casually observes the not-so-subtle change in his mannerisms.

"Yeah, I guess I haven't slept. I feel pretty good though,"

Aris admits. "I am happy to see you."

She takes her fourth sip, "So you were just with your sister?"

"We took my parents to the airport for their cruise yesterday. She's house sitting for my parents while they are away."

"Monte Carlo, right?" Rose asks.

Aris nods. "You have pepperoncini, right?

"I think so. They'd be in the door."

Aris finely dices the tomatoes, cucumbers, pepperoncini, and olives. He mixes the vegetables with a bag of baby greens, Greek dressing and feta. "Eggs and bagels." Aris turns on his heels to locate the toaster. "I bought everything bagels. I hope you don't mind."

Rose watches silently, gulping down her coffee. She is trying to process what is actually occurring in her kitchen. "Aris?"

"Yes, Rose," he responds.

"It's still dark out," Rose says.

"Sunrise isn't until 6:53," Aris states the matter-of-fact and then looks at the kitchen clock to note the time.

Rose turns to look out her window, and then back at Aris. She adjusts her footing and sits completely on the island stool.

"What have you been doing for the past eleven days?" Aris asks with a smile masked by a twisted pucker. "It actually has been eleven days."

"Eleven days – they seemed like…"

"Years?" Aris interjects.

"Years," she repeats. "What have I been doing? I don't know – work."

"How's work?"

"Aris?" Rose says with an exhausted tone.

"Breakfast in two minutes," he answers.

Rose stands and walks to her dish towel drawer and pulls out two placemats from underneath the towels. She hands the industrial placemats to Aris. "Just in case you didn't enrich the uranium to 238."

The toaster pops.

"These are some pretty serious placemats; they weigh like two pounds each." Aris investigates their construction. "Lead?"

"You would think – yet I think it is just plastic," Rose shrugs. "I went to the home section in search of a durable placemat… just lucky, I guess."

"I also bought orange juice," Aris says as he pulls two wine glasses from the cupboard and fills them with juice. "Sit."

Rose takes the left rather than the right.

Aris notices. "I think you are sitting in my chair."

"I am pretty sure they are both mine," Rose says with a renewed tone of enmity.

"Grumpy. You sure are grumpy in the morning," Aris says sniggering. He places a beautiful bagel sandwich filled with Greek salad topped with a sunny-side-up egg, cut sharply down the middle. He garnishes the plate with red grapes.

Rose softens for a split-second then asks, "Dammit! Are you bribing me, Aristotle?"

"No, I think I'm feeding you." He cuts his own bagel and moves his placemat to the other side of her and takes the third barstool.

Rose reacts by hopping a bit to the right.

"Am I too close?" Aris asks seriously, slightly offended.

"I don't know. Maybe. I'm confused."

"Eat," he commands.

"I'm not hungry," Rose protests. "What are you doing here?"

Aris turns toward her and places his hands on his knees. "I missed you. I have missed you every minute of every day since I left." He looks at the clock. "This minute makes 16,567."

Rose's whole body starts to shake as she tries to not look at him. She, instead, focuses on her plate. She bites both of her lips and tries to breathe. "You can't just…"

"It's Tuesday," Aris says. "My favorite day of the week."

Rose exhales and sinks into her own back. "Aris, please…"

"You were right to be angry with me. It was insensitive of me to not talk about my promotion. My boss told me about it literally right before our first date, on the plane home. I wanted to tell you about it. I did. I knew it involved me relocating. At first, I didn't think I was going to take it. I thought that maybe, that maybe I was supposed to stay with you…"

"At first?" Rose says with a deep furrow setting into her brow and hurt setting into her eyes. "Oh my God, I can't breathe."

"Remember when I asked you to trust me?" Aris asks her while trying to take her left hand.

Rose retracts her hand and sits on it. "I remember."

"You reminded me that you were a dancer. You said something like… like you knew what it meant when a partner asked for trust."

Rose closes her eyes and exhales. She nods and whispers, "I remember."

"Rose, you need a partner that is strong enough to lead you," Aris says. "I think I was afraid that I wasn't strong enough."

Rose starts to hear Nicolas. "Aris, don't you understand that you have always been him. You have led me for years."

"You know that phrase, and I am not sure if it is an idiom or not, that sometimes you don't see what is right in front of you?"

Rose tries to think of an appropriate idiom to cover the sentiment. "I can't think…"

"So…" Aris reaches into his pocket and pulls out an envelope and places it on the counter between them. "This is the start of me trying to lead you."

Rose tentatively puts her left hand on the envelope. "Another envelope? What are you going to do, pull my strings?" she says harshly.

Aris inhales and exhales deeply. "Maybe? Do you think the 19th string is the heart string?"

"Ugh," Rose says. "Cheese."

"God, you really scare me."

Rose quickly looks into his eyes. She is sure that she has never really seen that emotion from him. "Scared? What's in the envelope?"

"You're going to have to find out," Aris says. "Open it."

Rose drags the envelope across the counter and then lifts it with both hands. She opens the envelope and then the letter enclosed. It is a letter from the State Scheduler for Senator Harkin. Aris has arranged a meeting for Rose with the author of the Cocoa Protocol.

"I need you to know how proud I am of you – for the work you have done," Aris reaches his right hand to touch the top of her ear and then stands to kiss the top of her head. "I want to help you get that piece of chocolate to Abdul. I am sure that Senator Harkin would love to help you find the people you need to be working with."

Rose starts to cry, the only reaction she could have.

Aris takes her arms and puts them around his neck. He picks her up and carries her to the couch. "The sun is rising." He sits down with her on his lap, her arms still around his neck and her nose buried in his shoulder. "Don't you want to watch?"

"You are holding me," Rose lifts her head to look at his profile. She places the side of her head on his shoulder and follows his line of sight out the window toward the east.

Aris tightens his grip and kisses her head every few seconds as they watch the sun rise. "I really missed you."

"How's Mina?" Rose asks trying to find normalcy.

"She's good. I felt like an Austen character running to my sister. I guess I knew then just how much trouble I was in," Aris says softly across her ear with his chin brushing her hair.

Rose gently smiles upon hearing his story and imagines him dressed in Victorian clothes talking to his sister.

"I told her everything. And do you know what she said?"

"I suppose not," Rose says.

"She said she was beginning to think I was an idiot and a coward. She said that the moment she met you she knew…"

"She knew what?" Rose asks.

"That you were going to be my wife." Aris pulls out a ring from his front shirt pocket and shows it to Rose.

"Did she?" Rose takes the ring from him and places it on her right ring finger. She admires the sight and then closes her eyes and moves her head to listen to his heart.

"Yes?" Aris says.

"Yes."

Aris sighs deeply. "Thank God. Are you hungry yet?"

"Thanks, God. Am I Hungry? No. Odd? There must be something wrong. I think that maybe I should probably call in sick today."

"I recommend bed rest," Aris says dryly.

"Bed rest?" Rose kisses Aris's cheek, and then swings her legs to stand. She extends her newly decorated hand to help him up with total forgiveness. "Yay! Good morning, Aris. I missed you, too."

"Good morning, Rose. I hope you know that I'm never going to leave you again."

Rose's mind turns over those words as she moves to turn on the fire. "Promise?"

"I promise," Aris says.

"Never?" she jibes.

"Never ever," Aris says hugging her to a near point of suffocation.

Rose looks up at him and says with her remaining breath, "So, a State Scheduler? A meeting with Senator Harkin and Representative Engel – together? How'd you swing it?"

"Impressed?" he says, displaying a proud chin as he lets go. "First of all, I thought a State Scheduler was a totally made up thing. Turns out, they do exist. For some reason I am thinking about M&Ms." Aris smiles and returns to gently embrace. "Anyway, in order to get a meeting with a State Scheduler you need to go through a Constituent Advocate. Sam helped me get a meet with the Constituent Advocate."

"A Constituent Advocate?" Rose asks.

"Yep, the government has great titles. Lousy pay, but great titles," Aris states.

"This is the most romantic thing ever," Rose says looking at the letter.

"I don't know, I thought that the proposal at sunrise was pretty good," Aris says smugly.

"You really want to marry me?" Rose says looking at her hand and then at him.

"On second thought, I don't know…Do you really think that the letter is more romantic than the proposal?"

"I'm in trouble, aren't I?" Rose says coquettishly.

"Nothing that you can't get out of. Speaking of…" Aris slips his hand under the shoulder of her robe. "What are you wearing?"

"A gift," Rose responds. She drops her robe to her elbows to show him the red negligee he bought.

"You missed me."

Rose does her impression of the Mona Lisa. "What do you think?"

"I think I have been in love with you since the day we met. I am sorry it took me so long to get here."

"You really want to marry me? Really?"

Aris smiles. "I do."

With a gentle peck to her lips, he picks up the plates and takes them to the microwave. He removes the grapes and closes the door.

"30 seconds," she instructs.

He delivers the re-heated sandwich to Rose.

"For some reason, I still cannot eat," she admits setting

down her sandwich.

"Loss of appetite... hmmm, I recommend lots and lots of bed rest."

"Bed rest?" Rose says. "Really? You really want to marry me? Really?"

"I want to be your husband even more."

"My husband," Rose utters contently.

"I still feel like I owe you an apology for not understanding where you were at – eleven days ago. My sister tried to explain to me what you were going through – giving away something you really cared about, something that you put your heart and soul into. I should have been more sensitive. I wasn't really there for you, was I?"

"To be fair, I am not sure if I understood what I was feeling. I spent the last eleven days wondering how I could apologize to you, but at the same time couldn't figure out what I wanted to apologize for. I wasn't wrong, but I wasn't right either."

"Also, I think I have to admit that I may have been a little jealous of Abdul." Aris gives her an embarrassed smile. "Before you say anything, I know how ridiculous that sounds. My sister even made fun of me for it. The thing is – you really seem to love him and have never met him. I don't know, I guess that scared me. How can you feel so strongly about a person you never met?"

Rose looks at Abdul on her refrigerator. "I do love him. I still do."

"Then I remembered your definition of love – Love inspires," Aris quotes Rose's definition from a previous conversation.

Rose tries again to take a bite of her sandwich and realizes that she is still unable to eat. "What is wrong with me? I should probably call in." Rose walks to her bedroom and immediately calls her manager. She leaves a message about a sudden onset of a very high fever. Rose hangs up the phone and turns to the mirror to look at herself in her red dress and ring.

"You are truly beautiful," Aris says as he stands at her bedroom door, gripping the frame. "So, ya wanna play a game of chess?"

Rose smiles and nods. "Work up an appetite?"

***

"You'd be surprised about how often I think about bathroom chess. One of your most brilliant ideas to date – both strategic and commonplace."

"One of my most brilliant ideas, eh?" Rose carries the board and the pieces to the coffee table.

"So you are going to meet with Senator Harkin the Tuesday after Easter. I love Tuesdays."

"I thought about you a lot yesterday, a Monday," Rose says. She picks a pawn from each and shuffles them behind her back. "Gentleman's choice."

"Right," Aris says as the hand reveals black. "So are you nervous? I know you think that you do not interview well."

"No. I don't think it. I know I don't interview well," she says. "Yet, I am very interested to meet him. The guy really wanted to fix the problem and made an effort to force legal action to stop the abuses. I'm pretty sure he encountered a ridiculous amount of closed doors – yet he did get something – a signed promise, and in many circles, honor is still key. I suspect I will be meeting a gentleman, not a politician."

"A gentleman Senator that actually gets stuff done. I didn't know that they still existed."

"Me neither. They are probably as rare as gentlemen. Speaking of…Are you sure you want to marry me?"

"I'm sure. So about your interview…" Aris smiles and moves his pawn "…I could help you practice. I actually received government training." He watches her response and then takes her pawn with his knight. He continues in an affected deep male voice, "About your personal life, Miss Isope, how is it that you can resist Mr. Irwin?"

"Sir, I can tell you that it is not without its difficulties. My best defense is clothes – lots and lots of well-layered clothes," Rose lowers a strap from her shoulder.

"I see." Aris's eyes sharpen. "Last question… Any questions for me?"

Rose bats her eyelashes and games, "We are in the middle of a game here and you are supposed to be helping me with my interview skills – not teaching me how to flirt with a State Senator."

"Didn't I tell you I received government training?" Aris says dryly.

"Ha ha," Rose says and then naturally laughs.

Aris castles. "I need water."

"I'll get it," she stands and walks to the kitchen as she contemplates her next move. "Yesterday I was reminiscing about the day that I first really learned about the Harkin-Engel Protocol. I met with you at the coffee shop, remember?" Rose asks.

Aris nods. "Of course, I remember. The penalty of greatness."

"You told me that the practice of these corporations was common knowledge. Anyway, I was thinking about all of the wrongs in the world today and well – its common practice. I mean, we all know about the sweatshops in China and all pay lip service to how horrible it is – yet more than 90% of my wardrobe, well minus the vintage, is made in China. Where is the penalty?"

"I think you mean to ask, where is the greatness?"

"It makes me nervous," Rose says.

"I don't understand. What do you mean - nervous?"

"Why don't we care about these things? I mean, why do these things still exist. Don't we know better?" Rose hands him his glass of water and takes her seat.

"You mean *we* as in humanity? Not to change the subject, or anything, but I think this is why your interviews go badly," Aris interjects. "You are too easily able to jump from chocolate to sweatshops."

"Maybe. But I don't know about it being an easy jump..." Rose looks to her left to consider the thought. "Anyway, the cocoa thing and the sweat shop thing and the Mexican border thing... all those things make me think about an overarching civil rights thing. During the American Industrial Revolution, there were champions that helped children and miners obtain civil rights. Later in the sixties, there were champions that helped African American people lift their voices and station." She moves a pawn and takes a drink of water. "I guess they had their greatness. I don't think we have that anymore and it makes me nervous. I think we mostly champion mediocrity and our banner says something like, 'It's not our problem.'"

"I don't think you are being fair. There is Senator Harkin, Nick, Rebekah and...God, you look stunning in red."

"Fair, enough," Rose says lowering her eyes. "And thanks."

"Fair trade?" Aris asserts, "I have been reading about cocoa's fair trade organizations."

"They really need to build the schools first. Mafeking," Rose says gripping her ankles. "Speaking of ... May-fee-King...I had another thought yesterday that I really wanted to share with you, but I couldn't. Did I ever tell you my favorite historic find from the 60s?"

"No. Well, maybe." Aris laughs while holding on to his queen. "You are pretty much all over the board right now, aren't you?"

"It was a long eleven days. I swear it felt like eleven years," Rose winks and catches his eyes with her own. "The find is 'Letter from a Birmingham Jail' as Martin Luther King's revision of the novel *Catcher in the Rye*. I read 'Letter from a Birmingham Jail' in the first year of my Masters. I found a small bound version at this combination used book store sandwich shop called 'Skylight Exchange.' I devoured the exquisite prose supposedly written on toilet paper because they would not give the *man* paper. In it, he basically sets up a beautiful theological argument answering those who are criticizing his timing. Many theologians and Christian leaders at the time were concerned about the violence and about riots and about… themselves, I guess."

Rose takes a breath and looks at Aris who is still dangling his queen. "It was in the second to last page, if memory serves me correct, that I saw his perfect sight. He made this delicate argument of why the time was now. And he leads the reader to this perfect hallowed precipice and then he takes a step back." Rose looks down at her chess board. "He was right there. He knew he was right there. And I mean completely right. And he took a step back. He had the courage to not take the last step. He gave up the lead." Her entire body trembles with the memory as she looks to Aris.

"You and your incessant prattle," Aris smiles at his wife-to-be.

She squeezes her eyebrows together. "Am I not making sense?"

"You are a genius, Rose. It's just no one believes you. And I don't know why. I really don't." He moves his queen to threaten her king.

"I think it has to do with my petite frame." Rose smiles as she looks down at her body.

"You look so good in red," Aris states.

"You should see me in buff."

"Now?"

Rose flexes her bicep. "Buff."

"Nervous?"

"Yeah, I guess I am a little nervous about that, too," Rose says meekly lowering her gaze.

Aris melts. "So Rose, question…If you met Abdul, I mean actually got to meet him at his desk in his school – what would you say to him?"

Rose rests her chin on the table and contemplates the question. "Interesting question…I guess I would have to learn

French."

"Oui," Aris says.

With a smile naturally settling on her face, Rose says, "I guess I would say something like… Roses are Red, Violets are Blue, Sugar is sweet and I still think we owe you. I think I would probably tell him the fable of the Ant and the Dove and let him know the moral – one good turn deserves another. I'd tell him how much he inspired me. And I would thank him for the chocolate."

"That's a lot of French. They have loads of language classes available in the D.C. area."

Rose looks at the board. "I see I am in check, mate." Rose smiles and shifts to her knees and leans over the table asking for a kiss. "Mate."

"I love you," Aris says as he grants her a kiss. "And Mate, you *are* in check."

"You love me." Rose hears his words, sighs, and looks at the board, "Have you figured out that I really don't know how to play this game? I learned the opening; I just never learned the end game." She moves her queen to the absolute worst spot on the board, smiles and winks. "I guess I am just tired."

"Tired? I suppose we could go lie down."

"And rest?"

"Rose, I would love to teach you how to play," Aris proposes. He stands and walks to the kitchen and reaches into the grocery bag and pulls out a box. He returns to Rose, "Starting with this…"

"Another present?" Rose asks smiling and giggling.

"I think this is more a gift for me," Aris answers and returns to his cushion. "I swear that I felt like the universe was dropping anvils on me these past eleven days."

"The universe?" Rose unwraps the white and gold box and finds a small marble and onyx chess board.

"For our future bathroom," Aris says smiling.

"Check mate."

"Happy?"

"I am so happy I am actually scared."

"What is it that you say – just a day like any other?"

Rose admires her right hand's adornment. "No. This is not a day like any other. This is the first day of the best of my life."

"Do you want to call your parents?" Aris lifts his hands to her shoulders, slipping his warm fingers under the spaghetti straps. "You really do look beautiful in red."

Rose intertwines her fingers in his. "I feel beautiful."

Aris cups her face and kisses her gently.

"That's it. Doctor's orders."

POST-FACE
THE SCORPION AND THE LADYBUG

A SCORPION befriended a Ladybug who became a loyal companion to him. A time came when she struggled to cross a challenging and dangerous river, and so the Scorpion offered to take her to the other side on his back. He had come to care for her and promised he would never harm her. But, safely across the river, he allowed his tail to dip upon her with its venomous sting. As she lay in greatest pain, she said, "... but, you promised... why?" He shrugged and said, sadly, "Because it is my Nature." –Aesop

THE MORAL: Regardless of our wishes, or even our intent, it is to our Nature alone that we will be faithful.

http://www.cocoainitiative.org/

http://www.harkin.senate.gov/documents/pdf/HarkinEngelProtocol.pdf

http://thecnnfreedomproject.blogs.cnn.com/

ABOUT THE AUTHOR

She wrote this book. She has Bachelor's degree and a Master's degree. All the same, she is pretty certain that these things really don't matter to the reader. She cares about this particular issue sincerely and has every intention of donating whatever she can afford to this cause. She does ask the reader to tell one other person about the goings on, if you could call it that, in the world's cocoa fields. If the reader tells just one person, at the very least, one more person will know. Thanks.

Made in the USA
Charleston, SC
13 March 2014